Somebody's Lover

JASMINE HAYNES

BERKLEY SENSATION, NEW YORK

THE BERKLEY PUBLISHING GROUP
Published by the Penguin Group
Penguin Group (USA) Inc.
375 Hudson Street, New York, New York 10014, USA
Penguin Group (Canada), 90 Eglinton Avenue East, Suite 700, Toronto, Ontario M4P 2Y3, Canada
(a division of Pearson Penguin Canada Inc.)
Penguin Books Ltd., 80 Strand, London WC2R 0RL, England
Penguin Group Ireland, 25 St. Stephen's Green, Dublin 2, Ireland (a division of Penguin Books Ltd.)
Penguin Group (Australia), 250 Camberwell Road, Camberwell, Victoria 3124, Australia
(a division of Pearson Australia Group Pty. Ltd.)
Penguin Books India Pvt. Ltd., 11 Community Centre, Panchsheel Park, New Delhi—110 017, India
Penguin Group (NZ), 67 Apollo Drive, Rosedale, North Shore 0745, Auckland, New Zealand
(a division of Pearson New Zealand Ltd.)
Penguin Books (South Africa) (Pty.) Ltd., 24 Sturdee Avenue, Rosebank, Johannesburg 2196,
South Africa

Penguin Books Ltd., Registered Offices: 80 Strand, London WC2R 0RL, England

This is a work of fiction. Names, characters, places, and incidents either are the product of the author's imagination or are used fictitiously, and any resemblance to actual persons, living or dead, business establishments, events, or locales is entirely coincidental. The publisher does not have any control over and does not assume any responsibility for author or third-party websites or their content.

SOMEBODY'S LOVER

A Berkley Sensation Book / published by arrangement with the author

PRINTING HISTORY
Berkley Sensation trade edition / July 2006
Berkley Sensation mass-market edition / June 2007

Copyright © 2006 by Jennifer Skullestad.
Cover design by Rita Frangie.
Cover photograph of "Couple embracing in water on beach" by Malek Chamoun / Getty; cover
photograph of "Couple #2 & #3" by Masterfile.
Interior text design by Stacy Irwin.

ISBN: 978-0-425-21604-0

BERKLEY SENSATION®
Berkley Sensation Books are published by The Berkley Publishing Group,
a division of Penguin Group (USA) Inc.,
375 Hudson Street, New York, New York 10014.
BERKLEY SENSATION and the "B" design are trademarks belonging to Penguin Group (USA) Inc.

PRINTED IN THE UNITED STATES OF AMERICA

10   9   8   7   6   5   4   3   2   1

To Jenn Cummings,
for saying just the right thing
at just the right time.

Thanks also to Rose Lerma, Lucienne Diver, and
Christine Zika, for all their hard work.

CONTENTS

Somebody's Lover

---- # ONE ----

THE WOMAN LOOKED like Taylor, his brother Lou's wife. But this woman's lips were painted a deep shade of red, where Taylor always wore pink. The tight spandex top hugged her full breasts, and her leather skirt revealed endless, captivating legs encased in shimmering nylon. Taylor didn't own a leather skirt, and to her, spandex was for jogging. Fuck-me high heels rested on the bottom rail of the bar stool. Taylor abhorred high heels.

The look-alike flipped her auburn hair over her shoulders, the locks sparkling with golden highlights in the flash of the strobe on the dance floor.

Jace Jackson cooled himself off with a slug of beer, his one and only bottle for the night.

Then she laughed. He shouldn't have been able to hear it over the voices, the semi-drunken laughter, or the beat of another country western ballad, but he felt it in his gut, the way he always felt Taylor's laugh, hard as he tried to ignore it.

Holy hell.

The woman didn't just look like Taylor. It *was* Taylor.

Jace slammed his beer down on the table, ignored his

drinking buddies' raised eyebrows, and rose to his feet when the guy Taylor was flirting with put his hand on her knee.

TAYLOR JACKSON KNEW she'd made a huge mistake the minute the man put his hand on her knee. She couldn't remember his name, Buddy or Bubba or Bucky or something, although Bubba seemed to suit him best.

It didn't seem right to be planning to seduce a man whose name she couldn't remember. Not that Bubba needed much in the way of a come-on from her.

She hadn't dated since Lou died. In fact, she hadn't been out on a date since she met Lou back in college. Not that she'd call what she was doing now dating.

Planning a seduction had been the easy part. Dressing for it even easier. The hour between dropping off the kids at her mother-in-law's house and finishing her final primp in her bathroom mirror had been like playing dress-up with her mom's makeup when she was a little girl. Of course, when her mother caught her, she'd blistered her butt. Taylor had started feeling jumpy on the drive over, out of Willoughby to the outskirts of Bentonville, the next town over, and home of Saddle-n-Spurs, a rowdy country western joint.

She'd chosen the bar because she wouldn't be recognized. No one she knew would come to a place like this. It wasn't a PTA/soccer-mom kind of place.

Jumpy or not, Taylor had climbed out of her minivan and headed inside. Her head had begun to pound with the din before she'd even taken a seat at the bar. She'd ordered wine to calm her full-fledged nerves and probably would have bolted before the bartender poured it if Bubba hadn't taken the stool beside her and paid for her drink.

She shouldn't have let him do that. Not that she felt like she had to sleep with him because he bought her a glass of wine. This wasn't how she'd planned it. In fact, the whole seduction plan seemed suddenly idiotic. If she hadn't felt so desperate, so needy, so out of control, she never would have considered picking up a guy in a bar for a night of casual sex.

It had seemed like forever since she'd felt a man's touch. For months after Lou died, maybe a year, she hadn't given sex a thought. She'd been too busy getting out of bed in the mornings, accepting the monumental changes his death wrought, wondering if she could handle things on her own, and helping Brian and Jamey cope with the loss of their dad.

Somewhere along the way, in that second and third year alone, she'd started remembering she was a woman. With needs. She didn't want a new father for the boys or a boyfriend or husband for herself. She only wanted the embrace of a man for a little while.

Bubba wasn't her idea of a dream lover. Reality didn't match the erotic fantasy she'd spun throughout sleepless nights. Now, she wasn't quite sure how she'd get rid of him, or for that matter, get herself out of the bar.

"Get your damn hand off my wife's knee."

Oh Lord. It couldn't be. She glanced up and almost choked on her sip of wine. It was her brother-in-law. And Jace didn't look like a happy camper.

In the next moment, she was terribly glad to see him as the hand on her knee suddenly shot back where it belonged.

"Your wife?" Bubba sputtered.

Jace's hand closed around her upper arm. "Yeah. My wife."

"But she ain't wearing no ring?"

How could she have considered that a man who didn't have proper command of grammar would know how to bring a woman fulfillment of her deepest desires?

"Where's your ring, sweetheart?" Jace shot her a feral grin.

She smiled sweetly. "On the kitchen counter, where I left it after I caught you with that hussy in our bed. The hussy being my dear sister." What chigger had bitten her bottom? But now that the immediate Bubba crisis was over, she felt giddy with relief.

Bubba stood and backed away, holding his hands out in

front of him. "I don't want no part o' this," he said, loud enough to draw attention.

A semicircle suddenly opened up around them, and the bartender froze, beer mug still tipped beneath the draft tap.

Jace tugged on her arm. "Why don't we talk about this at home . . . sweetheart?"

She wasn't mad at Jace. In fact, he'd saved her from an unpleasant scene.

"I'll only go if you promise not to beat me black and blue again. And you have to stop screwing my sister." She almost giggled, despite less than half a glass of wine.

Jace merely glowered.

Spoilsport. Still, she climbed off the stool and let him half pull, half drag her across the bar to the entrance. The patrons parted like the Red Sea. No one stopped him. What if they hadn't been joking? What if he really was a bully who'd beat her once he got her home? Didn't anyone care?

Once the door of the bar had slapped shut behind them, the question didn't matter.

"You don't know how glad I was to see you."

Jace didn't answer, nor did he turn to her as he hauled her down a long aisle of cars and trucks.

"You can stop dragging me now."

"Get in the truck."

"The minivan's there." She pointed a couple of rows over.

"I said get in the truck." He opened the passenger door and practically shoved her up on the front seat.

He was actually mad. Her brother-in-law was a pretty easygoing guy. She couldn't remember ever seeing him quite so angry. He stomped round the front of the truck, raking both hands through his short, brown hair and muttering to himself. Climbing in, he slammed his door.

Then he turned to glower at her. "What the hell did you think you were doing in there?"

"Well, it's a tad embarrassing to explain." A tad? Who was she kidding? "Maybe we could talk about it tomorrow."

"We'll talk about it now." He emphasized with a stab of his

finger in the air. "Don't you have any clue what could have happened to you in there?"

Yeah, she had a clue. She'd made a mistake. Next time, she'd try looking for someone down at the PTA. Right. "I thanked you for coming along at the appropriate moment to rescue me." She refrained from asking if he was going to tell his mother. Taylor knew Evelyn wouldn't understand.

Jace stared her down.

"All I wanted was a little drink." Boy, she couldn't look at him when she fed him that lie.

Which he didn't buy. "You went for a drink dressed like that?" He swept her attire with a slash of his hand. "To a meat-market bar twenty miles away from home?"

She smiled. "Yes."

"Are you crazy? You're the mother of two kids, for Christ's sake. You're my brother's wife."

Her smile died. "I'm your brother's widow. And I wasn't here looking for a replacement for him."

He shoved his hands once more through his hair. He looked a lot like Lou. Brownish hair only slightly longer than the buzz cut Lou had preferred. Brown eyes, laugh lines, and a killer smile. That's what she'd noticed first about Lou. His smile. Even then, back in college, he'd had laugh lines.

Jace hadn't laughed much since his brother died. Except with the boys. He was great with her boys.

He puffed out a loud breath. "You were here to get laid. Jesus Christ, I can't believe it."

"I was here for a drink."

Jace's gaze traveled from her throat to her breasts to the short skirt that barely covered the essentials when she sat, and finally to her shoes. She'd stood in front of the full-length mirror admiring those shoes that Lou had once forbidden her to wear.

Sudden anger spiraled deep. How dare Jace judge her? He'd done his share of catting around over the years. One woman after another, partying up a storm, though he'd calmed down since Lou died. Still, that didn't give him the right to castigate her.

"Men go out and get laid all the time," she pointed out.

"Dammit, Taylor, you're not a man. There're different rules for women."

"What are they?" She shook her head. He was almost laughable, if he wasn't pissing her off so much. "Lou has been gone for three years. And what, I'm supposed to go off to a convent?"

He looked straight ahead through the windshield. "You could try dating, you know."

"Like who?" Willoughby wasn't jumping with candidates.

"How about Joe?"

"He's ten years older than me and still lives with his mother."

"That makes him respectable."

"I don't want to date Joe. I don't want to date anyone. I'm not looking for Lou's replacement." To the family, Jace included, she was Lou's wife, not Lou's widow. Keeping his memory alive meant never letting her move on. They wouldn't like her dating a new man, and God forbid she should ever want to marry again. Which was fine with her, really it was. She was self-sufficient, and Lou's family, her family now, meant more to her than having a man around the house. She didn't want a husband. Most of the time. Except in the middle of a dark and lonely night as she climbed into a cold, empty bed.

"I need—" She stopped. She couldn't tell Jace that it wasn't true what they said about vibrators. They were not a woman's best friend. They couldn't replace a man's weight, a man's body, or his hardness inside her.

He smacked a hand on the steering wheel. "You're a mother. With my brother's two kids at home. You can't pick up men in bars."

If he said that one more time, she'd reach across the seat and belt him. She was Brian and Jamey's mom to him. He couldn't see anything else. None of the family could. She loved them, she never wanted to lose them, never wanted to hurt them, but sometimes, she wanted to scream. Suddenly all those bottled up feelings spilled out over Jace.

"I am not just somebody's mother. Or somebody's wife. Or somebody's daughter-in-law. And I'm not just somebody's sister-in-law." She wanted to be somebody's lover. Leaning over, she stared him down glare for glare. "I'm a woman, Jace. A woman."

"I know that." He backed off.

"Do you?" To him, she was his nephews' mother, his brother's wife. "Do you really?"

"Yeah, uh, sure."

Right. She was a sexless thirty-three-year-old. Forget the word *woman*. It didn't even fit in his definition of her. Later she wouldn't be able to say what had snapped inside her. She barely remembered diving across the space that separated them, but she did remember fastening her lips to his.

He tasted of yeasty beer and smelled like some cool aftershave. She pressed her breasts to his chest, wrapped her arms around his neck, and hung on as he braced his hands against her ribs and tried to push her away. Taylor wasn't letting go.

She angled her head, sucked at his mouth, then ran her tongue along the seam of his lips. Her nipples peaked through the spandex as she rubbed against him. Then she forgot it was Jace. She forgot he was her husband's brother. She simply reveled in the feel of a man's lips beneath hers. His thumbs began to stroke the soft undersides of her breasts.

He opened his mouth to her tongue, tested her, tasted her, then leaned her back against the steering wheel and kissed her as if she was somebody's lover.

Lord, he felt good, so good. Her body moistened against her minuscule panties. She throbbed. Her nipples ached for the rasp of his tongue on them. She wriggled in his lap and moaned against his mouth. His hand rose, cupped her, taking her nipple between his thumb and forefinger. She almost came—it had been so long since she'd felt like this. He shifted, his hips surging up to rock his erection against her.

She was actually wondering how she could get her nylons off and not let go of him.

Then the horn honked. Long and loud. Taylor snapped

back to reality, pulling away from the steering wheel to stop the racket.

Still cupping her breast in his hand, Jace stared at her, a weird shell-shocked grimace on his face. Dilated pupils, air puffing in and out of his lungs, his Adam's apple slid as he swallowed.

Oh Lord. She jerked from his lap, yanked down on her skirt where it had ridden to the top of her thighs, and lunged back to her side of the truck.

She'd been ready to straddle his lap right there in the front seat. In a parking lot. Jace. Her husband's brother.

"I'm sorry. I don't know what came over me. I'm really sorry. I . . ." Lord, the things she'd revealed. All her turbulent, needy emotions. She'd told him everything.

He stared at her, and her face heated with humiliation.

She almost stammered trying to get her words out. "I've got my car. I'll see myself home." She grappled with the door handle, wrestled it open, then almost fell out. "Thanks for helping me. I don't know what I would have done . . ." She was babbling.

She dug in the pocket of her skirt where she'd stashed her car key and alarm remote, then slammed his truck door. Where was her minivan? There! She stumbled in the high heels, caught herself on the truck bumper, then took off like a mortified teenager.

She fumbled with the remote. His truck door opened, and he called her name. Then she was in, thank you so very much, God. She slammed and locked the door, cranked the engine, and pulled out in a spray of gravel and dirt.

"I can't believe you did that," she said to herself.

She couldn't believe he'd tasted so good, felt so good.

She saw his headlights following her, at least she thought they were his. She hoped they were his and not Bubba's. The drive took forever, absolutely forever, but finally she was in her own driveway, and the house key was under the doormat where she'd left it because she'd intended on traveling light, only a twenty-dollar bill, her license, and her car key in her pocket.

Jace idled at the end of the driveway.

She bumbled her way inside and slammed the front door.

Lord, she'd just thrown herself at Jace. At her brother-in-law, whom she'd known for almost fifteen years. Since she was nineteen and he was sixteen. Since the first time Lou brought her home to meet the family.

The worst part? Taylor was hoping Jace would get out of his truck and follow her in to finish what she'd started.

JACE WHITE-KNUCKLED THE steering wheel as if that would somehow keep him from rushing in after her. He'd followed Taylor home to make sure she arrived safely. To make sure she actually went home. At least that's what he'd told himself.

But sitting there, his cock hard, his balls blue, her taste on his tongue, and remembering the sensation of her nipple between his fingers, he knew far more had driven him.

God help him, he knew she was a woman. He'd always known.

She'd been the woman in his wet dreams from the first time he met her. In youthful arrogance, he'd hoped she'd leave his brother. He'd been young enough and stupid enough to pray for it. She'd married Lou when she graduated from college, and Jace put away his fantasies about his brother's wife.

He'd stuffed them into the back of his mind for so many years, he'd almost forgotten the need that had practically crippled him. Even after Lou's death, those fantasies hadn't surfaced. Far from it. The responsibility he bore for his brother's death kept them where they belonged, in the darkness of his soul.

He'd tried his damndest to make it up to Taylor for what he'd done. Anything she needed around the house, he took care of it. He fathered the boys the best he could. He never partied, never more than one beer on a Saturday night with a couple of friends. He stopped dating entirely. He acted the part of role model for her kids. He tried to give them back what he'd stolen, their father's closeness. He tried to give Taylor everything.

Except the thing sometimes a woman wanted most. A touch. A caress. A rustle under the covers and a warm body to fill her up. To make her laugh again.

Her laughter had always tied him in knots. But she hadn't laughed like that in a long time, and he'd been safe.

Until tonight. Until she'd laughed with another man.

Until she'd thrown herself at him in the truck and kissed him like there was no tomorrow. Like there was no Lou. Like Jace was the only man on earth she needed.

He rammed the truck in gear and laid rubber before he succumbed to the memory of that kiss. His first, only, and last taste of her.

TWO

THE NIGHT BEFORE Taylor had been embarrassed. Today she was mortified. Evelyn, her mother-in-law, had brought the kids home at about ten-thirty this morning, then stayed to help Taylor get ready for the family barbecue. Every Sunday, rain or shine, the family got together. Taylor, Evelyn, and Connie, Evelyn's second daughter-in-law, took turns playing hostess. This week was Taylor's turn.

She'd put the high-heeled shoes in their box on the top shelf of the closet and hidden the leather skirt and spandex shirt at the back of her underwear drawer in case Connie wanted to borrow some clothes. They often swapped outfits instead of buying something new, especially when Connie claimed Mitch was being tight, as he was recently.

Jace arrived at noon and got the barbecue going, because that was man's work. Taylor hadn't been able to meet his eye, so she didn't know if he'd even looked at her. She crossed her fingers, hoped and prayed he wouldn't say anything to anyone about having seen her last night.

It would have been a lot easier to forget if he didn't look so good in jeans. His chestnut hair was starting to wave as it dried in the sun. He looked so hot, her heart did a little rat-a-tat-tat against her breast.

She'd always thought he was good-looking. She'd never felt guilty about admiring his butt in jeans before, because she'd always stopped herself right there. Well, almost right there.

Evelyn wouldn't understand about last night. As much as Taylor told herself she wouldn't be tossed out of the family if she one day invited a boyfriend to the Sunday barbecue, her heart told her otherwise. She was Lou's wife, and widowed or not, she always would be.

The family never talked about Lou's death. They never even said the word *dead*. Sometimes it was as if Evelyn and Arthur pretended their eldest son was away on a trip. She couldn't hurt them by dating a new man. She didn't want to. She got all she needed from being a part of the Jackson family.

Almost all she needed. Now Jace knew her dark secret. She prayed he'd keep it to himself.

"Since our men and the kids are all busy," Evelyn said with a nod at the horseshoe game well under way, "I'll finish up this potato salad." She scooped the last glob of potato goo onto her plate. "Connie, you eat the rest of the coleslaw." She skipped Taylor because her plate was still half full.

Connie plopped two spoons of slaw onto her plate before waving fondly at her kids. She and Mitch had been married nine years, with Pete coming along just shy of the first year and Rina a couple of years later.

"Go, Rina," Evelyn yelled when the little girl's horseshoe came within two feet of the spike.

Her mother-in-law's short cap of gray hair bounced in her excitement, and laugh lines crinkled the corners of her eyes. Her smile took five years off her age of fifty-seven. Terrified of crow's feet, Taylor's own mother hadn't laughed extensively. Not like Evelyn did when a grandkid spouted something outrageous or one of her boys jokingly gave her a hard time. Her sons would always be boys to her, though they ranged in age from David's thirty-four years to Mitch at thirty-two and Jace at thirty.

Lou would have been thirty-six. Taylor knew that Evelyn missed him every hour of every day. Truth be told, there hadn't been as much laughter or joking since Lou died. Most times, any gaiety centered around the children.

Lou had left a hole none of them had been able to fill. But Evelyn tried, insisting on the barbecues every Sunday and sharing all the holidays together.

"Arthur, have you got your sunscreen on?" Evelyn called, before popping the last fork of potato salad in her mouth.

Arthur patted his bald head. "Dear, we're in the shade."

"The sun's moving round. You don't want to look like a pink Easter egg." Then she lowered her voice, "Actually, he's cute when he has a little pink on top, don't you think, girls?"

"He's adorable no matter what, Mom." Taylor loved the way Evelyn talked about her husband. Never a snide remark or a cutting glance. Unlike Taylor's parents.

"He's an old fart," Evelyn scoffed and smiled at the same time. "But he's my old fart."

This is what she'd dreamed of having for herself someday, but she'd put those dreams aside after Lou died. Instead, she had his family. They were everything to her. When Taylor's parents died in a car accident at the end of her second year in college, Evelyn had taken her under her wing like a chick kicked out of the nest. Or like the mom her own mother had never been. Trundled off to boarding schools or put to bed by au pairs when her parents were traveling, Taylor had been a lonely child, an only child. But not once she met Lou's family. First daughter-in-law, mother of the first grandchild, Taylor also liked to think of herself as the daughter Evelyn never had. Evelyn was certainly the only real mother Taylor had ever known.

She wouldn't risk hurting either Evelyn or Arthur.

Still, she found herself staring at Jace. At his rear end actually, in those jeans. She remembered last night, the taste of him in her mouth, the feel of him against her breasts. And she knew she was in trouble.

"You know, girls, we're outnumbered. Look at all those males, and one teeny-tiny girl. We need to get David married." New daughters-in-law and new grandkids were fine for Evelyn.

A new boyfriend for her son's widow wouldn't be, Taylor was almost sure.

"David's too mopey to find a wife," Connie snorted.

"David does not mope, Connie."

"What's he doing right now, then?"

They all looked. David, the second boy, now the eldest. He'd never been the happy-go-lucky kind, but since Lou's death, he'd become downright standoffish. Even now, he stood back, arms folded over his chest, watching, not participating. He always came to the barbecues, that was Evelyn's rule, but he hadn't seemed a part of them for a long time.

"He's fine," Evelyn said, but a frown puckered her brow. She knew as well as anybody that David was not exactly fine.

"What about marrying off Jace?" Connie suggested.

Taylor wanted to kick her under the picnic table.

"That boy is not done sowing his wild oats."

Taylor's stomach did a little heave-ho. Jace's wild oats and wilder women had never bothered her before. Besides, he didn't flaunt his women anymore. He was actually pretty circumspect, probably out of respect for being the boys' Little League coach.

So why did his wild oats bother her now?

Because she'd tasted him and she'd loved the way he tasted. That kiss had changed the way she thought of him. For a woman who professed she didn't want change in her life, she'd brought on a doozy last night.

He'd probably been intending to pick up a woman at the Saddle-n-Spurs.

Instead, Taylor had picked *him* up. Sort of.

Connie twirled her fork around her plate. "What if I were to tell you your wish might come true?"

Evelyn practically beamed like a ray of sun. "You found a wife for David?"

"No-oh." Connie frowned. "I meant another little girl."

"Don't tell me." Evelyn's brow frown deepened.

"I'm late," Connie said. "Very late. Don't tell Mitch."

Evelyn was silent a second too long. "Honey, you have to tell Mitch. You should have told him before you told us."

"You know how he is," Connie sighed. "He'll start running numbers in his calculator and freak out about not knowing where to come up with the money for diapers and clothes and stuff."

Not to mention medical bills, insurance, and on and on. A new baby was very expensive. Taylor didn't voice the thought. Connie was sweet, loved her kids more than anything in the world, and was the best mom, but she could be a bit unrealistic at times. She'd probably invented rose-colored glasses.

"Because Mitch worries is exactly why you have to tell him," Evelyn insisted. "Have you been to the doctor yet?"

"No. I wanted to wait another week or so."

"Have you at least peed on the stick?" Which was Evelyn's euphemism for home pregnancy tests.

"I don't need to. I can feel the changes. I didn't need the stick to know Rina was coming along."

"Heavens, girl, you better tell Mitch soon."

Connie's usually perky lower lip trembled. "I thought you'd be happy. I think it's another girl."

"I am happy." But the laughter had faded from Evelyn's eyes. "But that boy's the worrywart in this family, always trying to keep up with his brothers as if he thinks he's got something to prove." She sighed, gazing across the yard. "And I don't like keeping secrets from my boys. So promise you're going to tell him."

Connie nodded. "I promise. As soon as I get a test. There isn't any sense in worrying him before I'm positive."

"There's a good girl." Evelyn patted her hand.

They sat in silence for a few moments, watching the game's progress. Childish laughter and whooping rang out across the yard as Brian made a perfect throw. Jace, always wonderful with her boys, gave him a high five.

"Jace is looking mighty fine today."

Taylor shot Connie a look. The younger woman sat with her chin propped on her hand, her gaze on the very part of Jace's anatomy Taylor herself had been watching too much that day.

Why had she said that? Taylor's mind started working overtime. Connie hadn't noticed something different, had she?

Taylor suddenly needed to busy herself. "I'll take these inside." She hastily gathered empty bowls and stacked the dirty paper plates.

"I'll help you in a minute," Evelyn said as she clapped for another well-aimed throw, this time by Taylor's youngest, Jamey.

Taylor headed for the house, but couldn't resist one more glance at the game. At that moment, Jace looked up. At her. Even from this distance, she could see the smolder in his eyes.

He hadn't put last night out of his mind either.

"WILL YOU LOOK at that?" Connie mused.

"What?" Evelyn pulled together the plates Taylor couldn't carry.

"That." Connie nodded at Jace with her chin. "He's been watching Taylor all day."

Evelyn looked. She didn't see anything. Jace was helping Rina get ready for another throw, demonstrating the proper stance. "You've got a fertile imagination."

Connie's eyes twinkled. "Fertile is right."

Evelyn felt a little catch in her throat. She loved Connie. She loved both her boys' wives. But Connie sometimes got things set wrong in her head. Evelyn debated briefly about pulling Mitch aside tomorrow and telling him about the maybe-baby, but discarded the idea. That's one thing she'd vowed she'd never do, get involved in her boys' marriages, any of them.

She ignored Connie's little joke. "Jace is acting the same way he always does."

"No. He keeps watching Taylor. Whenever she's not looking his way. And she's doing the same thing." Connie gave a sly smile. "Something's going on there."

Taylor and Jace? Evelyn gave her youngest a long look. She used to wish he'd find a woman like Taylor. Someone who would settle his oats, calm him down a little. He was her baby, her wild boy, the one who had given her quite a few sleepless nights.

Though he'd changed since Lou's death. There were times he brooded over things that weren't his fault, she knew. A mother who'd always been able to talk to her sons about anything, Jace's guilt was the one thing she'd never been able to bring up with him. He'd walk out of the room rather than listen to her. It wasn't something she could discuss with Arthur either. Arthur never talked about that day, and she certainly couldn't bring up her worries over Jace. She'd been married to Arthur for almost forty years, but that was a subject over which she couldn't predict his reaction. So she let sleeping dogs lie. Jace needed to deal with it on his own. He'd taken to treating Lou's boys like they were his, coaching their Little League team, taking them to father-son days at school or camp. He fixed whatever Taylor needed fixing around the house. He changed her oil when the car needed it, came over to mow the lawn. He did Lou's jobs. Atonement? Probably. Yes, for sure.

But something more with Taylor? That girl wasn't looking for a husband or a man. She was fine with her boys and the family. No one would ever replace Lou for her. If Jace thought otherwise, he was in for a big heartache.

"Hey, Jace," Connie called. "Come here."

He ambled over politely, but darn if his glance didn't stray to the screen door through which Taylor had disappeared and might reappear at any moment. A shiver ran down Evelyn's spine. She didn't want her boy hurt, she didn't want her family hurt, especially not Arthur. She didn't think he'd be able to handle the day Taylor found another man. If that man were Jace? Heaven help them.

But Taylor wasn't interested in another. How many times had she said she was happy with her life the way it was? Selfishly, Evelyn prayed she meant it.

Connie kicked her under the table, then smiled at Jace. "Did Taylor tell you her faucet's leaking?"

"No, Connie, she didn't."

"Well, it is."

He nodded, his head tipped slightly. "Thanks for letting me know. I'll take care of it as soon as I get a chance." Then he backed away, giving Connie an odd, speculative look.

He was a good-looking boy. All her boys were. Big, strapping, brown-haired boys. But Jace looked the most like Lou. Sometimes, when Jace came up the walk at the house, her heart would give a little leap. For a moment, when she forgot Lou was gone, the joy overtook her and she thought her eldest was coming home after a long time away. Then she'd remember, and the memory would steal her breath and start an ache in her heart that wouldn't quit until she cried herself to sleep while Arthur watched TV in the living room.

Taylor and Jace? Evelyn prayed it wasn't so. He'd never be able to forget Taylor was his brother's widow, and Taylor would always be seeing Lou in Jace's face.

And Arthur? Well, she couldn't think about how Arthur would feel. Or what he'd do.

THREE

MONDAY MORNING TAYLOR had nipped down to the office after dropping the boys off at school. They'd be out for summer next week, and she'd do most of her work at home then. She did the accounts and payroll for Jackson and Sons Arborists. Evelyn acted as receptionist, accounts receivable clerk, and general office person. The only adult family member not working in the business was Connie. Rina would be starting school in the fall, but until then, Connie had wanted to stay home. With a new baby on the way, well, she wouldn't be starting work anytime soon.

Returning home, Taylor dropped last week's receipts and payables in the bedroom she used as an at-home office, then went back to the kitchen to start another pot of coffee.

After filling the carafe at the sink, she tightly twisted the faucet, but the drip didn't stop. If it had started last week, she'd have asked Jace to take a look. After Saturday night, she couldn't look him in the eye, let alone ask him for a favor. She could fix it herself. Lou was always showing her how to do things around the house. She'd let Jace take over Mr. Fix-it because it seemed to make him feel good. Same as it did when he took the boys for an outing. She knew he felt like he had to make up for Lou's death. Though they'd never talked about it, guilt racked him for not being there that day. But they never *would* talk about it, the whole subject taboo in the family.

Just then, Jace's truck pulled into the driveway. Taylor's hands started to tremble, and she almost dropped the carafe.

What was he doing here?

He slammed the truck door. A black T-shirt molded his chest, and his jeans hugged him in all the right places. She'd felt exactly how right against her the other night. Lord, he looked good. Too good. He took her breath away. With a bag tucked under his arm, he flipped through his keys as he walked up the path to the front door. Sunlight gleamed off his hair.

The key rattled in the lock, then the door opened. She'd given him his own set because he often came over to take care of a job when she wasn't home. She hadn't expected him today. In fact, she'd brought the paperwork home in order to avoid him if he dropped by the office.

She smelled him first, a clean, recently showered scent. When on earth had she started noticing the way he smelled? Thinking like a woman in heat.

Fishing in the bag as he entered the kitchen, he stopped. Then lifted his head. Taylor's skin prickled. The room temperature rose. She swallowed, her throat suddenly dry.

"I thought you'd be at work," he said.

"I'm working at home today. I thought you'd be out on that job with your dad."

"It didn't need four of us." He pulled a box out of the bag. "Connie told me yesterday that your faucet was leaking. I brought a new one."

"It's probably only a washer. I don't think it needs a whole new faucet set."

"I'll return it if it doesn't. Got some washers, too."

She was still standing at the sink, with the carafe resting on the counter. Her fingers hurt from holding the handle so tightly. "Well, thanks. I was making coffee, if you want some."

"Great. I'll take a look while it's brewing."

He hadn't moved, maybe because she hadn't moved. He didn't want to get too close, probably thinking she might throw herself at him again. Lord, this was difficult.

She finally managed to cross to the other counter, where she busied herself measuring out scoops and pouring water. In a few moments, the rich scent of fresh coffee filled the air. But she could still smell him, as if he filled her head like the bubbles in a glass of champagne. The bag rustled, the cupboard under the sink where she kept the small tool chest creaked open, then the box plopped on the linoleum. Metal chinked against metal as he sifted through the tools looking for what he needed.

She chanced a quick glance. His gaze was on her, rising from the hem of her shorts to the sliver of bare skin between the waistband and her shirt. Her nipples suddenly tensed and ached.

She spoke before his eyes touched her breasts. "I'll get my stuff organized while the coffee finishes." Then she rushed out of the kitchen all the way to her office and closed the door. She leaned against the wood to catch her breath.

He'd looked at her. Not in any way he'd ever looked before. It didn't mean anything. He was probably wondering if she'd bring up Saturday night at the bar. In his truck. That look might have been curiosity as to how she'd handle the situation. Maybe he was wondering how *he* should handle it.

It was obvious they couldn't ignore it.

All right, buck up, kiddo. Get out there and deal with the mess you made of a very nice relationship.

HE SHOULD HAVE hightailed it out of there the minute he realized Taylor was home. He'd been ready to leave a strong note telling her she forgot to lock the damn front door again. But then he'd found her standing there in the kitchen. In a shaft of sunlight that made her hair glow with tones of red and gold.

He'd lost his voice and started thinking with his dick. Pretending to look for the right tools while she made coffee, he'd watched her legs, her butt in those shorts, the soft rise and fall of her breasts beneath the shirt. His gaze got caught on the outline of her nipples. He'd stayed in a squat beside the toolbox so she wouldn't notice the raging hard-on in his jeans.

God had been looking down on him when she said she'd take care of stuff in her office. He didn't want coffee, all he wanted to do was fix the damn faucet and get the hell out.

Before he put his hands on her.

She was right. The faucet only needed a new washer, but he'd bought the whole assembly in case, so he wouldn't have to make a second trip. A second time might be his undoing. If this first trip wasn't.

He tensed as her sandals pattered on the linoleum, but he didn't turn. "It's okay, I don't need any coffee. Almost done here. It was a washer, like you thought." The job complete, he turned the water on and off. "See, no drip."

"Jace, I think we need to talk."

The wrench slipped from his hand and hit the sink with a metal twang.

"Uh, yeah, sure." He picked up the wrench, then hunkered down by the toolbox on the floor. "What about?" He didn't look at her, instead futzing with the tools. Refitting stuff that already fit fine.

"About the other night."

He almost crushed his thumb as he slammed the lid closed.

"I don't want this to be an uncomfortable thing that sits between us."

The thing that sat between them was the way he wanted her. The way he'd always wanted her. Saturday night in his truck had merely proven that. While he'd pretended he didn't feel that way anymore, the need had rumbled around in his gut waiting for the right moment to burst forth. This time, he wasn't going to be able to put it away again.

"Don't worry about it, Taylor." He hefted the box back under the sink, then stood, brushing the dust off his hands in a simple gesture. He'd never brush her out of his system as easily.

"I embarrassed you, and I'm sorry."

She'd made him want to push up her skirt and drag down her panties. She turned him inside out, with her firm legs, that bit of skin showing beneath her shirt, and the slight peak of her nipples. His mouth went dry as a dust bowl.

"I want you to know that I'm over it." She spoke to her toes. "I'm not going to do anything weird like that again. So you don't need to worry."

Did that mean she'd stop being a woman who needed a man, or that she simply didn't need *him*? He couldn't stand the thought. "You're not going out to bars anymore?"

She wrapped her arms around her waist, plumping her breasts. Did she know what she did to him?

"No, I'm not going to bars anymore," she answered softly.

"Maybe you ought to look at me when you promise that."

He'd told her to look at him, but he was the one who couldn't meet her gaze once she did. He couldn't tear his own off her luscious nipples. He could swear they were tighter and harder than they had been a moment before. Bursting. Begging him to touch, to taste.

"Jace." Low, husky, hot, her voice reached inside him.

His cock took on a life of its own. So did his feet as he walked to her until he could breathe her in. She tipped her head back to look at him.

"You're lying," he murmured. "You'll do it again. You'll have to." He'd turn to murder if he caught her. "You're still a woman. I know you are. God help us both."

Her eyes, the color of warmed whiskey, darted to his lips. Her tongue flicked out, leaving a glistening trail.

He slowly wrapped her hair around his fist and held her still. "No more bars. No more slick cowboys. I'll give you what you need, Taylor." It wasn't a conscious decision, merely a need pulsing in him that matched hers. He'd be damned to hell rather than let her give herself to anyone else.

He arched slightly to rub his cock against her. She moaned.

With every fast breath she took, her nipples stroked his chest, lighting a fire deep in his belly. He knew it was a freaking bad idea, but worse was imagining her sneaking off to fill her needs elsewhere.

"Jace . . ." She licked her lips. "We shouldn't—"

He couldn't let her finish. "Deal, Taylor? You come to me when you need a man?"

He took care of the kids. He took care of the house. He'd take care of this, too.

Jace tipped her chin up with his finger. "Answer me, Taylor."

Taylor's panties were drenched, she'd gone light-headed from lack of breath, and more than anything, she wanted to taste him. All of him. His lips, his tongue, his skin, his semen. It had been so long since she'd taken a man in her mouth. He smelled salty and hot, felt hard and insistent.

She threw herself at him for the second time in two days. She started the kiss, but he took over. His mouth opened, then his tongue and lips devoured her. She tasted and savored and wanted. Pressing her breasts to his chest, she rubbed against him, the ache in her even stronger than the other night. This was stupid. It was crazy. They'd both regret it later. But right now, she didn't care about later.

Slipping her hand between them, she cupped him. God, he was hard. And big. And she needed him. Now. Pushing him away, she slid down his body until her knees touched the linoleum. Fingers fumbling, she tore at his belt, undoing it and going for the snaps of his jeans. Then she felt his hands in her hair and looked up.

His eyes were dark and oh so readable. His penis flexed against her throat as she leaned in. And she had to know. "Have you ever imagined me doing this to you?"

He swallowed, tipped his head back, then finally looked down at her again. "All Saturday night. All last night, too. And the whole time you were walking around your backyard yesterday."

Lord, she so pathetically needed to hear that. She dragged

his briefs down until he sprang free. A drop of moisture pearled on the tip. She licked it away, then closed her eyes to relish the salty taste. Jace groaned.

"More," he whispered.

Taking him in her hand, she guided his cock between her lips. Oh, oh, it felt so good. Filling her. She glided all the way down, meeting her fisted hand with her lips. His fingers tangled in her hair, pulling, the slight pain adding to the luxury of his taste. Swirling her tongue, she rose again, then sucked on the very tip. He cupped the back of her head and pushed gently. Taking him all the way, she removed her hand at the last moment until he touched the back of her throat. Her muscles tensed around him, dragging yet another choked groan from him. Faster, she took him, sucking harder, grazing him with her teeth. His hips began to rock with her motion, and his hands massaged her scalp, sometimes biting, sometimes soothing.

She gave his body's movements free rein as she grabbed onto his hard thighs to steady herself. His muscles bunched beneath her fingers.

Then suddenly he pulled free. "Christ, I can't hold off. You have to stop or I'm gonna lose it."

"I want you to come. In my mouth. Please."

"Oh God."

She took that for a yes and drew him back between her lips, back home, where she wanted him. Then he came, crying out, holding himself deep as he poured inside her, trapping her head against his belly, holding her with his legs.

She drank every drop as it if were wine. She memorized every jerk of his body, every sound falling from his lips.

It was heaven. She learned it wasn't only her own orgasm she'd needed, but his. The sound of a man's pleasure, the rumble of his desire, the grip of his fingers in her hair as if she were the only one who could wrench such a powerful reaction from him.

She licked him clean as his throb in her mouth died, then looked up at him.

"Jesus Christ, Taylor, Jesus." His gaze was slightly unfocused and his breath rasped in his chest.

Even on her knees, she felt powerful. She felt wonderful. She felt like a woman.

Then a car door banged.

"Holy shit, it's my mother."

Jace jerked away and began buttoning his jeans. "Christ, your lipstick's all over the place."

It was all over his mouth, too.

Taylor rose as if she had all the time in the world, as if they weren't standing to the left of the kitchen window, where, within a few seconds, Evelyn would be able to see them.

As if she hadn't just swallowed his essence and loved it.

She smiled, swiped her hand across his mouth to wipe off the traces of her lipstick, then leaned close. "You answer the door. I'll just . . . freshen up."

"I can't answer the door like this." Panic threaded his voice.

She leaned back and tipped her head. "Like what?"

"Like—like I've been—"

She wanted to laugh at his wild-eyed look. "Like you just came in my mouth?" What they'd done made her feel wild in a completely different way.

"Shit, Taylor."

"She's not going to know. You answer the door and let me fix my lipstick."

Then she left him, scampering across the living room.

Lord. She hadn't felt this good in . . . well, in over three years.

FOUR

HIS BODY STILL hummed. It was seriously not a good feeling to have around his mother.

But Jesus Christ, Jace wanted more of Taylor. If his mother hadn't arrived, he'd have dragged off Taylor's shorts and taken her right there on the kitchen floor. Then on the counter. Then probably on the table, too.

She'd blown his mind as well as his body. He'd never seen a more beautiful sight than Taylor on her knees before him. Jesus. His brother's wife. The feelings he had for her were so damn wrong. Yet what she'd done felt so damn right.

His hand shook slightly as he opened the door, and he'd only just gotten his breathing under control. "Hey, Mom, I'm fixing Taylor's faucet. She's back in her office, I think."

His mom looked him over, as if he were fifteen and trying to sneak out of the house with one of his dad's beers.

"Hi, Mom." Taylor's smile was cheery and her lipstick perfect, but the soft pink glow of lovemaking still tinged her skin. He hadn't tasted her nipples or the sweet flesh between her thighs. He hadn't had near enough of her. Nowhere freaking near enough. But dammit, he couldn't have more. He wouldn't.

Looking from him to Taylor, his mom finally said, "You forgot the time cards when you rushed off earlier."

Taylor tapped her forehead. "Silly me. You didn't have to bring them, I could have come back." She held out her hand.

"I had to go out for some envelopes anyway."

"You want some coffee? I made a fresh pot for Jace. He fixed the faucet for me. It was a washer and didn't need the whole thing replaced."

His mother looked from one to the other again, and Jace knew they'd made one too many faucet references. Then she said, "Sure. I'd love a cup. But don't let me overstay my welcome."

"Never," Taylor said, leading the way into the kitchen.

"I have to meet Dad and the guys out at the Carmichaels', so I'll take off." His dad didn't need him, but Jace needed to get out of the house badly. He grabbed the door.

"Thanks, Jace. For fixing the faucet." Taylor gave him a smile, and he was damn sure she wasn't thanking him for the new washer.

Fishing in his pocket for his keys, he was already making plans for how he could come back during lunch. How he could sneak off for another taste of her. Despite knowing how bad an idea that was.

Dammit. He was losing his mind.

He was almost to his truck when the door flew open. "You forgot the other faucet."

Maybe he could drag her into the truck and drive off.

"Thanks." He took it, his fingers brushing hers. Electricity seemed to jolt up his arm.

"No. Thank you. You didn't have to rush over, you know."

He wondered if she was shooting him some subliminal message he wasn't getting. Then he didn't care, and the words were out of his mouth before he could stop them. "Ask my mom to take the kids Friday night."

Her eyes went wide, the playful smile dying on her lips. "What?"

He let his gaze travel her face, then fall to her breasts. Her nipples were still hard. Or hard again. He liked the effect too damn much. "We didn't finish. You didn't come. I didn't come inside you. We won't be finished until that happens."

He was on the road to rack and ruin, because he knew he'd never be finished with Taylor. He'd crossed a line, and there was no going back to the way it used to be.

She bit her lip. He wanted to suck it into his mouth, touch his tongue to hers, and rub his cock between her legs.

"Meet me by the old barn at Miller's Pond Friday at dark. Eight-thirty."

She stared at him. In the heat of the moment, she hadn't thought ahead to the real meaning of what they'd done.

"Say yes, Taylor." He knew how wrong it was, but he wouldn't allow her to turn back now.

"Jace, we can't. If anyone finds out—"

He shushed her with a look, though he wanted to put his finger to her lips, one more caress to stop her words, to sear his touch into her mind. "No one will know if we're careful."

Doubt clouded her eyes. His heart shriveled. He was her brother-in-law. Worse, Lou was dead because of him. In her mind, now that the conflagration between them had cooled to a simmer, what they'd done held a caste of shame. He was crazy to ask for more. What he'd get was big trouble. But he couldn't stop himself. "Be there."

She shook her head, her eyes dazed with the enormity of what had happened in her kitchen. He didn't think he even had a fifty-fifty chance of her showing up. But he'd be there, waiting, dreaming, praying.

He tossed the bag with the faucet onto the front seat, a hand on the truck's door, and added one final inducement. "And Taylor, don't wear any panties."

DON'T WEAR ANY PANTIES.

Taylor kept hearing Jace say that in a husky whisper. Over and over. She couldn't concentrate on Evelyn's conversation.

The euphoria had lasted fifteen minutes, maybe less, before the guilt and fear set in. She knew she couldn't meet him.

But Lord, he'd tasted good. So good. Felt good.

She put too much creamer in her coffee and not enough sugar. Did Evelyn suspect anything? She'd tossed about lots of odd, assessing looks. But Evelyn couldn't know, not for sure.

Don't wear any panties.

She couldn't get the sound of Jace's voice out of her head. Lord, the way he made her feel. Like a woman again. Powerful. Wanted. Sexy. Desirable. Things she hadn't felt in so long.

But he was her husband's brother. She couldn't touch him again. Not that way. She couldn't hurt this family.

Jesus Christ, Taylor, Jesus. Her name on his lips as he came, filling her mouth, filling her heart. Lord, he was right. They hadn't finished what was between them. They'd barely begun.

And Evelyn was staring at her with another of those assessing looks.

Taylor knew she shouldn't. It was insane, risky. She could rip her family apart. But she needed one more taste of Jace. Just one more, then she'd stop. Swear to God.

"I was wondering if you could take the kids Friday night. For a little while."

Her mother-in-law gazed at her, then blinked and said, "Sure. You know we always enjoy having the boys over."

Her stomach tied itself into guilty knots. "Thanks. I appreciate it."

"Need more alone time?"

Twice in a week, Taylor had asked. Saturday night, she'd said she needed some alone time. The lie hadn't set well. This was so much worse because it was Jace. Still, she searched for an excuse. "Actually, I have a meeting with Brian's teacher."

After Lou died, she'd had a lot of teacher meetings. Brian went through a bad time, acting up in school and picking fights with bigger boys. Things had gotten better, though, when Jace stepped in, spending much of his spare time with the boys.

"Is everything okay?"

"Yeah. It's sort of an end-of-year meeting. Like a checkup." She felt like she was digging her own grave.

"In the evening?"

"The teacher will be out of town for the day. He asked me to meet him at eight-thirty. Is that okay?" Lame, but Evelyn's reaction to the truth worried her. She didn't feel comfortable saying she had a date. Let alone that it was with Evelyn's own son.

Evelyn sipped her coffee. "Sure. All right. Do you want them to spend the night?"

If she really had a meeting with a teacher, Evelyn wouldn't need to take the kids for the whole night. "No. I should be able to pick them up before ten. No later than ten. Promise."

"I really don't mind having them spend the night."

"I wouldn't think of it, Evelyn. You had them on Saturday. Jamey said he beat his grandpa at checkers twelve times."

Don't wear any panties. The husky whisper tingled along her spine. Her cheeks heated, her body warmed, and her breath quickened.

Good Lord. She was talking to her mother-in-law about her kids and checkers and their grandpa.

But the taste of Jace was on her mind and on her tongue. Not even hot coffee nor the trace of guilt could wash it away.

She started to babble, and when Evelyn left, she couldn't remember a thing they'd talked about.

Except the lie and Friday night.

And *Don't wear any panties.*

THE GIRL WAS giddy. Now, Connie was giddy, and Rina was equally as bad as her mother. But Taylor always had her feet on the ground. Good heavens, Connie, the little matchmaker, was right. Something was going on between Taylor and Jace.

Not to mention that story about Friday night. Meeting

Brian's teacher? School was almost out for the year. Why would a teacher ask for a meeting at this late date? And at night?

No, it was Jace who asked for the meeting. Or a date. Or an assignation. Evelyn had been watching out the window. Taylor had stayed on the front path as he drove away. Watching.

Heavens above.

Arthur would have a heart attack. To him, Taylor was the epitome of a mother. The mother of his eldest son's children. In Arthur's mind, she would always be Lou's wife. He wouldn't understand if Taylor turned to another man. To Arthur, no one could replace Lou. No one. Not even Jace. Especially not Jace.

She didn't want to believe that Arthur blamed Jace for Lou's death. He'd never said it, not once. Except one small hint the day they put their boy in the ground. The worst day of her life. Burying Lou made it all real. Arthur had held her hand and whispered, almost to himself, "If only Jace had done what he said he was going to do."

The words themselves were blame enough.

Taylor and Jace.

Evelyn prayed the family didn't come apart at the seams.

"IT'S ME."

Taylor didn't have to ask who "me" was.

The TV was blaring, Brian and Jamey were yelling about something Spiderman had just done. Her house was a mess, popcorn all over the coffee table, and her sons were out of control.

All Taylor cared about was the way the deep timbre of Jace's voice over the phone melted her from the inside out. The thing she'd done to him yesterday morning in her kitchen kept popping into her mind at the oddest moments. Like today, when she'd made a pot of coffee while the boys were getting ready for school.

But what did you say to a man you'd taken in your mouth

just yesterday? Her son saved her from thinking about it. "Jamey, do not spill that soda on the carpet."

"Is that *Spiderman 2* I hear in the background?"

"That and those dastardly children of mine destroying the house. And how do you know we're watching *Spiderman 2*? You're not a closet Spidey watcher, are you?"

"They made me watch it three times the other weekend. And they got every line right just before Spiderman said it."

"Them's m'boys. A movie hasn't been watched enough if they haven't memorized the lines." It felt so easy to talk to him, like it had been before Saturday night. Except for that lazy heat running through his low voice and elevating her body temperature. She snuggled into the couch, pressing the phone intimately to her ear.

"Will my mom take the kids on Friday?"

She didn't want this conversation, not now. "She'll do it," she said, soft and low so the boys wouldn't hear. Somehow it came out sounding sexy, matching Jace's tone. "I told her I'd be back by ten." She modified her conversation for the boys. Little children had big ears when you least expected it.

"You'll only be on your tenth orgasm by ten o'clock, just getting warmed up."

Her body started to buzz in reaction. The boys had quieted down, the Coke didn't get knocked over, and Jace was turning her into a puddle of mush. But she wouldn't reply in kind.

"You're driving me nuts," he whispered.

He was doing exactly the same to her. Jace made it so hard to be strong.

"Who ya talking to, Mom?"

"Nobody. Watch the movie." She rose and carried the portable phone into the kitchen.

"Nobody? Did it feel like nobody when I came in your mouth?"

"No." It felt like heaven.

"You liked what you did to me, didn't you?"

"You know I did." She'd loved it. She still tasted him.

"Put the boys to bed, and I'll come over."

"That's not a good idea." Oh so tempting, but a very bad idea. She had to make him see the risks in what they were doing. "It'll be the only time. Friday, I mean. Then we have to get back to . . . normal." She knew they never would.

He was silent a moment. "I know." He exhaled, his breath teasing across the phone lines. "That's why I'm going to make sure it's so damn good you'll never forget it. You'll never feel like going alone to a bar."

She already had some very big hints of how good Jace would make it. A stranger in a bar would never be enough now. "I told you I wouldn't do that again."

"You'll be tempted. You're too much woman not to need it."

"I'm stronger than that." The man she wasn't strong with was him. Maybe Friday night was a really bad idea. If she knew the full scope, could she stop herself from going back again? And again. "Maybe we need to rethink this whole thing."

"No." He seemed to catch his breath, catch himself. "One time. Then it'll be out of your system."

She closed her eyes and dragged in a breath. She wanted so badly. She needed. It was like a drug, a habit harder to break the longer you did it, the deeper you went. "I really think—"

"You think too much, Taylor."

"Wrong. I haven't been thinking at all." Except about what she'd done to him in her kitchen. And how badly she wanted more. Her nipples peaked against her T-shirt. Her panties dampened. And her good sense circled down the kitchen drain. "Tell me."

He hesitated. "Tell you what?"

It was dangerous. Reckless. Her kids were sitting in the other room. She slid further into the darkened kitchen, further from her children.

"Tell me what it'll be like on Friday."

"Taylor . . . where are you now?"

"In the kitchen. They can't hear me. And I won't say anything. I just want to hear you say it."

He was silent several heartbeats, then he gave in. "I'll suck your breasts until your nipples are tight and hard, and you're arching into me for more. Begging." His breath came a little faster than before. "And when you think you can't take that without coming, I'm going to spread your legs and taste you the same way you tasted me."

The thought of his mouth on her had consumed her last night as she tried to fall asleep. "Yes."

"I'm going to lick you till you scream. I won't leave an inch of skin untouched. And when you think you can't come one more time, I'm gonna slide inside of you, and drive you fucking wild. Christ, Taylor, you don't know what you're doing to me."

His breath was ragged. She knew what he was doing. She wanted to be there to catch him in her mouth. Her legs felt weak, her heart hammered. "Do it," she whispered. "Now."

"I want to be inside you so fucking bad."

Something exploded on the TV in the living room as Jace came with a groan and a long sigh, then, "Shit."

She wanted to slam down the phone and run from what she was doing with Lou's brother. She wanted to carry the phone into her bedroom and touch herself with his harsh breath rasping in her ear. Leaning back against the counter, she closed her eyes and squeezed her thighs together.

"Mom, Brian won't share the popcorn."

Lord. Her children were calling. What on earth was she thinking?

"That's only the beginning, Taylor." Jace seduced her with his voice. "Then we'll do it all over again."

"I have to go."

"Think about how good I'm going to make you feel."

She wouldn't be able to stop herself. "Only the one time. Just that night. Promise." A panicky thread ran through her voice.

"I promise," he murmured, "to make you feel better than you've ever felt. And I won't ask for it again after Friday."

She punched the end button without another word, but his

voice still rang in her ear. As did that hot, heavy groan when he came. He wouldn't have to ask again. She'd come begging.

Back in the living room, she clapped her hands. "Bedtime."

"But the movie's not over."

"It's school tomorrow." She started gathering popcorn bits. "And you already know the ending."

Jamey moaned and griped, but did as he was told. Brian tried to eke out another few minutes. "Go, Brian. Both of you brush your teeth, and I'll be there in a minute."

Grumbling, Brian followed his little brother down the hall.

Lord. This was crazy. Maybe even a little sick and perverted. She'd had phone sex with her boys sitting in the next room. She was losing it. Out of control. Obsessed.

And Friday felt three too many days away.

HE'D LIED. ONCE would never be enough.

Jace stood under the cold shower. He'd called only wanting to hear her voice. But he'd crumbled when she wanted to "rethink" and lost his mind when she wanted to hear the things he planned to do to her. All these years, he'd maintained his distance, separated thought from action. One kiss in the front seat of his truck had shot that distance to hell, and he'd lost all perspective. The memory of Monday morning in her kitchen pulsed in his blood. He'd been damn near dangerous at work today, his mind in his pants, his cock in her mouth. Not a good thing to be thinking about when you're thirty feet up a tree with a chain saw in your grip.

The family had a rule. Work smart and no working alone. He wasn't alone, but he sure as hell hadn't been smart up there. His head had been filled with images of Taylor on her knees.

He needed to get this thing under control. Or he'd end up like Lou.

Hell, at least this time, the death he caused would be his own, not his brother's.

FIVE

IT WAS ELEVEN-THIRTY in the morning, close to ninety on a summer day, and Jace was sweating buckets. He downed a bottle of water, then swiped his arm across his forehead.

"We're making good progress," his dad said, wiping his own brow. "Should be done tomorrow right on schedule." They had another job in Bentonville on Friday, which would carry through to next week.

They cut in the mornings and hauled in the afternoons, so the homeowner wasn't left with loads of crap cluttering the yard. Mitch and David were topping and shaping the last few branches on the oak. It had needed to be trimmed back off the roof for both winter-storm protection and to keep the carpenter ants from infesting the eaves. The two-acre lot around the house would be trimmed to retain the view and give the trees room. Like his dad and brothers, Jace knew every species of tree common to the area and its required maintenance to promote healthy growth. The underbrush needed clearing out, too. Willoughby and the five small surrounding towns nestled in the mountain foothills provided year-round work for Jackson and Sons. Primarily, people living in the foothills didn't maintain their yards with lawns and flowers. The only ones who did were flatlanders, recently moved from suburbia. Most residents let the forest grow around them, chopping it back only when it became a fire hazard.

"You put your sunscreen on, Dad?"

"You sound like your mother."

Jace grinned. When he'd left the office this morning, Mom had told him to ask every half hour.

At fifty-nine, his dad still had a few good working years left. He let his sons do the higher climbing, but he hauled his share of the load. At damn near forty years in the tree business, he deserved more time on the ground.

"If you want, Mitch and I can finish up here tomorrow and you and David can start the Bentonville job."

Jace didn't suggest doing it the other way around. David hadn't partnered him since Lou died. It was Mitch or Dad. Always.

His dad removed his cap and scratched his head. "Nope. We'll stick to the schedule."

In other words, he didn't trust Jace alone with Mitch, even if they'd only be finishing the clearing, hauling, and mopping up.

Together, they watched Mitch and David complete the job with synchronous teamwork. At one time, Jace had worked that way with Lou, each anticipating the other's moves. Timing and skill. You counted on each other to be there.

He hadn't been there for Lou that day. He'd been sleeping off too much partying the night before, and Lou had started without him.

Jace glanced at his dad, wondering how often he thought about that day. Hell, most likely every day. Dad had been the one to find Lou before Jace got there. His brother hit the femoral artery with the chain saw, though God only knew exactly how it happened. Alone in the midst of a nine-acre lot, Lou had been gone in a matter of minutes.

His father never said one bad word to Jace, never accused Jace of breaking his trust, of letting his brother bleed to death all alone. But Dad also never scheduled a job that put Jace alone with one of his brothers.

Shit. Jace popped another bottle of water and dug out the sunscreen tube for his father.

"You hungry?" his dad asked, smoothing a palm of SPF 30 on the back of his neck.

"I'll make the run," Jace offered. The job wasn't far out of town, so they weren't packing lunch. "Sandwiches okay?"

"Sounds good."

His brain crammed full of everyone's preferences, Jace took off, calling in the order so it would be ready when he arrived.

The moment he set the cell phone on the seat beside him, he started thinking about her. Taylor. Her shimmering hair, her nipples, and the way she stroked him with her tongue.

Like yesterday and the day before, she'd consumed his daydreams. He'd have thought the relief he'd given himself last night would have lessened the tension. Instead, he kept remembering the heat in her voice on the phone. *Do it. Now.*

Considering his thoughts of a few minutes before, he should have felt guilty for thinking about her. He was too far gone for that. His guilt over Lou would never be over, but wanting Lou's wife was a whole different matter. That guilt could be relegated to the back corner of his mind with the simple tactile memory of her mouth taking him to heaven.

Damn. Just like that, his pants were too tight, and his cock rock hard.

There was time before the sandwich order was ready. Just enough time. He picked up the phone and punched in the office number, hoping she was working today.

Taylor answered instead of his mom. He took it for a sign. "What time are you picking up the kids?"

"One. It's a short school day."

He glanced at his watch. Plenty of time. "Meet me at your house. Leave now."

"You know I can't do that." She lowered her voice. "And you promised."

"That was for Friday. This is for now. Meet me." He'd beg if he had to.

She was silent so long, he dredged up pleading words.

Then she simply breathed her answer in his ear, "Fine," and cut the connection.

He didn't have a condom on him. He doubted she would have one in her bathroom cabinet. For what he planned on doing to her, he wouldn't need one.

LIE NUMBER THREE. Taylor felt awful. Wasn't that what criminals and addicts did? Said they were sorry, but kept right on doing it?

"I've got a couple of errands to run before I pick up the kids. I'll take this stuff with me and finish it at home this afternoon while the boys are doing their homework."

Her hands trembled as she stuffed papers into her briefcase. Eleven-forty-five. She'd have to leave for the kids in exactly one hour. Lord. She hadn't had a quickie since before she and Lou were married. Lou always said marriage and babies put a damper on that sort of thing.

But with Jace? The anticipation was overwhelming, the fear and guilt debilitating enough to make her light-headed.

"See ya tomorrow," she called as she barreled out the door. She hadn't even looked at Evelyn. She felt like she had a neon sign flashing LIAR over her head.

Lies and sneaking around never did anyone any good. And sneaking around with Jace? She didn't even want to think about the family's reaction.

Just until Friday. It would be over then. They'd have their fill of each other. She'd have her thrill. And things could go back to normal.

Jace's truck was in the driveway. She pulled in beside it. Leaving her purse and briefcase on the seat, she raced up the walk to the open front door. She heard water running in the kitchen. Her heart pounded, her skin blazed, and when she saw him standing by the sink, she almost threw herself at him.

He'd sluiced himself under the tap. Water dripped from his hair down his naked chest. After years working out-of-doors, he was tanned and muscled and exquisitely delicious.

"I'm sweaty. Want me to take a shower first?"

He looked good enough to eat. And he smelled of honest sweat, all male heat. And suddenly she was so damn frightened she couldn't breathe. As much as being near him turned her inside out, so did the fact that the family wouldn't understand.

"This is crazy, Jace. You can't call me up at work like that anymore." She put her hands to her flaming cheeks. "Good Lord, Jace, you're Lou's *brother*."

The sexy smile on his face died, and his eyes darkened. "I know that real well, Taylor. But at least I'm not some hick you picked up in a bar."

He'd neatly sliced and diced her to pieces. "Do you have to remind me about that?"

"Yeah, I do. Because I can't stand the thought of you doing it again." He turned, shoving his hands through his damp hair, his muscles rippling.

His desperate words wrapped themselves around her heart. She needed to be desired this way. A nameless guy she found in a bar could never do this for her. She weakened, wanting to reach out to him.

After a deep breath, he faced her. "Look. I'm here. You're here. The damage, if there is any, is already done."

They were together. Alone. Whatever Evelyn was going to think she was already thinking it. Heat rushed through her. He was hers for right now. She could do all the things she'd dreamed of. She could fill herself with him.

Something lurked in his eyes. Lust and something else. Fear. As if her answer meant more than he wanted to say.

She closed the few inches separating them and plastered herself to his body. "My turn," she whispered.

He pulled back at her abrupt turnaround, his hands on her shoulders holding her away. "Taylor?" Just her name, as if she'd caught him off guard. Maybe he thought he'd have to work harder to get her to do what he wanted. But she had so many wants of her own.

She tugged his hand down, bunching the material of her skirt to mold his fingers against her center. "Make me come."

He froze, his fingers unmoving. She tracked the movement of his Adam's apple as he swallowed. Then finally, endless moments later, his breath fanned her face as he murmured. "Jesus."

Cupping her face, he took her lips, then her tongue. He was wet and hot, and she went up on her toes to wrap him in her arms. Oh, he could kiss. He kissed like he couldn't get enough, plunging deep into her mouth, retreating, coming back for more. He walked her backward until her butt hit the table.

She'd worn another shortie T-shirt, her usual summer wear, and a thin bra. He slid a hand up from the bottom to her nipple. She moaned. Then, pushing the chair aside, he put his hands to her waist and lifted her to the table. "I'm gonna make it so damn good."

She arched into his fingers. "Yes. Please."

He shoved his hands up her skirt, holding her butt. "Up."

She rose, and he whisked her panties down her legs. She wriggled, and together they got her skirt up over her hips. He pushed her legs apart and stepped between them.

"You are so pretty down there."

No man had looked at her in three years.

Jace leaned his forehead against hers and trailed a finger along the crease of her thigh, then across the curls there.

"I want this," he whispered, then slipped inside to touch her clitoris.

She nearly shot off the table, the feeling so intense it was almost an orgasm.

"Easy, baby, it's gonna get better."

He caressed the hard nub. She bit her lip and dug her fingers into his arms. "Oh God, Jace." Closing her eyes, she let her head fall back. Tiny sounds, a moan, a quick breath.

He slid a finger inside her, keeping his thumb on her clitoris. Pulling her legs up, she locked her feet behind him and leaned back until her head touched the tabletop. His touch was nothing like her own. It was rough, callused, extra texture, extra sensation.

"Look at me."

She lifted her head, opened her eyes. His gaze was bright with heat, his brown eyes black with passion. He stroked her. She leaned forward to loop her arms around his neck.

"Kiss me while I fuck you this way," he demanded.

She loved that word on his lips. Dirty. Tantalizing. Want and need and craziness all rolled into four letters. She pressed her mouth to his. He sucked her tongue and pumped her with his finger. Hard, fast. When she came, she screamed. Into his mouth. Rocking against his hand, driving the feeling on and on.

She shuddered in his arms when it was over. "Oh Lord, Jace. That was so good. I can't tell you how good."

He smoothed her hair back from her face and forced her to look at him. "It'll be even better when I use my tongue."

She turned her wrist to look at her watch. Grabbing her arm, he held her. "Don't look at that goddamn watch. We have time. I won't let you be late for them. But I will taste you. And I will make you come in my mouth."

Pushing lightly on her chest, Jace set her back against the table, then hooked a foot around the chair, and pulled it up. Sitting, he soothed her inner thighs with his palms, then spread her to receive him. Taylor leaned on her elbows to watch him.

"So pretty." He blew on her. She moaned and bit her lip. "Beg me, Taylor. Beg me to kiss you here." He traced the tip of one finger across her clit and down her slit.

"Please, Jace. Put your mouth there. Please."

He wanted her to beg. He wanted to hear her say his name in that soft, breathy voice. He'd dreamed of tasting Taylor for almost half his life, dreamed of making her come the way she just did. Lost to herself, completely his.

For one panicky moment there when she'd told him to

make her come, he'd been afraid that reality could never be as good as the dream. Now he knew it could be so much better.

She jerked when he put his tongue to her. Moist and tangy and hot, he sucked the juice of her last come, then drew her clit into his mouth. She moaned and writhed. He pulled both legs over his shoulders and grabbed her hips to hold her to him.

He'd been with women. He'd enjoyed them. But no woman had ever been like this for him. Using his tongue and lips to drive her wild, he took her with his mouth, and he gave her everything he had. Her soft curls tickled his nose. He burrowed deeper. Her moans and cries hardened his cock to a monumental ache.

When he left her today, he wanted her to remember this, wanted her to carry the memory with her day and night.

Her fingers found their way into his hair, twisting. She rocked against his mouth. Panting, she said his name over and over. Her thighs tightened around his head, and the first quake of her orgasm began. He sucked on her, hard, worrying the nub of her clitoris with his tongue, and she exploded with sound and taste, flooding his mouth with the sweetness of her orgasm. He took it all, every cry, every moan, holding her to him until her pleasure was so great, she couldn't take it anymore.

Then he raised his head and looked at her. Her breasts rose and fell with her erratic breath. Her lashes rested against her flushed cheeks. He leaned down, blew on her once more, then swiped his tongue across her clit.

She jerked. "Oh Lord, no more. I think I died."

Jace stood, then pulled her upright by the arms. Her head lolled on her neck. Boneless. Weightless. In the ecstasy of orgasm. He put her limp arms around his neck.

"Oh, Jace." She opened sleepy, lazy, replete eyes.

Dipping his head, he kissed her, gave her the taste of herself on his tongue, then pulled back. "Monday was mine, today was yours, Friday, we'll come together when I'm deep inside you."

He'd tasted her. She'd tasted him. He didn't have to be in-side her to know he'd never get enough of her. She filled his heart the way her taste filled his mouth. She pushed him to ex-tremes, to the point where he'd risk anything to have her.

Only Lou's memory stood in the way.

TRUE TO HIS word, Jace made sure she left the house in time to pick up the boys. Her legs still felt wobbly, and she kept gulping air as if she couldn't get enough.

Lordy-Lord, she'd gotten everything she was looking for that night when she ventured out on the wild side. She simply hadn't figured she'd find it with Jace. She hadn't imagined he could take her the way he had, make her feel such glorious sensations.

This morning, she'd thought about doing a no-show Friday night. Now that was out of the question. Right or wrong, she craved what Jace could give her. She wanted to feel him inside her. She needed the memory when Saturday morning, and the rest of her life, dawned.

The boys clambered into the backseat, their excited chat-ter filling the minivan. "We caught frogs today, Mom," and "Peter got in trouble on the playground today, Mom." She loved their prattle, the enthusiasm of youth, the battle for each to tell her his news first, tripping over their words, laughing.

Today, however, in the midst of all their babble, she won-dered how on earth she was going to serve dinner on the same kitchen table where Jace had given her such pleasure.

SIX

"TAYLOR, ARE YOU sure this is right?"

Friday morning. Each minute ticking by seemed like an hour.

"What's the matter, Evelyn?"

"This says the checking account has a negative balance."

That couldn't be right. Frowning, Taylor punched up the file. It *was* negative. Where had she gone wrong?

Don't ask that. She'd gone wrong the moment she'd thrown herself at Jace in his truck. She'd gone wrong in her kitchen. Twice. But she didn't regret it. Not one single moment. She merely felt sad that it would have to end.

"I'll go through it, Evelyn." Scanning a couple of pages, she saw her error immediately. She'd put an extra zero on one of the checks she'd entered. Could happen to anyone. Except that she usually double-checked everything she input. Then triple-checked the balance. "Here it is. I'll fix it."

"Is something bothering you, Taylor?"

Taylor stiffened. Her mother-in-law had already been at the front desk when she arrived. They'd shared coffee, talked about what Taylor was supposed to bring for Sunday's barbecue, and what time she'd drop off the kids tonight. Nothing unusual in all that. Nothing suspicious.

"Everything's fine, Evelyn. Why do you ask?" Now, that was a stupid leading question.

"You seem preoccupied. It isn't like you to make mistakes."

It was only one. Except that yesterday she'd forgotten to take the receipts down to the bank. And she'd forgotten to pass on a message from the Montgomerys about some additional work they'd wanted done. Which had sent David and Mitch back out to the property to finish up.

What was she supposed to say?

I've been unfaithful to your eldest boy's memory with your youngest son. And I'm afraid I won't be able to stop after tonight.

"I'm a good listener, honey."

Taylor smiled. "I know you are, and I love you for it." And for the first time since Saturday, she didn't lie to her mother-in-law. "I need to work this one out on my own."

After tonight. After she'd finally done the dirty deed with Jace. That would be the cure. Then she'd stop the insanity. She had to.

HE'D NEVER GET her out of his system.

It had been all Jace could handle not to call Taylor since he'd made love to her in the kitchen two days ago. He hadn't come, he hadn't even gotten inside her, but what he'd done to her was making love.

This morning, he'd done all the loading and hauling while David, Mitch, and his dad did all the cutting. He hadn't trusted himself in the trees or with a chain saw in his hand.

He was counting down every hour. Ten hours till Taylor. Six hours till she was in his arms. Four hours until he filled her with everything he had, everything he was.

He quit at five and headed to his apartment. He wasn't a guy who gave a rat's ass what he wore, but he picked black for tonight. Black jeans and a black button-down shirt. Taylor always looked at him when he was wearing black, and he'd long suspected she had a thing for the color. He took his truck by the car wash, stopped at the superstore for a blanket and a bottle of wine. She liked the sweet stuff. He chose a white burgundy for something unusual.

He pulled up next to the old barn at Miller's Pond before eight. The sun hadn't quite set, and it shimmered across the water. He wished Taylor could see it that way.

Miller's Pond and the old barn was a hot make-out spot when he was in high school. In recent times, the pond had taken a backseat to the video game craze and the call of the mall.

Kids these days didn't know what they were missing.

At eight-thirty, she hadn't arrived.

He started to sweat at eight-forty.

At eight-forty-five, fifteen minutes late, she pulled in beside him. She didn't get out right away. Instead, in the last of the twilight, she simply looked through her window at him. His heart jumped to his throat. She'd changed her mind. But at least she was here. He could change it back for her. All he needed to do was put his hands on her.

He grabbed the blanket and the wine off the seat beside him and climbed out. She hadn't opened her door when he got to her. Reaching past her through the window, he took her keys out of the ignition and threw them on the passenger seat next to her purse.

"What are you doing?"

"Making up your mind for you. Get out."

"I wasn't going to—"

"Yes, you were. You were going to tell me you couldn't go through with it." He died a little inside thinking about it. If she said it, he'd go crazy.

Her dress rose up her thighs as she slid out. Barely more than a flowery slip with little straps holding it together and a row of buttons down the front, he wanted to rip it off and bury himself inside her right on the front seat of her minivan.

He shook with how badly he needed her.

Taylor put her hand to his cheek, a sweet scent rising up from her hair to captivate him. "I'm sorry I was late. The kids were making a fuss. But I'm not leaving, Jace. I want you."

He held her palm to his lips and closed his eyes. *You're losing it, man.* Christ, he'd lost it over her a long time ago. He just hadn't known how badly.

"We have tonight. But then it's over."

It was on the tip of his tongue to say it didn't have to end. But he'd promised he wouldn't ask for anything. He prayed she'd do the asking for him. Fear that she was stronger than him cleaved his heart in two. "I know."

"You brought me wine." She took the bottle from his hand.

If tonight was all he'd get, he'd take it. "I forgot the glasses."

"It doesn't matter. I haven't drunk wine from the bottle in . . ." She laughed, a light sound that burrowed beneath his ribs. "Well, I guess I never have. It'll be a first."

He needed to give her a lot of firsts. The first time she came under the moonlight with him. The first time she'd had a man buried to the hilt in three years. With her hand in his, he led her down to the water. Later in the year, the mosquitoes would be out. For now though, the night was warm, the lap of the water at the reeds gentle.

Slipping the blanket from beneath his arm, she spread it out on the grass, then sat.

"You look pretty in that dress."

"You look nice in black."

She said it so shyly, his heart flipped over. Pulling the bottle opener from his back pocket, he came down beside her, then worked the cork. "Ladies first."

She drank, a sip. "Mmm, that's good. Nice and sweet."

He felt like a teenager, wanting to make everything perfect. "I remembered you liked it sweet."

Her lips glistened with wine. He swallowed, then leaned in to touch those luscious lips with his. Her flavor and the drink's sweetness burst in his mouth. He pulled away before he dragged her down and had her right then. They didn't have a lot of time, but he wouldn't rush this.

Stretching out beside her, he propped his head on his hand, holding the bottle loosely in front of him. "How was your week?"

She smiled. Her eyes sparkled in the first light of the rising moon. "It was good, Jace. How was yours?"

"Fine." Better than any he'd ever known. He'd touched her, she'd touched him. That was everything he'd ever wanted. "Are the kids looking forward to summer?"

"Yes. Brian's going to camp at the end of July for a week. And Jamey's doing junior camp at the same time."

"You'll miss them." She'd be lonely. He could only hope she'd need him to ease the loneliness, but July seemed too far away.

"Yeah. But they like it." She smiled again and took the bottle out of his hand for another sip. Then she laid down beside him, tucking her hand beneath her cheek. "Cork the bottle, Jace, so it doesn't leak."

He did as she said, tossing it down to the bottom of the blanket. He'd planned to seduce her, but she touched him first. Just her hand on his chest, smoothing down his abdomen, then back up to his right nipple.

"Thank you for what you did the other day."

"Dessert," he murmured, concentrating on the mesmerizing feel of her palm caressing him. "You were like dessert."

"I was nervous when I drove up just now."

"I know."

"But I'm not nervous anymore." She tugged on his hand, pulling it to her breast. "Remember what you said on the phone?"

"Which part?" He undid the first button, then the second, until suddenly her dress was open to the waist.

"The part about teasing my nipples."

He slid his hand in the opening, cupping her firm bare flesh. "You're not wearing a bra."

"I figured that when you said not to wear panties, you meant I shouldn't wear a bra either."

Oh God. He'd forgotten about the panties, though how he could have, he'd never know. "Are you naked under this?"

"Uh-huh." She punctuated her words with a nod and a smile.

"You make me nuts, you know."

"Ditto." Then she laid flat on the grass and spread the opening of her dress.

She had the most beautiful breasts he'd ever seen. They weren't large, but they were high and firm beneath his fingers. She'd carried two children, yet remained perfect. He dipped his head and took a nipple in his mouth. She arched into him, stroking the back of his neck as she held him to her. She tasted of strawberries or some other sweet fruit. He cupped her other breast with his hand and played with the nipple as he sucked her. She wriggled, moving closer into him.

"Lord, that's good," she sighed. Then she reached down and undid the rest of her buttons. All the way to the hem.

He looked down the length of her as the dress fell open. The slight roundness of her belly, the soft thatch of hair at the juncture of her thighs, and legs, endless legs. He remembered them wrapped around his head.

"Take off your shirt," she murmured. "I want to feel your skin against mine."

He sat up, jerked at the buttons. Damn, he should have worn a T-shirt. So much easier. She helped him push it off his arms, then tossed it to the other side of the blanket.

He came down on her, glided a hand along her thigh. Her skin was so soft, so smooth against his. Then he took her lips, played with her tongue, angled for a deeper, sweeter penetration of her mouth.

He'd show her how good they could be together. He'd make her need him.

Her leg slid along his, her thigh to his hip. She caressed his back and sides with long strokes. "You feel so good, Jace. Make me feel good."

Make love to me, Jace.

Taylor trapped the plea inside. He'd thought she'd changed her mind. He couldn't know how badly she wanted this. Too badly to consider backing out. Badly enough to lie and sneak.

"I'll make you feel better than you've ever felt, Taylor."

He worked his way down her body, from her throat, to her breasts, across her belly to the place he'd been before.

He parted her with his fingers, sliding across her clitoris. She closed her eyes. "Make it better than the other day." Which was a tall order. A huge order.

He pushed two fingers inside her, then put his tongue to her, working in and out, hitting all her sensitive spots at once. She rose on her elbows.

"I want to watch you."

Under the moonlit sky, the sight of him between her thighs was the most erotic she'd ever known. He touched her with total concentration, igniting a fire in her body, playing her like he was a sexual prodigy. She reached the peak, exploded, and fell over the edge before she'd even known she was starting the climb. Her orgasm rushed over her like a hot, wild wind. She knew she cried out, she knew Jace held her down, stretching the pleasure peak out until she couldn't move, couldn't speak.

He crawled up her body, resting his hips between her legs and rocking gently against that same spot so that she couldn't completely come down from the orgasm.

"Was that better?"

"The best," she whispered. "Now I want you inside me."

He reached to his back pocket, came back with a condom packet, then slid off her body to his side. He was quick, practiced, the jeans popping easily, the wrapper tossed aside, and the condom in place. She felt a momentary twinge. But then she'd never minded his bad boy image before. She hadn't thought too much about how many women he'd had.

Or how long he stayed with them. Jace grew bored quickly.

"Come here." He pulled her on top.

She straddled his hips. With the feel of him between her legs and his hard cock slipping slightly inside her, she stopped caring about anything else. She wanted him. She wanted Jace.

She rose above him. He slid in so easily, filled her so deeply. "Oh God, Jace."

"Fuck me, Taylor. Please."

He put his hands at her waist and guided her movements, his hips rising to meet hers, driving home.

"I am so glad it was you, Jace. Nobody else. Just you." She leaned down and took his lips, sealing her mouth to his in rhythm to their grinding hips.

Then suddenly she needed more, something she hadn't realized was so important. "I want you on top. Please, Jace. Make me come with your body on mine."

He held her ribs, then rolled them until he was above her. She opened her eyes to meet his glittering gaze.

"Say it again. Say it's only me." He slid out, then drove back in, hitting a spot high and deep that made her gasp.

"Only you, Jace."

Then he pulled her leg to his waist, intensified the angle of his thrusts and pushed her until she screamed. He shouted her name, pulsing inside her, then let his arms collapse.

She took his full weight, breathing hard, hugging him close. She wrapped both legs around his hips and both arms around his neck. "Don't move, please don't move. Stay like this, please."

Stay like this with me forever.

JACE KNEW HE was crushing her, but she wouldn't let him go, her grip on him tight and all-consuming.

She'd screamed, she'd begged, she'd whispered he was the only one, only him. At least that's how he heard it.

I am so glad it was you, Jace. Nobody else. Just you.

Isn't that what her words meant? Only you. Just you. Nobody else. Shit. He didn't know what she meant. Could have been nothing more than she was glad she picked someone who knew his way around a woman's body.

Shit.

He eased off slightly, holding himself on his elbows to let her breathe. Why was he ruining what they'd done together?

"You okay down there?"

Her eyes still closed, she smiled. "I'm more than okay. What time is it?"

He pulled out and rolled off.

"Hey."

"Sorry, my arms were breaking." Something was breaking, and it wasn't his arms. He angled his watch to the light. "It's a little past nine-thirty."

"I was late getting here. I'm sorry."

He turned to peel off the damn condom. What was he supposed to do with it except litter? He tossed it in the lake with a plop.

Was it good for you, Taylor? Jesus. That was a female line. He'd knew it had been good for her. But was it good enough?

"You're mad."

He pulled up his pants, wishing he'd taken them all the way off to feel her skin against every inch, and flopped back down beside her. "How could I be mad, Taylor? That was the best."

She was gorgeous in the moonlight. A slight breeze caressing her hair, her skin all dewy and sweet, her dress rumpled around her sides and thighs, her body bare and beautiful.

"It was the best," she agreed.

Can we do it again? Soon?

Christ, if he said it, he'd sound like an adolescent.

"You better go." Before he begged. "You don't want to be late picking up the boys."

She rose to her knees, straightening her dress, buttoning up. Then she stood, looked at him. "Thank you, Jace."

Rising to her, he closed his eyes, waiting, aching. *Say it won't be the last time. Please.*

But she didn't utter a word.

He opened his eyes to find her backing away. He wanted her to stay just a little longer. But ten o'clock was closing in fast. If she left now, she'd make it back to his parents' with five minutes to spare. Maybe. She turned at the side of her van, lingered a moment, then climbed in. Leaning over, she checked her makeup and hair in the rearview mirror. Fixing herself, wiping away the traces of his lovemaking.

Then she closed the door, the dome light went off, and he couldn't see her anymore as she backed out and turned the minivan around.

His heart ached as her taillights disappeared at the bend in the road.

SEVEN

TAYLOR HAD LEFT Jace standing on the blanket with the moonlight through the trees flickering over his hard face. Shirtless, his pants over his hips but undone.

She'd wanted so badly to go back, to beg for one more time. How could she give up something as wonderful as what they'd done?

But she had to. She couldn't fall in love with him. What they'd shared tonight was as much as she could ask for. One glorious week.

She pulled off to the side of the road in a dark spot, snapped on her bra, then rolled on her panties. She couldn't pick up Brian and Jamey naked underneath the dress.

Her body was more than satisfied. Yet something didn't feel right. Something was missing. Something terribly important. Maybe if she'd had fifteen minutes more to lie in his arms. Afterglow. Instead, this felt like aftermath.

The lights at the Jackson house were blazing when she pulled into the driveway. Evelyn would have let the kids stay up since it was Friday, no school tomorrow, and because Taylor wasn't going to be late. She checked her lipstick once more and smoothed her hair. She found a blade of grass and pulled it out.

Closing her eyes, she breathed deeply and smelled Jace's clean scent all over again. He said she drove him nuts. Well, he drove her crazy. She'd done things no mother of two growing boys should do with her brother-in-law. And she could never ask for it again.

The kids were bouncing off the walls when she walked in. Evelyn had been feeding them sodas and cookies again.

Taylor smiled brightly. "Hey, guys, were you good for Nana and Grandpa?"

"Like little lambs." Evelyn beamed.

"Yeah, right," Taylor scoffed. Her little hooligans? "Time to go, get your things." Which meant bags of toys, video games, a couple of battle tanks. Arthur bent on one knee, helping.

"How did it go?" Evelyn asked as they watched the kids pick up their stuff.

"Fine. Like I said, it was a checkup. He's doing fine." Was she supposed to meet Brian's teacher or Jamey's? Lord.

"Bri's a good boy. He'll be fine."

Brian. "Yeah. He's going to be fine."

"Jace taking them out sometimes really helps," Evelyn added.

Her heart stuttered, then slammed in her chest. "Yeah. Jace has been great." Her mouth dried up, and she couldn't look at Evelyn. Why did her mother-in-law bring Jace up now?

The boys bounced over to her, and she ruffled each head. "Kiss Nana and Grandpa good-bye."

Arthur gave them each his usual bear hug.

"Thanks for having them. We'll see you on Sunday."

The kids scampered out to the car.

"That's a pretty dress, Taylor," Evelyn called.

Taylor looked over her shoulder. Evelyn smiled. Not her usual big smile, a small one. Almost sad.

"Thanks." It was all Taylor could think of to say.

First that bit about Jace and the boys, then a comment on her dress.

Liars and sneaks. They always came to a bad end.

ON SATURDAY, SHE took the boys hiking in the county park.

"Am I still in trouble at school, Mom?"

"No, Brian. Why would you think that?" Taylor swung out the stick she'd found along the path, pushing up the short hill while Jamey scampered ahead looking for arrowheads.

"If I'm not in trouble, why'd you have to meet my teacher?"

Lord. She was a bad, bad mother. She hadn't told him the lie, couldn't bear repeating it, but obviously Evelyn had mentioned where she was going.

"It was a checkup. You weren't worried, were you?" She put her hand on his head as they walked. "I'm sorry, Bri."

"Was it Mr. Henderson?"

"Yes." For a split second, she couldn't remember a single name. Henderson was as good as any.

"But I saw Mr. Henderson at school on Friday. Nana said he was out of town, and that's why you had to meet him so late."

Brian wasn't questioning her or doubting her. But he was a brooder. And he'd been brooding over what his teacher was going to tell her about him. She'd been very foolish. And selfish.

She bent down, taking her son's arms. "He said you were a wonderful student. He wanted me to know how proud of you he is."

He blinked sad, brown eyes. Sometimes her little guy seemed much older and much younger than his ten years. "Truth?"

"I wouldn't lie about a thing like that, Bri. Not ever." She was filled with lies and ached with guilt. "Give me a hug," she whispered, almost crying when his arms went around her neck.

Then suddenly all better, like little boys could be in the blink of an eye, he rushed after his brother.

Taylor told herself the lies were over. But she couldn't stop the rush of warmth that came with a sudden image of Jace.

LATER IN THE afternoon, Jace stopped by to take the boys out for pizza. They'd climbed all over him like monkeys, and he appeared to enjoy every minute of it. She'd always appreciated how good he was with the boys. They missed their dad, but Jace did a good job filling the void. Today, her heart ached watching them. She wanted to beg to go along, but it was a guy thing. Moms weren't allowed. That had never bothered her before.

After all the activity, the boys had tumbled into bed almost as soon as they got home. Jace hadn't even come inside, simply watched them from his truck as they barreled into the house, then he drove away. They hadn't exchanged a word about last night.

She went to bed at midnight, but sleep wouldn't come. Had Jace gone to Saddle-n-Spurs after he dropped off the boys? Had he met a woman, taken her home?

She was going crazy in the dark. She had to stop thinking about him. Rolling over, she tucked the pillow beneath her cheek. A dog barked in a neighbor's yard. A car passed in the street. She rolled again, this time lying flat on her back.

When she closed her eyes, the soft breeze through the window caressed her face like Jace's fingers. She kicked the covers off and imagined his touch between her legs. Oh God.

The digital clock flipped to twelve-thirty. The portable phone lay on the night table. She grabbed it and hugged it to her chest. She wouldn't call. It was over. It *had* to be over.

She'd called him a hundred times. For this and that. She'd never worried or hesitated before. Before, she didn't carry the memory of him inside her.

She'd promised herself she wouldn't make love with him again. She'd promised she wouldn't lie to her boys. And now she was in danger of breaking that less-than-twelve-hour-old promise.

When she pushed the talk button, the numbers lit up. Biting her lip, she hesitated. She dialed the first three, hung up. But she couldn't put the phone back on the nightstand. This time she dialed all the numbers and let it ring.

HE JUMPED ON the phone when it rang, praying it was her.

"Jace?"

"Yeah." He'd chased her, begged her, cajoled her, waited for her, and now she was calling him. Sooner than he'd hoped. His heart was so high in his throat, he almost couldn't speak.

"I wanted to thank you for last night."

"You did thank me. And it was my pleasure." Pleasure that had lasted only until she'd asked the time. That one act on her part had ridden him like a sore that wouldn't heal. "It's late. Where are the boys?"

"They're asleep."

Duh. "Where are you?"

"In bed."

Silence. He could hear her breathing. A deep inhale, then a long sigh. Why had she called?

"What are you wearing?" He almost hated himself for asking, but he had to know.

"A T-shirt."

"And?" Panties? Or was she bare?

"That's all." Then finally, she added, "No panties."

Ah, Christ. He wanted—needed—to be there, beside her in her bed. Touching her. Making her come with his fingers, his tongue, and his cock.

"Touch yourself for me, Taylor."

"Jace. This is crazy. It's not why I called."

"Isn't it?"

She exhaled. He felt it all the way to his cock.

"I'm sorry. I shouldn't have called. I just wanted to—"

"Wanted to what, Taylor? Tell me that one more time would be okay? Just one more?" He was angry and hard, wanting more than just her voice over the phone.

She sighed. "I've rationalized that it was okay if it was only on the phone."

He squeezed his eyes tightly shut against the ache in his heart. One more time would never be enough. The phone wasn't enough. He had to face that he wanted nothing less than forever with her.

"It won't be just this once, will it, Taylor." Not a question, a solid fact. She'd call and tear his heart apart every time.

"We have to stop."

"No. *You* have to stop. *You* called me." He prayed she'd never stop. He would always sew his heart back together in the morning.

"I won't do it again, I swear."

"You were the one who said it had to end after last night. You. Not me. What is it you really want?" His eyeballs ached, praying she wanted the same things he did. Time. Together.

"I don't know, Jace. I really don't. First, I just thought I wanted sex."

And now she wanted more, more, more. His mind screamed for her to say the words. His gut rolled and twisted, and then he took a chance. "What we did was more than sex."

"Yes. It was."

God, yes. But how much more?

"It can only end badly," she whispered. "Your parents."

"Screw my parents."

Her long silence after his outburst wore him down, forcing him to back off, retrench. He didn't want the secrecy, but if it was the only way, he'd do it.

"If we're careful, they don't have to know." He lowered his voice. "I want to have you again." He closed his eyes. "I want to make sure you never have to go looking elsewhere." The thought of it killed him.

She didn't answer, but he could hear her quickened breath.

He didn't let up on her. "You're too much woman, too hot, too desirable to ever stop needing a man altogether. Don't deny it."

"Jace, please. I . . ."

"I want to hear you come," he whispered, seducing her with his voice and her own needs. "I want to imagine it's me between your legs. Touch yourself for me. Do it. Now." He gave her own words back to her. "Tell me what it feels like."

He could hear the hitch in her breath. She wanted it. He had to get her to do it for him. It was more important even than making love to her last night. Last night, she'd wanted finality. Tonight, he saw a chink in her armor.

"Think about how it felt to have me inside you, on top of you. How hard you came. How good it was. So damn good."

Taylor had lost her voice.

"I can still taste you. You were so fucking sweet and hot."

Jace was right. This was exactly why she'd called. To hear his voice. To remember the way he'd made her feel. She couldn't give up those sensations now that she'd discovered them. And this wouldn't hurt anybody. It was the phone. Merely his voice, the memory of his touch, and her own fingers caressing her nipple. No one ever had to know.

She pulled her shirt up, exposing herself.

"More, Jace," she whispered.

"Tell me what you're doing."

She closed her eyes and pinched lightly. "I feel you take my nipple in your mouth. You suck and I feel it all the way down between my legs."

"I'm kissing my way down your abdomen, licking your belly button."

She dipped her finger into her belly button, her hand following his voice.

"Spread your legs, baby. Let me feel how wet you are."

She felt his quickened breath in her ear as if he were right there. Dipping her fingers, she found herself dripping, ready.

"Oh God, Jace, it aches when you touch me like that." She moaned for him.

"I wanna use my tongue on you. I wanna make you come."

She caressed her clitoris, arching, her fingers biting into the phone. "Please make me come."

"Put your finger inside yourself."

All the way in, then she slid deliciously back out, with a soft murmur. "I'm so wet and slippery. Does it turn you on when I touch myself, Jace? Does it make you want to take your cock out?"

"It's already out, baby. And I'm so fucking hard listening to you. Have you ever come over the phone before?"

She twisted in the bed, spread herself wider as if he were lying between her thighs. "No."

"It'll blow your mind," he whispered. "Keep playing. Rub all that sweet juice over your pussy."

She didn't think she'd ever been so wet or so hot. Her hips moved, rising to meet the push of her fingers. She couldn't talk, couldn't breathe, could only moan and writhe and never let go of the phone, listening to his soft whispers, his hot words.

"Come on, baby, come for me. Come now. Oh, Jesus. I can't hold it. I need to fuck you. Aw, Christ. You don't know."

She came as he did, in an explosion of color and light behind her lids. Jace cried out, his voice wrapping around her, part of her, inside her. She bit her lip to hold everything inside, a soft moan sliding out anyway, even as she gathered in every sound he made, gathered them all to her heart.

Then the phone went dead.

Her body quivered and quaked. Why had he hung up without even saying good-bye? Taylor rolled over, pulled her knees to her chest, and hugged the phone. She was still so wet and hot and needy. Needing Jace.

What was happening to her? How could she keep doing such crazy things? Maybe it was best that he'd cut off so abruptly. Next thing, she might have been begging him to come over. Just playing with him on the phone wasn't enough.

She knew better than to promise herself she'd stop. He'd proven to her that she couldn't.

* * *

JACE LAY THERE, filling his chest with great gulps of air.

God, I love you, Taylor.

He was so fucking crazy in love with her.

Crazy enough to shout it to the world. And to her over a goddamn phone line. He could only thank God he'd managed to disconnect before he'd completely let loose.

He'd been in love with her almost half his life. He was more than used to the idea. But it was too soon for Taylor. She needed more time to accept. He could wait. He would have to because he'd just made a deal with the devil. His silence in return for her body, but not her heart. At least he'd have time to work on her. Until he was as important to her as her next breath. Until she couldn't imagine life without him. Until she was as addicted to him as he was to her.

Until he was sure she could forgive him for having caused Lou's death.

EIGHT

JACE TOUCHED TAYLOR every chance he got. Her elbow as she stepped out of the house carrying the plate of hamburgers. Her fingers as she passed the coleslaw. Her thigh with his as she sat next to him at the picnic table, something he'd engineered.

Connie sniped at her kids, Mitch seemed sullen and uncommunicative, Mom chattered at Taylor's boys, and David and Dad engaged in a heated discussion regarding the proposed bond measure for sewers to replace septics in their water district.

No one noticed as he put his hand on Taylor's knee under the plastic tablecloth, then slid it up to the edge of her shorts. Dangerous, but sometimes women liked a little danger. He slipped down to stroke her inner thigh.

For a moment, she squeezed her legs together, then she stepped on his foot. Satisfied with her reaction, he let go and bit into his burger. Even the simple act of eating made him think of her, his mouth on her sweet pussy.

"Basketball anyone?" David climbed off the bench. "Rina needs practice with dribbling."

Rina, Mitch's youngest, was doing fine with dribbling, splashes of mustard down her white shirt and a glob of coleslaw at the neckline. Connie scooped away the offending splotches, then patted her daughter's behind and sent her after her uncle and grandpa. Mitch followed, as did Jamey and Brian.

"I'll finish making the fruit salad for dessert," Taylor said as she lifted her legs over the bench seat and stood.

"I'll help clean up before I go out and play." Jace wanted an excuse to trail Taylor into the kitchen.

He stacked plates, heaped silverware, and shoved empty cups into each other. Damn, he felt good. It was pathetic what a little hope could do. And last night on the phone had given him hope. He wanted to hear Taylor moan again, drink in the sound of her pleasure, her hitched breath as she came. He wanted to touch her all over.

Connie dragged two lawn chairs over to the side of the backyard basketball court. "You want to watch, Mom?" she called.

His mom looked at him, then the leftover barbecue mess. "Go ahead," he told her. "I'll take care of it."

She rose slowly, then rested both palms on the table. "Tell Taylor to call us when the fruit salad's ready."

Yes. A few minutes alone in the kitchen, a soft word, a touch. Taylor would be crazy, and the salad would be late.

"Sure, Mom."

Taylor stood at the counter slicing bananas when he entered. "I thought only the grilling was man's work," she said without looking at him.

He dumped the load of plates by the sink. "Oh, I think a man's work is far more than flipping burgers. Especially if he wants to keep a woman happy."

She gave him a sideways glance, then pointed with the tip of her knife. "Put the cutlery in the dishwasher and throw the plates in the garbage under the sink," she said, then added, "Please."

He closed in on her. "I've got a better idea. Why don't I show you my boyhood room?"

"No," but she smiled as she said it. "I've seen your boyhood room. Two twin beds, one for Brian and one for Jamey when they sleep over."

"Ah, but have you lain down on one of them?"

"No, I have not. Now start loading the dishwasher or I'll call your mother and tell her you're not pulling your weight."

She started peeling an orange, the citrus scent wafting up from her fingers as he leaned in to blow lightly against her hair.

"I'll load after you lie down on the bed with me. Five minutes, then I'll let you up." He dragged his thumb down her bare arm, his finger brushing the side of her breast.

She drew in a breath and stopped slicing oranges. "Five minutes? What can you do in five minutes?"

He circled her ear with his tongue, then whispered, "I can make you come. Twice."

She shivered and held onto the edge of the counter. "Oh God, Jace, this is idiotic. We can't go to your room. Someone could walk in on us."

Dammit, he didn't care. He moved behind her, rubbed his cock in the crease of her ass. "I'll lock the door."

"It doesn't have a lock." This time, she held onto the counter with both hands.

"I'll put a chair under the doorknob."

"No. It's too risky."

"Sometimes the risk can be worth it." When she didn't respond to his underlying message, he cupped her breasts. He worked her back and front, rubbing her nipples until they hardened against his fingers, and pressing into her bottom, letting her feel how damn hard he was. For her.

Outside on the basketball court, there were shouts of triumph and squeals of laughter.

"Or," he murmured, "I could put my hand in your shorts and make you come right here."

She elbowed him back, then rounded, holding the knife in front of her. "Back off, bud. Or I'll have to slice up your little banana."

"Little?" God, he wanted her, that smile, her laughter against his lips, her body in his hands.

"Very little."

He held up his hands. "I'm wounded immensely."

She jabbed with the knife. "Back three more steps or you're in big trouble, buster."

He backed up until his butt hit the kitchen table. "Playing with a knife is dangerous."

"I'm not playing." She feinted once more, her eyes sparkling.

If he could get her to go back to his room with him . . .

"What the hell?" David slammed the kitchen screen door behind him.

"He refused to load the dishwasher," Taylor said, recovering quickly, but her eyes had gone wide, and Jace read her thoughts. Almost busted.

Part of him wanted David to have caught him fondling Taylor's breasts and ass. At least they'd be out in the open then, and Taylor would have to make a decision.

He might have gotten her to agree that it wasn't over between them, but acknowledge their relationship out loud? It was too soon. At this point, he was sure she wouldn't make the choice he wanted.

"Loading the dishwasher is woman's work. I cooked the hamburgers. Tell her, David."

A tick of silence. David had forgotten how to tease. He'd forgotten how to smile. Then, surprisingly, he said, "I cooked the burgers. You just watched. Better load the dishwasher, buddy, or she might cut off the family jewels. Women can be sensitive about things like that."

Jace looked at him. Damn. His brother had made a joke.

Taylor pointed the knife at David. "Dad cooked the burgers. You have to load the dishwasher while Jace gets the rest of the dirty dishes."

The door opened again, and this time it was his mom.

"Mom," David said plaintively. "Taylor's trying to make us do the dishes. Tell her we cooked. It's a rule we don't have to clean up if we cook."

Taylor's lips twitched. Mom's didn't. She was good at playing possum and hiding expressions when she wanted to.

"Finish the salad, Taylor. Both of you boys get the rest of the dishes, and I'll load the dishwasher. Men suck at loading."

David laughed. Everyone looked at him, but he didn't seem to notice anything was different. "You can't say *suck*, Mom. That's a bad word."

"Suck. There, I said it again. I'm the mom, and I can say anything I want." Then she flapped her hands and moved aside. "Now get on with it you two."

David pushed Jace out the door ahead of him. "See what you got me into, asswipe."

"*Asswipe*'s a bad word. I'm telling Mom."

"Not if I beat the crap out of you first."

Damn. They hadn't had fun like this in three fricking years. Taylor was good for him. She was good for all of them.

Everything was going to work out.

MERCIFUL HEAVENS, THIS was awful.

Should she talk to Jace, ask him what was going on? Evelyn never interfered in her sons' lives. If Connie came running with some nitpick about Mitch, Evelyn remained neutral. She wouldn't choose her daughter-in-law's side against her son, but she wasn't about to do it in reverse either.

What would she say to Jace anyway? Are you making a mistake? Is she going to hurt you? Are you going to hurt her? Are you in love with her, or is this some meaningless fling?

Can you ever mean more to her than Lou did?

No. She couldn't ask any of her questions. The answers terrified her. As did the thought of having to tell Arthur what she'd found out. Goodness knows, she couldn't do it. It was better not to ask.

Evelyn had watched them all afternoon. Jace couldn't keep his hands off Taylor. He couldn't take his eyes off of her either. Then he'd followed like a hound dog when she'd gone into the kitchen.

No one else had seemed to notice, except perhaps Connie. If Connie mentioned her suspicions to Mitch . . . well, Evelyn didn't know what he'd say or do.

And that scene in the kitchen, oh my heavens. She'd wanted so badly to laugh with them. The family laughed and played with the kids, they all enjoyed that, but between themselves, when the children were off being children, all the gaiety seemed to have died when Lou died.

But David had laughed. He'd actually laughed. And joked. Like the old days. Before Lou died.

She should have been delirious. It should have signified her family was on the mend.

Instead, she feared worse times were coming.

NINE

TAYLOR KNEW WHAT that whole scene yesterday in Evelyn's kitchen was about. Jace wanted to see how far he could push her.

How far *would* she go? She wasn't sure. But she did know that if David hadn't walked in, she'd have followed Jace to his old room in his mom's house and gone down on her knees for him.

She knocked her morning coffee over all the papers on her desk. "Darn it."

Evelyn hurried over with a roll of paper towels, and they mopped and sopped together.

"You've seemed pretty preoccupied lately."

Taylor avoided Evelyn's gaze. "Too much coffee. It makes me jittery." That had been her first cup of the day.

Taylor couldn't think of another single thing to say, but her mother-in-law stood there a little longer, waiting. All of a sudden, Evelyn had started making Taylor nervous.

"Really, Mom, everything's fine and dandy."

After one last look, Evelyn sighed. "I'll go to the bank

then. Arthur didn't give me last week's receipts until this morning."

"Bad Arthur," Taylor said.

That won her a smile, and her tension eased. A tiny bit.

Evelyn fluttered around her desk, gathering her purse, the deposit bag, her keys. Then she waggled her fingers and left.

Lord. Taylor took her coffee mug back to the kitchenette to refill. The front door opened. Boots stomped across the floor, and everything inside her went still. Jace stopped in the doorway, legs apart, hands in his back pockets. The stance pulled his T-shirt tight. She almost fainted with need.

"Where's Mom?"

"She went to the bank." Gone for at least an hour.

"How long ago did she leave?"

"A few minutes." She couldn't breathe thinking of the possibilities.

"We need to talk." They could no longer just talk, but he went on before she said that. "These phone calls make me nuts."

"They make me nuts, too," she whispered. They weren't enough. Her heart pounded. She bit the inside of her lip so hard she tasted blood. She felt hot, needy, and dangerous. Then she grabbed his hand, pulling him past the small refrigerator, microwave, and coffeemaker.

"Taylor, what the hell are you doing?"

Opening the bathroom door, she shoved him inside, then turned the lock and leaned back. "I don't want to talk."

He blinked, his breathing harsh. "Taylor." That was all. It held a wealth of meaning. Evelyn might return. The risk. The hurt, if anyone found out. She knew all the reasons why they shouldn't and was too addicted to care.

"I didn't wear panties today."

His eyes widened, darkened. "Christ, you're killing me."

"Then put us both out of our misery."

His fingers flexed. Right and wrong warred with need. He lost the battle. Putting his hands on her waist, he pivoted and set her against the sink with her back to him. His hands skated beneath her jean skirt, pushing it high. "I can't think I wanna fuck you so bad."

She held onto the sink with numb fingers. His words, laced with heated longing, almost made her knees buckle. In the mirror, she saw him rip open a condom with his teeth and bend his head. The backs of his hands brushed her bottom as he rolled it on. He might not have planned this outcome, but he was prepared.

Then he stopped, gazing at her reflection, his fingers twitching on her hips. "Are you sure, Taylor? Now? Here?"

He was making the decision to stop irrevocably hers. The choice hers, but the act would belong to both of them. "God, now, please."

He closed his eyes and put his head back, dipping to run his hand between her legs. Stroking her clitoris, testing how wet she was. How hot.

"Come first, before I do you," he told her. "So I can watch."

He withdrew, then came back at her from the front. She moved with his hand, meeting his gaze in the mirror.

"Does it make you feel out of control?"

She nodded, then gasped as he pressed a finger deep inside. He shoved her up on that cliff edge ready to dive off, then pulled her head back by her hair and kissed her. Long, deep strokes of his tongue in time with his finger.

"Come on, baby. Open your eyes and watch." He held her face to his cheek and made her watch herself.

Her skin flushed to pink. She breathed through her mouth, small pants, soft moans. Then she couldn't keep her eyes open. Squeezing them shut, she cried out, soft and low, as her orgasm pulsed up from his touch and shot through. She trembled, would have fallen if he hadn't wrapped an arm beneath her breasts.

He licked her ear and rocked against her bottom.

They weren't done, far from done. "I want you inside me."

"Your wish is my command." Leaning back, he bent her forward with his hand on her spine, then dipped and spread her to receive him. Hot and hard, he filled her. She wanted to close her eyes to savor the feel of him, how easily he slid inside, how perfectly he fit. But more, she wanted to watch his expression.

Hair rumpled on one side where he'd rubbed against her cheek. His mouth open to grab air. His eyes half-lidded as he buried himself in her heat.

"That feels so fucking good. I missed it so bad."

She held onto the edge of the sink as he began to move, thrusting high, withdrawing, pushing her up to the brink again.

"Look at me," she whispered.

Rich brown eyes the color and depth of the earth itself. She reached back, pulled his face to her throat and threaded her fingers through his hair as soft and as thick as fur.

Over her shoulder, he watched as he pumped inside. So hot. So good. So strong.

He put a finger to her clitoris and she flew clear through the roof. Biting down on her throat, he came, pulsing inside her even as he thrust one last time, hard and high and deep, then held her tight to his body.

Their hearts raced together, their breath mingling. Taylor floated back down to earth in his arms. And opened her eyes to stare at their reflection.

Lou stood behind her, holding her.

For a brief moment, he looked so much like Lou, she thought she was dreaming.

But it wasn't Lou. It was Jace. And Lou had never made her feel the way Jace did. Never. Not even in the beginning.

Jace tipped his head. "What?"

She swallowed. Lou had never made her want to throw all thought and caution to the winds.

"That was good," she whispered. Lou had never taken her so completely out of herself.

"Yeah. Fucking perfect," Jace murmured, turning to kiss the slight red mark his bite had left.

Lou had never made sex perfect.

She'd fallen in love with him the day she met his family.

His mother, his father, his loud, obnoxious brothers. His big, open, loving family so unlike her own. She'd fallen in love with all of them. She'd wanted them for her very own.

Lou had been the way to make sure they loved her, too. But he'd never made her feel the way Jace did.

"What's going on in that mind of yours?"

Jace made her hot, bothered, crazy, needy, wonderful, wanted. He made her feel like a woman. Not just somebody's mother or somebody's wife. But somebody's lover. His lover.

She was too unsure of her newfound realizations to answer.

"You're getting freaky, Taylor." He pushed inside her, as if he thought she needed reminding that he was there.

She couldn't forget. She wanted him again. She wanted to taste him, swallow him, keep him inside.

She'd loved Lou, had thought she'd fall apart when he died, but he'd never made her ache for one more touch. Not the way Jace did. She tried telling herself it was just sex. Because it had been so long. And she'd been so needy. But it was so much more.

Lord. Jace. She closed her eyes and pulled in a long, deep breath until her chest hurt.

She'd loved Lou. But she'd loved his family more. Now suddenly, Jace had become more important to her than Lou had ever been. The disloyalty of it ate at her from the inside out.

More than the family stood between them. Lou himself did. The way he'd died. The way Jace felt about that. She didn't know if she had the courage to talk to him about it. If she ever would.

She didn't know if she had the courage to admit she'd never loved Lou the way she should have.

SHE SCARED THE shit out of him.

He pulled out of her, aching to stay, then tossed the condom in the toilet, flushed, and did up his pants.

She shimmied her skirt down, not meeting his eyes. "You looked like Lou for a minute."

Christ. Shit. Lou. His dead brother. The brother he let down. The brother he let die.

What the hell did he expect? He'd been doing her for a week. Lou was years ahead of him. She wouldn't forget Lou, not after a week. Or a month. Maybe not even a lifetime.

"I'm not my brother's replacement." He wanted to ram his hands through her hair. He wanted to lay her down on the floor and fuck her until she didn't remember who the hell Lou was.

"I know you're not Lou."

What did that mean?

She pulled her skirt down and smoothed her hair. "I have to think. I need to think."

Don't think. Please don't think. Don't remember. Choose me. He wanted to howl like a wounded animal. He would pay for what he did to Lou for the rest of his life. He deserved to pay. But he couldn't stand here and watch her slip away from him.

"I gotta go. I'm meeting Dad and the guys out in Bentonville."

He'd seen his mother driving away and had known Taylor would be alone. He'd taken to carrying the goddamn condoms in his pocket, but she'd been the one to yank the rug out from under him, dragging him into the bathroom. For a minute, he'd freaked out, but then he'd been lost in her. Until she remembered Lou.

He unlocked the door.

"Jace."

Christ. She was going to tell him she couldn't do this again. She was going to tell him to take a hike. Couldn't she tell he was dying here? If he turned to her, he'd wrap his hands in her hair and drag her with him kicking and screaming.

"What?"

"Kiss me before you go."

He couldn't breathe. He closed his eyes and squeezed the doorknob until his hand was close to the breaking point.

"Please, Jace."

She ran her finger down his arm in the softest caress. Taken in by her touch, he did what she asked without a clue to its meaning. *Don't-ever-let-me-go kiss? Or good-bye kiss?*

Cupping her face, he stroked her lips with his tongue. Then he took her mouth with all the love in his heart. She didn't touch him with anything but her mouth, yet that kiss was the sweetest damn thing he'd ever tasted.

He let go and backed out of the bathroom.

"Thank you, Jace."

"Don't thank me." *What does it all mean, Taylor?*

At the door of the kitchenette, he ran smack dab into Connie.

Startled, she bounced back like a little butterball despite the fact that she was a tiny thing.

"Jace"—she tilted her head around his arm—"where're Evelyn and Taylor?"

How long had Connie been standing there? Behind her, the front door stood open. She'd dumped her bag on Taylor's desk.

"Mom's gone to the bank, and Taylor's getting some coffee."

Taylor appeared, coffee in hand. "Hey, Connie, what's up?"

Cool as an ice queen. Those minutes in the bathroom might never have happened. He, on the other hand, hadn't sewn his heart back together yet. "Gotta go."

Connie didn't move out of his way. He was in the mood to brush her aside.

She looked from him to Taylor and back again, then got that little Connie-flash in her eyes. Connie-the-know-it-all. Connie-the-I-know-your-secret. Mitch's wife packed a punch into every look.

"Taylor, I came by to ask if you'd let me have the boys tonight. Peter wants a sleepover because it's the last day of school. He wants to celebrate." She gave Jace another Connie-flash, this one saying she was setting him up but good. "I know that means you'll be all alone tonight, but pretty please."

That said it all. Connie knew something was up. He checked his jeans. Thank Christ his zipper was closed. Connie had her teeth into something, and pretty soon his mother, father, and brothers would know Connie had almost caught Taylor and Jace doing . . . something. He didn't give a flying rat's ass. If it was out in the open, Taylor wouldn't be able to hide from it either. She'd have to make up her mind.

He'd need to ask her the question first.

"Of course, the boys can come over." Taylor hadn't moved, neither closer to him nor farther from him. "I don't mind being alone for a night."

He glanced at her, only to find the look in her eyes unreadable.

Well, she wouldn't be alone tonight. Then tomorrow morning, he'd ask his question, and she'd need to figure out her answer.

He couldn't stand sharing her anymore. Not even with her husband.

TEN

"NOW WHAT DID you really come over for, Connie?" Because Connie could have *called* to invite the boys for a sleepover.

Just like that, Connie burst into tears, where moments before, she'd been smiling.

"I'm not pregnant."

Taylor patted Connie's hand and murmured, "There, there."

It was a blessing in disguise, not that she'd convince Connie of that. Children were an awesome responsibility, not one to be taken lightly. And no matter what anyone said about how three was cheaper than two or two was cheaper than one, it was crap. Personally, Taylor didn't know what she would have done without Lou's life insurance.

"And Mitch doesn't even want to touch me anymore," Connie buried her face in her arms.

"He must have touched you if you thought you were pregnant."

"I mean after I told him I might be pregnant." Connie shifted enough so that her words were muffled in her arms.

Taylor sat back. "You said you were going to wait until you were sure."

Connie raised her head. "I couldn't help myself. I was so excited. And I cooked this gorgeous dinner and put the kids to bed early, and—" She threw herself across her arms again. "And it all went to hell in a handbasket."

"When was this?"

"Friday."

Friday. When Jace had been making glorious love to her. Well, that was a melodramatic sentiment. He'd been fucking her. Didn't he always call it fucking instead of making love? It hadn't bothered her until this moment. In fact, the word was sexy when said in that husky, needy way of his.

"He won't talk to me," Connie moaned.

Ah, the silent treatment. Lou had been an expert. But she couldn't think about Lou now. She needed time alone for that. For reflection and analysis. Like tonight, after she'd dropped the boys off at Connie's. In the bath—a nice, steamy bath with a tangerine fizz ball scenting the water.

While she waited for Jace to arrive.

She knew he would. He had to. She wanted to believe he couldn't help himself. How far she'd sunk. Their affair would eventually blow up in her face, but taking him in the bathroom *had* been an irrevocable decision. She'd chosen not to stop, to have him whenever she could. She just needed to figure out how her revelations about Lou changed everything.

"You're not listening to me."

"Of course, I am." What had Connie said?

"I said my period started this morning. I feel all bloated and ugly and achy and I hate it."

She knew Connie hadn't said all that. "Did you take some ibuprofen?"

Connie scrunched her lips mutinously. "I don't need drugs. I need a baby."

The truth hurts, but sometimes it had to be said. "You know, Mitch has got to want the baby, too."

"But I'm the one who carries it. I'm the one up all night feeding and diapering and soothing. I take care of everything."

"And Mitch pays for everything."

"You sound just like him. A big family was something we always planned on having." Connie glared.

Well, she'd said her piece. Connie didn't want to listen. Done. "What did he say when you told him you weren't pregnant?"

"I haven't told him. He'd already left."

"Well, at least it will give you a chance to work out a compromise."

"How do you compromise on a baby, Taylor? You either have one or you don't. There is no compromise."

"You can compromise on the timing." She patted Connie's hand. "You're only twenty-nine. There's time." She wondered if Jace wanted children of his own. He was so good with the boys.

The ultimate quick-change artist, Connie dried her eyes and sighed. "You're right. I'm just feeling sorry for myself." She touched Taylor's hand. "I don't know how you put up with me."

"Because I love you like a sister."

Connie sniffed one last time. She was never down for long. "Mitch and I will work it out. I'll convince him somehow."

"I know you will." Taylor wasn't sure of that, but she didn't want Connie to start crying again. "What time shall I bring the boys over?"

Connie's eyebrows popped up. "Better make it around four. Are you sure you're going to be all right on your own? You could come, too, if you want."

Right. That is not what Connie had planned. Taylor didn't know how she felt about Connie playing matchmaker. Connie didn't really get all the family dynamics. Everything was black and white to her. She had a baby, or she didn't. What Mitch wanted was irrelevant. Taylor wanted Jace, or she didn't. What Evelyn and Arthur thought about it was immaterial.

Things weren't that simple.

Maybe they would be after tonight. After she'd slept in Jace's arms and woken up beside him in the morning.

JESUS, HE WAS freaking nervous. He parked around back on Lou's old motor-home pad so his truck couldn't be seen from the road, since he intended to leave it there all night.

Taylor had turned off the outside lights. The kitchen and family room were dark, blinds closed, as well as her bedroom. The only beacon guiding him, besides the moon, shone from the small bathroom window.

Unlocking her front door, Jace stepped into a collage of scents and candle flame flickering across the walls. She'd left four candles burning on the table. The main bathroom was to the left of the family room. Steam spilled out into the hall-way.

He braced himself with his hands on either side of the doorway.

The long, narrow room smelled like tangerines. Steam beaded on his forehead. She stood in front of the mirror, hair streaming over her shoulders, torso wrapped in a towel, and her left foot on the counter. Smoothing lotion from her calf to her knee, she then delved beneath the towel to knead the cream into her thigh.

Je-sus. He went up in smoke.

She put her foot down and held out the tube to him.

"I haven't done the other leg. Do it for me."

Squeezing a generous amount in his hand, he went down on one knee. "Give me your foot."

She raised her leg, the towel falling open with a tantalizing sneak peak. Starting with her foot, he spread the lotion up her calf and thigh, his fingers lightly brushing the curls at her center. Taylor shivered.

He started over at the bottom, rubbing in the excess, first her instep, toes, ankle. She steadied herself with a hand on his shoulder, kneading him the way he did her.

"You give a good rub," she murmured, her voice a low caress.

"I give good other things, too."

She put her head back. "Mmm. I know."

She had no idea how good he could be. After tonight, though, she would. After tonight, she wouldn't be able to turn him away. He started on her thigh. A moan escaped her.

He tugged on her towel. "You don't need this."

She freed the upper edge, and the whole thing pooled behind her on the rug.

She took his breath away. He couldn't move beyond the simple touch of his gaze on her. She was perfect. Plump breasts, creamy, rounded belly, and dusky curls at the apex of her thighs. Moisture glistened there. He leaned forward to tongue it away like the sweetest wine.

She rewarded him with a sharp intake of her breath and a soft sound in her throat.

He nosed her belly button. "You're beautiful."

"I've got stretch marks times two."

He put his lips to each and every one. "They're gorgeous."

She ran her hand through his hair, then fisted her fingers and pulled his head back. "You are a freak."

He grinned. God, he loved her. Like this. Making him laugh. Making him hot.

"Hey, I'm trying to be romantic here, and you're throwing my compliments back in my face."

"You don't have to be romantic to get what you want."

His smile died. "Tell me what you think I want."

She pushed her hips against him. "To fuck me."

He'd never heard her use that word, and he took so long to speak, he knew she doubted he'd answer. He gave her what she asked for. The truth. "Oh, yeah. I want to fuck you. Over and over. Until you don't ever want me to stop." Taking her butt in his hands, he brought her to his face, breathed her in, held her scent. "Not fucking ever, Taylor."

She combed both hands through his hair, massaging his scalp, his temples, the back of his neck. "Then get started."

She didn't understand what he was saying, but he let it go. For now. Pushing her to the wall, he put his hand between her legs and opened her to his touch.

He'd have her this way now, her body, her orgasms. And hope like hell she'd give him her heart and soul someday soon.

She already owned his.

ELEVEN

JACE TONGUED HER moist center with slow circles. She forgot her gentle massage in his hair and tightened her fingers, pulling at the roots. He only went at her harder, faster.

"Oh God, Jace, you look so hot doing that."

He raised his head long enough to lock gazes with her.

"Don't stop," she begged and guided him back.

The sight of Jace, holding her still, his head between her legs, his black-clad shoulders against her naked skin was incredibly erotic. A fresh burst of moisture filled her. Taylor had never imagined how sensual the light could be.

Jace made her feel beautiful. She preened for the mirror, arching her back, biting her lip, pinching her nipple. Heat shot down through her belly to her clitoris. She jerked against his mouth. He gripped her bottom harder, pushed deeper, then sucked her clitoris into his mouth in a rush of mind-blowing pleasure.

Leaning her head against the wall, she watched herself in the mirror through half-closed lids. A woman on fire. A woman dazed. A woman taken completely by the man between her thighs.

She raised her foot, stroking him with her calf until he let go with one hand and pulled her leg over his shoulder. Now fully open to him, he pushed two fingers into her. Her toes curled, she moaned, cried out, leaped to the sky, and closed her eyes.

"Don't ever stop, please don't ever stop. God, Jace." She panted and squirmed. He wouldn't let her go, branding her with his mouth and his tongue, his fingers still inside her.

Lou had never made her feel this way.

Jace eased off, lapping at her lightly, keeping her close to the edge, hungry for more, but back in her own body.

I want to fuck you. Over and over. Until you don't ever want me to stop.

It was the closest he would ever come to telling her how he felt about her. Taylor understood that. She'd learned that this morning, along with her own set of revelations. She rubbed his head, needing to feel him beneath her fingers. Then, her hands on his cheeks, she made him look at her. His eyes were dark pools, and his lips shone with her moisture. She bent to lick it off, then eased down on her knees between him and the wall, resting her head in the crook of his neck.

Her own taste along with his lingered in her mouth. His heart beat next to hers, hard, fast, as if what he'd done had turned him inside out just as it had her. He freed the tangles she'd somehow gotten in her hair.

"I'll never stop. Not until you want me to." His voice rumbled against her chest, her lips. She kissed his throat.

She feared talk of the future, of his parents, of telling each other dreams they might never share together. She feared learning the real reasons he seemed to want her so badly. She had the boys, the family, and a life that included Jace in a role he'd played all his life. Not the role he'd played this week.

Reaching between them to palm his erection, communicating with her touch, she put her worries and her ghosts aside. Until tomorrow. For tonight, she'd take this, Jace in her hands, her mouth, her body. "We shouldn't stop yet."

Pulling back, he put his hand over hers, and together they

brought him once more to hot, heavy breathing and rock hardness.

"Let me handle the whole thing while you keep your clothes on." She liked his black jeans and shirt next to her nakedness, the rasp of the rough material against her bare skin was unbearably sexy.

Pushing him back to rest on his elbows, she undid his belt and popped the buttons, being sure to let her fingers brush him time and again.

"Don't make me come. I want to be inside you for that."

"Shh. We have all night."

She grabbed the waistband of his jeans and briefs, pulling them over his hips as he lifted slightly to make the job easier. His erection jumped free.

He stroked himself. She batted his hand away. "Stop that. I get to do it all."

"You loved listening to me do it the other night."

She had, more than she'd ever thought she would. "I'd rather lick you myself." She climbed between his legs, taking him in her hand.

He pulled her hair off her face, fisting it into a ponytail. "Yeah. I like watching you do that, too. But one day, I want to stand at the foot of the bed while you make yourself come."

"That is so bad." The idea turned her insides to jelly. "You're messing with my concentration here."

He kept talking when she took the tip of his penis into her mouth and sucked. "It would be the most beautiful thing I've ever seen. Except when you dropped the towel." He pushed gently on her head, and she slid down his length. "Oh shit, that's so damn good." His hips rose, driving him deeper.

He talked, a nonstop litany of compliments and curse words. Lou had never talked or laughed during sex. Jace turned it all into something about her, about the perfect feel of her hand at his base, the incredible swirl of her tongue, the absolute rightness of her sucking the tiny drop of semen from his slit.

"I love watching you do that. Your lips are so red and so sweet. You're so fucking good for me."

He moved her head, angled her, thrust up against her, drove harder as if he were making love to her mouth.

"Jesus, Taylor, fuck."

His words, his sounds, his groans of pleasure made her body weep with need. When he began to throb in her mouth, when he was close to pumping himself into her, his hands on her head drove him as deep as he could go. She dug her fingernails into his sides, squeezed her thighs, and came at the moment he exploded.

His body jerked, he shouted her name, and held her as she drank from him. When he was empty and she was full, he lay prone on the floor. She collapsed across his hips and rested her face on his belly. Gently stroking her hair, her cheek, her lips, he whispered words she couldn't hear over the pounding of her own heart and the rush of air in and out of her lungs.

She'd have stayed that way forever if the phone hadn't rung.

Lord, the kids. Calling to say good night.

Taylor jumped up, grabbed the towel, and ran into the family room. Where on earth was it? She found the phone on the floor between the coffee table and the couch.

"Hey, Mom, you sound out of breath."

"I was trying to find the phone because *someone* didn't put it back in the cradle." Half-truths came so easily now.

"Jamey used it last."

Then she heard Jamey's little voice in the background, "I did not, he did, Mom. Brian did it."

"Are you all having fun?"

"Peter got a cool new PlayStation game. But Rina keeps wanting to play and messes everything up."

"Men have to learn tolerance around women, Brian."

"Uncle Jace always says that."

"Uncle Jace is right."

Uncle Jace came up behind her, slid his arms around her waist, then sucked on her neck.

"What's that noise, Mom?"

"The phone's crackling." She wriggled against him, trying

to get loose. Jace pulled the towel from her death grip and threw it across the couch.

"Do you miss us?"

"Of course I miss you, sweetheart."

Jace cupped her breasts and tweaked both nipples. She almost squeaked.

"What time are you picking us up in the morning?"

"Noon. Don't stay up too late." They'd be up past midnight telling scary stories in Peter's room.

Jace slid both hands over her belly and between her legs.

She bit her lip as Brian promised not to stay up too late.

"Jamey wants to say good night."

"All right, sweetheart. Sleep tight. I'll see you tomorrow." She clamped her thighs on Jace's questing hand and tried to elbow him.

"Mom?" Jamey, her baby.

"Hi, sweetie. Are you having fun?"

"Girls suck, Mom."

"Jamey!" Where on earth had he heard that? "You don't say that about girls."

Standing so close he could hear everything, Jace whispered in her other ear. "Girls do suck, Mom."

This time, her elbow connected.

"I'm sorry, Mom," Jamey muttered.

"Promise you won't say that again. Did you say it to Rina?"

"No. Peter said it to Aunt Connie when Rina jumped in the middle of the checkerboard."

She tried not to laugh. Then Jace put his hand through her legs from behind to find her clitoris with unerring accuracy. Lord. "You didn't promise, Jamey."

"I promise."

"Now say good night, Mom," Jace whispered, his breath hot in her ear.

"Good night, Jamey. I love you, honey. Bye."

Jace grabbed the phone and tossed it onto the couch. And didn't miss a beat of his sweet massage between her legs.

"You're hot down here. And wet. Really, really wet."

"You're terrible doing that to me when I'm talking to the kids." God save her soul, she'd loved it, the play, the uniqueness of being touched in secret. Something totally apart from the boys. Something more than simply being their mother.

"I'll try to do better," Jace said, then pushed his fingers up hard and fast inside her. She gasped, teetering on the edge.

"Ready to fuck me, Taylor?"

"I like it when you say the word *fuck*," she said, then felt her face heat after she said it.

"Fuck." Then he laughed, withdrew his fingers, turned her around, and pitched her backward onto the sofa, landing on top. "So you like dirty talk, huh?"

She buried her face against his throat. "Yeah. Am I bad?"

Bracing himself on his elbows above her, he held her face in his hands. "Say it. Tell me what you want me to do to you."

Something broke loose inside her. "Fuck me, Jace. Hard."

His eyes were dark wells except for a single point of light from God knew where. "Christ, you make me so fucking hot and insane."

"Please fuck me *now,* Jace."

"You're killing me, woman. Clothes on or off," he murmured in her ear.

"Off." She wanted every inch of his skin against hers.

"If it's a no-clothes affair, then we better take this to the bedroom where I can spread you out like a feast." He rose, snuffed the candles, then led her down the hall to her bed.

Lord. There were so many things they hadn't felt and done yet. But they had all night. She wanted to savor every moment.

TWELVE

JACE LAY FOR long minutes before opening his eyes, savoring the feel of Taylor's skin against his. Always getting out the night before, he'd never woken up beside a woman in the morning.

Taylor was his first.

Blue jays squawked in the front yard trees, and a squirrel or some other small animal scampered across the roof. Boneyard the cat mewled from the window ledge outside.

"She always does that," Taylor muttered. "My little alarm clock. What time is it?"

An ache started above his eye, a stab of pain so real he had to shut his eyes against it until it quieted to a steady throb.

Why did she always have to know what time it was?

Because she was a mother. He'd always admired her mothering abilities, the way she used to hear Brian cry in his crib before anyone else did, the way she could ferret out their agonizing boyish secrets, then kiss the hurt away.

"Kiss me good morning." *Kiss the hurt away.*

She looked at him, smiled, her lids at sleepy half-mast. "I haven't brushed my teeth yet."

"Neither have I."

The kiss was delicious because it was her. Life was freaking worth living because he'd woken up beside Taylor this morning. Because he'd made love to her before falling asleep. Because her sweet tush pressed into his exceptionally hard cock in the middle of the night. Pulling her leg over his, he'd taken her from behind, slipping inside her before she was fully awake. She'd come, crying out loud enough to disturb the cat outside the window. Sleep again. Only to wake to her mouth sucking him and her hand priming his balls. He'd taken his fill of her once more as dawn broke through the window.

Yet he wanted her again. Now.

"Something's up, Mr. Jackson."

Her hand billowed the covers as she found him.

"Don't you want to know what time it is?" His last word split in half by his groan.

"I already looked. It's eleven. We overslept. But I think we can manage a quickie before I have to pick up the boys."

"You're a very organized woman."

"Why, thank you." Then she grinned. "Now fuck me, Jace."

Last night, she'd said it right before her orgasm. *Fuck me with your fingers, fuck me with your mouth,* and plain old *fuck me.* The woman had gone wild with the word.

Nothing had ever made him hotter.

He rolled her beneath him, then reached for the last condom on the side table.

"I get to put it on this time."

"It's tricky." He dropped the packet onto her palm.

Taylor wriggled from beneath him. "Get on your back."

He let her go at him. "If you don't hurry, this won't be a quickie." Not quite true, because if she fondled him much longer, he'd lose it before he ever got inside her.

She sighed. "Ah, I think I did a perfect job."

"Too fucking perfect." Damn near close to combustible. "Now get on top of me."

He hoisted her aboard with his hand on her butt. Rising

above him on her knees, she took him in her hand, then stroked his cock along the center of her slit.

"Shit." She was sizzling hot and creamy wet, and he wished to God he could have her without the condom. "Fuck me, Taylor."

Her chocolate-sweet eyes deepened to the color of rich liqueur. "You can't say *fuck* in front of the kids."

"I've never said *fuck* in front of the kids."

"You can only say it to me."

"I promise. Anytime you want. Fuck me now, please."

Sliding him deep, she threw back her head and moaned as she settled. "Oh Jace. You feel so good. You make me want to come without even moving." She flexed around him, heightening her own pleasure with her inner muscles.

He damn near burst off the bed, pushing up into her, then grabbing her hips as he started to pump.

Steadying herself on the bed, she matched the rhythm he started. He couldn't hold it with her. She took him, turned him inside out, and brought him to the edge of orgasm in seconds.

"Don't ever stop wanting this." He gritted his teeth around the words, held on long enough to say them.

"I'll never stop, Jace. Not ever. I promise."

And he lost everything he had, everything he was. Heart, soul, body, and mind as he poured himself into her, as she cried out his name when she came.

He hadn't quite caught his breath, but he managed to open his eyes when he felt her stretch. She arched, ran her hands through her hair, over her breasts. Then she smiled.

"That was very, very good, Jace."

"Jesus Christ! What are you doing?"

Taylor shrieked and dove beneath the covers, Jace's cock popping free of her and flapping in the wind before he even thought to pull the sheet up.

David stood in the doorway.

The adrenaline high pumping through Jace's veins set his skin on fire. "Why the hell didn't you knock?"

His brother's lip curled. "I knocked. You were too busy screwing to hear me."

"Shut your damn mouth."

David shoved his hands through his hair and turned a circle in the doorway. "I can't believe this."

Taylor hadn't moved, but he heard her muffled breath, hard and fast, beneath the mound of bedclothes. He knew. Her worst nightmare. That someone would find out. Too soon. She wasn't his yet. They needed time.

He wanted to howl or beat the shit out of his brother. "Get out, David."

His brother fisted his hands and marched two paces into the room. "I didn't come here to bust up your little screwfest."

He'd kill him for that, smash him face first into the dirt.

"Jamey's hurt. Connie and Mitch took him to the hospital over in Bentonville. And we've all been trying to call Taylor, but her damn phone was busy." The last ended in a shout.

Taylor shot from her hiding place. "Jamey?"

"Yeah. *Mom.*" David fairly snarled the word at her.

She didn't even flinch, her whole concentration on Jamey. "Is he okay? What's wrong? What happened?"

"He fell out of the big oak in Mitch's backyard. I don't know if he's okay."

She clambered from the bed. Naked. Whispering, "Oh my God. Oh my God," as she slammed drawers looking for her clothes. Panties, shirt, no bra, jeans. She dressed in front of them both without a thought, even as she cried. "Oh Lord. Oh Lord."

Jace couldn't stand it. "Wait in the family room, David."

"Sure thing. *Brother.*" The same snarl on his lips. "In fact, I'll meet you in the emergency room. After you clean up."

Then he was gone, and the front door slammed. A moment later, his tires squealed in the road.

"Oh my God, Jace. What if he's dead?" She flopped on the side of the bed, her sandals in her hand.

Jace threw aside the sheet and pulled her to his chest. "He'll be fine. Kids fall out of trees all the time."

Lou fell out of a tree and bled to death when he sliced open his femoral artery.

She jerked out of his arms as if she'd had the very same thought. "I have to get to the hospital."

"Wait a minute and I'll take you."

"I can't wait. I need my purse." She was out the bedroom door before he made it out of the goddamn bed.

"You can't drive like this."

The front door slammed for the second time that morning while he was still in the freaking hallway. Naked.

She hadn't brushed her hair or her teeth or wiped away her own come from between her legs. And she hadn't needed him.

Her kids would always come first. He knew that, wouldn't have had it any other way. But he wanted to offer his strength on the drive to the hospital, his arms to hold her.

And he was a freaking pantywaist. Jamey was hurt. Damn David for not being able to tell her more. Jace tossed out the condom, yanked on his jeans and shirt, shoved into his shoes.

On the end table in the family room, the phone cradle was empty. He found the portable stuffed down between the cushions. Where he'd thrown it last night before he made love to her.

Before he'd fucked her.

She hadn't pushed the end button when he took the phone away. No one could get hold of her because he hadn't let her alone long enough to cut the connection.

Out back, he rammed his truck in gear and backed up, barely missing the neighbor's fence.

He'd been idiotic all those years ago when he'd fallen in love with his brother's wife. He'd been reckless when he'd drowned his misery by drinking himself into a stupor. He'd been criminal the day he'd overslept as his brother waited for him on a nine-acre property in the middle of freaking nowhere.

Lou had died because Jace hadn't been there to help him.

This time, he'd separated Taylor from her son. He'd never forgive himself if anything happened to Jamey.

*   *   *

SHE'D BEEN WITH Jace when her baby needed her. It was the only thought in her head. Her baby needed her, and she'd been thinking only of herself. Only of *her* needs.

She shouted at Jace that night in his truck. *I'm not just somebody's mother.*

Oh yes, she was. That's exactly what she was. And she hadn't been there when her baby needed her.

She did not drive like a crazy person. She did not cry, because she wouldn't be able to see if she did. She needed to get to the hospital in one piece. That was her duty as a mother. And she wouldn't shirk it. Not ever again. Jamey and Brian came first. Always. *Please, God, let him be all right.*

She didn't think about how Lou died falling out of a tree. If she did, she'd wreck the car, and let her baby down again. Nor did she question why she hadn't heard her cell phone or why her other line was busy. Inconsequential. All that mattered was getting to Jamey. And never again leaving him alone.

She parked in the hospital lot without getting a scratch on the minivan. She ran across the pavement without losing her sandals or falling. She performed with perfect execution.

She would be the perfect mother from now on. As soon as she made sure her sons were all right.

TAYLOR WASN'T IN the emergency room when he got to the hospital, but he'd parked next to her van in the lot, so Jace knew she'd made it there safely. His mom entered through a door on the right. Dad, Connie, Mitch, David, and the kids were clustered in the corner. Nobody saw him.

"Taylor's with him. He'll be fine. He broke his arm."

Jesus, thank you, God. He wasn't dead, he wasn't maimed.

Connie started crying. The way she was nestled into Mitch's arms, Jace figured she'd started and stopped several times. "It's all my fault, Mom. I wasn't watching carefully enough."

His mom snorted. "Kids are kids. They're into trouble before you see the smoking gun. Mitchie, take your wife home."

Mitch hadn't been Mitchie since he was nine, which only went to show the stress his mom was feeling.

Then she saw him. "Jace, where were you? I kept calling."

David had obviously kept his mouth shut, though now, seated next to Dad, he glowered through slitted eyes. He could ask David to keep Taylor's secret, his secret. He could hope Taylor would let him close enough to try again. He could lie to his family. And keep on lying until Taylor either blew him off or said she couldn't live without him.

He might have gone on hoping if Taylor hadn't walked through the door at that moment, Jamey's right hand securely in hers, the little guy's left arm in a sling.

"Jace was with me."

The entire family stared at her. Taylor didn't offer an explanation, but her tone told them the story. Her stark eyes revealed everything. He hadn't been over there fixing her faucet or riding her lawn mower, and she was done lying about it. She was done with him.

"Come on, Bri, let's go home. Connie, thanks for bringing Jamey to the hospital."

"I'm so sorry, Taylor."

Taylor shrugged off the apology. "Don't be silly. Jamey's fine. You acted quickly." Easy words, but she'd aged five years since this morning when she'd told Jace to fuck her. "Mom, Dad, thanks for coming. I'm glad you were here for the boys."

His mom answered her. "We're always here, Taylor."

"My butt hurts sitting on these chairs, Mom." Peter bounced to his feet. "Can we go home now?"

Mitch took his boy's hand, then Connie's. "Sure." He turned to Taylor. "We really are sorry, Taylor."

"I know. It's over now. Don't worry."

Then Connie scooped Rina into her arms and followed Mitch.

Taylor turned to Evelyn. "I'll call you and let you know how Jamey's doing."

"Give him those pain pills if he needs them."

"I will. Bri?" Taylor held out her hand, and her son took it. Jace watched her until she disappeared around the corner.

It's over now. Don't worry.

She'd referred to far more than the terror of those moments when David said Jamey was hurt. Knowing that, he died inside.

He'd almost messed irreversibly with her life again. Almost. God had been on their side this time.

Jace would make sure it never happened again.

THIRTEEN

JACE NEVER EXPECTED his dad would be the one to ask.

"What were you and Taylor doing together?"

They'd left the emergency room together, halfway to his truck, halfway to the rest of his life without Taylor. Would she even let him see the boys?

"What do you think he was doing, Dad? Changing her oil?"

"David." Mom gave his brother the evil eye.

But David didn't give a shit. Not this time. "David what? David, don't tell the truth? David, don't hurt him? Somebody should have told him the truth three years ago."

She backed away in the face of his fury. "David, please."

"He was screwing her, Mom. In his own brother's bed. He was screwing Lou's wife."

Jace balled his fists. "Don't talk about her like that."

"Like what? Like she wasn't fucking her husband's brother."

"Stop it, you two," his mom cried.

No one listened to her.

Jace wanted to smash his brother's face. He would have if Mom wasn't there.

"Lou's dead. She has a right to a life." Even if it wasn't with him, Taylor had a right to love again.

"Yeah, he's dead. And why, Jace? Because you couldn't get your sorry ass out of bed. Because you were drunk, like usual. Because he couldn't count on you."

"Stop it, stop it." Mom was crying, but Jace couldn't stop David, not even for his mother.

It was the truth. They'd all been dancing around it for three years. It was time somebody said it, long past time he heard what they all thought. What he knew.

"Yeah, he's dead because I messed up. I wasn't there. I let him die. I know that. I live with it every night and every day." The blood, sometimes he still smelled it. "But that has nothing to do with Taylor. Don't use the word *fuck* about her."

"Why? Because she's your *fucking* whore?"

"Don't you ever say that about her." His arm back, poised to punch his brother's nose through his face, David's fists came up. White hot fury stabbed behind Jace's eyelids.

Then someone grabbed his arm. Held him back while his mother cried. It was the saddest damn sound he'd ever heard. Worse even than the day they'd gone to tell Taylor Lou was dead.

"Back off, David." His dad's voice, his dad's hand on his arm.

The eyes, it was all in his brother's eyes. Hatred. Far more than anger. Pure hate. But David stood down when his father told him to.

"Arthur. Let's go," Mom begged. "Please let's just go."

"No, Evelyn. We have to talk about Lou. And Jace."

He couldn't breathe. He couldn't face it. He'd always known he couldn't face his father, but he turned to him anyway.

Tears glimmered. One slipped from his father's eye, caught on a lash, then slid down his cheek. Jace had never seen him cry. Not that day, nor when they buried Lou. Never.

"I'm sorry, Dad. But I know it won't ever bring Lou back."

"What's our rule?"

Mom opened her mouth, but his father held her off with his hand. "What's the rule, Jace?" he repeated.

"You don't let your brother work alone."

"No. That's not the rule. It never was. The rule is you don't work alone."

"He didn't have a choice because I didn't show."

"He had a choice. He made the wrong one."

"But—"

"Lou made the wrong choice."

He stared at his father. "It wasn't his fault."

"I loved your brother. When he came along, before the rest of you, I used to gaze at him and wonder how I could possibly have made him. I died when he died." Another tear joined the others. A river down his father's face.

Mom gripped his arm. His dad didn't take her comfort.

"I loved him with everything I had, but your brother was a lot like me, and he could be an arrogant SOB when he chose to be."

Jace shoved both hands through his hair and squeezed the back of his head.

"He made the wrong choice. It was his mistake. I never wanted to say that. I even tried not to think it. It was some-how . . . sacrilege. But it's true. And sometimes when I'm alone, I hate him for that."

"Jesus, Dad." David took a step toward him.

"He made a stupid move. He broke the rule. Jace didn't make him do that. And you know that, David. None of us wants to say it was Lou's fault. But you can't go on blaming Jace because you don't want to admit the truth."

"I didn't blame Jace."

"You did. Like I did. Because he was alive and it was eas-ier to blame him with Lou in the ground."

David hung his head, and Dad turned to Jace. "I'm sorry. I should have said that a long time ago. I don't even have the excuse that I didn't know you blamed yourself. I did know. I just didn't know what to do about it. I love you, Jace. I'm sorry I let you down."

"Christ, Dad. You didn't let anyone down. I've always known what I did."

"I don't blame you for oversleeping. We've all tied one on. That never meant you had a hand in your brother's death."

Something lifted off him, a mantle, chains. He would always regret that he hadn't been there, but his father had given him a precious gift. Forgiveness. And the ability to forgive himself.

"You've changed since it happened, son. I can count on you. Taylor can count on you, too." He wrapped his palm along the side of Jace's neck and held him. "Lou's dead, Jace. He isn't coming back, and Taylor doesn't deserve to live with our ghosts. Are you in love with her?"

"Yes."

"Then I guess you better make sure she knows that."

"Yeah."

His mom wiped at her streaming eyes. Jace hugged her beneath his chin and kissed the top of her head.

"I'm sorry I put you through that, Mom." Then he eased back to look at her. "Forgive me?" It seemed such a blithe and easy phrase, yet he needed it as much as he'd needed his father's forgiveness.

"Of course, I do. You're my baby."

He kissed each cheek and rested his chin a moment in her hair, filled with the scent of flowers and baby powder.

"Go tell Taylor how you feel. Tell her we're glad, too."

"She'll want your blessing, Mom. It's been bugging her, what you'd say about it." About someone taking Lou's place. Not just Jace, but anyone.

"I always knew it would happen someday, but I didn't want things to change. I didn't want to lose her."

He understood what his mother meant. Taylor had said the same thing in the truck that first night. Finding a new man would change things more than anyone wanted. It was long past time for that change, though. Lou was gone. They all had to face it.

"I'm not sure she'll choose me, Mom." But he would make

sure she knew she had a choice, that life as a woman hadn't ended the day Lou died.

She patted his cheek. "She'd be crazy not to jump at a man like you, honey. But I'll love her no matter what."

"So will I." Ignoring the ache around his heart, he turned.

"Jace." David's voice stopped him. "I was wrong. What I said about Taylor was wrong. I never thought that. I just"—he spread his hands—"Lou's death has been eating at me." He wiped a palm down his shirt as if he were suddenly sweaty. "But Dad's right. About everything he said. And I was way out of line this morning." It was probably the closest David would come to accepting that maybe Lou had made a mistake, too.

"It's fine, David. It's . . . it's really fine."

And it was. Jace couldn't pinpoint precisely why, but it was. His family felt whole for the first time since Lou died.

He couldn't say the same for him and Taylor. He didn't deserve a damn thing from her if he didn't have the courage to tell her exactly how he felt.

Fuck was a good word in its place, but it didn't come close to the meaning of *love*.

EVELYN HELD ARTHUR'S hand. The heat had risen inside the truck cab until she'd had to flip the key in the ignition to roll down the electric window. Jace and David had long since gone.

"I love you, Arthur. I wish you'd told me how you felt."

"You wanted me to tell you I actually hated my son because of how he died?"

He stared through the windshield, a big handsome man even at fifty-nine. If she hadn't had Arthur, she'd never have made it through those dark days after Lou died. She realized now that she hadn't helped him through. He'd bottled it all up inside.

"You didn't hate him, Arthur. You hated that he was gone." She soothed his hand with a stroke.

"I did hate him, Evie. I hated him for going up without

backup, for being careless, for not listening to everything I taught him, for leaving his cell phone in the truck instead of taking it with him. I even hated him for leaving Jace with all the blame on his shoulders. I hated him for everything."

God in heaven, she'd had no idea the weight Arthur had carried. She stroked his cheek.

"Maybe you hated yourself for not being there that day."

He grabbed her knee, squeezed it almost to the point of pain. "I didn't want you to hate me for those terrible thoughts."

"Arthur, you're the most important thing in the world to me. I could never hate you. I'm so sorry I couldn't help you."

"No, Evie, I'm sorry. I wasn't good for you. All those nights you cried yourself to sleep, I wanted to hold you, I really did." He drew in a breath. She felt his pain inside her own body. "But I kept seeing him lying there, the ground beneath him dark with his own . . ."

She petted him, comforted him, wiped away the tears. "Shh, my darling. You did your best for me, for all of us." It was so easy for women to pour out their hearts. But a strong man couldn't let the pain out.

God worked in mysterious ways. If Jace hadn't fallen in love with Taylor, if Taylor hadn't returned that affection, if poor little Jamey hadn't fallen out of the tree. If David and Jace hadn't almost come to blows in the parking lot . . . Arthur would have carried his pain in silence and killed himself with the stress of holding it all inside.

"You can tell me anything, Arthur. I'll always love you, no matter what."

He turned to look at her, a tear teetering on his eyelashes, a tremble on his lips. "I miss him so goddamn much."

"So do I." Then she gave in to her own tears.

Arthur held her and let her cry. They held each other.

TAYLOR STOOD AT the kitchen window. The boys laughed in the family room. Brian had the markers out and was decorating Jamey's cast. There would be ink everywhere, but the stains would serve as a reminder to her. She desperately wanted a shower, but she was afraid to go where she couldn't hear them.

Instead she'd made coffee.

And remembered the expression on Evelyn's face, the look in Arthur's eyes. Horror. Disbelief. She'd been with Jace.

At least she didn't have to lie anymore. She wouldn't sneak out to meet him or call him in the middle of the night. He wouldn't be coming around again, except to take the boys out. She would never take him away from the boys. Nor would she indulge herself at their expense. She was done pushing this family to their limits.

She wasn't sure who to expect first. Evelyn on her own? Evelyn and Arthur together? Connie? David? God forbid. She'd paraded naked in front of him, and she hadn't been able to meet his gaze in the emergency room.

Jace was the first to arrive, pulling into the driveway. Cutting the engine, he sat for long moments. With the slant of the sun, she wasn't sure he could see her in the window.

She didn't have a clue what he planned to say, but she couldn't go on letting him try to fill Lou's shoes. He deserved more than that. He couldn't go on taking care of his brother's family as if he were to blame for what happened to Lou.

Lord, she'd miss the way he touched her, the way he made her feel. She'd ache when he would come over to play with the boys or take them out or drop them off after Little League.

But he had his own life to live, and she wouldn't steal pieces of him anymore to assuage her own loneliness.

As he climbed from the truck and tramped up the front walk, she steeled herself to do what was best for everyone. But Lord, it hurt.

BRIAN THREW HIS marker on the table when Jace opened the screen door. Jamey hopped up, holding his arm out. "See my cast, Uncle Jace, isn't it cool?"

He ruffled the boy's hair, then reached to ruffle Brian's as well. "Better than cool, man."

"Will you sign it? I want everyone to sign it." Jamey had to be in pain, but you'd never know it. Kids just seemed to be like that. When they weren't milking it for all it was worth.

"Sure, kiddo. Give me a pen."

Brian babbled excitedly about what he'd witnessed as Jace signed his name in bold red letters, then drew a skull and crossbones. Jamey bounced up from the couch to show Taylor.

"Will you draw a skull on my arm, Uncle Jace?" Brian didn't want to be left out.

Taylor nodded and Brian handed Jace a black marker.

Jamey tugged on her hand. "Mom, can I go over and show Ernie? He's never had a cast."

"You need to rest, sweetie."

"Aw, Mom," both boys moaned in unison.

Jace had never presumed to tell her what to do with her kids, but he knew her fear, the same he'd felt, his heart climbing into his throat. But she had to let it go or she'd end up smothering them. The way he'd tried to smother her after Lou died.

"It'll be okay, Taylor. Let them go for a little while."

Her indecision flashed across her face, fear darkening her eyes. She didn't want to let them out of the house, out of earshot. Out of her protective reach. Then she said, "Half an hour. Then I want you back to take a nap."

They rushed out of the house like a herd of elephants. She moved to the window to watch them stampede across the street.

"You'd think nothing had happened," she said.

"Kids heal fast. We need to talk, Taylor."

"I know. You want coffee?"

"Thanks, but no." He needed to say what he had to say. Prepping the coffee was putting off the inevitable. "Sit down."

She lingered a moment longer at the window, then moved to the couch, perching on the edge and clasping her hands in her lap. "I'm going to say my piece first."

She laid the words out like a law. Perhaps if she got out her objections, he'd find a way to show her how wrong she was.

"I'm listening." He didn't know whether to stand or sit, though he was sure touching her would be a mistake. He stayed where he was, miles too far from her.

"It's best that we end . . . what was going on between us." She sucked in her breath as if voicing the thought had been hard for her, even as she sliced him in two. "You've been good to us since Lou died. The boys and I wouldn't have made it without you. Everything you've done around the house, it's meant a lot."

"It meant—"

She held up her hand. "Let me finish while I can." She took another deep breath. "I crossed the line when you found me at the bar that night. I shouldn't have put you in that position. What happened after that wasn't your fault."

"Taylor."

She looked at him, silenced him. He didn't want to hear, but he would listen, for her.

"I've been feeling pretty weird lately, and that was all a culmination. But I'm better now. I'm sorry I took advantage of your generosity."

Shit. Generosity? He was crazy for her. Couldn't she see that? He shut his mouth on the words.

She rolled her lips between her teeth, worried them, then finally spoke. "I know you've always felt responsible for what happened to Lou. And you've tried to make it up to us. What you did for the boys. You went out of your way to help me even after the way I threw myself at you that night." She swallowed, her chest swelled with her breath.

Jesus. Is that how she'd viewed what they'd done? That he was selflessly helping her? He'd laugh if it wasn't so damn sad.

He wanted her to finish, so he could prove her wrong.

"I shouldn't have taken all you gave without telling you that I never thought what happened to Lou was your fault. Never, Jace. Lou was . . . Lou." She shrugged. "He liked things his way, and he probably thought he was teaching you a lesson by starting without you. He should never have done it."

Her words washed over him in a gentle wave. Cleansing him at last.

"It was so hard to talk about. Nobody talked about it."

No, they hadn't. They'd all let it fester. Even Lou wouldn't have wanted that.

He looked at her after that long silence. "Are you done?"

She twisted her hands. "I don't want you to think it's because I didn't enjoy what we did. It was wonderful. I mean that. But we both knew it was a . . ." She wriggled her brow, trying to find the right word for what they'd done. "Thing," she finally came up with.

He moved then, swiping the markers off the coffee table and tossing them back in their box. He shoved with his foot until there was enough room for him to sit in front of her.

"Is it my turn now?"

He wanted her to state every objection. He wanted to know every thought in her head, so he had an answer for it.

"Umm, yes."

What should he tackle first? "I have felt responsible for what happened to Lou." He bent his head, touched his lips to the back of her hand. "And I don't think I can ever make you see how badly I needed you to forgive me."

"Oh, Jace, there's never been—"

He put two fingers to her lips. "My turn. I've done a thousand and more things to show you how sorry I was. But I love the boys, and I never used them to get you to forgive me. I did it because they needed me. For that, I'm the one who's grateful. I needed *them*." He searched her eyes for a sign that she believed him. He couldn't read a thing. "Fixing stuff for you kept me busy, kept me from thinking too hard. But Taylor, I didn't touch you because I was trying to atone in some weird way. I touched you because I've always wanted to touch you. Always."

Finally, a reaction. She frowned, tipping her head.

"What do you mean?"

"I've loved you since the day Lou brought you home. I hated myself, but I couldn't stop the way I felt. I never would have touched you, I never would have told you. But when you kissed me that night, you suddenly handed me everything I'd ever wanted."

He let her absorb his meaning. He couldn't know how she'd react, but on the way here, he'd sworn to give her the whole truth. His guilty obsession with her was the most damning part.

"Always, Jace?"

"From the beginning."

"But I never even noticed."

He laughed, though his throat ached. "I know. You loved Lou. And I would never have tried to take you away from him." He'd dreamed about it, yes, but he'd never acted, never would have acted, if she hadn't begged him to see her as a woman.

"You were always a woman to me, Taylor. But you were also Lou's wife. Brian and Jamey's mother. My sister-in-law."

She didn't say anything, staring at her hands. Would she revile him for the lie he'd lived with for half of his life?

"I never fucked you. I made love to you. I just couldn't figure out how to tell you that." He waited, his chest aching, his heart pumping overtime. "Say something."

She looked up, her eyes wet and shimmering. "I don't think I can say this, Jace."

He died, a hundred times over, but he would take it. "You can tell me anything, Taylor. I love you. Whatever you have to say, it'll be okay."

I love you.

Taylor bent her head to her hands, pulling in air as if that would give her courage. What would Jace think when she told him the real truth? Everything she'd learned about herself over the past few days. Yet Jace had confessed his greatest sins to her, she could do no less for him.

She sat up, rubbed her fingers over her eyes, then met his gaze. "I loved Lou. He's the father of my boys. He was a good man. I've always loved you, as Lou's brother. But God help me, sometimes I looked at you when you were wearing a nice tight pair of jeans, and I had . . . thoughts." Oh Lord, this was so hard. "Small ones, Jace. Nothing explicit. But I did have thoughts." The number grew in her mind as she remembered. She'd had a lot of thoughts about Jace, and oddly, hadn't even felt guilty at the time. Because she would never have *done* anything. Never, not while Lou was alive. "But once I'd kissed you, I couldn't stop. I didn't want to stop."

"You didn't betray Lou, if that's what you're thinking."

"Yes, I did." She bit down on the inside of her cheek. "In the bathroom at work, when you made me look in the mirror, I betrayed him then." And understood a lot of painful things.

"He's dead, Taylor. You're not."

She shook her head. "You don't understand what I'm saying. I loved Lou, but I wasn't *in* love with him. I don't think I ever was. I wanted to be a part of your family, and Lou was a way to get there." It sounded so much worse when she said it aloud.

He took her hand. "You were a good wife. The best. A wonderful mother. In you, Lou got everything he'd ever wanted."

"But I . . ." She dropped her eyes to her lap and tried to pull her hand from his.

He wouldn't let her go. "Say it. Whatever it is, we'll deal with it."

Say it. He made it sound so easy.

"He never made me feel that way," she whispered. "He never touched me and set me on fire. I loved him, and I miss him, but the bed wasn't empty because Lou was gone. It was empty because I wanted someone to touch me. Anyone." Even Bubba at the Saddle-n-Spurs would have done. Until she touched Jace. "Then it was you, and now there'll never be anyone else. It was never like that with Lou."

He went down on his knees in front of her. "If you think I'm going to say I'm sorry that I make you feel that way and he didn't, you're wrong. If you think I'm going to let you feel guilty about it, you're crazier than me. I love you. I've waited fifteen years to hear you say that. And I'm not going to let you take it all back. Now look at me."

In the end, he lifted her chin. "I'll never replace Lou. I don't want to. I love you, and I want to marry you. I want to give you everything Lou never did, make you feel everything he didn't. I want to be a father to Jamey and Brian. I want you. Tell me you want what I want."

She scanned his face. He loved her. God help her, she loved him, too. More than she thought she could ever love any man. Jamey and Brian needed a daddy again. Jace would be more than they could ever have hoped for. But . . . "What about your family? What will they say?"

The clock ticked on the wall. Outside, the automatic sprinklers turned on. The timer was wrong. They should have come on early this morning.

Jace made a mental note to fix it. Then he gave Taylor the only other lie he ever would.

"If Mom and Dad can't see how right this is, then I don't give a damn. And I don't give a damn what David says either."

They'd already given their blessing. But if he told Taylor, she'd never be sure of herself. She'd always doubt, always think she made the choice for the wrong reasons. He couldn't let her do that.

"You have to decide, Taylor."

She took long moments, in which his blood thundered through his veins like a runaway train.

Then she put her hand to his cheek. "I don't want to be just somebody's lover, Jace. I want to be *your* lover. And your wife. And I think maybe your parents will understand."

He stroked a finger down her face. "I know they will."

After living in hell for the last three years, he finally got his taste of heaven. And he'd never let it go. He'd never let *her* go.

FOURTEEN

TAYLOR WAS GIDDY. Evelyn felt giddy herself at the Sunday family barbecue. Mitch filled the doughboy pool for the summer. Rina, Peter, and Brian splashed everyone that came in range, and Jamey sulked because he couldn't go in the water with his cast. David had actually laughed at something Connie said, and Arthur put on his sunscreen without being asked. They'd made love every night the last week. Evelyn felt like a blushing bride.

And then there was Taylor. She glowed, like when she'd first learned she was pregnant with Brian. Jace couldn't keep his hands off her. He smoothed lotion on her shoulders, dropped a kiss on her hair, held a finger when that was all he could reach. And he smiled. He laughed. Not just at the children's antics, but at everything. She hadn't seen him laugh like that in more years than Evelyn could count. Taylor did that for him.

They'd all miss Lou like the dickens. Evelyn would always talk to him before she went to sleep, as if he could hear up there in heaven. Her first born. Her big boy. She wasn't silly enough to think she wouldn't cry on the anniversary of his death or his birthday, or any day, just because she thought of him. But now she had Arthur to hold her. And he had her. Sometimes that was enough to bring you a measure of peace.

Especially when your grandchildren were as cute as bugs in a rug and your other sons had all learned to laugh again.

Except Mitchie. Mitchie was another story.

"Mitch isn't talking to me," Connie whispered to her.

In unison, they put their hands on their chins and stared across the lawn in Mitch's direction. With a whoop of laughter, the kids splashed him. He wiped the spray from his face and shook a finger, a smile creasing his lips. As soon as they turned, racing off to get Uncle David, Mitch's smile died.

Taylor and Jace were worries off Evelyn's plate.

But there was David. He needed a wife to make him complete.

And Connie and Mitch who needed . . . well, something.

Evelyn never interfered in her boys' lives. They'd have to work it out for themselves.

Of course, she could always give Connie a suggestion or two. And maybe find a sweet little gal for David. She'd have to put on her thinking cap.

Somebody's Ex

ONE

"YOU CAN'T JUST quit on me like this, David."

"I'm not quitting, Dad." David Jackson sighed and leaned his chair on its back two legs. He'd known this wouldn't be easy. "I want to fix up the house, and Rich Morrisey is going to take me on so I can pick up some of the skills I'm lacking."

It was the God's honest truth. He wanted to do some re-modeling around the place he'd bought a couple of years ago. Though he was handy with his tools, he needed to learn precision, optimum-materials use, and practical shortcuts. Working for Rich part-time would teach him the homebuild-ing trade.

"But what about a replacement?"

"You can hire some green kid to help with loading and hauling." Which comprised a good portion of the work Jack-son and Sons Arborists did. "I'll still do tree work when you need me." The family tree-trimming outfit could run without him a few days a week. Dad would still have Jace and Mitch.

"But why?"

"It's a good opportunity for me." Not to mention that he needed a little time off from the family.

"I knew something was up when you didn't make it to the last two barbecues."

The Sunday family barbecues were a tradition his mom hadn't allowed to die when Lou did. David had needed time off from that, too.

"Look, I know this whole thing with Taylor and Jace has gotten under your skin."

Taylor and Jace. His youngest brother and his eldest brother's widow. Since the announcement six weeks ago, he'd been telling himself they hadn't betrayed Lou. Taylor had a right to move on.

But marrying Jace? There was something *wrong* in that.

"My decision has nothing to do with them." He'd struggled to keep his feelings to himself since that day at the hospital, but the effort was wearing on him.

"David, I might be almost sixty years old, but I'm not stupid. I suspected you had a thing for Taylor, and I know it's hard to watch her with Jace."

Balanced on two chair legs, David almost fell backward, shock hitting him first. Then he tamped down a burst of anger. That was the most telling symptom of his current malady, a temper too close to the surface. In the past, he'd been slow to anger, but recently, the slightest thing set him off. He dropped his chin and stared at his dad over the top of his sunglasses.

"You've gotta be kidding. Where did that come from?"

"I've got eyes. You've been twitchy around her for months."

He'd been twitchy because Lou's death had ripped a hole the size of California in the family, tearing apart the very fabric by which they lived, and filling his big brother's shoes had been a helluva lot harder than he'd thought.

But wanting Taylor for himself? Christ. "Dad, I never had a thing for Taylor." The thought of being a secondhand dad to her boys petrified him.

He wanted out for a while. He'd worked for the family outfit since he was old enough to load the scrap left behind after a job. Over half his life. The last three years had been the worst, though, since Lou died and keeping the family together had always fallen on his shoulders. On his watch, they'd damn near crumbled beneath the weight of Lou's passing. He sucked at being the eldest.

His dad was still giving him the eye. David felt the need to repeat himself.

"I'm happy for them. I don't have any hidden passion for Taylor. And I've made my decision."

His dad's lips flattened. "I don't know how I'm going to tell your mom. She's going to be heartbroken."

He should have known Dad would play the guilt card. David took a deep breath, then let it out long and slow.

"Mom's going to be fine, and you know it."

Arthur Jackson sighed, and resignation eased the tense line of his jaw. "She should hear it from you. She'll want to be sure you're happy with this move."

"I planned on dropping by to tell her tomorrow."

"And you're coming to the barbecue on Sunday or she'll think you're mad at us all."

He was thirty-four years old yet his father still seemed to think he needed to be told how to handle a delicate situation. It wasn't a dig, it was just his dad, but he'd never heard his father remind Lou about the basics.

David hadn't handled the situation well on the day he found out about Taylor and Jace. In fact, he'd been way out of line. He'd apologized to both of them for the shitty things he'd said. But something changed that day, as irrevocably as life had changed the day Lou died.

He no longer felt a part of his family, and he'd go away until he could figure out why. He'd leave before he let loose with something even more damaging than what he had already said to his brother.

THE ENGINE CHUGGED, stuttered, then died halfway up the hill. The truck, rolling back a short distance, barely made it to the side of the road, the two left tires still on the macadam.

Dammit. Damn it.

The gas gauge hadn't worked for over a year. Randi Andersen measured her gas consumption in miles, but she'd forgotten to reset the trip the last time she'd filled up, then, dammit, she'd forgotten that she'd forgotten. Mick, her ex, was fond of saying she'd forget her head if it wasn't screwed on.

"This is not my day." First, Royal went ballistic in the middle of the night, barked her fool head off, and got herself sprayed by a skunk. Two baths and three quart cans of tomato juice later, the dog's coat still emanated eau de skunk.

Then Randi had punched off the alarm without fully awakening and fallen back to sleep for another two hours.

She and Royal were supposed to be at the vet's by eight-thirty for the dog's yearly shots. Even running late, Randi would have made the time easily, except now she'd run out of gas.

Royal bumped her with a wet doggie nose as Randi beat her head on the steering wheel. The dog still stunk, a potpourri of wet fur, tomatoes, and semi-acrid skunk spray.

"Looks like we're going to have to hoof it." The country road was sparsely traveled, making the chance of vehicular rescue nil. Calling for help wasn't an option. Her cell phone needed a new battery since the charge didn't hold longer than a day. Yes, she'd forgotten to put it in the charger last night. Thank God she didn't have to put her head in the charger nightly, although that might have done something about her chronic forgetfulness.

Randi snapped on the dog leash. Leaving Royal in the cab wasn't a consideration. The heat of a summer day in Willoughby, California, even this early, would bake her brain. Two and a half miles to town would take less than an hour. Randi looked at her platform sandals, which were not made for hiking. Make that an hour and a half, unless she wanted to risk a sprained ankle.

She shoved at the door with both hands. It groaned but didn't budge. The damn thing was getting harder to open every day. She threw her shoulder into it and practically fell out of the truck, the door flying wide. Saving herself by slamming her sandal on the concrete, she jerked her head up at the shriek of tires on the roadway just in time to see a three-quarter-ton pickup bearing down on her.

Amidst the sound of squealing tires, her life flashed before her eyes like the old cliché. The knee-holes in Mick's jeans on their wedding day in that cheesy Nevada chapel. Her divorce papers with Mick's illegible scrawl. Her mom's fish balls sprinkled with curry powder. That day her pops stopped talking to her when she was thirteen, the day that lasted almost a year.

Her last thought before she died: *I really am a loser.*

Her body must have been flattened beyond pain because she didn't feel a thing except warm sunshine heating the top of her head and the pungent aroma of burnt rubber in her nostrils.

"Lady, are you insane opening your door like that?"

No, I'm dead.

But wait, the angry drawl didn't sound like the angel Gabriel. Or was it Peter who was supposed to meet you at the pearly gates? And hey, what about the tunnel of light?

Randi opened her eyes to an enormous truck bumper staring her in the face. Brilliant sunlight bouncing off the chrome blinded her. Her neck hurt from the awkward angle at which she held her head, looking back at that terrifyingly close grill. Her little truck was a mere ant compared to the monster pickup only a few inches from her rear bumper.

Hands on his hips, booted feet spread wide, and his chin jutted forward so he could stare her down, Randi decided the man was too pissed to be an angel.

He'd asked if she was insane. She had to admit that statement was a darn sight better than what Mick would have said. *Are you a fucking idiot?*

One foot in the truck, the other out, she was suddenly aware of the awkward spread of her legs, and the three popped snaps on her jean skirt. Only two remained holding it together.

Holy Moly! If he came any closer, he'd see her thong.

She hastily snapped the buttons on her skirt. Hopping out too quickly, she stumbled, catching herself with a hand on the top of the door.

"My door was stuck."

One side of his mouth curled. A snarl, not a smile. "So you figured you'd just stick it out so someone could rip it off? Not to mention ripping off the top half of your body."

He perused her top half with fiery eyes. His sunglasses swung from the fingers of his clenched fist, and the sun made his gaze burn. With her five-inch platforms, he was only an inch or so taller than her, but he seemed to tower. And glower.

He took a giant step closer.

Royal started to growl.

Randi shuffled forward and slammed the door hard. Of course, that brought her less than two feet from him, so close she could now see his eyes were the color of a Hawaiian black sand beach. Glitteringly dark with silvery flecks.

He arched a brow.

"It doesn't like to shut," she explained, in case he thought she'd slammed it out of pique. "The dog doesn't bite, but I've never been threatened before, so I'm not sure how she'll react."

"This is not threatening. This is mildly pissed off."

"Mildly?" Half joke, half fear. Her breathing had returned to normal, but her heart pulsed a beat too quickly.

"If I was really pissed, I wouldn't have stopped. Or gone around."

He looked up the hill at the blind spot, communicating his thought that going around her open door might have resulted in a head-on with someone coming the other way.

When she didn't comment, freak out, or even apologize, he tipped his head. "Were you threatening to sic your dog on me?"

"If I was, I wouldn't have closed the door." She made a placating little moue. "I'm sorry about the door. I couldn't open it. Then it just . . ." She spread her hands. "It just popped." Like the snaps on her skirt.

Instead of answering, his gaze dropped to her skirt, and

she realized she hadn't properly snapped all her snaps. She reached down, but then his gaze rose to her breasts, which were now a little too close to falling out of her low-cut Spandex top.

The man was ogling her. And she liked it. She hadn't been ogled in a long time. A look at him revealed buff thighs, chiseled abs, nicely shaped chest muscles, and brown hair streaked with several shades of blond, probably from days spent working out in the sun.

"You're leering at me," he said. "I feel like a cheap piece of meat." He still glowered, but the hint of a smile curved his lips. He put on his sunglasses before she could detect an answering glimmer in those intriguing eyes.

"Not cheap. Very expensive." Her voice came out deep, husky, and way too seductive. Damn. There went her mouth again, spouting off before her brain had time to catch up. Her pops, and Mick, really hated her tendency to babble.

But Holy Moly, she'd just flirted with a man who'd almost creamed her and her truck. Not to mention squishing the dog. Of course, it wasn't the guy's fault. But, well, he could get the wrong impression about her with a comment like that.

"I didn't mean that the way it sounded."

She sure as hell had, David hoped. He'd lost his irritation the minute she'd bent down to button her skirt.

She was a wet dream come true. Long blond hair, brilliant blue eyes, plump cherry lips, and a pair of ta-tas the sight of which damn near knocked him upside the head. And if he looked at her bare legs one more time, he'd expire in unfulfilled lust.

It didn't matter a whit that she was ditzy. He could have killed her. The thought of that beautiful chest crushed between his bumper and her door gave him heart palpitations. He still hadn't come down off the adrenaline high, which explained his explicit wayward thoughts.

A man, however, couldn't be blamed for becoming fascinated by such a lovely creature, especially with that pretty blush blooming on her cheeks.

David pulled his thoughts out of his shorts. "Stopping almost in the middle of the road probably isn't a good idea."

She rolled her eyes, her long lashes catching his attention. "I didn't do it on purpose." She looked at the side of her dusty, beaten truck. It might have been rust-colored or a long-since faded red. "I ran out of gas."

Ahh. Why did women seem perpetually out of gas? He eyed a can in the truck bed.

She quirked her mouth wryly. "I'm pretty sure it's empty."

He hefted the container and sure enough, it weighed almost nothing. "Might be a good idea to keep it full." He glanced at her face. "For emergencies."

She closed her eyes and heaved a sigh, scrambling his thoughts all over again.

"If one were prepared for every eventuality, life would be like having to watch Julia Roberts in *Pretty Woman* every day. Not that *Pretty Woman* is bad, but once in five years is enough." She tipped her head, her hair falling across her breasts. "Gives you a chance to forget the ending."

He agreed with the chick flick assessment. But how could she forget the ending? Didn't all chick flicks end the same way? She went on, though, before he had a chance to ask.

"Then again, if it were Vin Diesel in *Pitch Black* . . ." Eyes closed, arms held slightly away from her body, she shuddered. He almost lost control as her husky voice swept through him. "Well, twice a day wouldn't be enough."

Pitch Black. Definitely sounded like a movie to have a girl watch on a Friday-night date.

She shook herself. "Where were we?" Then she batted her pretty blues. "Oh. I was going to ask if you could help me."

He squeezed between her truck's rear and his bumper to set the can in his bed, then opened the passenger door. "Hop in."

She glanced back at the dog face staring at her through the rear window of her truck. Some sort of husky breed, he presumed, wearing a beseeching expression.

"I can't leave Royal."

"He can hop in the bed."

She tipped her head from side to side, then said, "*She* is strictly an in-cab girl. You know, dust and dirt in her poor little eyes. I can wait here"—she did that batting thing again—"if you wouldn't mind bringing the gas back."

He'd have to come back anyway, unless he forced her to walk, and he wouldn't leave her. Mom would flay the flesh from his bones if he did.

He slid his eyes to his cab-plus. "Bring her on."

She smiled. Whoa, Nellie. The knock-em dead beam almost blinded him with its brilliance. With that smile, the lady could get a man to do for-freaking-sure anything.

She yanked hard on the door, and the dog sprang out, its leash trailing, to bounce all over the concrete. *"Bli,"* she said. Obviously a command, the dog now bounced in place.

Not a husky, much smaller, he wasn't sure of the breed, but she was pure something. Just like her owner. The woman grabbed her backpack, then the leash, and led the animal over. Sniffing a boot and a pant leg, the dog seemingly pronounced him trustworthy and started snuffling the truck tires.

"She's really very good. She won't drool all over the seats. This is Royal."

The dog actually looked at him as her name was said, as if she understood she was being introduced.

"What breed?"

Leaning over, she put the dog's paws on the bottom sill of the open door. *"Hoppe,"* she murmured in that odd dog language, then patted the interior carpet. Royal scrambled into the back behind the seats. "She's a Norwegian elkhound."

"Never seen one before." But it explained the lilting commands the woman used. He'd have guessed Swedish, but presumed the two languages were similar. Multilingual. Maybe the woman wasn't as ditzy as he first assumed.

"So you speak to her in Norwegian?"

She huffed, hands on her hips. "Well, duh. That's the only language she understands."

Was she kidding? The blue sparkle in her eyes said yes. "And you are?"

"Randi Andersen." She gripped his proffered hand firmly. The warmth of her skin left a lasting impression with him.

"David Jackson." He flourished his hand. "Hop in."

She looked at the height of the sill, and he had the perverse vision of helping her in the way she'd helped the dog. His hands on her hands, his body pressed to her backside.

"You need a hand?" Oh man, he'd give her one.

She raised a brow. "I'm fine." She waited expectantly.

David didn't move, entranced by her blue eyes.

"All right. I can see you're going to make me say it. Unless you want the shock of your life, I am not getting up in this truck until you back off." She looked down pointedly at her short skirt, then the height of the truck's sill.

Shock wasn't what he felt, but he was a gentleman, at least in deed if not in mind. He backed off and rounded the end of his truck, the image of the snaps on her skirt popping open.

His body might never recover from the vision.

MORTIFYING, BUT REALLY, how else was she supposed to say, *Shove off, buddy, before I flash my privates.* As it was, Randi barely got her skirt back in place—as in place as it could be due to its brevity—before he climbed into the driver's seat.

Was he clueless or had he been waiting for the peep show? Maybe a bit of both. Nice. But not too nice.

David Jackson. Such a nice, normal, boy-next-door name. Not like Spike or Slick or Hellboy. Or Mick. David was a Mr. Nice Guy name. He looked the part, too. Clean-cut, no two-day-old whiskers on his chin or holes in his jeans. His white truck was spotless, and his fingernails were clean.

Though she did have a thing for the bad-boy type—much to her everlasting damnation, torment, and wicked delight— David seemed the kind of guy of whom her dad might actually approve.

Pops never liked Mick, but he'd liked her divorce less. *Now you are just somebody's ex.* She could still hear his derogatory tone. She shoved away the voice of disapproval.

While not a bad boy by any stretch of her limitless imagination, David was quite hunky. Not to mention the military-style boots. She had a thing for boots.

His nose twitched. "What's that smell?"

Her vision of him in boots and storm trooper uniform winked out. She rolled her eyes right, then left.

"My perfume?"

Mr. Nice Guy who was driving her all the way to town and back again glanced at her. Then he gave her a devilish smile. "There's no way you smell like"—he sniffed—"skunk."

"Royal thinks she's a mighty hunter. The skunk won." Maybe she should have told him before he let the dog in the truck. "It won't get on your carpet. Cross my heart and hope to die."

She did just that, the crossing part, not the dying part, then realized that was a big fat mistake when his gaze dropped to her stretchy spandex top. She just could not seem to do or say the right thing with this guy.

Talk about the dog, without the hand gestures. She stuck her hands under her thighs. "She usually sleeps on the bed, but it was so warm last night and she was panting and squirming around and I've never seen her so hot and bothered and . . ." She stopped, stuck on an image of hot, bothered, panting, squirming animals on her bed. And it wasn't Royal.

David tugged off his sunglasses, dropped them in his lap, and glanced at her with those black-sand eyes of his, heating her from the inside out. Her nipples tingled, and she didn't have to look down to know they were stark against her spandex top. Her skin flushed from her throat to her cheeks, and she licked her lips. He watched that, too, before finally dragging his gaze to the road.

Holy Moly. When would she learn to keep her mouth shut? "I give up. I'm not talking anymore. Nada, zippo, *nei*, *nyet*."

David Nice Guy laughed. It was nothing like Mick's laugh, which had sounded like Snidely Whiplash toward the end of their marriage. David's was deep and full and shivered in her belly.

Royal obviously felt the same tummy tingle because she

leaned forward to stick her nose in David's ear. Which made Randi laugh. Then they were both laughing.

He had the nicest laugh. And he had an even nicer gaze when he was letting it roam all over her upper body.

Randi batted at Royal's snout. "It's impolite to stick your nose in a man's ear until you know him much better."

David shot her a sideways glance. "And just how well does she need to know me before it's okay to nose my body parts?"

"Your ear, probably a couple of weeks. Other places, it's always impolite."

The side of his mouth quirked.

Give it up. She wasn't capable of shutting up nor of saying the right thing. But it didn't matter. She'd made him laugh.

"Thanks for helping me with the gas thing."

"You're welcome."

What a nice, polite guy. David wouldn't be sticking his nose where it didn't belong on short acquaintance. Mick hadn't known please and thank-you from "get your fat ass in there and get me a beer."

She stopped herself just short of asking if David liked her ass. "I'd like to repay you somehow."

He was silent a long moment.

Her skin prickled waiting for his answer.

"How did you want to repay me?" A slight harsh note laced his voice, then softened as he added, "I don't accept cash for saving a damsel in distress."

He probably saved damsels a lot, which deserved more than a coffee or a donut. *She* wanted more than coffee and donuts.

She'd come back to Willoughby a year ago for a lot of reasons: helping her parents, getting her life in order, divorce recovery, self-esteem recovery. Settling down, whatever that meant. She felt far from settled. Maybe, like her father always told her, she needed a man to take care of her. A nice guy, not a Mick who, while he could be sweet as banana cream pie and make her fall in love all over again, had a mean streak a mile wide. He had never beat her, but he knew just the right words to make her feel as dull and as stupid as a potato. Nice guys didn't do that. Nice guys cherished, loved, and protected. They made a girl feel special. Didn't they? Here was her chance to find out. Her dad would be pleased she'd finally set her sights on a nice guy.

Randi smiled and jumped in with all her wits about her. "Dinner. Tonight. If you'd like."

David tipped his head, the look he gave her lasting longer than the other glances. They were nearing town, and she noticed Royal pressed a wet doggie nose to his side window.

Finally, David answered. "Dinner sounds good. I'll pick you up. What time?"

"I meant I was going to make you dinner. Picking me up on the side of the road deserves more than restaurant fare. How about seven?" That would give her time to clean the house.

He maneuvered into Four Corners Garage, pulling up to the pump and shutting down the engine before he answered. Then he retrieved his sunglasses from his lap and slid them up the bridge of his nose.

"Seven sounds fine."

Holy Mack Moly, she'd just invited a man over for dinner. And she didn't know how to cook. She'd call her mother for the recipe for Norwegian meatballs as soon as she got back from the vet. The store was closed on Monday, and her mom was sure to be home. Meatballs couldn't be that hard to make.

Could they?

"BUT DAVID, EVERYTHING'S starting to get better now. We feel like a family again. Why do you have to leave?"

David winced at the pain in his mother's voice, etched into the lines on her face. But getting better? Nothing was normal, not with Taylor and Jace getting married. Hiding his feelings about that was getting more difficult every day.

He hated to cause his mom pain, but a man had to do what a man had to do. "I'm not leaving the family, Mom, I'm just working for Rich."

"What's wrong?"

He resisted rolling his eyes. Mom was as bad as his dad. Making a change automatically meant something was wrong. It pissed him off that he had to keep explaining, but his mom's concern didn't deserve the anger.

"Nothing's wrong."

He braced himself for some of the same irrational crap his dad had thrown at him. It never came.

Instead, his mom rose from her chair, came around to his side of the desk, and pulled his head to her shoulder, hugging him as if he were a kid.

"I'm sorry. Your father and I can't expect you to live your life our way. But with Jace settling down, I was sort of hoping you'd find the right woman, too."

An image of Randi Andersen's short skirt and tight top flashed across his mind.

He'd always been the cautious one, always done what was expected of him. Even the women he'd dated were somehow family-related. He'd had three serious relationships, and they'd all been with women his family approved of: the daughter of Mom's best friend, a friend of his sister-in-law, the sister of a friend of Lou's. And David would have fallen right in with the family pattern, if he'd actually fallen in love with any of them.

Randi seemed anything but the homemaker type even if she was cooking him dinner tonight. He was damn glad of it, too, because right now he wasn't looking for anything serious.

"Mom, I'm getting a crick in my neck."

She let go, then put her hands on his cheeks, and forced him to look up at her. "I just want my boys to be happy."

She wanted her family to be normal again. They never would be. Lou's death had changed them forever, but he wouldn't squash her fantasy.

"I am happy."

He stood, patting his back pocket where he'd stowed the piece of paper with Randi's phone number and address. She lived near him out on Griswall Road, a few acres down. Now that he thought about it, he'd seen her faded, dented truck before. He'd just never seen the driver.

"I gotta go. Dad's expecting me by noon."

"You're a good boy." His mother patted his cheek.

Yeah, he was a good boy. He'd always done what was expected of him. That was constricting him, too.

Randi Andersen seemed the perfect antidote.

DAVID HEARD THE dog bark even before he killed the engine. Randi Andersen's house appeared little more than a run-down shack. There were more weeds than grass poking out of the hard-packed earth, as if the place hadn't seen a drop of water since the last rain back in May. Her dented truck sat forlorn beneath a large oak as if it had been abandoned. The porch was missing several boards. Despite the shabby exterior, lacy curtains fluttered at the windows, and a brightly colored wind chime tinkled in the breeze at the far end of the porch.

The house was a bit like the woman, seemingly rough around the edges but softened on the inside. She'd thanked him politely for everything he'd done that morning. From driving her to the gas station, paying for the gas, taking her back, letting her use his cell phone, and following her to the edge of town once again to make sure she made it.

He couldn't pigeonhole the woman.

Avoiding a missing board on the front step, he knocked on her door.

When she answered, he almost ran for his truck.

"Hi." She smiled with softly pink-tinted lips.

This morning's hot, bare-legged woman with the uncensored mouth had morphed into June Cleaver, the personification of the fifties housewife. Pearls circled her throat, her summer dress poofed at the waist, and her blond hair was neatly braided. In flat sandals, she was five inches shorter than he remembered.

"Hi." He had little more to say, sort of stunned by the

transformation. Then he remembered the wine bottle in his hand. "To go with dinner."

"You didn't have to do that. I'm supposed to be paying you back." With a curve of her pink lips, she opened the door wider, took the wine, and drew him in.

Man. He felt almost guilty about the condoms in his wallet. A guy wasn't supposed to lust after Beaver Cleaver's mom.

Trying to take his mind off of Randi's assets, he perused the front room. The interior was as shabby as the outside. A ratty couch dipped in the middle, its once-blue fabric sunbleached to gray. The coffee table, draped with a flower cloth, was the exact size of a powerline cable spool. The television looked like it had been born in the sixties and still had rabbit ears, though one was bent in the middle. Threadbare carpets covered hardwood floors that might have once been gorgeous, but needed stripping and refinishing some ten years ago. The three scented candles she'd lit couldn't extinguish the musty mildew odor.

She sighed heavily. He was suddenly aware of her beside him, of her eyes seeing the same thing his did.

"Well, this is . . . cozy."

She snorted softly. "Cozy," she murmured. "Yep, it's cozy," she repeated, almost to herself. Then she brightened. "But it's clean. I cleaned all afternoon. I haven't done that much cleaning in years." She covered her mouth. "I mean, I clean once a week. But the dog hair—" She spread her hands.

"Hey, the barking's stopped."

"She heard me close the door. That means I let you in and I'm safe and she has to stop barking." She clapped her hands together lightly. "Dinner's almost ready."

Pearl earrings dangled at her lobes, and her braid swished across her shoulders as she turned. He saw the deep cut of her dress, baring her delicate skin almost to the middle of her back. All that bare flesh flushed comparisons to the Beave's mom right out of his head, and he followed her into the kitchen as if she were a siren crooning his name.

The kitchen was little better in the shabbiness quotient, with enamel-chipped appliances, stained Formica countertops, and a refrigerator that chugged as if taking its next to last breath. Post-it notes covered almost every inch of the freezer door, though he was too far away to read the tiny scribblings. But the place sparkled as best she could make it, and mouthwatering scents bubbled from pans on the ancient stove.

The kitchen table sported more stained Formica, but she'd picked wildflowers and set them in the table's center in a jelly jar. Mismatched china and cutlery sat in two place settings, next to each other rather than opposite.

"The table looks nice." It was the best he could come up with.

Randi's house didn't have much going for it. Then again, with her in it, who cared?

THREE

RANDI WANTED TO CRY.

David's gaze wandered over her possessions with wide-eyed horror. They weren't exactly her possessions, of course. Most had come with the house rental. She couldn't afford to be picky, but she'd scrubbed and cleaned for hours and put out candles and flowers and still . . . he was looking at a dump.

Worse, it smelled like a dump.

Her mother's expression had been tight-lipped shock and dismay. Her father had simply turned around, walked out, and hadn't spoken to her for three days. David Nice Guy was at least struggling to say something . . . nice.

It was sweet, but she still wanted to cry. She hadn't even been able to find an appropriately circumspect dress. The front was fine, but her back was naked. Though his eyes had followed the line of her shoulder blades, she felt . . . unsexy. Having a man in her house—this was her first date since the divorce over a year ago—wasn't in the least bit exciting or sensual. It just made her nerves act up.

No point in crying over spilt milk, as her mother loved to say. She wouldn't think about the bad stuff, only the good. He was a man, he was cute, he was nice, and he was in her house. There, four good things. She struggled to find at least five good things that happened every day. One more, one more . . . ah, he filled out his jeans to perfection, back and front.

Okay. "Let's eat. It's ready." She tipped her head. "Gee, it actually smells good, doesn't it?"

After dishing up, Randi set the plate in front of him, then took her own seat. The sauce was a little runnier than her mother's, but that didn't mean it wouldn't taste as good.

"This is my mother's special Norwegian meatball recipe, straight from the old country." Hmm, the first bite wasn't so good. The noodles had stuck together like they'd been glued and the meatballs were a bit . . . well, completely tasteless. Had she forgotten to add some necessary spice?

"Your parents are Norwegian?" David cut a meatball in half, scooped up some sauce with it, and put it in his mouth. Odd expression, that, as if he'd just eaten sawdust.

"Yeah. They came over to the States in the sixties. I was born here." Randi decided to go for the carrots next. Were they supposed to be as soft as mush?

She'd forgotten the meal cooking on the stove while she was getting ready, worrying about her hair, her dress, her makeup.

David valiantly ate on and plied her with polite conversation. "They don't happen to own that Scandinavian grocery store down on Main, do they?"

"Please, it's not a grocery store. Scandia Haus is a place of culinary delight." The name wasn't Norwegian, her parents deciding they needed something Americans could at least pronounce, but it still had the right flavor.

"Sorry. I didn't realize."

"Which means you've never even been in it."

He raised both hands in surrender. "My secret is out."

"Well, you don't know what you're missing. When I came back here after my divorce—" She stopped. Maybe she shouldn't mention her defunct marriage. Well, the cat was out of the bag now, so she went on. "That was a year ago. Anyway,

I set up a website for my parents and you wouldn't believe how the Internet business has grown. It's practically taken over."

"Impressive. There must be a lot of Scandinavians around."

"Yeah. They used to have a store down in L.A., but they moved up here when I went away to college. L.A. wasn't their kind of town. You know, I think the mountains around here re-mind them of home a little bit."

"So you work for them?"

She smiled. "I take care of all the Internet traffic, orders, shipping, site maintenance, all that stuff." She rolled her eyes. "My dad freaks when he gets too close to a computer."

"And you like doing it?"

She tipped her head. She had to think about that one. Did she like it? Or was it a place to run to after the divorce? A hideout. Finally, she said, "It's fine. I don't know what else I want to do with my life, so it works."

He gave a soft snort of laughter. "I know the feeling."

She put her chin on her hand and gazed at him. He hadn't eaten very much.

"So tell me about yourself."

Something flickered across his face, then his eyes seemed to shutter themselves. "Not much to tell. I'm a contractor. It's good work."

Well, that was a lot of info. For some reason, he didn't want to talk about himself. Maybe she'd get him to open up later. Randi set down her fork.

"Well, I appreciate that you tried to eat my dinner. But the truth is, it sucks." She shook her head. "I don't know what I did wrong, but whatever. You don't have to force the slop down."

"It's not slop. It's very . . . interesting." He wore the sweet-est smile when he said it, but he wasn't a very good liar. He couldn't look her in the eye. And *interesting* wasn't exactly a compliment.

She laughed. In the midst of catastrophe, the best thing one could do was laugh. "It's total crap, but thanks for being po-lite. I'm sure I've got something else in the refrigerator."

She'd actually stocked up on stuff when she went shopping for the meatball mess. No, no, she wasn't beaten. Not yet. "Why don't you take the wine into the living room"—the wreck room, meant literally—"and I'll bring out some treats."

He raised a brow, and she tried to discern the suggestive nature in what she'd said. Treats, maybe?

She heard him carrying plates to the sink as she rummaged in the refrigerator. She really needed to get out of this dress and into something more comfortable. The skirt underlining was scratchy, the bottom of the short sleeves were too tight, yet the shoulders kept threatening to slip down her arms. She'd bought it a couple of years ago for a fifties Halloween party. She'd wanted a poodle skirt, but found only this dress.

"Need any help?"

He was right next to her, gazing not into the cold depths, but at her. His breath played across her hair and tickled her ear. She suddenly wasn't cold at all.

"No, no, you sit down. It's a surprise."

He blinked and his mouth quirked.

"Better than the meatball surprise, I swear."

"Dessert?" He glanced at her lips as if they could pass for dessert.

She was warm all over now. "This is something better"—she let her eyelashes fall seductively—"than dessert." She hadn't made dessert. Forgotten all about it. But she'd think of something really good when the time came. She pushed at his chest. "Now, go. I'll be there in a minute."

The wineglasses chinked as he picked them up, then his footsteps faded into the living room. Ah, she could breathe again. Now where was the caviar? A-ha!

Five minutes later, she carried a plate of cheese, crackers, and a tube of caviar into the living room. He'd sunk into the center of her couch. Oops, there was that missing spring. She should have warned him.

"Here we are," she said brightly, setting down the plate, and taking a spot on the edge of the sofa. "This is Jarlsberg cheese, and that's caviar."

David eyed the tube with its foreign writing. "I've got to admit I've never had caviar before."

"A Scandinavian delight from my parents' store. It's not like the black beluga stuff. It's a paste, and you squeeze it on crackers."

This time he eyed her as if she were one of the delights.

"This is Norwegian caviar. I like it better than the Swedish stuff. And the cheese is Norwegian, too."

"I can definitely see the Norwegian in you. With all that blond hair."

Right. The man was definitely not thinking about Norwegian *food*.

"Take your hair down," he murmured, his voice suddenly huskier. He tugged lightly on the braid down her back. "Hair like yours should be loose."

Her cheeks warmed. His voice sent shivers down her arms despite the heat flooding her body. Unable to take her eyes off his gaze, she reached behind and undid the braid. He pulled the freed tresses forward, the backs of his fingers grazing her collarbone. Everything was getting warmer, hotter, and she suddenly felt the need to fan herself. He had a way of looking at a woman, his gaze scanning her face, lingering on her lips, then dipping down to the pearls nestled at her throat.

She wasn't a seductress by any stretch of the imagination. The men in her life, including and especially Mick, had swept her along with their magnetism, telling her what they wanted in rough, hot words. David was somehow gentler, sweeter, but he made her no less hot.

She pointed at the plate. "Do you want to try?"

"Oh yeah." His words trickled along her nerve endings as if he were answering a question that didn't apply to food.

Picking up the tube, she squeezed a dollop on her index finger. "Here, taste."

His eyes glittered with that enticing black-sand sparkle. Then he took her hand and guided her finger to his lips. First he licked, then he sucked the caviar from the end of her finger. A sharp pang of need shot through her.

She hadn't been with anyone since the divorce. She suddenly realized how much she missed a man's touch, the seduction of his tongue, his lips taking hers.

"Do you like it?" she whispered, because she couldn't manage more than that.

"Yeah, I like it." He took the tube from her other hand. She was surprised she hadn't dropped it. "You should try it the same way. Hand-feeding adds something to the flavor, I think."

He squeezed a line across his palm, then held out his hand. "Lick if off and tell me what you think."

Randi bent her head to his hand. She'd never done anything like this. Sweet, seductive play. Mick didn't—she shoved aside the thought. Mick wasn't here. David was. And he held his hand out as if he were offering the world.

The tang of his skin mingled with the flavor of caviar. She licked his palm, savored his taste, then licked again, harder, longer. As if she were devouring something completely different, completely male. His wrist in her hand, she could feel his pulse beat faster.

Then she lifted her head to look at him. "You're right. It's much better that way."

"My turn again." He moved aside her strand of pearls, squeezed a cool dab at the crook of her neck, then put his mouth to the spot. Her head fell back and her eyelids drifted closed at the heavenly caress. His clean male scent tantalized her. Beneath her fingertips, his hair was soft and beckoning. She couldn't help sliding both hands into it, holding him close. His tongue and lips stroked and sucked much longer than it took to lick away the caviar.

Then he raised his head, captured her with his hot gaze, and held out the caviar. "Your turn."

She thought about his lips, licking caviar from his mouth, then kissing him until she couldn't breathe. Or she could undo the buttons of his shirt and dab it on his nipples. Her hands trembled as her mind pondered possible scenarios.

"Do you want me to show you where I want it?"

Her eyes automatically dropped to the bulge in his jeans. Holy Moly.

He tipped her chin up with his forefinger. "That's rushing things. You don't want it to end too quickly, do you?"

"Where then?" She mouthed the words because her voice seemed to have deserted her.

He unbuttoned his shirt to his abdomen, then grabbed both her wrists and fell back with her. She landed with her elbows on either side of his chest. The springs that still remained were probably poking his spine.

Bronzed male skin gleamed at her. He didn't have a hairy chest. She didn't particularly like hairy chests. He plucked the tube from her fingers and squeezed a line down the center.

Not his nipples. No private parts. But an erogenous zone, nonetheless. She wanted to lick caviar off his chest more than she'd ever wanted anything in her life.

"Taste it," he urged.

Her lower body sprawled across his legs, she held his shirt open with her fingers and started at the bottom of the line of caviar. Right above his belly button. She licked and tasted and relished. He grew against her abdomen, his body pulsing at her stomach as if he were a part of her. She made it halfway, sucked his flesh into her mouth, then nipped lightly.

He groaned and tunneled his fingers into her hair, kneading her scalp.

She slid higher in quest of more caviar, more flesh, more man. David thrust up against her. When she reached the last delightful bite, licked his entire chest clean, she folded her hands, rested her chin on top of them, and looked at him.

"Did it taste good?" he asked.

"Did it feel good?" It had, she knew it had, but she wanted him to say it.

"I can show you what it felt like."

Her throat went dry. She couldn't simply unbutton the front of her dress, she'd have to take it off.

As if he saw the glimmer of fear, he slid out from beneath her. Lying on her stomach, she was suddenly cold.

Warm fingers skimmed her spine. "Close your eyes."

She did as he told her, resting her cheek on her hands. Something cool followed the line his fingers had traced, then the warm slide of his tongue. He took his time, tasting her flesh, nipping, sucking, devouring her along with the caviar. Her legs started to tremble with need, and moisture built inside her. This was total eroticism, the glide of his tongue, the suction of his lips. She quivered in response. Her legs moved restlessly. She was suddenly out of control, breathing hard and fast, arching up into his body where it rested against her buttocks. He licked the last of the caviar with a long delicious swipe along her spine, then stretched out his legs, flattened his lower body against her, and thrust. Her legs parted. He slid a hand between them and under her dress, skimming along her wet center on the outside of her panties. She moaned, rocked against his fingers, and squeezed her eyes shut until she saw stars.

Then she couldn't breathe at all as orgasm swept her away.

When she came to herself, David was stroking the hair back from her face.

"Can I assume that felt good?"

She nodded because she didn't seem capable of opening her mouth and certainly couldn't open her eyes. Wow. Although it was a tad embarrassing to have come without him even putting his hand in her panties. Maybe he *expected* embarrassment. But gee, it had been too damn good for that.

David dropped a kiss on her shoulder.

"I'll have to drop by your parents' store for more caviar." He nuzzled her hair. She smelled like an exotic flower, and her skin was as soft as a kitten's tail. "You're amazing."

"Amazing is right. I haven't had an orgasm in a year," she glanced up at him, then rolled her eyes. "Okay, it's been longer than a year." She covered her mouth. "I can't believe I just told you that."

He laughed. He truly had never met anyone like her before in his life. She was completely uncensored. He wanted more.

"I think we should take the caviar in the bedroom and use

it with all your clothes off." He rolled with her, pulling her on top of him. "Who the hell knows how good it could get?"

One helluva lot better, he was sure. She fascinated him. He wondered how she'd make him laugh next. How she'd take him by surprise.

"I know just where I want to squirt caviar next." He smiled, very slow, very sexy, letting the curve of his lips tell her exactly what body part he'd smear with caviar. And how long he'd take licking it all off.

FOUR

RANDI FLIPPED ON the light in her bedroom so David wouldn't trip over the worn spots in the carpet. He set the caviar on her side table. It wasn't exactly a side table, but a couple of wooden boxes stacked one atop the other and covered with a flowered cloth. The bed was hers. She couldn't sleep in what her landlord had left behind. She'd set the box spring directly on the floor so Royal's hair couldn't drift underneath.

"Do you want a refill?" He tipped the wine bottle at her.

She held out her dime-store wineglasses for David to pour, wishing she didn't live in such a dump. What must the man think of her? But Randi always tried to look on the bright side of things. He was in her bedroom, and he'd said she was amazing.

She sipped the wine, planning a host of absolutely amazing things to do to him. Then Royal started a ballistic bark out in the backyard. And did not stop.

"Mountain lion?" David asked, one eyebrow raised.

"I'd prefer that over a skunk." Please, not a skunk. Please, please, please.

As soon as she opened the window to shout at the dog, she smelled it, the acrid odor stinging her nostrils. Oh man.

David crushed close to her backside and leaned out beside her. "Is that mountain lion or skunk? I'm having a hard time telling the difference."

She elbowed him in the ribs. This was *not* funny. She'd ruined dinner, her house was a junk pile, her life a mess, and now this. "Royal, get your little miscreant butt over here."

The miscreant cantered into the window's pool of light.

"Ewww." The stench actually hurt, her nose stinging and her eyes watering. She slammed the window, but it was too late. The odor had permeated the room.

Beside her, David plugged his nose, but his eyes glimmered with laughter. Could the night possibly get any worse?

"I'm really sorry, but I have to take care of this now or I'll never get it out of her fur."

"I'll help you," he said with a nasal twang, his nose still pinched between his fingers.

He was going to stay? "This is very embarrassing."

He let go of his nose to hold her chin in his big, warm hand. "It's amazing," he whispered.

"This is *not* amazing," she whispered back, almost fiercely.

"I've never given a dog a bath on a first date. That is definitely amazing."

A first date? As in not the last date? Randi wouldn't ask. But she could hope. She could really, really hope.

THREE OUTDOOR HOSINGS on the back porch and three cans of tomato juice later, Royal's fur oozed skunk stink only when David stuck his nose against her head.

"I'll dunk her in the tub," Randi said. "I think she's still got tomato juice clots in her fur."

Randi truly was amazing. He'd never had so much fun. Not even with Lou's or Mitch's kids. He'd splashed her with the hose, she'd thrown a cup of tomato juice on him, then hosed him down again. They'd taken more of a bath than the dog.

Randi's nipples had burgeoned against the wet bodice of her dress. He wanted to strip her out of it. Now.

A towel had fallen through one of the broken boards on the end of the porch, and Royal was pushing an empty tomato juice can all around the wooden deck.

"Royal, *komme*."

"You know, I have the irrational need to hear you use that command on me."

She scooped the dog into her arms. "David, *komme*."

He would. Over and over. He opened the door for her and her burden. In the bathroom, she plopped the dog into the tub and ran the water, testing the temperature with her fingers. On her knees at the tub's edge, she soothed the shivering animal.

David almost moaned at the sight of Randi's swaying backside. "What do you want me to do?"

Man, the things he wanted to do. What was it about this woman? Her very liveliness made his cock stand at attention.

"Can you hand me the shampoo? It's in the cupboard over the toilet, and there's a little jug in there, too."

The bathroom had the bare minimum—toilet, standing sink with a mirror over it, combination bath and shower. She must have added the cabinet to store her various personal items.

That was another thing that intrigued him. She didn't have a preponderance of stuff. He'd never known a woman that didn't. There was very little closet space in the place, but she didn't have stuff stacked knee-deep.

"Douse her while I hold her head, would ya?"

David knelt shoulder to shoulder with her, scooped water into the jug, and wet down the dog. Randi squeezed shampoo. Her sleeves slipped down her shoulders as she worked in the lather. Christ, even that made him hot as he imagined her soaping him up. In the shower. A hot tub. Anywhere. She had long, beautiful fingers with short nails and no polish.

Randi Andersen was a girl of bare minimums. He liked that.

He slid two fingers down the back of her dress.

She wriggled away. "Not in front of the child, dear."

"Sorry." He wasn't. Next he pulled on the shoulder of her dress, slipping it further down her arm. She wriggled again, but this time he already had his lips to the soft flesh between her neck and shoulder.

She'd gotten wet and she smelled ever so slightly like tomatoes, which shouldn't have been erotic in the least, yet it tantalized him.

"Do I have to squirt you again to get you to behave?"

He smiled. "You really don't want me to comment on that."

She blushed prettily. He could see straight down the front of her dress as she leaned back on her haunches, her hands still soaping the dog. Her dusky nipples beckoned. He ached to lick them. The evil eye she gave him only heightened the need.

"Pour the water over her and rinse her off. And be good. Or is sex all you think about?"

"Oh, I'm very good. And I've been known to go a full minute without thinking about sex." But not here and not now. He poured and rinsed. "How much do you think about sex?"

Her Scandinavian skin flushing to the color of her nipples, she shrugged. "Not much. Usually."

He leaned in for a quick nuzzle of her hair. "How much did you think about it today?"

"Not much."

"Liar."

Then she laughed, turned, and smiled up at him. "Okay. I thought about it at the grocery store which made me drive to the drugstore so I could buy something which would be necessary if I was actually going to do something about sex rather than just think about it." She tipped her head, her eyes dancing. "Then I thought about it when I was cleaning the house."

She'd bought condoms? Christ. It was all he could do not to scoop her up in his arms right now. "Cleaning the house? That makes you think about sex?"

"Oh, when you're cleaning, your mind can wander, and

then you start thinking about all the things you could do on that very clean kitchen table or a sparkling countertop—"

"Stop. I give up. You win, and you're driving me crazy. Is this dog done yet?"

She batted her eyelashes. "She's done." Then she leaned over to pull the drain plug with a long, exaggerated stretch.

He wanted to run his hands over her backside, cup the flesh. Ah hell, he wanted to climb right up behind her and press his cock to the curve of her ass.

And she knew it, if the glint in her eye meant anything.

"Towels. Where are the towels?" In the cabinet over the toilet, he remembered.

He rose, watching intently as she squeezed water from the dog's fur with yet more exaggerated moves that drew his gaze to the smooth length of her back.

Then she wriggled her ass.

"Tease." At that moment, he'd do anything she wanted.

Wrapping the dog in the towel, he lifted her. And felt the soft glide of Randi's hand across his cock. Up, down, a squeeze, then it was gone.

"Don't drop the dog," she said.

Together, with two towels between them, they dried as much as possible, then Royal squirmed free. The minute her feet touched the floor, she bounced into the hallway, then shook herself, leftover water flying everywhere. Randi squealed as the spray hit her, then David slammed the bathroom door.

A moment later, he hauled her into his arms, pulled her high, and backed her up against the door. She had no choice but to wrap her legs around his waist, her full skirt bunching at her hips and flowing all around him.

"Time to pay the piper for all your teasing." He rocked gently against her, his gaze rising from her luscious lips to her luminous eyes.

She looped her arms around his neck. "Right here?"

"I'm not sure I can wait." He wanted inside her badly, the need building in him all night and coming to a crescendo as he watched her on her knees.

"You haven't even kissed me yet."

She was right, he hadn't, at least not a long, slow kiss to savor her mouth. "Yes, ma'am, whatever you want, ma'am."

"I knew you were polite. Now kiss me."

She tangled her fingers in his hair, pulled his head down, and he lost himself in her taste laced with the lingering sweetness of wine. Her tongue flirted with his, then he took her, deeply, hungrily, pushing her flush against the door. She clung to him, devouring him even as he consumed her, the night's teasing adding a touch of desperation between them. Her legs tightened at his waist, and he dipped his knees, then thrust against her with the same sweet rhythm of his tongue in her mouth. His head swam with her scent, her taste, the warm glide of his hands beneath her dress.

She pushed away, gulping air. "I can't breathe." Then her teeth sank into her lower lip. With eyes the dark blue of the ocean's depths, her gaze traced his features. "I can't do everything I want to do in this tiny bathroom."

He let her legs slide gently to the floor. "We need a bed. A very big bed."

She tipped her head. "My bed's not very big."

He kissed the corner of her mouth, the shell of her ear, then whispered, "It's big enough."

Randi's legs trembled, and she could barely stand, let alone walk. David made her a little nutzoid. Mick had never done that, no one had. David didn't kiss like Mr. Nice Guy. He kissed like the baddest of the bad boys. Better than Mick. Better than anyone. Which made him a dangerous man. He wanted her, it was there in the depth of his kiss, the hitch of his breath, the darkening of his eyes, and the slight tremor in his hands under her skirt. But was amazing the same as special? Maybe, maybe not. A girl could get carried away, mistaking lust for love. Randi had made the blunder before.

She wouldn't again. She'd have hot, intense sex with him—she was dying for hot and intense—but she wouldn't go expecting promises or vows of undying love. At least not right away.

Instead, she'd let him make her feel like a hot, sexy woman for the first time in over a year. Not somebody's ex and not her father's no-good daughter.

Randi grabbed David's hand, flung open the door, and pulled him across the hall to her bedroom before he could change his mind. Before she could.

She flipped off the overhead light, then crossed the room to turn on the bedside lamp. Softer lighting revealed less shabbiness. Then David's hands went to the buttons at the back of her dress. Granted there weren't many of them, but the damn things were so tiny she'd had the devil of a time doing them up on her own. David made quick work of them, then slipped his hand down to the bottom of her spine.

"I like the feel of your skin. Smooth and soft." He nuzzled her ear as he spoke.

Moisture pooled between her thighs. "Will you lick my ear?" She had such sensitive ears.

Warm breath, the glide of his tongue. She tingled all over. Arching her back, thrusting her breasts out, she let the hot sizzle slide through her body.

"What else do you like?"

She liked that he asked instead of just doing whatever made him happy. "I liked it when you licked my back." She'd had that first orgasm when he did that.

He slid the dress from her shoulders, pushing the too-tight sleeves down her arms until her upper body was naked. Sitting on the low mattress, he pulled her between his legs, his hands stroking forward to her abdomen, then up to cup her breasts as he laid his lips on her back. Electric shocks jolted through her.

His tongue tickled and sent shivers to her fingers and toes. She squirmed against his mouth, but his hands clasped her close. Tweaking both her nipples in his fingers, he nipped below her shoulder blade, the combination sending another lightening quick jolt to her clitoris.

"You do that very well," she said, her voice husky, her lids drooping.

"I'm a fast learner."

He turned her in his arms so quickly she had to grab his shoulders to steady herself. His eyes blazed—for her. She wanted to melt into that gaze and pretend she was the most important, special person in the world to him.

"You're dangerous," she whispered, the words falling from her lips without her meaning them to.

He laughed. "That makes me hot. A dangerous guy. Yeah, that really makes me hot." He grabbed one of her hands from his shoulders and put it on the bulge in his jeans. "See?"

She raised one brow. "You're a very big man."

"Keep talking, woman, while I feast on these." He latched onto a nipple, sucking it into his mouth.

"How am I supposed to talk when you're doing that?"

He didn't answer, testing the bead of her nipple with his teeth, laving with his tongue, then sucking once more.

"Do you like my breasts?" They weren't large, but they filled his hands. And his mouth.

He hummed his pleasure, the sound vibrating through her. Then he switched to her other breast, giving it equal attention.

"Could I please take off this dress now? The lining is really itchy." And she didn't want to miss a single sensation.

He kissed her between her breasts, licked her tummy, then caught the waist of her dress and dragged it over her hips. A small embroidered rose adorned her otherwise plain white cotton thong. He stopped at the sight of that rose and the cotton riding high on her hips.

"I have never dated a woman who wore a thong. I thought they were all made of a tiny scrap of lace."

"You're kidding, right?" She didn't even address his misconception. Cotton was much more comfortable than lace.

He smiled up at her. "Still think I'm dangerous?"

"I'm not sure. Maybe I have to ask a few questions."

He slipped the dress down her legs, waited for her to step out of it, then tossed it aside. "Okay, ask."

With the box spring set on the floor, he was at the perfect height for what she wanted. "Have you ever . . ."

He rubbed his nose along the elastic at her waist, then planted a kiss on the rose just below her belly button.

"Have I ever what?"

"Have you ever made love to a woman with your tongue?" Mick had been very skimpy in that department. Since it wasn't about him, he didn't care for it.

"I might have done that a time or two." He opened his mouth against her panties and blew warm air across her.

Oh yeah, he'd done that.

She flicked the elastic of her thong to catch his attention. "If you've only done it a time or two, maybe you should get a little more practice now."

"I like that about you," he murmured, gazing up at her.

She stroked her fingers through his lush hair. "What?"

"That you know what you want, and you don't mind asking for it. It's pretty damn refreshing."

Right. Her, know what she wanted? *Yeah,* right. That's why she was divorced, worked at her parents' store, and lived in a hovel. Ha!

But that was another thing entirely. Right now, she *did* know what she wanted. Mick had grown tired of pleasing her. But here was a willing man. She pulled her bottom lip between her teeth and sucked on it in conscious imitation of what she wanted. "You're taking too long."

David grazed his teeth down the cotton's center. Hooking his fingers in the top of the panty, he let the material slide down her legs, caressing her all the way with his tongue and his touch. Then he came back to the juncture of her thighs.

He probed with his tongue, a light, questing pressure. Then he parted her with his fingers, his hand between her legs forcing her to a wider stance. The first brush of his fingers across her clitoris had her grabbing for his shoulders.

"Am I doing all right so far?" His eyes twinkled with mischief and pleasure.

"I need more just to be sure."

This time he slid a digit deep inside her. Her head tipped back, and a moan fell from her lips.

"I guess you must like it because you're very, very wet. I wonder how you taste?"

Oh please, please, please. He cupped her butt in his hands and pulled her flush against his mouth, opening over her, taking her with his tongue and his lips. Her clitoris throbbed, her legs shook, and she plunged her fingers into the neck of his shirt, hanging on for dear life.

There was nothing quite like the feel of a man, the sight of him pleasuring her, the kiss of soft hair against her belly, and the insistent pull of his lips on her clitoris. He was beautiful. He made *her* feel beautiful and special and wanted.

She started to pant as he sucked harder, holding her close. Tangling her fingers in his hair, she pulled him deeper. He dropped a hand from her butt to her thigh and pulled her leg up over him to open her more fully to his mouth. She moaned as he thrust a finger deep and swirled his tongue over her clitoris.

When she would have fallen, he held her up. When she started to come, crying out his name, he only increased the pressure, making her come harder and longer than she could ever remember doing. Made her come until her legs felt like the bones had melted, and her ears started to lightly hum.

Somehow he swung her to the side, and she flopped weightlessly across the bed, unable to open her eyes. Light fingers stroked her belly.

"So, did I do okay?"

She cracked one eyelid. "You lied big time. You've done that more than once or twice."

He smiled. Dangerously, all gleaming white teeth and kissed-to-perfection lips. "I have *never* done that before."

"Which part?" She narrowed her eyes suspiciously.

"Made a woman scream like that."

"I didn't scream."

"Yes, you did."

Maybe she had. The ringing in her ears had drowned it out.

He stroked a hand down the side of her face, over her breasts, across her belly, and into the thatch of hair at her apex. "Oh, baby, you screamed, and I almost came."

Wow. "You've still got all your clothes on."

"I can do something about that." His shirt still halfway unbuttoned from their earlier bout on the couch, he simply pulled it over his head and tossed it on top of her dress.

She ran a hand down his chest. He unbuckled his belt, the rasp of his zipper filling the quiet room.

"Let me stand up." He eased her back as he rose, her gaze traveling up with his. Then he shucked his jeans, reached for her hand, and wrapped her fingers around his cock.

He was long and thick and very, very hard. Her throat dried up. Yes, he was beautiful there, too.

"You look at me like that much longer, I'm going to come."

She stroked his length.

He stopped her. "Get in the middle."

She moved to the center of the bed, then turned to watch him as he leaned down to his jeans, pulled out his wallet, and extracted a condom packet.

He glanced at her over his shoulder. "Hope you don't mind. I did come prepared."

"I don't mind." She'd prepared, too.

He let her watch as he rolled on the condom, then crawled across the bed on his hands and knees. Sinking his hand between her legs, he slid a finger over her clitoris. She moaned.

"You want the top or bottom?" he murmured.

"Top." She wanted to watch as she guided him inside.

He flopped on his back beside her, then pulled her over him. His cock nestled at her juncture. She rubbed lightly against him, then rose. Stroking a hand down the condom, he lifted to her opening. God, he was hard. She closed her eyes a moment to relish the feel of just the tip inside her, then she leaned forward on both hands, watching as he filled her.

"Christ, that feels good."

Air rushed from his lungs as she took him all the way and then settled, loving the feel of him inside her. His hands on her hips guided her, forcing her to rise, then fall once more. Again. When she found that perfect rhythm, he took her breasts, molding them with his fingers.

"I knew you'd feel just like this. Hot and wet." He rose, taking a nipple in his mouth and sucking until a bright shot of pleasure zipped to her clitoris.

She slid down against him, taking him deeper and rubbing herself against his coarse hair.

He stiffened, suddenly, and not in a good way. "Houston, we have a problem."

FIVE

"THERE'S SOMETHING BETWEEN my legs, and I really don't think it's supposed to be there."

Randi twisted to look behind her. Royal had crept up onto the bed and was sprawled between David's legs.

Holy Mack Moly. "Royal, down." She couldn't even remember the damn Norwegian command. Her face flamed.

Mick had hated, absolutely hated the dog on the bed.

After Royal slinked away, she turned back to David. "I'm sorry. I forgot to put her back outside or close the bedroom door." She'd forgotten everything in her haste to have him. "She's used to sleeping with me. You're not mad, are you?"

He cocked his head. "Why would I be mad?" He waggled his eyebrows. "Though I have to say I'm not used to a dog trying to nuzzle my nuts."

Oh, this was mortifying. He'd leave now. Just pull out and leave. "I'm so sorry."

He ran his hands up her forearms, then pulled her down by the elbows. "It's all right. I don't care. What's wrong?"

She'd cooked dinner to mush. She'd forgotten the dog, left her outside to get sprayed by a skunk, then allowed her to crawl up between his legs. What else could go wrong?

He shook her lightly. "It's not a big deal."

Stupid, stupid, stupid. What must he think? Terrible thoughts spiraled through her head, gaining momentum, spinning out of control. Looking on the bright side didn't work.

David rolled her beneath him and stared down at her. Tears pricked her eyes. And she knew.

She wanted him to fall in love with her. She wanted him to come back. Tomorrow. The next day. The next month. Holy Moly, she'd done it again. Mixed up lust and love, and really, she couldn't tell the difference in what she felt about David.

It was all so like her relationship with Mick. He'd wanted her badly, at first, so she'd fallen in love, hopped into bed, then jumped into marriage so quickly she hadn't a moment to *think* about what she was doing. It had taken three years to finally admit her mistake. She was a little slow on the uptake.

But here she was repeating the pattern all over again.

David moved inside her, gently. He pecked at her lips, then licked the seam with his tongue. "You're perfect, Randi, you don't have to worry about anything but this."

He dipped down to suck her nipple in his mouth, let it pop free, then blew warm breath on it. Her body involuntarily arched into his.

"You're not going to make me stop, are you, sweetheart?"

With a hand beneath her bottom, David pulled her closer, angled her for a slightly deeper penetration. He hadn't a clue what was running through her mind, but he wouldn't let her go now. It wasn't about fucking the hell out of a delicious woman, it wasn't even about getting off. It was about a warm sense of comfort that being inside her gave him. It was her laughter that still rang in his head. It was the taste of her, the scent of her, the feel of her skin along his body.

He slid deeper. "Say it," he murmured. "Say, 'Don't stop, I want you to keep going, I love what you're doing to me.' "

She bit her lip. "Maybe I overreacted about the dog."

He pulled out, pumped fast twice, then hit deeply again.

She moaned. "Yes, I definitely overreacted. Don't stop."

She raised her legs to his hips and her arms to his neck. "I love the feel of you inside me."

Ah, yes. He rocked against her, thrusting higher and deeper. Then he braced himself on one hand and reached between them, finding her clitoris, stroking it. She groaned, and he loved the sound. Her eyes closed, her lips gently parted, and he knew she was lost to the sensation of his cock inside her, his fingers on her.

She tightened around him, inner muscles working, and she cried out. He thrust harder, keeping her on the edge, riding it with her until he couldn't keep his eyes open any longer, until the wave slammed into him, tumbled him over, and he shouted her name as he lost a part of himself inside her.

THEY'D FALLEN ASLEEP with the light on. David had slept like the dead, better than he had in weeks. Randi's hair, splayed across the pillow, shone golden in the lamplight. She lay on her side facing him, both hands tucked child-like against her chest. Long lashes fanned beneath her eyes, and her porcelain skin glowed.

He hadn't intended on falling asleep. But maybe this made things easier, even if it was cowardly. He hadn't intended on feeling anything for her either, besides just the plain fact that she'd intrigued him. Shitty, however true it might be.

If he'd felt nothing for her, though, he wouldn't be slipping out while she slept. Hell, he hardly knew her. He didn't want to *feel* anything for her. He didn't need another complication.

And wasn't that one helluva typical male excuse.

He climbed from the bed as gently as possible, gathered his jeans, shirt, and boots, then carried them into the living room.

The dog lay curled up in the center of the carpet. In the dim light spilling down the hall from the bedroom, she raised her head to gaze at him with the saddest eyes. Dogs had that woebegone expression down pat. Randi had thrown her out of the bedroom, and the dog had not come back but had lain on the carpet moping.

"Look, girl," he whispered, because hell, when she gazed at him so steadily, unblinkingly, he had to say something. "You shouldn't be going into your mom's bedroom and sticking your nose where it doesn't belong." The dog blinked. "You're cute and all, but you just can't be crawling into bed when she's got company. It's not polite." Dressed, he bent to tie his boots. "It's like being caught by the kids, ya know." She stared, then finally she whined, laid her head down, and closed her eyes.

David felt oddly rebuked, as if the dog were saying he wasn't worth listening to since he was sneaking out in the middle of the night.

Shit. Definitely a guilty conscience talking there. Should he wake Randi? Should he go?

In the end, he just acted like a dickhead and left. He really didn't know what he'd say to her. He didn't have any promises to give.

WELL, THAT WAS that. She should have stayed in bed and let him leave. She shouldn't have hidden just inside the bedroom door and listened to him talk to Royal.

Randi had started letting the dog sleep on the bed the night she left Mick. He'd hated Royal. Hmm, *hate* was a strong word. He thought Royal was prissy and high-strung. He'd have been happier with a Doberman. Something manly. But Royal was like . . . royalty. There wasn't a prissy bone in her body. Mick, however, had treated her like . . . a dog.

David had actually talked to her. And Randi fell in love.

Just like that. Less than twenty-four hours. She was such a sucker. She'd done it all over again, opened her heart up to a world of hurt. Not much she could do about it now.

She was in love with a guy who'd said good-bye to the dog but left without even waking her. Which said a lot about the development of this non-relationship.

Randi used the bathroom, washed her hands, then climbed beneath the covers on her bed. Reaching to shut off the bedside lamp, she saw the caviar tube. After washing the dog, they'd forgotten all about it. It sat like an ugly reminder of what might have been. Closing her eyes, she bit her lip to ease the sudden pain in her heart. Then she clicked off the light and clapped for Royal, who came bounding in, careened onto the bed, and nuzzled her nose into Randi's armpit.

That was the thing about animals. They loved you unconditionally, were always happy to see you, and didn't sneak out in the middle of the night.

DAVID FELT LIKE shit. He hadn't slept well after he left Randi's. In fact, he hadn't slept at all. Then his dad had kept him and his brothers humping at the day's job site with barely a word between them. Sweating like a pig, David downed four bottles of water over three hours. In the summer, it would have been nice to start early and cut off shortly after noon, but for some reason, people didn't like the sound of a chain saw before seven in the morning. Gee, go figure.

They'd finished hauling the last load to the dumps at around three, and finally, dog-tired, David had hit the shower by three-thirty.

So why, at four-thirty, was he at Randi's with a load of two-by-fours in the back of his truck?

Oh yeah, to fix the front steps and porch so she wouldn't break her neck in the dark. The dog had set up a ballistic racket when he arrived, so he'd let her out of the backyard to wander around while he worked. She bounced around like a Ping-Pong ball, then settled down on the porch. She didn't run away, and damn, the little beast actually looked like she was listening when he talked to her.

"Was she pissed when she woke up this morning?"

Royal panted, and David gave her some water.

"All right, don't answer that question."

It really didn't matter if Randi was pissed. Not much he could do about it now. "And I am not fixing her porch to make amends. It's just the neighborly thing to do since she made me dinner." And gave him the best freaking night of his life, sexually speaking.

"All right," he told the dog, "I like her. Christ, I even like you. But I'm not looking for any of the serious stuff right now." She stared, sad brown eyes unblinking, just as she'd gazed at him last night. "Don't look at me like that."

The dog flopped over on her side to ignore him.

David leaned on the board he'd just finished cutting. "Fine, I'll tell her the truth. She has a right to know."

All he got was another doggie stare.

Years of doing the right thing, the expected thing, allowed a niggling glimmer of guilt to slip through. In his world, a man didn't have casual sex.

Worse than the guilt was the notion that last night was anything but casual. Randi was funny, sassy, bright, and somehow sweetly childlike in her penchant to babble. She was also deeply passionate. He had the feeling there wasn't a casual bone in her body.

Dammit. David laid the board in and screwed it down.

By six, he'd replaced four of the rotted or missing boards in the porch and fixed the steps. The dog raised her head, then jumped up for an exuberant barking session before David saw Randi's truck bumping through the ruts in the gravel drive.

She climbed from the truck, bending down to fondle and chatter to the wriggling mass at her feet. Then she leaned back into the truck, her jean skirt stretching across her backside as she reached to the passenger seat for a grocery bag.

"Hi."

David sensed a forced brightness in her greeting and her smile. He felt the need for a little forced small talk himself.

"Hope it was okay I let the dog out of the backyard."

"Yeah, that's fine." Randi looked from his truck, to the sawhorses he'd set up at the side of the drive, to the new planks in her front step. "What are you doing?"

What *was* he doing? Being a good neighbor? Or searching for an excuse to wait for her on her porch? Honestly, he had to admit it was more of the latter than the former, despite what he'd told the dog. Despite what he'd been telling himself. He might not be ready for any sort of serious relationship, but he wasn't done with her yet. Not by a long shot.

"I figured if you got home late and didn't leave a light on, you'd be liable to break your neck on those rotten boards."

"You didn't have to do that." She stared as his boots as she spoke. "But thanks. I've been asking the landlord for a while now. He doesn't listen well."

She should have been more insistent, but he opted not to voice the thought.

"I'm almost done now." He was usually good at polite conversation. But with Randi and all the crap roiling in his gut, he felt stilted and uncomfortable.

"Thanks. I bought burrito stuff. Can I offer you dinner to pay you back?" She shifted from one foot to the other, edging nearer to the porch, the dog milling about her feet.

"Burritos?" He searched for something to lighten the mood, the tenseness, the proverbial morning after the night before. He dropped down past the new porch steps, closer to her, within touching distance. "Another Norwegian delicacy?"

The only Norwegian delicacy he wanted was her.

She smiled self-consciously. "Since I wasn't so hot last night, I figured I'd better get back to the basics." Then she blushed, belatedly realizing, as he did, the innuendo in her words. "What I mean is, I thought I'd try something besides meatball mush."

He tipped her chin, forcing her to look at his face instead of his footwear. "No sense dancing around the issue, Randi. Last night was hot, and we both know it. I didn't come back for dinner or solely to fix your porch. And I shouldn't have left last night without waking you up to say good-bye." Serious intentions or not, that had been just plain wrong.

Randi shuffled her feet. The last thing she'd anticipated was to find him drilling screws into new slats for her front stoop. She hadn't expected to see him at all. The sudden punch of joy followed quickly by a sheer drop into despair had left her feeling off balance.

"I didn't expect you to wake me up." She didn't expect to fall in love with him in a day and a heartbeat.

He didn't let go of her chin when she tried to avoid his gaze. "Look, last night was fantastic. I think we should . . ." He paused, searching her eyes as if he'd somehow find the words he wanted hidden there. "I think we should explore this thing."

"Explore?"

"We were good. Really good. And I'd like to see you again." He glanced down at Royal this time, as if *she* had the answer. "I'm not looking for anything . . . permanent. But I don't see why we can't get to know each other better."

In the biblical sense. Yep, that's what he meant. "You don't have to hem and haw. We were very compatible in bed, and you'd like to try it again. Right? Well, that's okay with me. I like you. You fixed my porch. You didn't complain about the meatballs, and sure, let's get to know each other better."

She was a glutton for punishment, but she was used to surviving on crumbs. She'd done it long enough with Mick, and the sex had never been as good as it was with David.

"For a nice guy," she went on, "you're a wild man in bed." She hadn't had a man in her bed for a long time, wild or not, so what the heck. "Let's go for it. I'm on the rebound," kind of, "and it isn't good for me to get into anything serious anyway. You know the whole rebound thing, mixing up feelings and stuff, so playing it low-key and all is really the best thing for me anyway. So, burritos for dinner. Yeah, that sounds great."

She smiled. Her heart was not breaking. Because really, she *was* on the rebound. For sure. Hadn't David sparked her interest because he seemed to be the exact opposite of Mick? Yes, he had. So casual was a good thing.

She sidled by him and tested her new porch step. "Hey, this is great, wow, thank you. Come on, Royal, it's dinnertime. I'll feed her first, then get the burritos ready." She smiled even though it seemed to hurt oddly, feeling brittle at the edges. "There's a couple of boards left, and I just know you want to get to those before dark. I'll call you when everything's ready."

She juggled her purse, the grocery bag, and her keys. David stepped up on the porch beside her, took the keys, and unlocked the door. Royal rushed in like a whirlwind of dust.

Leaving the keys hanging in the door, David leaned down to bring his lips to hers. Soft, undemanding, he stroked her lower lip with his tongue, then sucked gently until she opened her mouth. It was sweet, yet the meeting of their tongues promised hot, carnal pleasures later in the night.

He released her, patted her on the butt, and turned her to the kitchen.

She'd told David she hadn't had an orgasm in over a year. It had been too embarrassing to admit she simply hadn't had one with a man. A man in her bed was better than sex by herself.

Now *that* was looking on the bright side.

HER NEXT AWKWARD moment came right after dinner. What now? Did she suggest coffee? Wine? Popcorn and a movie? Sex? Maybe she should do the dishes first. She wasn't shy about sex, something she'd proven well enough last night. But tonight David made her shy, or rather, her feelings about him did.

"I just have to sort a load of laundry. I'd planned to stop by the laundromat on the way home from the store tomorrow night." That *was* her plan for the evening. Honest.

Standing abruptly, Randi piled his plate on top of hers, then crushed the paper towels they'd used as napkins and tossed them on top. As she went to pick up the whole mess, David held her still by the wrist.

"I've got a washer and dryer at my place. Why don't you bring your laundry over tomorrow night?"

She stopped, still, stock-still. "You want me to do your laundry as well?"

He tilted his head up and to the side. "I did it this weekend. I was just thinking that I could make you dinner, and it would spare you having to go to the laundromat."

She really did hate the laundromat. The dryers were too hot

and were hell on her clothing. Not to mention that creepy guys littered the place. She didn't say that, asking instead, with a hint of breathy awe in her voice, "You can cook?"

"I'm thirty-four years old and I've been living on my own since I was twenty. Yes, I can cook."

"Beans on toast?"

"Scallopini."

"Ooh." The sound slipped out with yet another touch of awe. "And you're going to cook scallopini for me? But you fixed the porch. Last night's dinner was to pay you back for rescuing me on the road and tonight it was for the porch, so you don't owe me anything." Mick would never have considered that one good turn deserved another.

David slipped his fingers down to hold her hand, his thumb caressing her palm.

"It's self-serving." His voice had dropped a note, quieter, huskier, and his eyes simmered with the hot glow of last night. "If you do laundry tomorrow at my place, you don't have to sort it tonight. And if I make dinner, then you'll be eternally grateful and turn to putty in my hands."

She was already putty in his hands. He scooted his chair back, took her other wrist, and reeled her in between his legs.

"There were several things we didn't get to last night." His voice, soft in the early evening, seduced her.

"What things?"

He put her hands on his shoulders. She laced them behind his neck.

"Where's the dog?"

She tilted her head at his non sequitur.

"She's too young to overhear what I'm about to say."

She laughed, the first unstilted, honest-to-goodness laugh she'd had all evening. "You're just afraid she'll jump on the bed at a crucial moment and break your concentration."

He shook his head. "Nope. I'm afraid she'll see what I'm going to do to you right now and be traumatized for life."

"Hmm, well, in that case, I put her out back earlier so we could eat in peace."

David grinned. It was perhaps the most evil, lascivious grin she'd ever seen on a nice guy.

"That was the magic word."

"Which one?" She suddenly knew even as she asked. "Oh."

His gaze heated her as he caressed the bare skin above the waistband of her skirt.

"You did do that to me last night." She'd practically begged him to lick her to orgasm. He'd been sweetly obliging.

"I didn't do it to you in the kitchen." He winked. "On that nice, clean countertop."

The whole conversation from last night came back to her. She'd told him cleaning the house made her think about sex, and the memory of that hot, sexy talk heated her. Talking was as much a part of foreplay as touching.

"How about it?" he coaxed in a husky whisper.

How about it? He didn't want a serious relationship. But he did want her now. A girl had to work with what was presented to her.

Randi dropped gracefully to her knees between his legs. "You know, it's only fair that since I made dinner, I get to decide what's for dessert." Her gaze fell to the front of his jeans. He filled them out a little more even as she watched.

"And what did you want for dessert?"

She let one side of her mouth curve in a smile. Some women felt that doing that particular thing to a man was demeaning. It gave him the power. Randi knew the opposite was true. She might be the one literally on her knees, but taking a man in her mouth metaphorically put *him* on his knees.

Besides, she relished doing it to him.

She placed her palm over him without exerting pressure. Just touching, a barely discernible stroke. "I'd like to have *you* for dessert. We didn't do *that* last night." She couldn't have forgotten doing that. Selective memory. She only forgot what she didn't want to think about. Tasting him would have been ingrained in her brain.

"If you insist." He put his hand over hers and rubbed

harder. "I think I might like that." His eyes darkened and that lascivious grin said he'd more than like it.

She tugged on his buckle, then his zipper. He raised his hips, helping her pull down the jeans and tight white briefs.

"You're beautiful," she whispered, in admiration of his majesty.

"Shucks, it ain't nothing, ma'am."

She sank back on her haunches, tilting her head to peek up at him through her lashes. "Don't you think you're beautiful?"

He cupped her chin. "Right now, I am whatever you say I am." All trace of laughter had left his eyes, leaving behind some message she didn't get.

"And I say you're beautiful." She urged his hand to the side of her throat and leaned forward to glide her tongue straight up his hard flesh.

He let out a long, delicious sigh that wafted over her, teasing the fine strands of hair at her temples. She gave herself up to the pleasure of his taste—warm male, salty flesh, and hot desire.

Holding his cock aloft, Randi rode the length with her lips, down, down, down, meeting the fist she'd made of her fingers. David shoved one hand beneath her hair, pulling the mass of it to the back of her head.

This was the essence of beauty, her plump lips around him, her fingers wrapped at the base of his cock, kneading gently. The feel of her mouth, the pure sensation of warmth and wet, the slight rasp of her teeth. She tongued his crown, and his eyes felt like rolling back in his head. His gut tensed, and heat built in his balls, an ache that was both pleasure and pain.

He slouched in the chair, widening his legs, pulling her closer, forcing himself deeper. She took every inch, a hum in her throat vibrating through him. Her little noises, sounds of pleasure and delight, hoisted him closer to the horizon, the peak, where only her mouth on his cock existed.

No woman had ever made him feel so intensely. No woman had ever made a simple sexual act seem like the sun, the moon, and the stars wanted to explode inside his head.

No woman had taken her own pleasure in the very process of giving him his.

She shoved her hands up to his hips, holding him tight, and took his cock deeper than he'd ever gone.

Want, need, and desire beat inside him, behind his closed eyelids. Heat pulsed from his balls to the tip of his cock, then raced to his extremities. He wanted to come deep inside her body, his cock buried in her warmth, but more, he wanted to fill her mouth, have her take him, swallow him, devour him, consume everything he had in him to give.

When he touched the sky at the back of her throat, he shot to the heavens and emptied himself inside her.

SIX

DAVID CAME TO himself to find his fingers tangled in her hair, massaging her scalp. His body jerked once, involuntarily, then he leaned forward to wrap himself around her body. She cuddled close, her cheek to his abdomen.

"No one's ever done that for me before," he whispered against the smooth, fragrant skin of her neck.

"Done what?" she whispered back as if they were deep beneath a pile of bedclothes on an intimate stormy night where only reverent whispers were allowed.

"Taken me like that. Made me come. Swallowed for me."

He heard how pathetic that sounded as soon as the words were out of his mouth. Shit. Yet in some weird way, the act had been more intimate, more intense, more powerful than losing himself inside a woman's body, even hers last night.

She smoothed her hands along his thighs, his butt, but she didn't say anything.

Yeah, he might be pathetic, but she'd given him something he'd never had, and damned if he would spoil the best freaking moment of his life. "Come here."

He pulled her up onto his lap and wrapped his arms around

her. She clung to him as he clung to her, still without a word. And as odd as it was that a blow job was more intimate than burying himself deep in her body, the silence rang with more meaning than any words could have done.

NO ONE HAD ever done that for him because no one had ever loved him the way she could. Randi trapped the words inside with a moment of silence.

Finally, after a minute, maybe two, who could tell, he reached up to brush the tangled hair from her face. "I think we should go to bed. I really, really want to be inside you."

He didn't call it making love, but he didn't say fucking either.

Okay? I'd love to? She settled for "Yes, please," then slid off his lap. He rose, tugging his jeans back over his hips as he stood, zipping up and rebuckling.

Holy Moly Mother, she just might cry if she said another word. That's how intensely she'd loved the feel of him in her mouth. The heaven in his taste.

He bent his knees, scooped her up, and pulled her legs around him, clasping his hands beneath her butt. She steadied herself with her arms around his neck. Taking him with her mouth had left her wet and wanting. She'd almost put her hand between her legs and touched herself as she sucked him. Now, her body rubbed against his as he walked, and hot sensation made her gasp.

In the bedroom, he dumped her on the bed. She sprawled across the center as he turned on the bedside lamp, then fished condoms from his wallet and threw them on the side table.

He moved to stand between her legs. "Pull up your top."

She did, inching it across her abdomen, over her breasts, her pinkies dragging across lace-covered nipples. She left it bunched above the swell of her breasts and beneath her armpits.

He liked the show. He filled the front of his jeans, and his eyes, with the light behind him, were dark pools of want she could lose her soul in.

"Undo your bra." He spoke in a husky rasp.

She popped the front clasp, then did a deliberate graze of lace over her peaks. Her lower body squirmed with sweet intensity. The outline of his cock deepened inside his jeans.

Following his instructions to the letter, she didn't wriggle out of the bra, but left it lilting at her sides.

"Your skirt, tug it up to your waist."

She wanted to be naked, yet remaining half-clothed was naughty, erotic. Hot. She tugged, wriggled, revealing first the tops of her thighs, then a blue cotton thong, the embroidered daisy, and finally, her belly button. Before she'd been wet. Now, the cotton was drenched. His look, lids at half-mast, eyes dilated, dark, wanting, needy, stole the breath from her chest. The beat of her heart pulsed in her ears. Mick had never made her feel so sexy. So wanted. Not even in the beginning.

And she would not think about Mick *now*.

"Panties. Take them off."

Ooh, there was something delicious in being ordered about in that husky, raspy, heavy male voice. She hooked her fingers in the top of the elastic and dragged down the cotton. Slowly, sensuously, she swished her hips and lifted her bottom. When she'd tossed the thong to the carpet, he knelt between her legs dangling off the bed.

"Now this is pure beauty." He traced a finger down her abdomen, through her curls, and across her clitoris. "Christ, you're wet." He tested her with one finger, sliding in, out, back to her clitoris. "I don't want to use my tongue on you. I want to watch you while you come."

She writhed on the bed though his touch was gentle. The softness of it, the barely there pad of his finger excited her more than a rough, hard workout.

"Whatever you like."

He grabbed her thighs and hauled her butt to the edge of

the bed. His jeans chafed her inner thighs. "Watch me touch you. Don't look away."

She concentrated on the sight of his hand gliding across her, the lines of intent on his face, his gaze on her exposed pussy. He rubbed her with his thumb, using all her wetness.

"Does it feel good?"

She clutched the coverlet. "Yes." Her eyes wanted to close with the sheer hot passion engulfing her body, but she fought to keep them open, her gaze on his hand, his taut abdomen, his tanned arms against her paler flesh.

He entered her with two fingers, his thumb still circling her clitoris. Her pelvis rocked. She started to pant. With his other hand, he caressed her bottom, squeezed her flesh. Then he withdrew his fingers and worked her clitoris, around, beneath, straight on. Clasping her legs around him, she rose to meet every stroke, directing him with her body, gasping when he hit just the right spot. She bit her lip, but a moan of pure need slipped from her. She tossed her head, back and forth, as he concentrated on the tiny button. Her hips strained into his touch, her body trembled. White heat zipped to her clitoris, sucked all her energy, and threw her into climax. She bucked, writhed, and finally cried out, her ears ringing with the sound.

He leaned down to place a reverent kiss just above her mound. No tongue, just lips and warm breath as her body jerked in the aftermath.

She opened her eyes to find him looking down at her, his abdomen to her pelvis, his mouth close to her belly.

"That was the most beautiful thing I've ever seen," he whispered.

No man had ever made her feel so special, something beyond mere physical orgasm.

"Come here." She held out her arms.

He crawled up her body, divesting her of her clothes before he gathered her close and carried her more fully onto the bed. She rested and calmed in his embrace, the ringing in her ears finally abating as she nestled her chin to his throat. She didn't want words, she didn't want promises. She didn't want anything to steal the moment's magic.

She fell asleep, magic still singing through her body.

DAVID WATCHED HER sleep. He reveled in the fact that he had given her absolute pleasure and absolute sexual exhaustion. The image of her face would live in him a long time, the force and power of her orgasm, her eyelashes fanned beneath her eyes, her lips as she'd cried out his name. Her skin bore the rosy glow of satisfaction, and her hair fell like silk across his chest. She slept on, even through the gentle stroke of his fingers on her arm, the curve of her hip, her bottom, her thighs. She murmured something unintelligible and snuggled deeper into his embrace.

Sex had always been pleasurable. He'd missed it between relationships. Yet he'd never hopped into bed with an available woman, instead practicing self-satisfaction when the need arose.

He'd hopped into Randi's bed the first day they met and came running back like a horny goat. Yet these two nights had been far more intense than even his first sexual experience at the age of seventeen, regardless of acute teenage hormones.

He should run, as he'd done in the dark hours last night. Instead, he continued a slow caress of her body as she slept. Something had changed between this night and the last. He couldn't leave until he figured out what it meant.

The slow tick of the clock and the needs of his own body finally made him ease her warmth from his arms. She muttered, curled into a ball, but remained fast asleep. He took care of the necessities in her small bathroom. Unlike yesterday, female items cluttered the back of the toilet and the space around the sink. Sweet-smelling lotion, toothpaste, pots of makeup, an earring minus its back. At times, during his serious relationships, similar paraphernalia had made its home in his own bathroom.

He remembered his irritation. Randi's mess, on the other hand, made him feel at home.

In the bedroom, she remained in the small fetal ball, her feet tucked close to her bottom, hiding her bare essentials. He knelt at the side of the bed, trailing a finger along her thigh, then the seam of her butt. She mumbled and twitched. He delved deeper, up beneath her tucked feet to the soft curls. She was still wet, her moisture and heat making his cock jump to full alert. He stroked the outer lips of her pussy. She wriggled, then heaved a great sigh followed by a soft moan. And still she slept.

He left her long enough to shuck his clothes, put on a condom, and turn out the light. Moonlight streamed across the carpet, reaching the bed, falling across her skin and setting it alight. He wanted to wake her with his cock. He wanted to have her squirm sleepily beneath him, then open her eyes to see his face above her, to feel him deep inside.

With gentle strokes, he eased her flat to the coverlet. She licked her lips as he traced her nipples. A finger parting her, lightly caressing her clitoris, he got her to spread her legs. Climbing between them, he rubbed her with the crown of his cock.

He didn't know how she could sleep on even as her body reacted to him, but more than anything he wanted to awaken her with his lips on hers and his cock already deep inside her. Somehow, it was the most important thing in the world.

He'd think about how damn scary that was later.

SHE WAS HAVING the most marvelous dream. A female wet dream. Hot flesh, hard cock, and a tongue in her mouth. She wrapped her arms around a strong neck and raised her legs to lock her feet behind a taut male butt. She clung to him and let him pump her to oblivion. Hard, fast, sweet, deep. David. His voice. His body. When she came, she exploded with his lips on hers as he swallowed her cries. When he came, she felt the pulse and throb through her entire body, and she took his cries into her mouth as he had taken hers.

"Oh my," she whispered against his lips.

"When did you wake up?"

"I don't know. I might still be dreaming."

He rolled them beneath the covers which, at this time of year, were nothing more than the bedspread and a sheet. Even so, it was hot and steamy under there, the night breeze through the open window not enough to blow out the day's heat, but she liked the cling of their sweaty flesh.

"Was it when I slid inside you?"

"I'm not sure."

"When I kissed you?"

"Maybe."

It was when he whispered against her lips. *You are so beautiful.*

"You were awake the whole time, weren't you?" He almost sounded disappointed.

"No. Not the whole time. I was still dreaming at least until you were inside me. I'm sure of it."

He sighed. Satisfaction. For some reason, exactly what he wanted to hear.

Royal chuffed just outside the window. She'd been so quiet, Randi had forgotten her. An earsplitting bark soon escalated to a frenzy.

"Dammit." She shoved the sheet aside.

"Bring her inside."

She glanced at him over her shoulder. "Once she's inside, she'll be on the bed. And if I try closing the bedroom door, she'll just sit outside it and whine. It's very annoying."

She stopped. Without even thinking, she'd assumed he would spend the night. The idea had just been there in her head. Her heart cramped, missing a beat. She couldn't bear it if he sneaked out like he had last night.

He took four beats longer than necessary to answer. "Let her in. I don't mind if she sleeps on the bed. As long as she doesn't start sniffing places she shouldn't."

Randi padded naked through the house, let Royal in, checked her paws for dirt, then allowed her to run ahead.

Hurtling onto the bed, the dog shoved her nose in David's face, then settled at the bottom. Randi climbed in, scooting to David's side until she could feel him. Putting an arm around her waist, he tugged her close, right up to his chest, her body flush against his.

She couldn't stand it, she just couldn't. "Are you going to spend the night?" It was debilitating to ask, but worse to wake in the night as he dressed in the dark and scurried out the door like a thief or a rat.

He was silent for so long, she thought he'd fallen asleep. Except that his breathing lacked the soft rhythm.

"Yeah," he whispered. "I'm spending the night."

She didn't ask for a single other thing from him. The night was enough.

DAVID HAD WOKEN with the sure knowledge that two nights with Randi had given him more intensity than the entire three years with his first sweetheart, Betsy. More than the two and a half years with Eileen.

The realization was enough to make him want to jump from the bed, grab his clothes, and run like hell. Her butt nestled against his cock, the sweet scent of her hair, and her soft skin kept him right where he was until her alarm went off.

Royal didn't even twitch at the sound.

He'd wanted to make love to Randi one more time before he left for work, but hell, the dog was on the bed! Even if she hadn't cracked an eyelid.

Maybe he'd have Randi in the shower.

She pressed the snooze alarm and rolled back into him. Then her body stiffened against his.

"This feels too good. I have to get up." And she did, just like that, buck naked and practically running out of the room. The bathroom door closed, then water clanged through the pipes as she started the shower.

"Did I say something wrong?"

Royal raised her head, looked at him, then settled again.

Funny thing, Randi was right. It felt too good. He could see spending a lot more mornings waking up with her in his arms after a night buried deeply inside her.

And that just wouldn't work. Relationships muddled a man's thinking. He had his own shit to get together before he even attempted using the word *relationship* again.

When Randi left the bathroom, her face freshly scrubbed, wet hair pulled back in a ponytail, and a short, blue robe tied tightly at the waist, a different man stood in her living room.

But David had no intention of leaving this morning without saying good-bye. He owed her more respect than that.

"I have to change clothes so I'll shower at my place."

"Yeah, sure. That makes sense."

She deserved more than a peck on the cheek, too. He leaned down to kiss her lips. He didn't say thanks for last night because it seemed trite. "See ya."

A decent good-bye, noncommittal. As he started his truck, he remembered that he'd invited her to do laundry at his house tonight.

He wasn't sure she'd show up. While that shouldn't have mattered because they weren't having a relationship and he'd already told her he didn't want one, he knew he'd miss her if she skipped his place to go to the laundromat.

Shit.

DOUBLE SHIT. RANDI hadn't called his cell though David had given her the number. He didn't know if she was coming tonight.

He'd been thinking about her all day.

"I'm talking to you. Where's your head, David?"

In his pants. In Randi's pants. It wasn't prudent to tell his father that. Luckily, they'd finished the cutting over an hour ago, and all they had left was clearing the scrap and heading to the dumps. Jace had some wedding crap to attend to with Taylor, and Mitch lit out half an hour ago, too.

"Sorry, Dad, what was it?"

"I asked if you would talk to your brother. Some bug's been up his butt the last couple of weeks."

"And which butt would that be, Jace or Mitch?" David didn't really want to know.

"Mitch. Take him out for a drink and find out what's up with him, would ya?"

David snorted and shook his head. Mr. Fix-it. Talk with your brother and fix him up. He hadn't fixed things with Jace. He wouldn't even try with Mitch.

"Can't do it, Dad. Got a date." He threw an armload of branches onto the pile in the trailer.

His dad raised one eyebrow. "Should I be telling your mother anything important?"

"It's a date. That's all. Not someone serious." He'd screwed Randi, that was all. All that intensity crap was just that—crap. He didn't even know her. She was a good lay.

The thought made him wince.

His dad waggled his eyebrows, but laid off. "Tomorrow then, or Friday. I'm sure Mitch'll hold till you get to him."

Mitch could rot in his own self-made hell.

David sucked in a breath. Anger, seething, had risen so quickly it took his breath away. His gut ached with it, his blood boiled, his muscles tensed. He gritted his teeth.

"Later, Dad. Gotta go."

He eased his bunched fists. In a minute, he'd start yelling at his old man like a maniac. And for nothing. It wasn't his dad's fault that David couldn't get his shit together, much less Mitch, for that matter.

He took one more deep breath, then another. If Randi didn't show, she didn't show. He didn't give a damn. Yes, she was more than a good lay, more than a screw, but they still weren't serious together.

And Mitch could handle his own goddamn bug.

"That's it." He slapped the side of the trailer, flipped the tarp over the load, and tied it down. "Can you handle the dump on your own, Dad?"

"Sure."

"Good. I've got something to take care of."

He stopped at home long enough to shower off and change his clothes. It was four o'clock. Randi hadn't gotten home last night until close to six, which meant she'd probably still be working at her parents' shop. He'd find her there.

Dinner was still on, as far as he was concerned. He'd pleasure her again, better than last night. He wanted her to burn, hot, hotter, until this thing between them burned itself out. He needed her to burn the flare of anger from his soul.

SEVEN

THE SHOP WAS dark and cramped, the three aisles narrow, the shelves filled with cans, bottles, and packages jammed with candy. The checkerboard linoleum was clean but dingy. Two register stands stood to the left at the front of the store, and in the back, the refrigerated section hummed.

"May I help you?"

Short, plump, and white-haired, the woman was probably the same age as his mother, but the lines at her mouth drooped as if she frowned more than smiled.

"I was looking for Randi."

"Papa, he's looking for Randi." Her voice rang out with a singsong Scandinavian lilt. The name sounded softer and more feminine coming from her lips.

For a moment, David wanted desperately to perfect the lilt gracing the name.

Randi's father was no less round, but taller, and he had twenty years on his wife. He must have been middle-aged when Randi was born.

They stared at him with blue eyes identical to Randi's.

The man spoke first. "You're looking for my daughter?"

"Yes. She works here, right?" Somehow he felt like a sixteen-year-old showing up for a prom date and driving his dad's car for the first time.

"And you are?"

"David Jackson."

"And how do you know Randi?"

Carnally. Exquisitely. "Her car broke down the other day, and I helped her into town." He couldn't say why, but he knew in his gut that saying she ran out of gas would be the worst explanation he could give.

The old man grunted out a Norwegian word and flapped his hand. "That cursed truck. She's in the back. Working."

It would have been better to call her on her cell. He had a feeling he wasn't going to make it past Papa.

"I'll only take a moment of her time, sir."

Eyeing him, the old man seemed to think about the "sir," then finally waved his hand, this time in the direction of a swing door at the back of the shop.

Low-pitched whispering followed him down the aisle. Various meats and cheeses filled a dairy case, and on the bottom row, tubes of caviar. He still hadn't licked the stuff from any luscious body parts beyond her throat and back.

Tonight, he'd perform that duty. Tonight, he'd bury himself inside her enough times to quench this craving.

With a sudden intense need that bordered on insanity, he wanted her now. Manic. She screwed with his emotions as well as his mind. She was dangerous in ways he hadn't dreamed.

But he wanted her. Badly. Tonight was too damn far away.

THE WAREHOUSE WAS hot, muggy, and dusty. Randi had opened the windows along the rafters and turned on the fans, but hot air only produced more hot air. She'd stripped off her blouse sometime after the last UPS pickup, and now wore only a thin camisole and her shorts. Pops would pitch a fit, but no customers would come back here to see her.

Sitting on the top step of the ladder, she fanned the top of her camisole. Her makeup was melting. She'd prayed for air conditioning every night the first six months she'd come home, but Pops said it would cost a fortune to cool the warehouse. Perishables, including chocolate, were stored in a refrigerated room, but canned or bottled goods filled the racks around her.

Come on, she'd wanted to scream. The warehouse isn't that big. Pops hadn't listened. He never listened.

Today he was on the warpath. She'd forgotten a special order he'd left on the bench that should have gone out yesterday. *I told you and told you how important this was.*

She'd been thinking about David. And Pops had taped the note to the calculator, which she never used, instead of amidst the sticky notes lining the worktable's cubby holes.

She'd been a day late and a dollar short all her life. She'd overnighted the package, and it would still get there at the same time. She'd pay for it out of her own pocket.

Picking up her clipboard from the shelf, she got to her overheated feet. The tennies were boiling, but sandals were a no-no in the warehouse. What if she dropped something? Huffing out a breath of air, she began staging an order in the basket hanging from the side of the ladder.

Something tickled her leg just above her knee. Without looking, she swatted at the irritating insect. The thing skimmed the back of her legs, both legs, then delved straight up through the bottom of her shorts.

David grinned up at her. "I couldn't resist those cheeks peaking out at me."

"You are so bad." He was oh so good. Last night had definitely driven the point home. "What are you doing here?"

"I wanted to remind you about dinner and laundry."

She'd been trying *not* to think about it. That peck he'd given her this morning had spoken of run-and-hide. Then again, she'd done her own run-and-hide into the shower. Only she'd hoped he'd follow her. Instead, she'd found him dressed and ready to go in the living room.

"You could have called." She thrust her chin at the cell phone sitting on the countertop.

"But then I wouldn't have gotten to do this." He pressed higher, squeezing her bottom.

She slapped at his hand playfully. "Stop that. What if my dad walks out here?"

"We're two aisles over. We'll hear him before he sees us."

She almost smiled, but that would spoil the game. "He walks very softly."

"Then let's hide so I can put my hands all over you."

"Noo . . ."

Hoisting himself onto the second step, he grabbed the clipboard out of her hand, set it on a shelf, then lifted her down with a tight grip on her waist.

"You're kidding, right?"

His eyes burned. "I want to touch you. Now."

He captured her chin in his hand and took her mouth with a deep kiss, all tongue, robbing her of her breath.

"Now. Let me touch you. I can wait for the rest later."

"Just a quickie." She grabbed his hand and practically hauled him back toward the freezer.

David wanted her. She didn't care about anything else. She hadn't from the moment she first laid eyes on him.

Cool air rushed over her body as she threw open the walk-in's door. It felt so good. *He* felt good at her back as he hustled her inside, then closed them in.

"Does it lock?"

"No."

"All right. I'll be quick. I swear."

He backed her up against the wall inside the door. There wasn't a speck of light, just hot hands sliding up her shorts.

"Christ," he murmured against her throat, all warm breath and questing lips. He overwhelmed her, turned her upside down. She dug her fingers into his shoulders, then glided them through his hair, begging for his kiss.

Taking her lips with his mouth and tongue, he lifted her, pulling her legs to his waist. Openmouthed, he devoured her.

Pinned to the wall, her legs wide, she rode the ridge of his erection. He rocked into her, making love to her despite the layers of cloth between them. His hands found their way beneath her camisole, captured her breasts in an almost painful grip. Then his mouth followed his hands, sucking her nipple hard, kissing it, biting lightly. Electric shocks traveled straight down her center, pulsing in her clitoris.

He backed off slightly to yank the snap of her shorts.

"David." She gasped, tugging down her top to cover her breasts. "David."

He didn't listen to her protests, undoing her zipper by pulling on her waistband. She wasn't even sure if she *was* objecting.

"So hot, so freaking hot." He shoved his hand into her thong, a finger as deep into her as her shorts would allow.

She panted, hot and needy. "David, please."

"Come. I want to hear you."

"David."

"Come on, baby." He worked her, whispering encouragement.

"We can't." But she was so very close. Just a throb away, just a mindless scream, just a—

The door slammed open, and a pool of light spilled across the interior, passing just beyond their feet.

"Randi, what are you doing?"

Holy ever-lovin' Moly, dear God, I'm dead.

Jerking his hand out of her shorts, David pressed deeper against her to hide the gape of her open zipper.

"Pops."

Her legs slid down David's until her feet touched the floor. Her shorts were undone, and the scent of sex was all over them. She wanted to die.

Her father simply closed the door on them.

David let out the breath he'd been holding. "I'm sorry. I didn't mean to go that far."

He righted Randi's camisole over her breasts and belly, then reached down to zip her shorts.

Somewhere between touching her on the ladder and shutting them both inside the refrigerator, he'd gone from hot and hard to totally out of control.

"I'm sorry." It was easier to beg forgiveness when he couldn't see her eyes.

"It's okay. But you better leave." Her hands shook against him as she took over the task of fastening her shorts.

And suddenly he couldn't stand not seeing her eyes. "Where's the damn light switch?"

All she did was open the door a crack to allow in a stream of light. It wasn't enough to gauge her full expression, but it was enough to reveal the stark lines at her mouth.

"It's okay," she repeated. "I'm twenty-eight years old, and I've been married." She shrugged. "This is just embarrassing. He'll get over it."

"I'll tell him it was my fault."

She gently pushed away from him. "I think it's better for me if you just sneak out the back door so I can handle it."

He'd never sneaked out the back way in his life.

Shit. His MO was sneaking out the front door while she slept.

"Please. For me," she begged, her hand on his wrist. "Let me do it my way."

It didn't set well that her way was the easy way for him.

She pushed him away so she could once more smooth her top, then ran her fingers through her mussed hair. Her lips were plump and swollen, her nipples still peaked beneath the cotton.

She spread her hands. "Please, David, just go."

Two more minutes and he would have had his cock out of his jeans and buried inside her. Without a condom. With her parents only yards away.

He'd lost it. Completely. He hadn't cared when she'd told him to stop. He'd only wanted her like a wild man, the need to burn them up together greater than his common sense. Greater than anything.

She was right. He had to go. He had to clear his head.

Easing out the back door, he didn't even say he'd call her.
Outside, with the late afternoon sun blazing down on his head,
he stopped, leaning back against the wall. Searching for something. Some sort of explanation.

Things had gone totally out of control the day he found
Jace in Taylor's bed. No, long before that. Life had gone to
hell the day Lou died. Nothing had been the same since. Nothing ever would be. Taylor and Jace's marriage just made the
whole situation worse.

He didn't have a goddamn clue what to do about Randi any
more than he knew how to fix what had happened to them all
the day they laid his brother in the ground.

THERE WAS NOTHING else to do but go out and meet her
fate. Just as she had the day she came crawling back home to
tell her parents she'd left Mick.

With one last deep breath, she opened the walk-in. Her dad
probably wouldn't talk to her for a few days. Maybe a month.
But he'd get over it eventually, he always had. Even if it took a
year. As a last desperate attempt at reclaiming her modesty,
she grabbed her shirt off the stool and pulled it on.

She smelled her father before she saw him. He'd worn bay
rum cologne for as long as she could remember, the scent part
of her childhood—the good, when he patted her head for high
grades at school, and the bad, when the only communication
they shared was the waft of bay rum as he passed her in the
hallway of the small house she grew up in.

The burn of embarrassment still flamed in her cheeks as
she turned to him. "Pops, I—"

"You hussy." His complexion was more apoplectic than
hers felt. A vein throbbed at his temple, and his white hair
stood on end as if he'd tugged at the roots. "How dare you
comport yourself in such a manner in my store?" He stabbed
his chest with a thick forefinger. "*My* store. *My* work. My rep-
utation might have been ruined in this town."

He'd called her a hussy. From him, it was tantamount to calling her a whore. She shoved aside the pain.

"I don't think any customers would have walked into the freezer, Pops."

"That is not the point. You could have scandalized your mother. Did you think of that? How she would have felt walking in on that . . ." He sputtered, trying to find the word. "Walking in on that filth."

He had a point. She hadn't thought of that, not at all.

"You are a disgrace to this family. You have always been a disgrace. I have tried and tried to teach you properly, but you do not listen. You do not care."

"Pops, I do listen. I just forget sometimes. And I make mistakes."

He slashed his hand through the air. "Do not make excuses. No more. I am done speaking to you since it does no good."

David stepped from an aisle of racks. "Mr. Andersen, I'm to blame for what happened. It wasn't Randi's fault."

David. He hadn't left her. She almost sagged with relief. But how much had he heard?

The finger-pointing switched from Randi to David. "And you, I do not even know you, and you do horrible things to my daughter in my store. I do not accept your explanations."

This time the old man stabbed David in the chest for punctuation. David resisted the urge to break a finger already crippled with arthritis.

"Sir, I understand how you feel, but you're overreacting."

"Overreacting?" The elderly man's eyes bugged out of his head. "Overreacting, do you say? I do not speak to you either, despoiler of young women. I do not speak to you *ever*." Still glaring at David, he pointed yet again at Randi. "And never again do I speak to this harlot."

His blood boiled. If the man had been anyone but Randi's own father, David would have belted him. They'd been caught in a compromising position, but Christ, the old man was going way too far. For Randi's sake, he held on to his rising temper.

"Let's calm down. You don't have any right to call your own daughter a harlot."

Randi's dad threw his hands in the air, waving them almost in supplication or impotence, his rage was so great. "She is my daughter no more."

The moment was almost surreal. "Sir, we need to be reasonable and drop the name-calling."

Mr. Andersen's rage simply boiled over. "You, Mr. Pimp, get out of my store." Then he turned, his arms still flailing ineffectually in the air. The scent of his overly strong cologne hung behind as a tangible reminder of his words.

The silence was long and loud, broken only by the whirring of the fans and street traffic wafting in through the open windows. Randi didn't say word. She was in shock, that could be the only explanation.

"Jesus, I'm sorry. But he didn't have the right to say that about you."

Randi shrugged, then picked up her clipboard. "Don't worry about it. It was my fault. You didn't know."

What the hell? David grabbed her arm. "You're just going to let him say that shit to you?" He couldn't fathom. He'd come from the loins of a woman who'd taught him the meaning of sticking up for yourself. The meaning of self-respect. No matter what happens, never give that up. Admit you're wrong, sure, but you can't allow another human being to demean and degrade you, even your own father.

Randi hugged the clipboard to her chest. "You saw what good it does to challenge him. He didn't listen to you either."

"It doesn't matter if he listens. It matters that you . . ." He stopped, tipping his head to stare at her. He wanted to shake Randi. He had the sense to understand that while her father had not used a single swear word, he'd cut her to ribbons. Christ, it had been a freaking bloodbath.

And she just took it. No matter what she'd done, the old man *didn't* have the right. "You're just going back to work?"

"He didn't fire me. He only stopped speaking to me."

"I don't think I get what's going on here, Randi."

He'd been incredibly stupid coming here in the mood he'd been in, edged as it was with anger and some weird need to dominate her. His mother would have whupped him upside the head for the way he'd acted. He didn't know his own mind these days or understand half the things that motivated him.

But he did know that Randi Andersen needed more than a few nights of hot sex. She was on the rebound from far more than just a marriage gone bad.

She was on the rebound from a father that could call his daughter a whore. He could tell her old man he had no right to treat her that way, but it would take more than that to fix what was wrong with Randi accepting those words so blithely.

David didn't have a clue how to show her. He couldn't even fix his own freaking life.

She spoke first. "You know, I don't think I feel like doing laundry or having dinner tonight. If that's okay with you. Let's just skip it."

He realized now that's how she phrased most things, as a question, asking for permission. She cajoled him into helping her fill her gas tank, she let her landlord get away without making necessary repairs. Hell, when the dog had jumped on the bed that first night and practically nosed his balls, she'd freaked out like a little girl, afraid he'd get mad at her. She didn't allow just her father to mistreat her, accepting abuse was actually a part of her makeup.

He forced this decision on her. "Is that what you want? To skip tonight?"

She glanced briefly at the floor, her chest rising with a deep breath. David himself wasn't clear on what answer he wanted her to give. But at least she finally gave one.

"Yes, that's what I want." Then she shooed him toward the back door. "You better vamoose before Pops comes back."

She needed time. She needed space. Hell, Randi Andersen needed a lot more than that.

He just wasn't sure he was the guy to give her anything.

EIGHT

SHE ABSOLUTELY HATED that assessing look in David's eye. It reminded her of the way her father looked at her every time he stopped speaking to her for a day or a month or a year.

David had backed off just the way she told him to, along the aisle from which he'd first appeared. She knew he wasn't backing down from her father. He was backing away from *her*.

It had to happen sometime. At least the break came at the beginning of the relationship. Not that two dinners and two nights of some very hot sex made a relationship.

It was just rather debilitating that he'd seen her true weak colors. Somehow, it felt worse than the ending of her marriage, though exactly why, she couldn't say.

Randi tossed the clipboard onto the bench. It slid across the Formica and tipped over the edge, clattering to the concrete floor. She left it there.

Quitting time was another hour's worth of clock ticks. She couldn't stand it. Not one more tick, not one more tock. Outside, the sun hit her like a spear right through the eye, and she dug in her purse for her sunglasses. Not there. Not anywhere. She'd forgotten where she left them last, story of her life.

All she wanted was to lie on her bed, wrap herself around a loving bundle of fur, and forget. Forget about David—because he wasn't coming back—and forget about what happened in the warehouse. To forget. That's all she wanted right now.

It would have been easier if David wasn't sitting on her porch when she got home.

THE ANSWER TO his problems hadn't hit him like a bolt of lightning or the hand of God. Instead, it had seeped into his brain like a frosty mug of beer nursed over half an hour rather than slugged back in five minutes. The half hour of his ride from Scandia Haus to his own driveway. He'd sat for a minute, hands on the wheel, then flipped a U-turn.

It was simple, really. He'd failed to hold his family together after Lou's death. They'd almost fallen apart, drowned in the loss, and the fix, in the end, had not come from him. It had happened on its own. With Taylor and Jace falling in love. His mom was happy. His dad was happy. Everyone was happy. Instead of accepting it like a man, David had run like a green kid getting his first kick of sand in the face. A man did not run from his responsibilities. A man didn't quit his job or divest himself of his family. A man didn't pick up a young woman on the side of the road, then dump her three days later after *he* did an unconscionable thing.

Lou wouldn't have done that. But David could still fix things.

Randi needed him. He couldn't fight her battles for her, but he could make sure that she fought them for herself. She was special. He'd known that last night when she gave herself so sweetly. He'd known it when he watched her come. When he'd held her as she slept. The awkwardness this morning, even his anger with his dad, well, that had all been part of finding himself. And he'd done it. He couldn't walk away from Randi if he tried. She needed him. With care, he could help her reach her potential.

He only had to wait on her porch for fifteen minutes, the dog at his feet. He liked the picture they greeted her with.

Of course, as soon as she heard a commotion out at the road, Royal didn't stay put.

Randi's truck rattled through the driveway ruts and rolled to a stop, then she stared through the windshield at him.

Finally, she climbed out, dropping a hand to the dog for a quick scratch, a soft word, then she seemed to suck in a breath and close the distance between them. With him sitting the few steps up on the porch, they were almost eye level.

She shaded her eyes. "I didn't think I'd see you again."

"We have unfinished business."

Her gaze fell to her tennies. He looked at her bare, tanned legs, then the strip of skin between her waistband and the bottom of her skimpy camisole thing. On a guy, it would have been called an undershirt. Over it, she'd thrown a short-sleeved shirt, but hadn't buttoned it.

She fiddled with the keys in her right hand, then lifted her purse to her chest like a shield. "Unfinished business. You mean what we were doing in the cold room?"

There was certainly that. But there was also a lot more. He held out a hand, beckoning with his fingers. "Come here."

She shuffled a few steps closer.

He leaned forward, grabbed her hand, and reeled her in. "I think we should forget about the cold room."

She rolled her eyes and sighed. "Yeah. Let's forget it."

"I think we should start over."

She tipped her head, forsaking her shoes to look at him. "Start over how?"

"Well, first I ask you how your day was, and you say it was fine, but you're tired."

"Oh." The sadness in her eyes at the warehouse hadn't dissipated.

"How was your day, honey?" he murmured.

"It was fine, but I'm tired," she whispered.

"Then I take you inside, give you a glass of wine, run you a hot bath, fix dinner, and feed the dog while you're soaking."

"I don't have any wine, and I'm not sure there's enough of anything to make dinner."

"I'll improvise. Then after dinner, I'll carry you into the bedroom and make sweet love to you all night long."

She didn't smile or laugh or fall into his arms. "David. Why are you really here?"

"You had a bad day. I caused the problem. I want to fix it." What he didn't say was that after all that sweet lovemaking, he'd help her see that she had to tackle the issue with her dad. He'd go with her, hold her hand, whatever. But he'd tell her all that later, when she lay drugged with passion, when he could make her see what she had to do.

"I thought you wanted to keep things casual between us."

David stroked a smudge of dirt from her cheek. "I changed my mind. Is that all right?"

Randi knew something was wrong. Off. Like the sensation of being followed. You kept telling yourself you were being silly, but the hairs at the back of your neck wouldn't lay down. Taking flight seemed like the best solution, but if she ran, she'd never know if David could actually fall in love with her. She'd forever wonder what would have happened if she'd had the guts to stick around.

She'd jumped too quickly and too far with Mick. But was she too battle-scarred to ever jump again?

Maybe. Yes. No. She drew in a breath of calm. And jumped. "I think we should skip the bath, and go straight for the sweet lovemaking."

DAVID UNSCREWED THE cap off the caviar. "Where do you want me to squeeze it?"

"You decide."

He pushed with a finger on her chest. "Close your eyes."

She lay back on the bed, completely naked, and did as he said. In the end, they'd taken the bath together. She'd rubbed tangerine soap all over him. He'd chosen a cucumber scent to lather all over her. They smelled good. And Randi was in love.

He squeezed a cool line of caviar from the tip of one breast to the other. "Now what?"

"Lick it off, silly."

"Lick it or suck it?"

"A bit of both, please."

His lower half lay flush against her, naked flesh to naked flesh. It was a to-die-for sensation. Then he rose on his elbows and bent over her right breast. He blew, the hot-cold stimulation starting a slow burn between her thighs. With just his tongue, he taste-tested the caviar, going straight to her nipple, sucking both it and the caviar into his mouth.

She pressed against him, her mound to his abdomen, his erection nestled along the join of her legs. She would have opened her thighs, but he rocked in the spoon of her legs.

He pulled back, surveying his handiwork. One clean, wet nipple with a slash of caviar paste leading straight to her other breast. "A man's work is never done." He bent his head to the task, licking a path to the goal.

She curled around him, running her hands down to his buttocks. They tensed beneath her touch though he kept up the rock of his body between her legs. Opening slightly, she let him fall deeper in the lee, then clamped her thighs. He slid easier in the drop of moisture, his cock swelling, hardening.

But he never stopped licking. Not until he reached her left nipple and sucked it into his mouth. There was something about the suction, the heat, the direct connection between her nipple and her clitoris that made her arousal spike. She started to rock with him, thrusting.

He'd taken her with hot passion. He'd wanted her with a driving need. Now he seemed to savor her, first with long minutes of bathtub play that had her coasting along the water's edge to orgasm. Coasting without reaching, craving more, but unwilling to give up the sweetness of foreplay for the big bang.

And now this. His light tongue, his gentle sucking, his easy thrust and parry between her legs.

He raised his head and smiled, the bedside lamp glimmering in his eyes like a flame. "That was delicious. Now where do you want it?"

Her clitoris. Her vagina. His tongue, his fingers, his hot, hard cock. She craved all that, but more, she wanted the tempered rise of her excitement. She yearned for the peak, but she needed the climb to be long and slow. Two steps forward and one step back. Until she was absolutely mad, until all he had to do was blow on her, and she'd come.

That was how love should be. A little forward, a little back, a little give, a little take.

"Since you're not answering, I assume I should decide."

"Do it just right," she whispered. A test and a prayer.

He gazed at her, his chin resting between her breasts. Then he went for the gusto, sliding down her body and spreading her legs with his hands. "I know what you're thinking," he said as he moistened her with nothing more than that hot gaze of his.

"What am I thinking?"

"That I'm gonna wham-bam-thank-you-ma'am you since I've given you five minutes of sucking on those gorgeous nipples."

"I wasn't thinking that." Though her thoughts had been somewhere along that line.

He blew on her as if it were a punishment for the little lie. Her body shook with an involuntary quiver.

"You've got it all wrong."

She snorted softly.

"I've got stamina, sweetheart. And you're going to be screaming for me before I even get inside you."

"Talk, talk, talk," she teased. It didn't matter. She'd take whatever he gave. Hard and fast, or soft and slow. It only mattered that he'd come back.

"You're going to scream, that's a promise." Leaning on one elbow, he parted her folds with two fingers. "My, isn't this pretty." He jabbed the tip of his tongue on her clitoris, once, twice, two jolts of electricity, then he withdrew.

She bit her lip and watched.

Holding her open, he aimed the tube and squeezed. She squeaked as the cold caviar paste hit her hot, sensitized clit. Deep inside, her body tightened in need.

"I think that felt good," he said.

She nodded, loathe to speak in case her voice cracked.

"How shall I go about this? There's the fast suck where I go straight for the caviar and take your pretty little clit on a quick ride to heaven. Or there's the slow lick, where I taste each morsel individually. That may take hours."

She thrust up. Or rather her body did. Begging. Pleading. "Just suck and get it over with."

He laughed softly, his breath puffing over her. "The slow lick, individual particles of the delicacy savored separately."

Then he began to devour her, one atom at a time. It went on and on, the slip-slide of his tongue. The glide of his fingers entering her, retreating. No one touch enough to push her over the edge, the combination propelled her closer to heaven. She was so wet, she could hear the entry of his fingers. Her eyes teared up. Her lips ached from biting, and her fingers clenched and unclenched in the bedspread.

And each time, as her body tensed, and pinpricks of light burst before her eyes, he pulled her back.

"Not yet, baby," he whispered. "Just a little longer."

"Please."

He went at her again. His tongue delved, then his fingers. He pumped her as he swirled and sucked the swollen nub of her clitoris. She shook and writhed.

"Please, oh God, please." It might have been minutes, it might have been hours, the torture went on and on. Until she couldn't remember her own name.

Until he entered her deeply with two fingers, pushed the tip of his tongue against a spot just beneath her clitoris, and made her scream.

Nothing could have stopped the utter implosion of her body. She orgasmed from the inside out, rocking, thrusting, squirming against him as he pinned her legs to the bed. She tossed her head, gasped air that wouldn't go down, and still he held his tongue against her.

He made her come until she lost awareness of where she was. Of who she was. Until he was the only thing that existed, and she couldn't take another breath without him.

HE LOVED WATCHING her come. He loved knowing that he could make her lose herself. He loved that she screamed and didn't even hear herself.

She didn't even know when he entered her. But her body knew, gripping him, sucking him deeper. He pulled her leg to his waist, drove in until he touched heaven, and stilled.

When he came, she'd come with him. He could wait, holding himself motionless. The slightest tremor of her body threatened to push him over the edge, but he wouldn't go without her.

He hadn't known that he could come without a single pump of his cock, without a hand around him, a mouth on him, or the warm cocoon of a woman's body holding him.

Somehow, her pleasure, her release, her cries had almost driven him to it. His limbs had trembled, staving off orgasm. They still trembled.

He pressed a kiss to a closed eyelid. "Look at me."

She opened her eyes, her gaze glassy. He nudged slightly forward, his body rasping against her clitoris. She jerked, grabbed his shoulders, and dug in with her nails.

"Oh my God," she whimpered, then clutched at him, pulling her other leg to his waist.

He slid in to the hilt, not a breath between their bodies. Then he pumped, every muscle straining. He was so damn close that only three thrusts deep inside her made the blood rush in his ears and his balls ache with need.

"Come with me." He didn't even recognize his own voice. He didn't bother to question why it was so important. He simply took her, dragged her along with him, thrust her high up into the clouds, up to the sky, then he shoved them both off into a clear, pure, relentless orgasm that lasted till the end of time.

"I THINK I just died."

"As long as you went to heaven, then it's okay." David jostled her in his arms, pulling her closer.

"As in, I died and went to heaven because that felt so good?" she muttered against his chest.

"Exactly."

She sat up suddenly and looked at him. "David, I have to tell you something."

He stroked a hand down her arm. "All right, honey."

"I'm in love with you. I fell in love with you that first night when you sneaked out of bed and you were trying to tell Royal how you felt."

He pushed her hair behind an ear. "You were listening?"

"Yeah. I was listening. And I feel like such a scum for not telling you earlier how I felt."

"Why would you feel like a scum?"

"Because you might not have those same feelings for me, and if you'd known, you might not have wanted to go the extra step with this relationship, in case you thought I'd get hurt."

"You have a weird sense of logic that I'm only just beginning to appreciate." He tugged her down again, into his arms, then tipped her chin. "I have never felt this way about a woman. I've had three serious relationships, and I've never felt like this. Three *years* and I never felt like this."

"They all lasted three years?"

"Thereabouts."

She was silent several heartbeats. "That doesn't mean you're in love with me." She wiggled her toes as if that helped her think. "It's a good start. At least you're not running."

"I'm done running, Randi." He'd been running for weeks now, from Jace with Taylor, from the sheer incomprehensibility of it, from the final, irrefutable proof of Lou's passing, and from his own inability to set his family on the right path.

"Then I can say I love you again?"

"Yeah. What I'm feeling couldn't be anything else." Yeah, it was love. It had to be. He wanted to give her everything. He wanted to give her back her self-respect.

"Say it," she whispered.

He could feel her held breath, her body tense against him. "I love you, Randi."

"Holy Moly." She hugged him, going all gooey and pliable in his arms, then she hiccuped as if she were crying.

"That's why I feel like shit about your dad."

She lost all the pliability of the moment before. "I told you it's not a big deal. He gets upset, then he gets over it."

"Randi, I'm not saying we weren't over the line, that *I* went over the line. But so was he. Don't you see that?"

"You don't know my dad. He's from the old country, and he's got certain ways, and you just get used to them."

"Does he talk like that to your mom?"

"He hasn't caught my mom in the meat locker with some man's hand down her pants."

It was more than that. David knew in his gut. "But he's stopped speaking to you before. What'd you do to upset him?"

She shrugged, rolling away from him to the other side of the bed. "Just stuff that pisses him off."

"What kind of stuff?"

Nothing, absolutely nothing, deserved her father's kind of reaction. He would get the answer out of her. Then he'd help her fix the problem.

HER BACK TO him, Randi shrugged again. "Just *stuff* stuff."

David drew a finger down her spine. "Rand-i."

He wouldn't understand. He just wouldn't. "I can't remember exactly."

Why did he have to go and ruin everything like this?

His breath was suddenly in her hair, caressing her cheek. "Of course you remember."

She pursed her lips. "No, actually, I don't. I have a very selective memory, and I can't always remember things. Didn't you see those reminder notes all over my refrigerator?"

"But this is different. How could you forget the things that made your dad stop speaking to you?"

She shook her head. "I just do, okay?"

He cuddled up against her. "How long before he'll start speaking to you again?"

"Well, this time, he's really pissed. I mean *really* pissed. It could be a couple of years."

He rolled her to her back even as she tried to hang on to the edge of the bed. "Two years? You're joking, right?"

"When I was thirteen, he stopped speaking to me for a year."

His forehead furrowed. "Nobody stops speaking to their kid for a year."

She just blinked.

"But why?"

"I told you I don't remember." She put her hand over his mouth before he could call her a liar. "I don't. Not specifically. I forgot to do something. It could have been washing the car or taking out the trash or doing the dishes. I didn't *not* do what he told me on purpose. But I'd get busy with something else. And . . ." She spread her hands, her shoulders scrunching to her ears in that universal symbol of hopelessness. "And I'd forget. He said if I couldn't bother to listen to him, then he wouldn't bother to speak to me."

It made perfect sense actually.

"But the more he did that, the more I forgot. I just sort of got so worried about forgetting things, and I'd end up having so much stuff running around in my brain that I'd forget something. Not everything, but something. Then he'd stop talking to me for a while."

He gathered her close. "Jesus." A fervent, anguished whisper on her behalf. "That's so fucked up."

She laughed, a soft, achy sound that hurt her throat. Even more fucked up was that Mick, her husband of three years, had never even asked her about those silent times. Not once.

"You can't let this go on, Randi. You just can't."

She sighed. "Oh, it's okay, I'm used to it." Her dad's silences were easier to handle than Mick's digs and cuts.

"I'll go with you to talk to him."

"The offer's really sweet, but it won't do any good. He won't listen when he's not talking." And she just wanted to forget the whole embarrassing incident.

He tipped her head with his thumb beneath her chin. "Randi, look at me."

She hadn't even realized she'd closed her eyes.

"It isn't about him listening. It's about you having the gumption to tell him it's not right."

Gumption? Just what was he saying here? "David, you just don't understand."

"I do understand. Perfectly. You need to confront him."

She had gumption. Lots of it. By God, she'd show him, too. "I'm not doing it."

"I said I'd go with you," he coaxed.

"It doesn't matter."

"Are you afraid of him? Has he ever hit you?"

"No." She snorted.

"Then why won't you do it?"

"Why is it so important to you?"

"Because I think it's important for *you*."

He had very pretty eyelashes, long and tipped with gold. She hadn't noticed that before. He'd made love to her with sweet insistence. He'd taken her to orgasm with unrelenting gentleness. But he wasn't satisfied with who she was, what she was. "What if I refuse to talk to him?"

He grinned, but serious intent set his jaw. "I'll keep at you until you do."

She wasn't perfect, far from it. As Mick always said, some of her brains had leaked out her ears. She lived in a musty dump amidst someone else's castoffs. But she was a good person, and she had a lot of love to give to a man who could see beyond the exterior. A man who could see that she was special without making her prove it all the time. A man who would want her just the way she was, faults and all. A man who would love her at least as much as Royal did.

"David, I am never going to have it out with my dad. I am never going to tell him he can't say the kinds of things he said today. I have reached stasis, and I am not going to change."

"Randi, honey—"

She put her hand over his lips. "Take it, or leave it."

"But Randi—"

"No buts." It was a challenge, a test. Pass or fail.

"Randi, don't you see that—"

Fail. She pressed harder to shut him up. She was tired of men who didn't love her the way she was. Her dad had tried to change her by the simple act of not speaking to her. Mick had tried to change her by harping cruelly on her every fault.

And David? He wouldn't give up. He'd coax, cajole, make love to her, always gentle, always with the best intention, but he wouldn't give up until she talked to Pops. Eventually, just like Mick and Pops, he'd find a way to punish her for not doing what he wanted. For not being what he wanted her to be.

Living with a dog was easier. Royal loved her without expecting a thing in return, loved her when she scolded, when she dumped a can of tomato juice over her head. Royal would love her even if she forgot to feed her.

Men didn't have the capacity for that kind of unconditional love. Though she hadn't learned the lesson in three years with Mick, it took less than three days with David to finally get it through her thick head.

"I think you better leave."

She moved so quickly, he didn't have a chance to get his arms around her. "Sweetheart."

See, there he went trying to cajole with endearments. He'd withdraw them when she displeased him one too many times.

"I'd like to be alone."

He stared at her a long moment, his head tipped just like Royal when she couldn't figure out which hand held the biscuit.

"All right." He rolled to the other side of the bed, then glanced over his shoulder. "We'll talk when you're not upset."

Just like a man. *We'll talk about it when you're more reasonable.* She would *never* be more reasonable than she was in this moment. And righteously angry, too.

"Your clothes are in the bathroom." As she pointed, she steeled herself against the pure beauty of his naked body.

She would not be swayed. He wanted her to stand up for herself, and she would. She would no longer accept crumbs, not his, not any man's. Never again.

And oddly, miraculously, she suddenly remembered why

her father had stopped speaking to her when she was thirteen.

It wasn't as simple as forgetting to wash the car. It had been about a boy. A boy she'd tried to please. Her father, with that uncanny sense parents sometimes have, came home from the shop early and caught the boy with his hand up her shirt.

He'd called her a harlot then, too.

No one was ever going to make her feel bad for just being herself. Not ever again.

THAT WAS, BY far, the weirdest argument he'd ever had with a woman. Halfway to Mitch's house for that talk his father had asked him to have with his brother, David still wasn't sure what he'd done wrong.

She needed a little time, then she'd see he was trying to help. A couple of days, and she'd forget all about the tiff.

Jesus. That sounded too close to Randi talking about her father.

RANDI SLAMMED THROUGH the house, the front door, her bedroom door, the bathroom door, then slapped her hand against the shower taps. What she needed was a hot shower, the needlelike spray pounding against her head and back. She needed to vent this feeling. She didn't like being angry. For a moment there in the bedroom, it had felt cleansing. Now, it was just a roiling mass in her belly she needed to get rid of.

She washed off David's scent, washed off the caviar, his tongue, his kiss, his touch. At least she tried as the hot water ran to cold, but when she closed her eyes, she could feel him filling her, taste his kiss still on her lips.

Even the towel she dried her hair with smelled like him.

Ha! It had taken less than half an hour to lose all that wonderful power she'd felt. The dregs of it lashed around her heart like tentacles and squeezed.

Royal whined outside the bathroom door.

She'd forgotten poor Royal. The dog hated being shut out.

Steam and warmth rushed out as she opened the door. Royal lay in the hallway, her head on her paws, sad brown eyes staring.

"I'm sorry, baby, wanna come in?"

Royal blinked, snuffled, and let out a huge doggie sigh. But she didn't move. She'd probably miss the damn man after only having known him only a couple of days.

"He's gone, sweetie-pie, never to return."

Again, the dog blinked, then regarded her with . . . reproach?

"It wasn't my fault."

Royal's ear twitched.

"You don't get it. See, he didn't accept me the way I am. He wanted me to change. I can't change." She shut her mouth. "What I mean is, I shouldn't need to change." Her father should be the one to change, if anything.

Was that a sneer creasing the dog's mouth?

"This is complicated human stuff, you wouldn't understand."

Royal sighed. That dog made sighing an art form.

"He just doesn't get what my relationship with my dad is like. I can't explain it to him."

Her relationship *was* crazy. But it had always been that way. How was she supposed to change it? In a few days, everything would blow over. All right, it might be a year. Or more.

"Pops just thinks I'm still thirteen. What am I supposed to do about that? I can't get him to listen. I've never been able to. It's simply the way things are."

Royal just stared at her. Then finally, she closed her eyes as if she couldn't bear to look anymore. As if she hadn't another doggie sigh to give. Or another word to say. Just the way Randi's father ignored her. Even the dog made her feel like she was still thirteen.

Randi's legs gave out and she sat heavily on the toilet seat. She'd acted like she was thirteen today, letting her father call her a harlot. Again.

That's what David had seen and heard. And deep down in her most honest of hearts, she had to admit her anger hadn't been about him accepting her as she was. It hadn't even been about getting her father to change. It was fear, plain and simple. The fear of a thirteen-year-old to confront her father. It had been so much easier to get angry with David than to even contemplate approaching her dad.

Just how long was she going to be stuck at that tender age?

No matter what had happened with David, no matter how he felt about her, there would always be her father. Whether he spoke to her or not, he'd always be a specter in her life. The question was, when would she stop letting him treat her as if she were thirteen? When would she stop accepting that kind of behavior as if it was all she was worth?

Randi knew what she had to do.

TEN

MITCH TOOK A long swig of his beer, then set it back on the table. "This outing was Dad's idea, wasn't it?"

Thursday night wasn't particularly busy at Hennesey's Tavern. Someone had started a country ballad playing on the jukebox, and the hum of voices was low compared to the ruckus that was raised on a Friday or Saturday night.

David set down his own beer. "He seemed to think there was something wrong."

"Well, you can tell him I'm fine, Connie's fine, and the kids are fine. We're all fine." The tension riding his younger brother's shoulders told a different story.

"Good. Glad to hear it." David realized he'd have to draw Mitch out. His brother had not been happy to see him standing on the doorstep, nor had he seemed particularly interested in hanging out at Hennesey's. It was Connie, his wife, who'd practically shoved him out the door to join David. There had definitely been some strain back there in the house.

They used to talk, an easy, boots-on-table camaraderie. David remembered times his brother had sought him out, even over Lou's more sage brand of advice. Those days were long gone.

Another ill Lou's death had wreaked.

"Why didn't you tell me you were quitting, David?"

The purpose of the outing was to discuss Mitch's issues, whatever they might be, not his own crap. "I made the decision on the spur of the moment."

"That's not what you told Dad. We work together, David. We're partners. You should have told me yourself two days ago."

David twirled his beer mug in the moist ring it left on the table. "You're right. So you'll be the first to know I've changed my mind. After thinking about it, I realize I made a mistake."

Now *that* was a spur of the moment decision, but David knew in his gut it was the right decision this time. He'd been running on screwed-up thinking for weeks, but everything that had happened tonight had shown him he'd been heading in the wrong direction in order to solve his problem.

Mitch just looked at him. "I don't get you, David. Ever since this thing with Jace and Taylor, you've been a freak."

David almost laughed. Maybe that's what he'd needed to hear weeks ago. Trust a brother to tell it like it is.

"I needed to get used to the idea." But was he the only one that had an issue with Jace hitting on his older brother's widow? "Didn't you need a little time to assimilate it?"

Mitch shrugged and, in the same manner as David, twirled his beer in the wet rings it sat in. "Lou's dead."

"I know he's dead." But somehow, there was something just plain wrong about someone taking Lou's place, even if it was Jace. Especially if it was Jace.

"You're jealous, aren't you?"

Christ. "You know, Dad said the same thing. Where the hell are you guys getting the idea that I've got some sort of romantic feeling for Taylor?"

"It's not about Taylor. It's the way you think you have to act like Lou. You're jealous things got done without you."

"Since when have I acted like Lou?" He wasn't getting pissed. Not really. He just didn't get it.

" 'Here's what you need to do.' " Mitch's voice deepened in a very good imitation of their older brother's tones. "That's what he would have said. And you've started saying it, too."

"I've only ever offered brotherly advice."

"That's what I'm talking about. Lou and his advice. But he didn't give advice. He issued edicts. You didn't used to pull that kind of shit, David."

David threw his hands apart, another flicker of anger stealing over him. "Have I told you what to do tonight? Have I even insisted you tell me whatever the hell is going on with you that's got Dad so worked up?"

"Listen to yourself. Dad's a silent worrier. Mom's a vocal worrier. It didn't used to bother you. Now, it's all about the solution. Jace shouldn't be doing Taylor so big brother David has to step in and put a stop to it. Who the hell are you to decide?"

"I'm your goddamn older brother."

"Yeah, you're my brother. But I don't need you to tell me what to do. I didn't need Lou to tell me either. Why do you think I used to come to you? Because you *listened*. And somehow I figured out my own answers. But now Lou's dead, and I don't need to hear his voice out of your mouth."

"Don't you even give a damn about that? He's dead. He's not coming back. Somebody's gotta keep this family together without him." His chest ached. Even his breath in his throat felt as if he were dragging in shards of glass.

"Lou didn't keep us together. We tolerated his high-handedness because we loved him."

"You asshole." David slammed his mug down, beer sloshing over the side, then he slapped a bill on the table. Rising, he shoved his chair back, toppling it to the floor.

He needed to get out. He needed air. He needed to stop hearing his brother's voice in his head. Lou's voice.

Slamming through the tavern's swing door, his angry strides ate up the dirt as he headed to his truck.

Why don't you listen to what I say, David?
Why didn't you do what I told you to do, David?

Lou was the one who made them all strive to be better. Lou was the one who'd kept them on the straight and narrow. Lou was the one person in all the world David wanted to emulate.

And Lou, God rest his soul, would roll over in his grave if he knew about Taylor and Jace.

You don't fuck your brother's widow, even if your brother's been dead three years.

Roles reversed, Lou wouldn't have let it happen. Lou would have crushed them. Lou wouldn't have wanted Taylor to move on.

His head about to burst, David leaned over, breathing hard, his hands on his knees.

Lou could be an arrogant ass, but David had idolized him to the point of trying to fill the gaping hole he left behind. Doing what he thought Lou would do. Trying to *be* Lou. He saw his dad aging before his eyes, withdrawing. His mom struggling to pretend they were all fine. And Jace. Striving to atone for a death he hadn't caused.

"He was my big brother, David, and I loved him."

His ears roaring, he hadn't heard Mitch's boots in the dirt.

"We're never going to be the same without him."

David's eyes burned, but he couldn't say a word.

"But he wasn't perfect. You don't need to be either."

Lou *hadn't* been perfect. His way *wasn't* always the best way. Ultimately, he hadn't taken his own advice or followed his own rules. He'd paid with his life and plunged the rest of the family into turmoil with his passing.

David had only wanted to smooth the scars left behind. He'd wanted to fix it all. Instead he'd alienated his brothers and stolen a piece of the happiness Jace and Taylor deserved.

He'd also lost a good woman by telling her she wasn't good enough just the way she was.

How could he have missed all the answers?

Because he hadn't listened. Just as Randi's father never listened.

David rolled his head, eased the ache, then turned to his brother. "Little brother, how did you get to be so smart?"

Mitch shrugged. "Guess I take after you."

Maybe. When he wasn't walking around with his head where the sun didn't shine. David knew what lay ahead of him would be hard. He had abused relationships to repair, acceptance to give, and forgiveness to ask. Mitch. Jace and Taylor. And Randi. Most especially Randi.

"I know I invited you out for a beer, but I've suddenly got a pressing need to be somewhere else. Rain check?"

"Sure. Connie was pissed I went out anyway."

She hadn't been, having practically shoved Mitch out the door. But right now, David had his own mistakes to fix, just as any man had to find his own answers. The sooner, the better.

THE SOFT TONES of the TV filtered through the door of her parents' apartment over the store. Gathering her courage around her like a warm coat in a cold winter, or the comfort of David's strong arms, Randi counted to ten before knocking.

Her mother answered, her face grim, her jowls sagging lower than usual. Her mother had never been quick to laughter or a smile. Tonight, her lips drooped and the lines at her mouth were so deep it seemed her frown might be permanent.

Caught in the middle, her mother had always hated the silences as much as Randi.

"I want to talk to Pops."

Her mother glanced over her shoulder, quickly, stealthily. "That is not a good idea, Randi. Give him time."

Time. Her father always took his time. A day, a month, a year.

"No. He and I need to talk now."

Her mom had never known how to handle Randi or Pops, and acquiescence to any demand was the easier road. She stepped back and opened the door wider, allowing Randi inside the steaming apartment. The heat rose from the shop and warehouse below, turning the cramped set of rooms into a sauna.

Her father's white cap of hair peaked above the back of his recliner. A TV tray topped with an empty dinner plate sat beside him. He didn't greet her, and the TV volume rose.

Their silences had been punctuated by a louder than normal TV, and if he absolutely needed to tell her something, he spoke through her mother. Just as he did now.

"Tell that girl I am not at home."

"Your father is not at home." Her mother repeated whatever he said, even when Randi was right there in the room to hear it.

This isn't normal. The punishing silences had been so much a part of her life that long ago she'd begun to think of them as ordinary. As if every father treated his children this way.

It *wasn't* normal. It was dysfunctional. While rationally, she knew that, in her heart and her belly, she believed his conduct was no more than she deserved.

She rounded his chair and stood in front of him. He looked beyond her as if he could see the TV through a hole he sliced in her body. Under that non-gaze, her legs wobbled like jello and butterflies dashed about in her belly, but she couldn't back down now.

"We're going to talk, Pops. And not through Mom. You're going to listen."

This time the TV's volume didn't change when he pointed the remote. This time, Randi was in the way.

This time, she would make him hear her. "I'm not going to apologize. I did that this afternoon."

He rose on stiff legs, placing the remote very carefully in the cloth holder hanging over the chair arm. Moving the TV tray out of his way, he headed to the hallway leading to the bedroom.

Randi followed, pushing past him in the narrow hallway to stand between him and the bedroom.

"You either need to accept my apology or tell me not to come back. But whatever you do, you need to *say* it, Pops."

He went into the bathroom and closed the door in her face. Her mother watched her from the same spot near the front door. She hadn't moved.

The doors were thin. Her father could hear her breathe out in the hallway. She raised her voice only slightly.

"Come out of there, and we'll talk about it like rational adults."

He turned on the water.

She didn't shout, merely raising her voice to be heard over his childish antics. "I can't work for a boss who won't speak to me. Come out and talk, Pops, or you'll have my resignation by the cash register in the morning."

The water went off, and the door suddenly slammed open, crashing against the toilet on the other side. Her father's face beat a deep red, and his eyes flashed an angry midnight blue.

"Tell this person she cannot threaten me."

"Randi—"

She held her hand up to shush her mother. "I'm not threatening you. I am telling you that in a normal business relationship two people talk. If you can't give me even that much courtesy, then I can't stay." Her stomach crimped. She was quitting her job. She was quitting her family. But she wouldn't let him smash her down. Not again.

"In a normal place of business, the owner does not walk in on his employee doing the terrible things you were doing."

He'd actually spoken to her. She grabbed the triumph. "The door was closed, Pops. You didn't have to open it."

Even his scalp pulsed with anger, gleaming red through his thin, white hair. "I knew what you would be doing. With that man. I saw it in his eyes. I have always seen it in you."

He'd hoped to catch her. He'd wanted to humiliate her. He wanted to find fault. He always had.

"You have not changed. You were only thirteen and yet I saw the seeds. You do not listen. You forget everything I try to teach you. You do not learn. You marry trash, and now you are divorced and still you have learned nothing. You still allow men liberties."

She tipped her head as if that would somehow allow her to see her father clearly. "Are you trying to protect me, Pops? Is that what this is all about?"

"You do not know a good man from a bad man. You allow them to disrespect you. I will not have it." He slammed a fist against the bathroom door, sending it crashing once more into the toilet. "I will not have a man disrespect you in my store," he shouted.

She backed up until her shoulder blades hit the wall.

"He wasn't disrespecting me. He was loving me. And he is a good man. I know the difference." She smiled softly. "He thinks I'm special."

"You speak nonsense." This time her father didn't shout. His face was still red, and his hair looked like he pulled a rake through it, but he was looking at her and talking to her, without shouting.

"It's not nonsense," she told him. "People show how they feel in different ways. With David, I *am* special." He'd touched her with reverence. Those heated, frantic moments in the locker carried a special brand of homage. Even his desire for her to confront her father was steeped in his belief that she was special.

People showed how they felt in a myriad of ways, each utterly unique. She stared at her father as if seeing him for the very first time. He used silence to teach what he thought was the right path to follow. Punishment was love in order to guide. She'd just never seen things the way he wanted her to. That didn't mean he didn't think she was special.

"Pops," she whispered, "you have to talk to me. We can't go on if you don't talk to me. It just won't work that way between us anymore."

"I am talking to you." He rubbed a hand over his head, looked at the tiled floor of the bathroom, then finally back at her. "I do not like some of the things that you do."

"I know. I was wrong. That wasn't the time or the place. But he does think I'm special, Pops. He does."

After long seconds of silence, he said, "You did not finish

filling the orders for the morning's shipping. Perhaps you will come in early tomorrow. And later we will talk about this man who thinks you are so special."

She smiled. He couldn't change her with silence, and she couldn't expect to change him. He would never be a talker, but what he had said was his own form of compromise. It was enough.

"Yeah, Pops, tomorrow. I won't forget to be there." She didn't touch him. They weren't a touchy-feely family.

When she turned in the hallway, she found her mom. The permanent frown etched along her mouth was gone.

She left her parents with a lighter step than when she'd arrived. Life wasn't perfect, neither was her relationship with her dad, but things were . . . on the upside.

She took the stairs with a spring in her step, reaching the halfway point, and then she saw him leaning against her truck. David, legs crossed, his hands stuck in his pockets, the parking lot light shining down on his head.

"I'm special," she whispered, taking the last two steps. "He *does* think I'm special."

Warm night air fluttered through Randi's hair as she crossed the lot to David's side.

"Hi," was all he said.

"Hi," she answered, equally innocuous, a tentative note in her voice and a slight wariness in her gaze.

"I went by your house first," David admitted.

"Then you came here to see if I did what you told me to?"

He couldn't blame her for her suspicion. Earlier, he'd come off like a know-it-all ass.

"Actually, I didn't have any idea where else you might be." He shoved his hands deeper into his pockets so he wouldn't reach out to stroke an errant lock of hair that had blown across her cheek. Talk first, touch later, if she let him.

"Well, you found me." She tucked the strands he wanted to touch behind her ear.

He uncrossed his legs and straightened away from the truck. "I owe you an apology."

"For what?" She shuttered her eyes, her gaze falling to his shoulder. Her posture gave nothing away.

"I didn't like what your dad said to you. If it had been anyone else, I would have popped him one right in the kisser."

Her glance flashed to his eyes, then dropped to his lips as if she had to read the words as well as hear them.

"But I couldn't belt the father of the woman I'm in love with. And I felt . . . helpless."

"The woman you're in love with?"

"Yeah."

"But you've only known me two days."

He took a chance, running a finger down her cheek. "Three days," he corrected. "And that's long enough with a woman who's as open and honest as you are."

She toed the dirt lot. "You were right, you know. I've got a whole lot of crap going on with my dad and how he treats me, and I needed to do something about it."

He cupped her cheek, drawing her closer with a slight touch. "Your dad's your own business. You didn't have to do anything just because I told you I thought you should."

She took the final step to bring her body flush with his. "I didn't come over here for you, David. I came for me. And for him. But you were still right, it needed to be done. I shouldn't have thrown you out just because you told me what you thought."

He stroked her face. "What I said to you was for my benefit, Randi, not yours." He leaned his forehead against hers. "My oldest brother died three years ago, and I've spent the time since trying to fix everything for everyone because that's what he always did. I thought I could fill his shoes. I am only just beginning to realize that I don't have to do that." He pulled back to look at her. "I was trying to fix things for you, too. Tell you how you should run your life. I was wrong."

"I'm so sorry about your brother," she whispered. "But you don't have to fill someone else's shoes. You're perfect the way you are."

He touched his lips to hers. "So are you."

"And I'm glad you helped me realize I needed to have it out with my dad."

He breathed in her sweet scent. "How did it go up there?" If she needed to talk, he'd listen. He'd do anything she needed.

"It was fine, David. Just fine." She nuzzled into him.

He didn't know exactly what that meant, but whatever she did was fine with him, too. "Randi?"

"Hmmm?"

"You're special. So special that I can't promise I won't drag you into a meat locker or a closet or anywhere we happen to be because I need to put my hands on you."

She rose on her toes and wrapped her arms around his neck. "Ditto," she breathed against his ear.

"Say it then."

She crushed him close, her arms tight around his neck. "Oh, David, I love you."

Her words slid inside him to fill all the cracks Lou's death had fractured. The last three years had been a long, hard road, and he was sure life would throw more hurdles in his path. With Randi by his side, he could make the leap.

ELEVEN

HOLY MACK MOLY. Randi could hear the commotion even as she climbed down from David's truck.

It sounded like a herd of Jacksons in the backyard of his parents' house. She shivered, then David's arm slid around her shoulders, pulling her close.

"Don't worry. They're going to love you as much as I do."

He had a mom, a dad, two brothers, two sisters-in-law, three nephews and one niece—or was it three nieces and one nephew?—but the noise thundering out of the backyard sounded like multiples of that number on a logarithmic scale.

"How am I going to remember all their names?" She shuddered to think. She was terrible with names, just terrible.

"I'll remind you. Besides, no one in my family is going to give a flying rat's ass if you call anyone by the wrong name."

But she so wanted to impress them at this first meeting. She now knew David's entire history from the time he was born to the day he slammed into her life. She knew about his dead brother, and the other brother who was going to marry the widow, and . . . Oh God, please don't let her say something totally embarrassing in front of them.

David whipped her around as if he could hear all the fears running rampant through her mind and pulled her straight into his big, strong arms.

"I love you and they'll love you. I told you my mom was ecstatic when I said I was bringing a very special woman to the barbecue. You couldn't do a thing to ruin it."

Sure she could. A million things. Maybe she should have had David introduce her to his parents first instead of waiting for the big Sunday barbecue. Maybe she should have ... maybe she wouldn't do a single thing wrong, and they'd love her just the way she was. "I'm special," she whispered into his chest. "And they're going to love me."

He lifted her chin and kissed the tip of her nose. "Don't forget I love you, too."

She wouldn't ever forget. She would never tire of hearing it, never stop believing.

"Come on. I want to meet your sister-in-law."

If it was hard for her to meet his family, it was doubly hard for him to face his brother and the widow. She'd heard all about the terrible fight. But she'd be there to hold his hand just as he'd offered to hold hers when she went to her father.

Pushing through the gate, the sister-in-law was the one he took her to first. A pretty woman with auburn hair and brown eyes, she was laughing with a couple of boys Randi assumed were her own. The man beside her, a slightly younger version of David, tapped her shoulder.

They turned, a package deal, and David went to them, Randi's hand in his.

"Randi, I want you to meet my brother Jace and his fiancée Taylor." He didn't call her Lou's widow. The word choice was purposeful, carrying a wealth of meaning.

The barest of something flickered in Taylor's eyes, mirrored in Jace's. Relief? Happiness? Forgiveness? Then David grabbed Jace, giving him a hearty hug and a back slap, one Jace returned only a half second later.

Over his brother's shoulder, David smiled at Randi and mouthed, "Thank you."

Later, she'd thank him in return, in a hundred different ways, for showing her just how special she was.

RANDI ANDERSEN WAS a beautiful girl with an abundance of blond hair that glistened in the sunlight. David held her hand as if she might disappear if he wasn't attached to her.

Evelyn had so missed the pure beauty of her son's smile.

Heavens, she was floating on air. She'd been so worried about David. She'd feared he'd might leave the family forever over the whole business with Taylor and Jace.

Evelyn beamed, remembering that introduction half an hour ago. *I want you to meet my brother Jace and his fiancée Taylor.* David's words echoed in her mind, and there was acceptance and forgiveness in the simplicity of them. Oh yes, life was perfect in Evelyn's small world.

Well, almost perfect. She just needed to figure out what that frown on Mitch's face meant, especially since normally chatterbox Connie had gone completely mum on the subject.

Somebody's Wife

ONE

OKAY, THE STATE of the union, as plainly and with as little emotion as possible. Mitch was tired and worried. He was pissed that she wanted to trade in the old station wagon for a new minivan to shuttle around the Little League team. They'd been fighting more than they made love. In fact, he hadn't touched her in over two months. Which amounted to one thing—Mitch didn't want her anymore.

Or maybe he was having an affair.

Connie Jackson shuddered. More than anything, she didn't want to be somebody's wife whose husband was having an affair. She'd die if he was.

"Oh for Pete's sake." The candy-coated almond leaped out of the other side of the blue lace netting Connie was trying to secure it in.

With the back door open, Connie could hear the kids yelling and screaming out in the yard. The clock ticked loudly on the kitchen wall, and the coffeemaker belched one last gasp of air from its tubes.

Next to her, Taylor smiled, expertly tying a bit of pink ribbon around her almonds and netting. "Slippery little things, aren't they? But they were inexpensive."

Trust Taylor to plan her wedding frugally. Taylor was good at everything, whether it was doing her wedding on a budget, keeping the books down at the office, or making coleslaw for the Sunday barbecue.

Taylor patted Connie's hand. "And I thank all of you for coming over this afternoon to help me make the wedding favors."

Connie would never have considered *not* helping. Taylor and Jace were part of her family. Connie looked at her completed pile, then Taylor's, Evelyn's, and Randi's in turn.

"My pile is not up to snuff here."

Her ribbons didn't curl properly, the little names-and-date cards didn't sit straight, and she'd finished half of what everyone else had. "I baked and decorated eight dozen Santa cookies for Rina's kindergarten in one afternoon. I can squish six Little Leaguers into seat belts in the station wagon. I can pack for a camping trip and not forget a thing. So why can't I make these favors?"

Randi gasped. "You don't forget anything? Not even the mayo or the mustard or a sleeping bag?"

Connie shook her head gravely. "Nope. I don't forget a single thing. Ever."

"Wow." Randi's voice dripped with awe. David's new girlfriend was a sweetheart and a half. She'd attended the last two family barbecues, and well, Connie had to admit she'd made David into a new man. He laughed and joked a lot now, a definite transformation from his usual taciturn self over the last few years. Randi had moved in with him, and Connie was crossing her fingers for another wedding.

Evelyn tossed another favor in her done pile. "My Heavens, Connie, you've been bumbling around for weeks now."

A woman couldn't function properly without a solid nookie quotient. The baby scare two months ago—a scare only for Mitch, she'd been delighted when she thought she was pregnant—had put a big crimp in their sex life. He was too busy worrying about money. But they'd both wanted a big family, they'd agreed on it when they first got married, and now, with Rina going off to first grade . . . well, the timing was perfect for Connie. She'd just have to convince him somehow.

But first she'd have to convince him to make love to her. Connie sighed. At least they were speaking again.

Taylor grabbed the ribbon spool. "Maybe you and Mitch just need a weekend by yourselves."

Connie's mouth dropped open. How on earth had Taylor known exactly what she was thinking? Oh yeah, probably because she'd spilled her guts that day two months ago right after she'd found out she wasn't pregnant. She'd told Taylor everything about her Mitch problems.

Her sister-in-law once again read her mind and winked. "I remember a few sighs of my own sounding exactly like that." Taylor tweaked the little bow on her bundle. "You could go to some swanky resort and get his-and-her massages."

Evelyn handed Connie the roll of netting. "You know Arthur and I would love to take the kids any time you want to get away by yourselves."

That's what she loved about this family. They all pitched in. Even Evelyn, when most moms would have been horrified to even think of their grown sons having a sex life.

"Thanks, but I don't think we should spend any money right now." Mitch would have a hissy fit if she suggested it. Then they'd start fighting, then she'd get mad. And really, she was not a nice person when she got mad.

"How about some sexy lingerie?"

Evelyn was great. She might be close to sixty, but she thought like a thirty-year-old. She hadn't even batted an eyelash when Randi moved in with David.

"Ooh," Evelyn suddenly blurted out. "Crotchless panties."

"How do you know about crotchless panties?" Connie gasped.

Evelyn tut-tutted. "I read about them in one of those women's magazines while I was waiting in the dentist's office."

"Ha, Arthur bought you a pair, didn't he?"

"Girls, girls, with this old body, I wouldn't be caught dead in teeny-tiny panties."

"Good Lord, Evelyn, you're not old." Taylor pinched her mother-in-law's cheek.

"Right. So that's why your boys bought me that button saying I wasn't just old, I was older than dirt."

"They were kidding." Then Taylor smiled mischievously. "You should see what they're getting you this year."

"Heavens above." Evelyn raised her eyes to the ceiling. "Now, we were discussing Connie. She needs our help, not me."

Connie's heart warmed. The women in your family *should* be there to provide sage advice on difficult matters. God knows she couldn't ask her own mother. Between them, they didn't mention bodily functions.

"I've got too much sexy lingerie sitting unused in the drawer. I need fresh ideas."

"You could try some caviar." Randi tossed another finished favor on to her pile. "It works miracles."

Now that sounded interesting. "Is caviar some sort of aphrodisiac?"

Randi smiled with a wicked tilt. "Not as far as I know. But there's lots of different ways to use it."

"Isn't it really expensive?" Taylor, ever penny-wise, wanted to know.

Randi flapped a hand, an almond rolling across the table with her exuberance. "That's beluga. My parents have this really cool Scandinavian caviar paste at the shop that comes in a tube." She batted her eyelashes. "You can squeeze it on anything you want."

So that's what David had been up to, that bad boy. Connie always figured him for the missionary, once-a-week type, he was so staid and serious most of the time. Until recently.

"And you say your parents carry it at their store?" Evelyn asked, cutting off the ends of her bow with more concentration than necessary.

Randi leaned forward. "You can have it shipped straight to the house so no one even knows you bought it. Except me, because I do all the shipping."

Evelyn grabbed a cut sheet of netting. "Does it come in a brown paper bag?"

"However you want it packaged."

They were quiet a few moments, amid the clicking of the scissors, as they all absorbed the information.

"Mitch doesn't like fish." But the suggestion did give Connie an idea. They needed something new in their marriage, something fresh, something different. Like any couple married ten years, they'd hit a rut in the road.

She needed to create a little spark. Maybe she'd do a lingerie striptease for Mitch. She'd never done that before. Tonight, after the kids went to bed, she'd give it a shot.

THE KIDS HAD gone to bed, Connie was in the bathroom doing her nightly feminine routine—which meant she'd be in there for an hour—and Mitch flopped on the couch in front of the TV. The news droned, but he couldn't wrap his mind around any details.

Mitch was tired. He was worried. His belly ached as well as his head. And he didn't look forward to the next argument with Connie about the washing machine, which was on its last cycle, or the car. That station wagon of hers wouldn't last out the year before something else blew on it.

Life was nickel-and-diming him to death. And Connie wanted another baby.

The idea of another child gave him heart palpitations. Their medical insurance had gone through the roof this last year, not to mention the grocery bills, new clothes, and the million things a baby would need. Plus the house wasn't big enough. They'd have to add on. They had the sewing room, but Connie loved that room for her projects, and he wanted her to keep it. She'd offered to get a job, but she already had one at which she was an expert—mother of the year. He wouldn't have her feeling like she wasn't giving the kids her best. Nor would it solve his main problem: If something happened to him, he wanted Connie and the kids to be taken care of. Over the last three years, he'd feverishly used every extra dime to pay down the house mortgage and buy a good life insurance policy.

Still, terrible scenarios in which his family was living on the streets consumed his waking hours and crept into his dreams at night. His head knew that wouldn't happen, but his gut was another thing. The family business was doing fine. Taylor and her boys had made it through the devastation of losing Lou. And he knew damn well his parents wouldn't let anything bad happen to Connie and the kids. None of that mattered, because it was his gut that controlled his actions these days, no matter how much logic he tried to feed himself. Sometimes he wondered if there even was an amount of money big enough to stop the gnawing in his insides. When Connie thought she was pregnant a couple of months ago, he hadn't slept for two days. As badly as he wanted to, he hadn't been able to bring himself to make love to her since.

Holy hell, he was giving himself an ulcer. Even the antacids didn't help anymore. He couldn't stop worrying. Life could change in a few seconds. In one wrong turn of a chain saw.

How would his family make it without him? The bills, the car, the insurance, the washing machine . . .

Mitch didn't realize he'd fallen asleep until he heard Connie's voice in the hallway.

"Honey, are you coming to bed?"

His heart was racing. His worries had followed him into his sleep, and they hadn't danced like sugar plum fairies.

He eased off the couch, his muscles aching as if he'd been running in his sleep. Shutting off the TV and the lights, he padded down the hallway toward their room. Light spilled across the worn carpet. They needed new stuff, but that replacement was way down on the list of priorities.

The scent of Connie's flowery lotion seeped into the hall.

Inside, only one bedside lamp was lit, throwing the corners of the room into shadow and delicately lighting his wife's profile. Even after ten years of marriage and two kids, she took good care of herself. Some women went to pot, but not Connie. She was as gorgeous as the day he married her. More so, in fact. Those few hated extra pounds she'd never been able to shed after pregnancy gave her luscious curves and perfect breasts with the most enticing pair of nipples.

One leg raised to the stool at her vanity, she smoothed cream into her skin, long strokes along her calves, up her thigh, then back again. He watched, mesmerized by the silk of her skin in the soft lamplight and the rhythmic caress of her fingers. The lace thing she wore barely covered her butt cheeks, and her hair cascaded over her shoulder and down her arm.

She smiled at him. "Did you fall asleep out there, honey?"

He missed her smile. "What are you wearing?"

"Don't worry, I didn't just buy it. I was cleaning out my drawers this afternoon and ran across it." She dropped one leg to the floor, then raised the other and started the creaming procedure all over again.

They hadn't made love in two months. Almost three. He remembered it like a jailed man remembers his last taste of freedom. His mom had taken the kids after one of the barbecues, and the minute the door was closed, the curtains pulled, and the house silent, Connie unzipped his shorts and climbed on top of him right there in the front room.

He'd come after four fast, hard strokes inside her luscious body. His cock filled out his jeans. He'd slept well that night, really well.

Christ, he loved that she loved sex. When they were younger, it was anytime anywhere they could manage it. A little risk had made it even better.

After ten years and two kids, they'd grown past that stage. But Connie hadn't stopped liking sex.

He hadn't stopped either despite his constant worries. He wanted her now.

She'd started on her arms now, silking up those smooth limbs. Facing him as she stroked, she arched her neck and blended lotion into her throat, then her upper chest, her fingertips dipping down beneath the thin lace. Her dusky pink nipples peeked through the flimsy covering, tightening into nubs as he watched.

"Mi-itch."

"Huh?"

"I asked if you were tired."

"Oh. Yeah." The outfit was cut high on her hips, her pretty little bush clearly visible through the lace.

"That's too bad."

"What?" Her scent wrapped around his gonads. He couldn't think.

She jutted her hip, putting one hand on bare skin, her fingertips flirting with the lace edging. "I said, it's too bad that you're tired."

God, he wanted her, needed to sink inside her gorgeous flesh and come until he was beyond worrying about anything but the warm fit of her body around him.

Hell, he'd be satisfied taking one tight nipple into his mouth and sucking it like fruit. He could taste her, feel her. His gaze fixed on the ripe melons of her breasts. He licked dry lips, then murmured, "Did you take your birth control pill?"

"What?"

Her shrill tone shocked him out of his desire-induced haze. "Huh?" What had he just said? He couldn't remember. Damn.

"Of course I took my pill. I take it in the morning, every morning. Like clockwork."

All trace of her sultry tone had vanished and the lines of her body, moments before seductive and enticing, now tensed with anger. Connie had the beady-eyed stare down to a science.

"I didn't mean—"

"I know exactly what you meant. You don't trust me. You treat me like a child. I'm almost thirty years old, you know. I can actually wipe my own butt, thank you very much. And I don't need you to remind me to take my pill, okay?"

"Connie, honey-sweetie—"

"Don't honey-sweetie me." She glared, as if she were so angry she couldn't find her next words. "You know what, since you fell asleep out on the couch, you can just get back out there again. I don't want a man who doesn't trust me sleeping in my bed."

"Connie—"

She pointed. "Go."

Man. He'd blown it. Big time. He slinked away with his tail between his legs instead of arguing, because the truth was, he didn't trust her. He didn't think she'd miss a pill on purpose, but her desire to have a baby was so great that she might accidentally forget. Subconsciously, of course, but the result would be the same.

Mitch punched a couch cushion into submission, then flopped down. He ached. Not just tired work muscles, but now his cock throbbed and his balls ached, and Christ, he wanted nothing more than to crawl back into the bedroom, beg her forgiveness, and get off in her sweet, delicious body.

Hell.

Maybe he could talk her into using condoms as extra protection. Because this abstinence thing was going to kill him.

TWO

SHE SHOULD HAVE slammed the door in his face, but she hadn't wanted to wake the kids. Instead, she'd closed it softly but firmly. Shutting him out.

Ooh, she was mad. She'd almost had him. She could have mopped the floor with his drool and hung the laundry on his erection. Mitchie wanted her. Bad.

But not badly enough to wipe thoughts of birth control out of his mind. Who did he think he was, checking up on her? Okay, so she had forgotten to take a pill a couple of months ago. She hadn't discovered it until it was too late, until she'd already attacked him after the barbecue. She'd planned the attack, getting Evelyn to take the kids, but really, she hadn't planned to forget her pill. She wouldn't do that. They were a team. As much as she wanted a baby, she wouldn't do that to him.

And Mitch should know it.

Oooh, she was so mad. Not to mention horny. Yes, flat out horny like an ovulating bunny. Hot, wet, and wanting, she needed an orgasm. She wanted it now. And why shouldn't she have it? So what if she was alone in the bed? Who needed a man anyway? Maybe he'd hear her, know what she was doing, and come back begging. She should have left the door open.

She'd ripped her pretty lace teddy when she yanked it off, but at least she was naked beneath the sheet. Connie spread her legs, slid her hands over her breasts, down her abdomen, then into the thatch of hair at her apex. She was wet, dripping.

"See what you're missing, Mitchie," she whispered.

Her clitoris was already a throbbing nub when she put her finger to it. Almost on its own, her pelvis moved in tandem. She groaned without meaning to, then dipped her finger inside. It was good, but Mitch's penis would have felt so much better. She went back to her clitoris, using fast circles. Faster, harder, her hips rising off the bed for extra pressure. Then she squeezed her eyes shut and bit her lip as heat and sensation shot straight to the sensitive bead and threw her up into starlight. Collapsing back into the mattress, delicious quivers traveled through her body as her breathing returned to normal.

Hmm. The springs squeaked. She hoped they squeaked loudly enough for Mitch to hear out in the living room.

WHAT WAS THAT noise? A rhythmic squeak, then finally what sounded like a moan. Connie's moan. He knew it well, a soft, throaty exhalation of pleasure. Very soft, because of the kids.

Man, she wasn't . . . no, she wouldn't. Sometimes she did, when he was buried deep in her. Sometimes he asked her to because he liked the thought of her working herself from the outside while he worked her inside.

But she didn't do it without him.

Did she?

Oh man. The thought of watching her pleasure herself made him close to explosive. He needed a cold shower. He needed his wife's mouth on his cock.

And he really had to stop thinking about it. He had bills to pay and family responsibilities, and those were much more dire than the fact that he hadn't gotten any nookie.

If only he could get over his debilitating anxiety. Even he

realized it was unrealistic given the fact that he was surrounded by a family who would do anything for Connie and the kids. But he kept remembering Lou.

In the end, he slept less than an hour, trapped between the image of astronomical grocery-store receipts and the sweet scent of Connie's skin.

"I'M SORRY, HONEY, I acted like a jerk last night." If not for the kids, Connie would have used the word bitch to describe last night's tirade. She had to admit she'd overreacted.

Mitch jerked his head up, his cereal going soggy.

"I acted childishly."

Mitch stared at her as if she'd brandished a pair of pinking shears in a crowded post office. And still he didn't say a word.

"Rina, finish your cereal before it gets mushy," she said, eyeing Mitch's cereal bowl with a message light in her eyes. "And Peter, don't forget to put your Van Helsing monsters in your backpack."

With his cereal sucked down as if he were a vacuum, Peter hopped off his chair and dashed to his room. Their son moved on only two speeds, slow as a garden slug when he didn't want to do something or Warp Eight when he did.

"Can I get my Barbie pack, Mom?"

Connie leaned over to look at her daughter's bowl. Not completely empty, but better than usual. "Okay, sweetie."

With the children getting themselves ready, she turned back to Mitch to find him still staring as if she were one of Peter's space aliens.

"Finish your cereal like a good boy, honey." She'd flummoxed him. Good. "I mean it, I'm really sorry I blew up last night."

Last night had given her a wealth of new insights. A really good orgasm could do that. Even if she'd given it to herself.

First, she had been a bit hasty in accusing him of not trusting her. After all, that reminder about her birth control pills was *just* a question, and she couldn't blame him for being worried. He'd always been a worrier. Evelyn said it was because he was always trying to play catch-up with his big brothers, trying to prove he was good enough. But after Lou's death, he'd gone haywire, examining every little expenditure she made. She'd wanted to help by getting a job, but he'd vetoed that idea. Then she'd hinted he should talk to someone, a professional. Grief counseling. Oh boy, that argument had been ugly. Even she, who never backed down from a good fight, had to let that one go. They'd sidestepped Lou's death ever since.

She needed a different plan of attack, though *attack* was the absolutely wrong word. She didn't want to start a war. She wanted to start some loving in the bedroom, get them back on the track they'd fallen off of.

"We've been fighting too much lately, and I've decided I'm not going to fight anymore. I'll give you a calm household to come home to every night, where you don't have to fret about a thing. Where you can relax and shrug off the day's worries."

He tilted his head, first one way, then the other. Like a dog who couldn't figure out whether the steak in front of him was laced with rat poison.

"What's wrong?" he asked.

"Oh, honey. Nothing's wrong." She smiled. She'd make everything just *right*. She was going to keep his house, watch his kids, and match his socks. And when they turned the lights out she was going to blow his mind.

The plan had come to her in that expansive, lethargic state right after orgasm where genius took root.

"Now, I'm dropping Rina off at day care," which she did twice a week to keep Rina used to being away from home during the day. It was a friend's day care, and they swapped favors so it didn't cost Mitch a cent. Kindergarten had been a big adjustment for Rina—not to mention herself—and she didn't want the same problems with first grade.

"Peter's spending the day with the Daigel boy, they're going to play Van Helsing, so I'll see you tonight. Anything special you want for dinner?"

Mitch choked on his soggy cereal. At least that's what the noise coming from his throat sounded like. He didn't turn blue or anything, and finally managed, "Anything's fine with me."

She called the kids to heel, though it took another ten minutes to get them ready. Mitch was still seated at the kitchen table, a cold cup of coffee clutched in his fingers. She dropped a kiss on his head, then scooted her gaggle out the door.

Oh yeah, she'd blow his matched socks off tonight after lights-out.

"SHE ACTED LIKE a Stepford wife, I tell you. She even asked me what I wanted for dinner."

"She asked instead of telling?" David repeated, jiggling his ear as if he couldn't have heard correctly.

Mitch threw another small stump on the heap and nodded. "She never asks. She knows whatever she makes is fine with me."

"Interesting."

"It was scary, David. Damn scary."

Connie's act this morning was almost . . . creepy. Definitely like a Stepford wife, especially after the way they'd gone to bed. Separately. Didn't the wives turn on their husbands in the end and kill them? He'd never seen the movie. Now he was terrified to.

"She's planning something, I know it, and it can't be good."

They stopped jawing a bit to work on the last stump. Damn, he hated removing stumps. That part of the job took longer than cutting down the whole damn tree.

"Holy Hell."

"What?"

"She said she's getting rid of the kids for the day. What if she's planning to . . ."

He stopped. He hadn't told his brother about his money woes. He didn't need anyone else telling him he was a freak. But fear was now busting his gut. "What if she's planning to buy a new washing machine? Or a car?" God forbid.

David leaned on the end of his pickax. "She wouldn't do that. Not behind your back."

He tried to listen to his brother's voice of reason. But she'd been so pissed last night when he'd inadvertently let that stupid question slip out of his gullet. She would be royally pissed if she knew he'd sneaked into the bathroom after she left this morning and checked her packet of birth control pills. Hell, he couldn't even tell if she'd taken her daily dose, not having seen the number the day before. Just how pissed could Connie get? Deviously pissed. Thank God he didn't incite her wrath often. Although, the make-up sex was pretty damn hot.

"You know, Mitch, if you're in a bind, you can always come to one of us for help."

"In a bind?"

"Money. Cash. That's what family is for. To help out."

"No. Hell no. I'm fine. We're fine."

David put his hands up. "All right. Just checking."

Did he sound like he needed to beg? He stopped work long enough to pop another antacid. His stomach was roiling. He honestly hadn't realized he'd let his worries slip that much into his conversation. He'd have to watch that in the future.

Right now, he had bigger concerns. Connie. Damage control. He suddenly had the driving need to get home. But they had two more stumps to clear. He feared that when he finally did get home, it would be way too late.

SHE CERTAINLY COULDN'T look for what she wanted in Willoughby. Not that she thought she'd find it, but just asking would set the town tongues wagging. This might be California, but small towns were small towns with everybody's business being everybody else's.

She'd have to drive into Saint Lucia, which wasn't much larger than Willoughby, but it wasn't *her* town. Besides, she'd heard about that new shop, everyone had heard about it. Surely she'd find what she wanted, no, needed. And she had until two-thirty when she had to pick up Rina.

"Shop till you drop," she quipped, parking the station wagon in the next block over from the store. The engine knocked and pinged for fifteen seconds after she shut it off. She really had to convince Mitch they needed a replacement.

The store wasn't obtrusive or garish. Its window displayed a tasteful arrangement of feather masks, which *could* be used at Halloween two and a half months away, assorted beauty products like lotions and soaps, and a mannequin in a pretty, gauzy summer skirt and spaghetti-strap camisole. UP AND COMING, the shop's name, was arched in gold letters across the window and front door.

Up and Coming. Connie snickered. It was quite a play on words considering what the shop stocked in the back room.

A bell tinkled overhead as she opened the door. The interior looked like any old Victoria's Secret at the mall. Lace, satin, and silk hung on gold racks, lotions and sprays sat on glass shelves along the wall, a selection of makeup beneath a counter, flowered curtains adorning dressing rooms. Candles burned, scenting the air with . . . well, what was that smell?

"Oleander," came a voice from behind her.

Connie realized she must have been sniffing the aroma.

"It's good for relaxing all the muscles."

Gorgeous red hair flowed over the saleswoman's shoulders. Jeez, why couldn't she have hair like that? It didn't look dyed, with shades of gold and strawberry glittering through it. Her makeup was lightly yet expertly applied, which enhanced the disgustingly perfect features God had given her. Sparkling green eyes, plump red lips, which weren't all bubbly with collagen, and full breasts that fit her Marilyn Monroe hourglass figure. Silver ankle bracelets jingled as she crossed the tasteful rose-hued carpet. With the grace of a voluptuous fifties beauty queen, she was no skinny-minnie by any means, but why couldn't Connie's pounds fall into perfect place like that?

"Can I help you find something? We have some lovely lingerie."

Lingerie had *not* worked, and Connie would have felt inferior with this perfect woman enticing her to buy more frilly stuff that *wouldn't* work.

"I'm more interested in what you have in the back room."

The woman smiled like Eve picking the apple off the tree. "We don't call it the back room. It's the boudoir."

Who was this "we" anyway? There were only the two of them. "The boudoir would be fine."

The woman held out her hand, indicating the way through a doorway decked with pink and blue beads acting as a curtain.

"May I ask how you heard about us? Since we're fairly new, I like to get an idea of which promotion worked."

Connie laughed. "You're kidding, right? This place is the talk of the area. Everybody's heard about Up and Coming." Following the woman through the beads, she added, "Did you really intend the name to mean what it sounds like it means?"

The proprietress had a very sexy laugh. Connie wondered if she could imitate it without sounding like a braying donkey. Besides, dealing in . . . the things she dealt in, the woman probably practiced her walk, her laugh, even her speech modulation. The impression given when a customer entered was everything.

"This isn't a sex shop you'd find down some filthy big city alley. Up and Coming celebrates femininity in all its forms."

"But you do have sex toys, right?"

She smiled. "Of course. Quite a variety. My name's Jensen, by the way."

Connie gaped. She didn't have to give her name, did she?

"It's all right. We don't deal in brown paper bags here, but everything is confidential."

Jeez, it wasn't as if she were visiting the doctor for some female complaint. What harm could giving her first name do?

"I'm Connie."

Jensen lightly touched her arm, subtly directing her deeper into the "boudoir."

"Do you have a specific toy in mind?"

"Not really. I was just sort of wanting to look around." She hadn't been expecting a guided tour, which might end up being a bit embarrassing. But after looking at the sizes, shapes, and colors ornamenting the walls, countertops, and display stands, Connie did need a little explanation. "What's that?"

Blue and rubbery, it looked like a donut with nubs on it.

"That's a pleasure ring. It's placed around a man's penis. It enhances the man's pleasure, allows him to maintain an erection longer, and the nubs stimulate the woman's clitoris during intercourse."

"Oh." Connie didn't have much more to say on the subject.

"You'll see these on the Internet, but please, never buy stainless steel. Swelling can occur, making it impossible to remove. A man once had to have it cut off with a diamond saw."

"Umm, gee, guess I'll skip that then."

"Perhaps you'd like to try a pair of handcuffs. We carry an assortment from fur-lined to leather to a replica of what the police would use."

"My husband and I aren't into S&M." Connie knew all the appropriate lingo.

"Not to worry, we entertain married couples wanting to spice up their love lives. Handcuffs don't necessarily mean S&M. A little restraint and blindfold can be quite enjoyable."

Connie considered it. Seriously. Would Mitch let her handcuff him to the brass rails of the headboard? She thought about being handcuffed herself and having her eyes covered. She couldn't wriggle away when his tongue got too intense. The idea sent a thrill between her legs. Which made her feel extremely uncomfortable with company around.

"I'll keep it in mind."

"Perhaps you'd like to look at our selection of vibrators?"

She shook her head. "I want something we can use together."

The woman laughed again, throaty. "Vibrators aren't simply a solitary tool. They can be put to good use by both parties."

"Oh?" Connie quickly held up a hand. "Please don't tell me. That would be too embarrassing."

"In that case, we offer a very useful instruction pamphlet to accompany the purchase." She crinkled her nose. "With some helpful hints for getting the maximum benefit."

Connie found herself following Jensen to the opposite wall as if she were the Pied Piper.

"This model has dual ends which can be used . . ." Jensen glanced at Connie, obviously gauging her word choice. "It has dual penetration capabilities."

Leaning closer, Connie examined the brown device. It was curved and had two heads. Mercy, they looked like penises. Then it dawned on her exactly where one was supposed to insert the two heads. Ewww.

"No, I don't think so." She wasn't letting anyone use that thing on her, not even Mitch.

"How about something more standard?" Jensen pulled a purple silicon penis-shape from the wall bracket. "This particular model is equipped with three speeds and the ability to rotate and vibrate at the same time. One partner can be in charge of the controls while the other . . . submits."

"You mean . . ." Oh my. She felt another little thrill at the thought of Mitch putting it inside her and . . . pumping it.

"I think you understand. Manual stimulation can be used in conjunction."

My. Oh my.

"Batteries are included, of course."

Connie just stared. She wasn't a prude. She and Mitch used to experiment with position and location and created their fair share of interesting techniques. She'd read *Cosmo* magazine and learned a few tricks Mitch found quite impressive. But she'd grown up with a prudish mother, gotten married young, moved straight from her mother's house to Mitch's apartment, and certainly, after looking around Jensen's shop, her education seemed a bit lacking now. She felt almost generic.

"How much is it?"

"It's actually a mid-range since it doesn't have all the bells and whistles you find on some of the others you see here." Then she named an astronomical price.

Well, it wasn't really all that bad except when Connie considered how Mitch watched every penny. A few pieces of lingerie stuffed in the drawer had cost more. But he made her feel terrified of spending a dollar on a cup of coffee, for goodness sake.

"I'll include the instruction pamphlet for free."

This was about their marriage. About getting back the fire they'd lost. About not being afraid he might turn to another woman because she didn't satisfy him anymore.

Money was no object in light of her plan's importance.

"I'll take it."

Jensen smiled. "If you're not happy with it, please come back for a refund which can be used to purchase something that might better meet your needs."

"You mean I can return it?" No. No, no, no. That seemed sort of disgusting.

Shaking her head as if she were dealing with a child, Jensen carried Connie's new vibrator to the register. "Return, no, but I want my clients to be happy when they've taken my advice about a purchase. If they're not, it's my obligation to fix that. You can pick out something that will work better for you."

Well, maybe the handcuffs. And the blindfold.

Now, where was she going to hide the purple monstrosity so the kids didn't find it and ask Mommy what it was?

THREE

THAT HADN'T TAKEN as long as she thought. Connie made it home with two hours to spare before she had to pick up Rina.

She carried the flowered bag containing her brand new vibrator into her bathroom. Hmm, maybe there was a place to hide it in there, away from curious child eyes. She cut the plastic with a pair of nail scissors and removed the thing. Whoa. It was big, thick, and long. Bigger than Mitch? Maybe a little, but not much. Mitch had a very nice penis. She fiddled a minute with the batteries, then turned it on, hitting the rotate dial. Stifling a giggle, she turned it up to the third speed until it whirled around like a snake being charmed.

"Oh my God, Mitch is going to die," she whispered to the empty room.

There was a button to change directions, and another dial to put it on vibrate. She turned up everything to maximum until the thing twirled and hummed like it was on steroids.

They wouldn't be able to stop laughing long enough to use it. Laying it on the bed, she nipped outside the door, closed it behind her, then listened. Nope, the kids wouldn't hear.

Back in the bedroom, she stared at the thing jiggling on the flowered yellow spread. What would it feel like?

"You better try it out first, so you don't embarrass yourself to Kingdom Come in front of Mitch." She bit her lip, then glanced at her watch.

An hour and forty-five minutes. "Just to test it out. To make sure it works. For goodness sake, I'm a married woman and old enough to experiment."

Why on earth she needed to give herself a pep talk, she couldn't say. Women used vibrators all the time. She should have done this years ago.

Without a moment to change her mind, she whipped her sundress over her head, slid her panties down her legs, then climbed onto the bed.

She piled two pillows so she could see what she was doing, then flopped down on the bed. Flipping off the rotate switch, giggling once more, she held the hummer in her hand. Another giggle, then she spread her legs, and tunneled a finger between her lips to test her wetness.

Wow. To quote Randi. She was amazingly wet without even noticing. Spreading herself, she touched the buzzing vibrator to her clitoris. Oooh. It was sort of intense, like a shot of tequila zipping straight to her center.

This time, she held it longer. "Oh, oh." It did feel good, incredibly good, her clitoris thrumming as the vibrator buzzed, her hips pushing up and rotating almost without her thinking. Closing her eyes, she pushed her head back into the pillows and moaned, then tossed her hair. Sensation flooded her body, straight to her toes and fingers. Her whole body purred.

How would it feel to have it vibrating inside her?

THEY'D FINISHED THE stumps in record time and Mitch cut out early to let David handle the dump run. The stumps didn't need two sets of hands. He had sluiced with the hose at the client's house, then donned a fresh T-shirt and headed home.

He was terrified he'd find a new car in the driveway. Thank

God Connie's station wagon was in its normal spot, covering the oil stain.

He went around back so he wouldn't track dirt through the front room. Once inside, he toed off his shoes, threw his jeans on top of the washer—the same old washer, thank the Lord—and went in search of his wife.

He followed the faint hum from the other end of the house. She must be doing some sewing. Sewing was good. Making things like curtains and stuff was cheaper than buying. She was even making her own bridesmaid dress for the wedding. Connie could be really thrifty when she tried.

He froze in shock in the middle of the hallway outside their bedroom. His heart started racing, his breath whooshed out of his chest, and he suddenly had the most massive boner he'd ever known. Just like that. Two seconds flat.

Connie writhed on the bed, panting and moaning, hands between her legs holding some inhuman purple thing.

It was the most incredibly hot vision he'd ever had. Her body flushed pink, her hair was strewn across the pillows, and she bit down on her lip as another moan slipped from her throat.

Connie was going at it with a vibrator. Mesmerized, he watched it sink into her body, deep, eliciting a frenzied whimper. Then she lifted one hand to massage her clit at the same time. The vibrator, in, out, her finger swirling. She dug her heels into the bed and rose to meet the fake penis.

Incapable of doing anything else, Mitch palmed himself, stroking his damn near painful erection through his boxers. His feet carried him forward so he could see better over the brass rails at the bottom of the bed, close enough to see the glow on her cheeks, her tightly closed eyelids, her lashes fanning her cheeks. Close enough to hear the soft puffs of air from her lips and see the moisture coating her inner thighs as she rode the thing hard. Her gorgeous breasts danced, her belly flexed. She panted, with soft sighs and louder moans, then she chanted. "Oh, oh, oh." Over and over.

His wife cried out, long, low, a musical sound. Her body

stiffened a moment, then shuddered and finally she dropped
bonelessly back against the bed, her hands flopping to her
sides, the vibrator still buried deep inside her, only its white
base visible now.

"Oh . . . my . . . God." Her words were just a whisper on
the warm summer air while outside, someone started a lawn
mower.

Then she raised her head, saw him, and shrieked.

The scream galvanizing him, he jumped on the bed and
slammed his hand over her mouth.

She stared, her pupils dilated to the size of stoplights.

Then Mitch reached between her legs and tugged on the vibrator, pulling it out gently, then sliding it back in as deep as it
would go. Somewhere along the way, she'd turned off the
hum. He found the little switch and flipped it back on. She
jerked, tried to wriggle away, but he took his hand from her
mouth to hold her down on the bed.

"Let me do it, baby, please."

"Mitch, what are you doing here?"

"Watching you do yourself, baby. Christ, I almost came in
my shorts. Where'd you get this thing? Spread your legs. I
want to make you come with it this time." He didn't give her
time to answer, leaning down to take one of her luscious nipples in his mouth, sucking, then biting lightly.

She arched, pulled up her legs, and her knees fell apart.
Her pussy glistened around the vibrator as he pumped. She
was so damn wet, he had to have a taste. Curling across her
abdomen, he put a hand beneath her butt to support her, then
dipped his tongue to the sweetness between her legs. Her clit
was a hard jewel, the scent of her excitement swirling around
his head.

Christ. He'd never seen such a damn beautiful sight. Her
hot pink clit, the neon purple cock, her sweet-tasting juices.

She slid her fingers beneath his shirt and stroked his back.
"Put it on rotate, too," she murmured.

He didn't get it at first, then saw the machine's buttons and
flipped the second switch.

She started to hum louder than the vibrator. "Don't stop, please don't stop. Make me come."

"You want it hard or slow?"

"Suck me hard and fuck me hard, honey. Ohhh." She ended on an exhalation as he followed her instructions to the letter.

She wasn't one to use dirty language, but her use of it now sent a hot shot straight to his cock. Sucking her clit into his mouth, he teased, backing off to tongue her, all the while driving the purple people eater deep, deeper, deepest. She bucked against his ribs, dug her fingers into his back, and started that sweet chant once more.

"Oh, Mitch." Her pelvis rose, grinding against his mouth, begging for more tongue, more teeth, more of that vibration hitting her from the inside out.

Mitch gave his wife every caress, every stroke she desired. His own cock close to bursting, his insides aching, he fed her need, drove her higher, until she crashed on the other side.

She screamed. No namby-pamby gentle cry, she opened her mouth and yelled his name loud enough for the neighbors to hear if it weren't for the wail of the lawn mower.

Then she collapsed and lay motionless beneath him. With one last pump of the vibrator and an answering shudder of her body, he pulled it out, switched it off, and tossed it to the bottom of the bed. His heart still pounded in his chest, and his balls pulsed with his own unrequited need. He turned, pulling her down off the pillows. "Suck me, baby, please. Suck me off."

He wanted her mouth on him, her moist, warm mouth, clever lips, and exquisite tongue.

She looked at him through sleepy, satisfied, heavy-lidded eyes. Then she snapped the elastic band of his boxers. "Get these things off."

He rolled off the bed, yanked his shorts to his feet, then kicked them aside.

"Mitch, you're as purple as the vibrator."

"Yeah, and I'm gonna die in a minute, so get busy, woman."

She slid to her knees on the carpet and wrapped her hand around his aching cock. Squeezing tight, she stroked him with her fist. "Mitch, I think it's bigger than usual."

"Hell, yes, I'm so horny I think I'm gonna faint. Please, Connie. Please, baby."

She licked his slit, then looked up at him. "You're salty."

"You're playing with me. Suck it, baby."

"You want to come in my mouth?"

He wanted to touch the back of her throat. He wanted to reach the sky. He wanted to shoot in her and have her suck every last drop until she'd drained him.

"Yeah, baby. In your mouth."

She swallowed him whole, one long swoop of her lips down his length. And he did shoot to the sky, his head falling back as if he'd lost his spine. He'd do anything for her, love her, make love to her, crawl around after her on his knees.

She grabbed his hips as he shoved his hands into her hair, holding her face, feeding her his essence, his being, his everything. God, how he'd missed this. How he'd missed *her*. The sweet scent of her rising to him, the warmth of her mouth, the gentle yet inexorable pressure of her lips.

"God. Oh God, you're so good." Then he held her tight, pumped in her mouth, and lost himself inside her.

She nursed him like fine champagne as he came back down, stroking light fingers over his butt, licking the last drop of come from his tip. His hands were hopelessly tangled in her hair.

"I haven't come in your mouth since we were married."

She let him loose with a soft plop. He was still semi-erect. Connie nuzzled his hip. "You could come inside me."

But there was something illicit and enticing about having her swallow for him. He dropped to his knees.

"Kiss me."

"But I just—"

"I don't care. Kiss me." He wanted to claim. He'd taken part of her, she'd taken part of him, and he wanted to share it.

She opened her mouth and kissed him, sucking his tongue

as hard and deep as she'd sucked his cock. Their separate tastes mingled and coalesced into something completely new and unique.

He didn't know how he'd stayed away from her for over two months. It seemed incomprehensible now. He rolled to his hip, hiked her up against his side, and leaned back against the bed.

"So, you never told me you got a vibrator. How long have you had it?" He wondered if she'd been using it in the afternoons for months, years. If she even needed him anymore.

"I got it today. And I was only testing it out just to make sure it worked."

He laughed, outright, doubling over. "Yeah, right."

Her skin glowed pink with embarrassment. "It's true. I can show you the packaging. It's in the bathroom." She dipped her head to his shoulder. "I thought we could use it together." After a moment, "Or you could watch me using it. I know sometimes you like me to do stuff to myself."

The sight had sent him into the outer reaches of the universe. He still hadn't completely returned. And he wouldn't, for God's sake, ask how much the thing cost. It was worth any price. Besides, she'd go ballistic again just like she had last night when he asked about the pills.

"I loved it, Connie. Especially when you didn't know I was there."

She looked up at him through her lashes. "How long were you watching?"

"A little while. What did I miss? How did you start?"

"Mitch."

"Come on, tell me." The thought of her describing it was making him hot all over again.

She pursed her lips.

He kissed the closed seam lightly. "Tell me, baby."

She shrugged, put her head to his shoulder, then her murmur vibrated against his chest. "First I tested how wet I was with my fingers."

"How wet?"

"Really, really wet." Her voice dropped to a seductive note, then her nipples peaked, and he knew he had her. She was as into describing the scenario as he was.

"Then what did you do?"

"I put it on vibrate mode and stroked my clitoris." She matched the remembered stroke with her fingers along her thigh, a tactile sensation to remind her.

"How did it feel?"

"I almost came right away. It was so different. You know, with it right in the same spot as long as I could hold it there."

"Did you come?"

"Not then. I wanted to feel what it was like inside me."

"So you spread your legs and shoved it up your pussy?" They weren't big talkers during sex, and he suddenly realized what they'd been missing all these years. His cock was hard again. "Did it feel good pumping yourself with it?"

She snuggled against him, burrowing down, her fingertip caressing his nipple. "All right, I'm going to be perfectly honest here, honey." She paused, continuing when he didn't protest. "It was fantastic."

He puffed out a breath of air. "Better than me?"

"Not better. Just . . . different. Intense, you know."

"So you're saying you don't need me?"

She tweaked his nipple. "No, silly. I heard you come in."

"You did not. I was quiet as a mouse."

"Honey, you're more like a water buffalo. Anyway, you're interrupting. I heard you, and I was going to jump up and try to hide the evidence." She tipped her head back and looked at him with sparkling eyes. "Then I thought about how it would feel if you walked in on me. It made me hot. Really hot. And wetter." She shrugged. "So I put the vibrator back in, and I let you watch." She breathed out a satisfied hum. "It was so much more extreme with you watching. I thought I was going to die."

He cupped her face. "My God. I married an exhibitionist."

"I am not."

"And you said *fuck*, too."

"I did not."

"You begged me to fuck you with the vibrator."

Connie never cursed, not that it was against her morals, but she always claimed she'd forget and use a bad word in front of the kids.

She nipped his shoulder. "I might have said it. I've never come like that in my life, Mitch. Never. Both times. And the rotate feature was really good, too."

He considered whether all this was a good thing. Then he laid it on the line with a smile. "That session was way up there, baby. Waaaay up there. Close to our best." He couldn't think of another time that was better, not even the first time.

Christ, what a concept. Orgasmic intensity and no danger of pregnancy. He loved being inside her, he'd never give it up for all time. But what they'd done this afternoon might just be the answer to relieving his balls and his anxiety. Duty, bills, and babies didn't have to stand in the way of great, hot sex.

Yeah. People got married and started thinking that sinking inside your wife's body in your own bed anytime you wanted was heaven on earth. And it was. Hell, yes, it was. But it wasn't the only way, and after ten years, maybe it lacked some of the excitement of the backseat of a car or lover's lane or the lake late at night. Not to mention when he was driving.

He hadn't felt this good in three years. Three long years. Life was looking up. Connie hadn't mentioned having a baby once. Hell, life was damn near perfect.

FOUR

CONNIE FLOATED IN orgasmic nirvana. He'd called her baby. He hadn't called her that during lovemaking in forever. She wanted him to say it again and again. Baby.

"Oh my God." Her baby! She grabbed Mitch's arm and twisted his wrist to look at his watch. "Rina."

Mitch patted her bare bottom, then hoisted her up. "I'll clean up in here while you get dressed."

She gazed down at him. He wore his T-shirt, but his lower half was nude. He still had an erection. And she was still hot, ready to go at him again. She'd like nothing more than to climb onto his lap and ride him right there on the carpet.

"That was wonderful, Mitch. Thank you." He'd wanted her. He'd loved it. He'd shouted when he came. All for her. Maybe it was pathetic, but she felt happy and sated and loved.

"My pleasure, baby." He leaned across the bed and grabbed the vibrator. "Do I have to worry about you becoming addicted to this thing?"

She wasn't the least embarrassed by what they'd done, though at first she'd pretended for his sake. But no, when she'd felt his eyes on her, when he took his penis in his hand, pumping as he watched her on the bed, nope, there wasn't an embarrassed atom in her body. Tipping her head, she gave him what she hoped was a sexy little moue.

"I don't know, honey. I'll try to be good, but you just might walk in on me again accidentally."

"I might have to come home early every day."

Ooh, yes, please. "Why *are* you home early?"

He put a hand on the bed and pushed himself to his feet, then padded barefoot into the bathroom to run the vibrator under the tap. "We were clearing those stumps from yesterday, and we got done early."

"I guess that was a lucky break."

"Yeah."

Lucky for both of them. More than lucky. Serendipitous. Maybe even prophetic.

Connie stepped into her panties and pulled her dress over her head. She ached in unfamiliar places, but her muscles felt languid, relaxed, mellow. She felt marvelous. In fact, life was marvelous. Mitch wanted her again. Everything was fixed. Pretty soon he'd be begging to give her another baby, and they'd all be one big happy family like they used to be.

"MOM, TOMMY WANTS me to spend the night tomorrow night."

"Mrs. Daigel didn't say anything to me when she dropped you off this afternoon."

Peter scooped his baseball cards off the coffee table and into the tin his grandma brought him from the Coca-Cola museum in Atlanta. "She said it was okay. You could call her, Mom."

Connie glanced at Mitch over the rim of her coffee mug. Seated on the other end of the couch, he was looking at her, intently, his head slightly lowered, his eyes in shadows.

"Can I watch *Nemo*, Mommy?" Rina had crawled underneath the coffee table from the other side and now lay on her stomach, peering up, her chin propped on her hands.

"Mom, I'm tired of *Nemo*. Can't we watch *Shark Tale*?"

The last five minutes of the six o'clock news petered out on the TV. Mitch loved his evening news, but he wasn't watching, not now, not for the first twenty-five minutes.

He watched her. It set her nerves on edge, making her jittery and overheated and terribly excited.

"Why don't you ask your Dad what he wants to watch?" Connie ruffled Rina's hair as she leaned forward to peruse the grocery flyers for weekly specials. Tomorrow was shopping day. She only went to three grocery stores, that was all. If she couldn't get it on special, they didn't get it. She finished up at the grocery outlet over on the highway, which didn't carry name brands but probably saved at least fifty dollars per trip.

Mitch should be glad.

"Daddy, you want to watch *Nemo*, don't you?"

"Dad, remember how you said you hated *Nemo*."

"Peter, you know I didn't say I hated *Nemo*." Mitch slyly glanced at her. "And I think your mother already knows exactly what I want to watch."

Her. With her vibrator. That was his sly little message. She met his gaze. He was so bad, and so kissable with that quirk at the side of his mouth and the slow burn in his eyes.

"What does Daddy want to watch?" Rina tugged on Connie.

He was going to be in so much trouble for making sexual innuendoes in front of the children. She eyed him, sending him that clear message. He simply smiled.

"Daddy wants to watch *The Parent Trap*."

Peter whined. "*The Parent Trap*. It's old."

"Yes, but your father likes to watch it because it's about a very bad daddy who gets punished by the mom and turns over a new leaf. It's a very good moral, Peter." She gave her husband the evil eye over her son's shoulder.

Mitch just smiled, promising retribution with the look in his eye. Retribution she was sure she was going to like.

"I think we should watch *The Incredibles*," Peter went on.

"Mom, you never said whether I could spend the night at Tommy's."

Kids. They never forgot a thing. You could distract them for a few minutes, but they'd come back to it eventually.

"If Peter gets a slumber party, I get a slumber party, too," Rina whined.

Mitch leaned his head back against the sofa and clasped his hands over his belly, his feet spread wide along the coffee table. "Yeah, Mom, if Peter gets a slumber party, Rina should get one, too."

He was soooo bad. He wanted a slumber party to get both kids out of the house so he could have his wicked way with her. She really, really wished she'd picked up those handcuffs.

"Your father is being funny, Rina. Petey, I'll call Mrs. Daigel, and if it's all right with her, then it's okay with me."

School would be starting again soon, and it was good for Peter to get all his playtime done before the homework season came around.

"You better not be joshing me that she suggested it."

"I'm not, Mom."

She went into the kitchen to make the call. Mitch kept making those eyes at her, egging her on in her plan to get rid of her children tomorrow night, and Peter would be making moaning noises and pleading sounds to get what he wanted. Come to think of it, he'd learned that from his father. In five minutes, the arrangements were made.

"She says okay."

Mitch clapped his hands along with Peter. "I bet Nana would want you to have a slumber party at her house, Rina. What do you think?"

"Mitch. You need to call your mom first before you make promises." There was no way Evelyn would turn him down. She loved her grandchildren to distraction.

Mitch picked up the handheld, dialed, and handed the phone to Rina. "Ask Nana if you can stay with her tomorrow night."

Standing behind the couch, Connie whapped him lightly on the back of the head. My, it felt wonderful. Like the early years of their marriage when they'd conspired together to get some hot monkey sex time where they didn't have to worry about making too much noise or waking the kids.

She'd have plenty of time tomorrow to make it over to Saint Lucia to pick up the handcuffs.

"Nana says it's okay, but she wants to talk to you." Rina held out the phone to Connie.

"Give it to your father."

Rina toddled over and Mitch leaned closer for the phone.

"No, Mom, nothing's wrong." He glanced up at Connie. "We're gonna go out for dinner or something." Pause, smile. "Yeah, something like that, Mom." Then after one last pause, he nodded. "Sure thing," then hung up.

Connie raised an eyebrow. "So, we're going out for dinner."

He cocked her a wry smile. "Or something."

He got off the couch, crouched in front of the video shelf, pulled out *The Incredibles*, and handed it to Peter. "An hour and a half, kiddo, then it's bedtime." He reached down, picked Rina up, threw her high in the air, then settled on the couch once more, tucking her close under his arm. Peter sprawled out on the carpet in front of the TV. Mitch waggled his fingers at Connie.

"Come on, honey. Sit down here right next to me, and I'll tell you all about dinner. Or something."

That devious smile meant he was planning something big. The man had too many white teeth when he smiled like that.

She knew she was going to love whatever idea was sprouting in his predatory mind.

HE WANTED CONNIE badly. The hour and a half movie would surely kill him. But he'd wait. Patiently. Until he could get his hands on her again. He had an idea for a nice surprise, something they hadn't done in years.

Damn. A miracle had occurred. He was thinking more about sex than worrying about money.

MITCH GOT UP halfway through the movie to take a shower, though Peter vocally marveled that he could tear himself away from the excitement of *The Incredibles*. Then, once the movie was over, Mitch picked up a sleepy Rina in his arms.

"It's all right, sweetheart." He gave Connie an exaggerated smile, all teeth. "I'll put the kids to bed, while you get all nice and ready for bed." He pecked her on the cheek. "You just take as much time as you need, honey-bunch."

She was giggling like a newlywed as she kissed Rina and Peter, then Mitch sent her off with a pat on the butt.

She soaped and cleansed and lotioned and felt all fluttery inside. Like a teenager on her first date. Or a woman who hadn't seen her husband in a month. Giddy. It was the most wonderful feeling she'd had in months. Years.

She was almost done when she heard Mitch come in. "Did you leave Rina's door open and the hall light on?"

"Yes, darling." The door shut, followed by the soft snick of the lock. "I kissed them twice, one for you, one for me."

He was saccharine sweet enough to smack. Connie looked at herself in the bathroom mirror. Her hair shone, her skin glowed, and her eyes sparkled. She bit down on her lip until it plumped, giving her the hot, sultry look of a seductress.

She topped it all with a short satin nightgown held up only by a pair of thin straps.

She flipped off the bathroom light to find Mitch sprawled in the middle of their bed. Naked. Stroking himself.

"*What* are you doing?"

He was long and hard, and the tip of his penis glistened. He took her breath away. The boyish, mischievous grin on his face belied the size and obvious excitement of his beautiful, gorgeous, wonderfully hard penis.

"I fixed the toilet while you were picking up Rina this afternoon. Did you notice?"

She stepped backward into the bathroom, cocked her head to listen. Sure enough, it wasn't running anymore. She'd been too excited to notice.

"That was very sweet of you, honey."

"Yeah. I'm really sweet. You *could* pay me back, you know." He puckered his lips, then added, "If you want to."

It was so like the first days of their marriage when she paid him in sexual favors. The longer the chore took, the bigger the prize. There were days when the house had been immaculate without a single nagging word to get things fixed, days they couldn't get enough of each other.

"What's it worth to you?"

"A blow job. It was a reeeally hard project."

"How hard?"

He stroked himself faster, making sure she could almost feel the flesh in his hand. "Very, very hard, baby."

She shrugged. "I don't know. I gave you a blow job this afternoon." She couldn't wait to get her lips around him again. She couldn't wait to feel his head buried between her legs. The game heightened the anticipation.

"Yeah, but you had two orgasms and I only had one, so I need to catch up. Come on, baby." He pumped himself twice. "For all the hard work on the toilet."

She knelt, one knee on the bed, leaning down to place her hand over his. Curling her fingers, she let them close over his crown, working the small drop of come that appeared.

"That feels so good." Mitch's eyes glittered in the soft light of her vanity lamp, its yellow glow bathing his legs, casting the long shadow of his penis across his belly.

Sometimes she forgot how truly magnificent he was. Long, hard days of strenuous outdoor work kept his muscles toned and his skin bronzed. He was tougher, harder, and infinitely more virile than the day she married him.

She lifted one leg to straddle him, intent on working his penis with her hand for a little while.

Mitch grabbed her before she could settle, turning her to

face the brass rails at the end of the bed. "This way." He ran his hands over her butt, pushing her nightie to her waist.

She wasn't wearing a stitch beneath the satin. He planted a kiss on her right butt cheek. Ooh. She had a glimmer of his plan. They hadn't done *that* in long a time, pleasured each other simultaneously with their mouths.

Leaning forward, she stretched across his hips, reaching down his legs to caress the springy male hair on his calves. He rose, gently stroking his penis against her abdomen. Then she pushed back, giving him a home between her breasts. She rubbed, teasing his penis and peaking her nipples.

Mitch caressed the globes of her butt, then licked the outer lips of her pussy. "Ba-by," he called softly, "suck me."

Connie rose to her elbows, dipped down, and sucked just the tip into her mouth. His salty taste and soapy scent tantalized her. It had been so long since they took the time to fully excite, to explore with long minutes of exquisite foreplay. He reached between them to cup her breasts, then pinch her nipples. Heat streaked down to the spot where his warm breath bathed her. She took him then, all of him, humming her pleasure.

His hips rose, thrusting against her. "Oh, yeah, baby."

She sucked hard all the way back up his penis, licked the slit, then lunged back down until her lips met her hand firmly gripping his base. He'd always loved the dual action, her hand combined with her mouth, her lips, her tongue. He'd taught her how to please him. She'd taught him how to drive her wild.

As if he could read her thoughts, he slid a finger inside her, matching the rhythm of her mouth on him. She bumped and ground against the sweet invasion, sucking him deeper with each thrust of his finger. Oh God, oh God. He put his mouth on her, sucking her clitoris, then stroking his tongue inside her.

She could barely keep him in her mouth, barely force herself to move on him, her body wanting to orgasm, pulsing with need. Her legs and arms felt weak enough to collapse.

"Mitch, please, I can't." She couldn't do both, couldn't

suck him and let him take her this way, the sensations were too intense. "Please, I need you inside me." She wanted it so badly, her belly ached.

When she tried to wriggle away from him, his hands clamped down on her hips and held her fast. "I want to come in your mouth when you come in mine, baby. I'll do all the work, just open your mouth. Let me in, baby." Then he hit her again, flicking her clitoris with his tongue until she knew she couldn't do anything else but explode all over him.

Bracing herself on the bed, she went down on him all the way, until he touched the back of her throat. Then he took over, just as he promised, pumping her pussy as if he were buried deep inside her. Almost as if she weren't in control of her own body, her hips pressed against his mouth. She quivered, shuddered, then heat jetted straight to her center, and if he hadn't been filling her mouth, she would have screamed. She bore down as he shot her to orgasm, taking every lap he gave, flying high with it, exploding from the inside out while he pumped his hips frantically against her mouth.

When they came, they did it together, each filling the other, each taking the other.

She couldn't remember falling, but when she opened her eyes, she'd crumpled across his legs. He stroked her thighs gently.

"That was incredible, baby," he whispered.

"Oh my God, the kids probably heard us." Her voice was muffled against his hip.

"We were very quiet."

Yeah, right. She'd come like Fourth of July fireworks.

Mitch rolled her to her side, then shifted, crawling around to lay his head down next to hers. "That was so fucking incredible, Connie."

Her limbs incapable of movement, the only thing she could manage was a smile. "Ya think?"

He pushed the hair back from her face. "I think I sort of forgot how good it was between us."

She opened her eyes and fell head over heels for him all over again. "I love you, Mitch."

He kissed the tip of her nose, her eyelids, her forehead. "I love you, baby. I promise I won't let us drift apart again."

Now was the time. Ask about the baby. Beg. He couldn't turn her down now. He wouldn't. But she couldn't open her mouth. Her body felt tender, achy, worked over, exhausted. Somehow the words between them felt equally fragile. She was terrified to ask about the baby, terrified to lose the sweetness between them.

Tomorrow. She'd ask tomorrow night, when the kids were gone, when he was all hers for the night.

FOR THE FIRST time in God knew how many years, Connie fell asleep in his arms. It was so damn sweet, his eyeballs felt achy. He held her close, lightly stroking her bare arm, her sweet shampoo tickling his nose as her breathing fell into the rhythm of sleep.

He'd wanted to be inside her so badly his balls had throbbed. But what they'd done was better. She'd come hard, bucking against his mouth, gushing her pleasure, wrenching his orgasm from him.

What could have been better? Mitch closed his eyes. Being inside her. Watching her face as she came. Swallowing her cries.

It might have been better. But it wouldn't have been safer. He'd come so hard, surely he would have gotten her pregnant if she'd forgotten a pill.

Yet he'd promised her he wouldn't let them drift apart again. He meant to keep that promise. There'd be lots of loving in the household from now on. But hell, it couldn't all be mouths and hands. Christ, he didn't want only that. He wanted to bury himself deep inside her.

There was only one thing he could do. He needed to assure himself she took her pill by checking every day that another one was gone. Yeah. That's what he'd do. Connie would never know.

The next morning, though he felt low and sneaky, he examined Connie's pill pack while she fixed breakfast. One more pill was missing since yesterday morning. She'd taken it. Thank God. He could stop worrying.

At least for today.

FIVE

EVELYN COULDN'T TAKE Rina until three o'clock. Connie felt like she was rushing all day, but she knew exactly what was making her flustered. She wanted to get to that shop in Saint Lucia, and she sure couldn't take Rina with her.

She just had to get there. Handcuffs. Blindfolds. Sex toys. She wanted everything she did tonight with Mitch to be new and special. Off the wall. She wanted him to know she was willing to try *anything* he wanted. She'd even ask what he wanted her to buy for the next time. She'd felt shivery and weak all day, butterflies in her stomach. Like the first time he'd asked her out. She remembered it so clearly. She was eighteen, working at Foster's Freeze, and he always came to her window. She'd stutter and stammer and get his order wrong every time, but God, she'd felt so alive, so excited, every moment with him etched in her mind. There was nothing like being young and in love.

They could get that feeling back. They could keep it. She knew they could. Mitch wanted it as badly as she did.

She'd dropped Peter at the Daigels, done the grocery shopping, gotten Rina an ice cream, managed three loads of laundry, and if she was lucky, she could finish it all before Mitch got home. She'd left one load going in the dryer, and put the last one in the washer just before leaving to drop Rina off at the office. Evelyn would take her from there.

Rina wanted to roll her own bag into the office like a big girl. Connie could barely restrain herself, wanting to rush her little girl. Her baby was so cute, struggling to keep the bag upright, though really, it was nothing more than a backpack on wheels. She stuck her tongue between her teeth, her brow furrowed in concentration, reminding Connie of Mitch. He got that exact same brow pucker when he was thinking too hard.

"I'll help you, sweetie."

"I can do it." And Rina did, valiantly making it up the small set of steps while Connie held the door open for her.

Goodness, she was getting so big. In a few short weeks, she'd start first grade, gone every day, then before Connie knew it, she'd be in junior high, then high school. They grew up so fast. For a moment, her heart ached for another child, another little girl who would look just like Rina.

Soon. She'd convince Mitch very soon.

"How's my baby?" Evelyn held her arms open.

Rina dropped her backpack, rushing into her grandmother's big hug. "I'm not a baby, Nana."

Connie set the backpack on its rollers. "She's a big girl, Nana. She was just telling me that."

"I'm sorry. Of course you're a big girl. Do big girls still like homemade cookies?"

Rina bounced excitedly in her pink princess tennies. "Yes, Nana, big girls love cookies."

As Evelyn described all the different kinds of cookies they could make together, Connie edged toward the door. The blinds rattled as she grabbed the knob.

Evelyn looked up. "Heavens, girl, what bee have you got in your bonnet?"

"Nothing, Evelyn, gotta run. Give Mommy a kiss, sweetie." She bent down to give Rina a big hug. "And be good for Nana."

Evelyn waggled her eyebrows. "I see there's been some improvements in the household since the other day at Taylor's."

Big improvements. She smiled brightly, a laugh escaping her lips. "Everything's great, Evelyn."

"Then go. Rina and I will be fine." She shooed Connie out.

She drove too fast, she knew, but she made her purchases—gosh, how could handcuffs and a blindfold be that expensive?—and was back home before four o'clock.

Mitch's truck was already in the drive. She'd wanted to finish the laundry, and she didn't want him to see what she'd bought until she took it out of the bag tonight, when she already had him so hot, he'd be willing to do anything to get inside her.

Okay. Revised plan. She'd leave the bag in the car, then sneak back out to get it while he showered. Or something. She'd find some way to surprise him with her little bag of goodies.

MITCH HUNG ON to his temper with a thin cord of sanity. But dammit, how the hell could Connie go out and leave the freaking washing machine unmonitored? When he got home, water had been gushing out from beneath the back door. If she'd been home, she could have pulled the plug on the damn thing.

If, if, if. If he'd taken the washer apart. If he'd replaced it months ago when it first showed signs of a drainage problem. Shit.

He'd used a broom to sweep most of it out the back door, but it had still seeped beneath the linoleum. He'd probably have to tear the whole lot up and replace the floorboards so rot didn't set in. Okay, that was worst case. But dammit.

Out front, a car door slammed. She was home.

He wouldn't get pissed. He would not get pissed or yell at her. He would not ruin the evening they'd planned. He wouldn't ruin what had happened between them yesterday or last night. He'd made a promise, and he'd keep it. He wouldn't let them drift apart by starting the fights all over again.

He was sopping up the last of the water when he heard her on the back step. He wrung out the towel in the sink.

"What happened?"

He didn't turn around as he spoke. "The washing machine backed up and overflowed all over the floor."

"Did it at least finish the rinse cycle?"

Neither spoke. Mitch looked at her. Connie looked at him.

She wouldn't get mad. She would not. If he'd taken a look at the washing machine when she first told him it was starting to act freaky. If he'd bought a new one. If he'd done *something*. She wouldn't let him make her feel guilty.

All right, she shouldn't have left it running while she was out. But she'd had things to do. Didn't he know how busy she was? Running here, running there, three grocery stores so she could hit all the sales instead of saving time by buying what they needed at one store. She did her best to scrimp and save on every purchase. For *him*. To make *him* feel better. Which he never appreciated. He treated her like a child, as if she was incapable of managing the family budget or making necessary spending decisions on her own.

He would freak at her credit card bill when he saw how much she'd spent on the vibrator, the handcuffs, and the blindfold. He wouldn't even notice how much she saved on groceries and looking for the cheapest gas. Not to mention the fact that she'd *made* her bridesmaid dress instead of buying some humongously priced getup she'd never wear again.

She would not get mad. She'd be an adult and admit her mistake, then when he blew a gasket, the fight would be his fault because *she* had been calm.

"I'm sorry. I shouldn't have left until it was done."

That really cost her a lot to say. He better figure out just how much or she would lose it despite her best intentions.

He drew a deep breath, then relaxed his shoulders. "I should have fiddled with it yesterday instead of the toilet."

What? Mitch admitting he might have been wrong? She knew better than to say *that*.

"No, no, you did a wonderful job on the toilet. I should

have told you I wanted to do laundry today, and you would have looked at the washer instead of the toilet."

God, they sounded like polite strangers. *No, it's my fault. No, no, I beg your pardon, it's my fault.* It might actually be worse than fighting. She just knew what it meant for their evening. It was ruined, all ruined. They'd sit on separate ends of the couch. They'd politely ask what the other wanted to watch on TV. Mitch would probably even do the dishes for her. But on the inside, he'd be pissed, seething with passive-aggressive male bullshit. Popping his antacids and extra-strength aspirins. And by bedtime, they'd be screaming at each other like they always did these last few months.

Her breath came a little faster, and she could feel her heart beating harder in her chest. She wanted to cry. One day, they'd had one good day, now this. Why did the crummy washer have to give out today instead of next week?

The tense silence pounded at her eardrums.

"It's okay, baby."

Baby? He was still calling her baby?

She didn't realize she was standing with her eyes squeezed shut until she opened them. He was above her on the top step, his face in shadow, his startling brown gaze liquid and warm. The sun was hot on the top of her head and bright in her eyes.

"Aren't you going to yell?" She spoke as softly as he had.

"I promised I wouldn't."

"You did?"

"Yeah, last night."

He'd said he loved her. She remembered that. But he'd said that before and it didn't mean they hadn't gotten into the next fight. What else had he said? She couldn't remember beyond that incredible mutual orgasm they'd shared.

"Let's get some Chinese for dinner."

He wasn't going to yell at her and he was springing for Chinese food? She wouldn't look a gift horse in the mouth.

"I just have to fold the load in the dryer and put the other load in so it doesn't sit around wet."

He flipped the washer lid open. "It did get through the spin cycle. You go powder your nose, and I'll take care of the rest of the laundry."

Ha. She'd have to refold everything he folded. But she didn't care. He'd offered, and he was taking her out for dinner. Things weren't so bad. In fact, they were good, really good. "Okay, honey."

As she sidled by him, he trailed his fingers down her arm. "I love you, Connie."

She stopped, looked at him, searching for a flicker of insincerity in his too hot eyes. And found none.

This was getting too good. Almost too good to be true.

HE WAS MASTERFUL. He hadn't gotten angry. He'd even folded laundry. She was putty in his hands. She'd do anything he asked. Mitch was ecstatic. He should have learned years ago that arguing didn't turn Connie into a yes-woman.

They didn't need a quarrel to incite them to great heights. Yesterday was hotter than any damn make-up sex they'd ever had. And Connie had gone out to dinner without any panties. She'd told him that over the moo shu and almost blown off the top of his head.

He helped her up on to the big bench seat of his truck, then went around to climb behind the wheel. They'd lingered over the Chinese, and the sun was just going down.

Now they had all night to enjoy dessert. Lots and lots of oral delight.

OH BOY OH boy oh boy. Life could not get better, not one single bit better. Well, except if she were pregnant and in her fourth month after she'd gotten over the sickness but was horny as all get out every minute of every day. That's how she'd been with both Rina and Peter. She'd wanted Mitch *all* the time. Well, at least until she felt like a fat, bloated cow.

"You go inside, honey," she urged sweetly once they were home. "I need to get something out of the car."

"What?"

"Never you mind. It's a surprise."

Mitch backed off, then called from the front door. "It better be good."

"Oh, it will be."

Would he let her cuff him? Nine years of marriage and the truth was, she didn't know. A few years ago, she'd have said yes, but now, she wasn't so sure. Sometimes his reactions threw her off. Like his whole money thing. She knew Lou's death had made it worse, but she didn't know how to undo the damage.

She wouldn't think about that now. Diving down beneath the junk in the backseat of the car, she pulled out the special flowered bag, heavy in her grasp.

Inside, Mitch leaned against the kitchen doorjamb, two wineglasses in one hand, an open bottle of wine in the other.

"What ya got there, baby?" He pointed with the wineglasses at the bag clutched to her chest.

She wagged a finger. "It's a surprise. You can't come into the bedroom until I call you."

Holding the stems between his fingers, he poured two glasses of wine, then held one out. "Five minutes is all I can wait."

His eyes blazed. The way he'd looked at her when she told him she wasn't wearing panties had kept her moist all evening. On the drive home, she'd barely managed not to reach over and unzip his pants. Now, she'd get to do anything she wanted, and her whole body throbbed with anticipation.

Mitch wanted her, *really* wanted her, not just a hey-do-you-feel-like-doing-it-tonight want, but an I'm-gonna-die-if-I-don't-have-you need. Married women all over the world could comprehend exactly how wonderful and powerful that felt.

She smacked him lip to lip, grabbed her glass of wine, then scurried down the hall to prepare the bedroom. After fiddling with the first handcuff, she got the hang of it and had the other three on the brass rails in no time. The fuzzy blue fake fur clashed with her flower-print bedspread, but she didn't care. Oddly enough, the lined cuffs were cheaper than the brand preferred by cops. Of course, she could have gotten the leather cuffs which were lined with real lambskin, but Mitch definitely would have pitched a fit over how much they cost.

Ooh, bad thought, Mitch castigation was not allowed tonight.

She laid out the blindfold, which was really just an eye covering like you'd wear on planes to cut out the light, across the pillow. She didn't need scented candles, vases of flowers, sexy lingerie, bubble baths, or romantic words. She just needed him to want her again. She needed his excitement. The stage set, she called out, "Honey, I'm ready."

Oh boy, was she ready. First, she'd cuff him, then lick his nipples, because he said it tickled when she sucked them. Normally he wouldn't let her do that for very long, but this time she'd do it for as long as she wanted. Then she'd climb on top to ride him. At her own pace, fast or slow, well, she liked to start out slow, then fast. Usually, Mitch let her do it for a while, but in the end, he'd flip her over onto her back and pound. Which was nice, very nice, but . . . she wanted to be in control.

His footsteps stopped in the doorway. When she turned, he stood, feet spread, the wineglass hanging heedlessly in his fingers. Then he raised it to his lips and sipped, his gaze on the handcuffs at each post on the bed.

"What would my mom say if she knew you were into bondage?"

Connie smiled. "She suggested them."

His eyes went wide for a moment, then one side of his mouth quirked. "Liar." He winked. "I like that you thought it up all on your own."

He hadn't said a word about the money she'd spent.

"Take off your clothes and get on the bed," she ordered.

He twirled the glass in his hand, looked from the cuffs, to her, to the blindfold, then back to the cuffs. "I think you'd look better in fuzzy blue."

She shook her head. "No. They're for you. You can use them on me later."

He toed off his shoes, left them in the doorway, then sauntered to the end of the bed and focused on the coverlet as if something lay on it.

"You know what I see in my mind's eye?"

"No."

"I see you. Blindfolded. Naked. Spread-eagle." He leaned forward, one hand on the brass stead.

Her heart raced. She could see it, too. She could feel his words as if he were touching her as he spoke.

"I see your pretty pink pussy. It is so beautiful and so wet. It's begging me to kiss it. Lick it. Suck it."

He turned slowly, capturing her gaze with his. She saw her own reflection in his eyes, felt her breath trying to push past her throat, and tingled with a thrill that drenched her pussy.

"And when you start to come, I'm going to hold you down. I'm going to lick you until you can't help but scream, until it's so freaking intense that tears come to your eyes, until you think one more second and you'll die from the pleasure. And then I'll lick you some more."

Her mouth had gone dry. It hurt to swallow. She didn't recognize the huskiness of his voice or the heat in his eyes, as if another man had taken his place, as if she were the most important thing in the world to him. As if he wanted this so badly, he'd sacrifice anything to have it.

Connie couldn't have done a thing to resist him.

SIX

WITHOUT ANOTHER WORD, he reached out and slid one spaghetti strap down her arm. All she wore was the thin cotton dress, no panties, no bra. He pushed the other strap off her shoulder. The bodice caught on her breasts, her almost painfully hard nipples. Eyes locked with hers, he put one finger in the center of the neckline and tugged the dress down.

Hot, breathless, wet, achy, she felt as if his gaze consumed her. This was brand new, as if they were first-time lovers when the heat and the need were all fresh and untried. When she couldn't wait for his touch or the sound of his voice. When she'd go mad if he didn't take her right this minute.

The dress fell past her breasts. His finger continued the trail across her abdomen, but with the zipper fastened, the material wouldn't go over her hips. And still he gazed at her.

Tipping the wineglass to her lips, he let her sip the sweet wine, then he whispered a command. "Undo it."

She couldn't help herself. The wine went to her head. She unzipped because he told her to, then pushed the dress past her hips, letting it flutter to the carpet.

"Get on the bed."

She wanted, needed, to do whatever he said. She climbed onto the bed, hands and knees first, her bottom facing him. Then she flopped to her side, turned, and looked at him.

"Now lay down and spread your legs and arms." With a touch, he directed her to lay width-wise, so the bedstead didn't obstruct his view of her.

She'd wanted to tie him down, yet his voice mesmerized her, his eyes tawny like a lion, heated, powerful. He managed to find the one thing she'd thought about in the shop, being forced to accept the pleasure, not being able to get away, the intensity almost unbearable. Allowing him control over when she came, how hard she came, for how long.

He set his wine on the bedside table, then secured her leg in the first handcuff. Trailing fingers along her skin, wherever he could reach, he repeated the procedure with feet and hands until she was restrained and spread for his eyes alone. Standing behind her, he leaned over, kissing her upside down.

"You are so beautiful," he whispered, "and you're all mine."

Her heart tripped. She'd wanted this for so long, the words, the need. She'd wanted it, yet she'd forgotten how it made her soar, how it eclipsed every other thought in her head.

He padded once more around the bed, returning to the place he'd started. His gaze fixed on the triangle between her legs, he popped the buttons on his shirt and dropped his jeans. His penis jutted, a greedy length.

He climbed between her legs, reaching for the blindfold.

"No. I want to watch."

He shook his head slowly, dipping down to kiss, lick, then suck her nipple into his mouth. "You bought it, must mean you want it, so we're using it."

He slipped the elastic band behind her head and fit the material to her eyes. His chest flattened to hers, and he fiddled a moment with the bottom of the covering, making sure for himself that she couldn't see from beneath.

"I'd turn out the lights, but *I* want to see. Everything."

He slid down her body, trailing his tongue over her breasts, dipping into her belly button. Without sight, the sensations were all fresh, acute. His lips were softer, his tongue warmer, the pads of his fingers rougher. His scent, intensely male, intoxicated her, filling her head like a drugging incense. He turned his face, and his hair brushed her belly, the feeling electrifying. How many times had she run her hands through his hair, yet never had she felt each individual strand like this or savored its thick softness. The lack of sight intensified everything, made each single stroke the center of her universe.

He parted her folds and blew lightly. Her body arched. Her whole being became her throbbing clitoris.

"Mitch, please."

He prodded her with the stiffened tip of his tongue, then delved down to lap straight up inside her.

"Jesus, baby, you are so wet."

"I got turned on thinking about sucking you."

He followed up his tongue action with two fingers. "I like that sucking me makes you hot. Licking you is about to make my balls explode."

She wriggled as much as the cuffs would allow. They weren't tight, but she couldn't bring her legs together nor find the leverage to push her hips off the bed.

"Stop talking, please."

"Whatever you want, baby," he whispered, then assaulted her clitoris as if it were quarry he had to subdue. Fast, sharp licks, then a suck, followed by a slow swirl that quivered along every nerve ending, from the bud of her clitoris to each square inch of her skin. He set her on fire inside and out. She moaned, letting him know his effect. She was so wet and hot, moisture trickled down to the bedspread.

"Please don't stop, please don't stop." She panted, tossing her head on the bed. Spirals of near violent pleasure shot out and back. "Oh God, I'm going to come, I'm coming."

He slid down to lick her opening, and the force fled, the orgasm retreating.

She raised her head as if she could see him. "What are you doing? I was almost there."

He chuckled. "I know. But you weren't ready yet."

"I was, too. I was more than ready."

She felt him shake his head, his faintly stubbled cheeks caressing her inner thighs. "You weren't screaming and begging."

"Do it again, I'll beg, I promise."

Blowing on her, he started the whole thing over again, pushing her higher and higher, forcing a fast pant from her, until finally she keened for the come.

He pulled back again, this time nipping her thigh.

"*What* are you doing?"

He gave her that all-knowing chuckle again. "It can be better, baby, I know it can. Just be patient."

"Please, Mitch, let me come." There, she was begging.

He squeezed her thighs. Her skin felt near to bursting, on fire with his touch. She wriggled, presenting him with her so-called beautiful pussy and showing how needy it was, how needy *she* was.

"Please, Mitchie."

He didn't, he wouldn't, torturing her, shoving her to the precipice, holding her a moment away from orgasm. Beneath the mask, her eyes teared with need, she begged and pleaded, yet he kept her on the razor-sharp edge until she was delirious.

"Please, please, please, oh God, oh God, oh God." Her mind whirled, her thoughts, her feelings, everything centered on his tongue and her clitoris and the screaming, aching need. Flailing her arms and legs as far as the cuffs would allow, the chant pounded inside her head. She would implode. Cease to exist.

"Pleeeeease." A long wail escaped her lips, fell into the night, surrounding them both.

Mitch sucked her clit into his mouth, flashed his tongue over the hard bead, then stabbed the hot flesh repeatedly.

She went off like Mount Saint Helens, bucking and heaving. He held onto her hips, keeping her on the knife edge of orgasm, making her ride long and hard. He held her when she fought him, when the pleasure was at its peak, its intensity near painful, when she was no longer inside her own body. When everything centered on the orgasm. When she'd do anything for him.

He knew the feeling exactly. When he was inside her, when his mind existed only for her, only to come in her. He needed that now more than he'd ever needed anything. He needed her.

Without giving her time to come down off the high, he slid up her body, ripped the mask from her face, and drove inside her. Her dazed and glassy gaze didn't even focus on him. But her body took him, rippled beneath him, shot close to orgasm once more as he ground against her and inside her. She milked him with her muscles, caressing his cock as he thrust.

"Kiss me, baby." He wished now he'd removed the handcuffs. He wanted her wrapped around him, all of her, arms, legs, pussy. Taking her mouth, he ravished her lips, ravaged her body, and staked his claim far more thoroughly than any mere protestations of love could do. Then he lost himself in a violent, shattering orgasm that turned him senseless to anything but the feel of her body, the taste of her tongue, and the scent of her release.

HE LAY BETWEEN her legs, his weight pinning her to the bed. Mitch rolled to the side.

"I'm sorry, baby."

Connie's chest rose, dragging in the air he'd denied her.

"Are your wrists all right?" He glanced at her restraints. She'd fought them, hard. Hopefully the fuzzy blue material saved her from slicing flesh on the metal.

She turned her head, slowly, as if returning from a long distance. Closing her eyes, she rested a moment, filled herself with another deep breath, then gazed at him. "I can't feel them. I can't feel anything. I think I died and went to heaven."

"Me, too, baby."

"Mitchie, that was the best."

She called him that in extreme moments. Or when she wanted to piss him off. It was a testament to how profound the loving had been. For the life of him, he couldn't remember a moment better than when he'd flooded her with his essence, his soul.

Powerful and elemental enough to make a baby. Part of him soared, praying he'd given her that in the most spectacular moment of their marriage.

Another part trembled with fear. Jesus, what had he done?

He slid off the bed, unable to face her, unable to let her see the panic in his eyes or the tension suddenly riding his face.

"I better undo you. Are you sure I didn't pull too hard on your arms or legs?"

"You were right. That was better than if I tied you down."

The moment she came would live in his body, a tactile memory, for the rest of his days. No matter what happened. Her pleasure had brought him to the edge of reason. He could have done nothing beyond burying himself inside her. He couldn't have fought the need if he'd tried.

It was only now that his gut began its relentless trembling, when he realized what he might have done to their lives. Another baby, another mouth, another responsibility he couldn't face.

Four depending on him.

Had she taken her pill today? He'd checked this morning, but he couldn't remember the count. He had the overwhelming urge to check again, to assure himself. Would she remember tomorrow? Or the next day? Could he take care of them all?

His head spun. From heaven to hell in sixty seconds.

He undid the handcuffs, kissing each slightly reddened spot, then reverently setting her limbs upon the bed.

"I love you, Mitch. We're going to be fine. Aren't we?"

"Yeah, Connie, we are." But he couldn't look at her. He felt lower than low. He didn't know how the hell he would keep her and the kids safe. For now, he concentrated on her body, caressing her skin. "I do love you." Despite his fears, he'd never questioned that.

She sighed, a heavy, exhausted sound. "Cuddle me to sleep?"

It wasn't long past nine, but he was bone weary. Bodily sated. He pulled back the sheet, helped her crawl beneath, then climbed in and pulled her flush against his body. She was warm, pliable, and scented with loving.

"Thank you, honey." She said the words on no more than a sigh, then her breathing slowed and her body relaxed into his.

"You don't have to thank me," he whispered. "It's what I should have been doing all along." Making sure she felt loved and wanted and needed.

He just didn't know how he was going to keep her safe and satisfied at the same time. He didn't know how he was going to keep her happy without worrying himself into an early grave.

CONNIE ROLLED OVER in bed, stretching her muscles. She ached pleasantly, feeling every creak and groan. Oh, oh, that was wonderful. Without opening her eyes, she wriggled deliciously, then flopped over onto her stomach.

Mitch was gone, but she smelled him on the sheets, smelled their sex, smelled them together. She squinted at the clock on the other side of the bed. Three. Middle of the night. Yet she felt energized. She was ready to have him again. Her husband, her loving, wonderful husband.

Tossing aside the sheet, she rolled off the bed, then padded naked to the bathroom. A thin sliver of light shone through the crack in the open door.

"Ho-ney," she sing-songed as she pushed open the door. "I'm rea-dy. I think we should use the handcuffs on you this time."

He jerked, dropped something to the bath mat, then stared at it as if he were caught with his hand in the cookie jar.

Then she saw what he'd been holding. Her birth control pills. The container had landed facedown, the lid open.

"What are you doing with my pills?"

He bent to pick them up, held them without snapping the lid shut. He didn't stammer out an explanation. He just stared at her, not saying a word.

"You were checking up on me, weren't you?"

He still didn't open his mouth.

"You don't trust me. You want to make sure I'm taking them when I say I'm taking them." Her voice rose with each word, the deep lassitude of their lovemaking vanishing as if she'd never experienced it.

"Sometimes you forget. You admitted that."

"How can I forget with you asking me every ten minutes?" The screech hurt her throat.

"I only asked once."

She glared at him. "How long have you been checking?"

"Just today." He licked his lips. "And yesterday."

She grabbed her robe from the back of the door because she couldn't stand being naked in front of him. "You bastard. You think I lied."

"No, not lied."

"Fuck you, Mitch."

"Connie."

She'd shocked him with the curse word, and she didn't give a damn. She'd given him the benefit of the doubt the other day, telling herself he trusted her. But here was proof he didn't. He *was* checking up on her. She did everything he asked, watched every penny she spent, every penny he earned, and it wasn't good enough for him. She was so angry, she couldn't sort out her thoughts.

Except one. Suddenly . . . certainly, it was there.

"You don't intend to have another baby, do you? You've just been stringing me along for as long as you could."

"Connie, I—"

"Tell me the truth," she shouted, stretched past a limit she didn't know she had.

"I just don't think it's the right time." He stared at her with bleak brown eyes.

"You never do, but you promised. That's what we promised each other."

"We made that promise when we were younger, more naïve."

"You changed your mind, and you didn't tell me. You've been lying to me and checking up on me."

"That's not what I was doing."

She looked pointedly at the pills in his hand. "You think I'd trick you into having a baby. You think I'd miss taking a pill on purpose. How could you do that to me, Mitch?"

They were supposed to love each other. How could he touch her the way he had tonight, then sneak into the bathroom and check to make sure she hadn't lied?

Mitch didn't say anything.

She crossed her arms over her abdomen. "I don't know you anymore, Mitch. We had plans. We had trust. Now all you do is bitch and moan about money. It's the only thing that's important to you. How many dollars you have in the bank. What about your family? What about Rina and Peter?"

The calmness in Connie's voice belied the angry glitter in her eyes. Yet there was more. Lines of sorrow etched her mouth. The saddened tilt of her head. The way she pulled her lower lip between her teeth, biting down as if to stem the tears sparkling in her eyes. She broke his heart.

"I'm sorry," he said. He wanted so badly to grab a towel, something to cover himself with, anything. More than just his body lay bare before her. So did his soul.

"That's not good enough." She pulled her robe tightly closed at the throat. "Answer the question."

He didn't pretend he didn't know what question lay between them. "Connie, please, let's talk about this." His life was shattering at his feet yet he clung to the small hope that he could talk his way out of it.

"I'm done talking. That's all we've done since Rina turned three and we were supposed to start on the next baby. You need to be honest. Are you giving up our dreams of a big family?"

They stared at each other for long moments. He could see the ultimatum in her eyes, feel it in his heart. His life with Connie flashed before his eyes, laughter, passion, joy at watching his babies grow in her belly. Her arms around him the night after Lou died. He'd cried. She'd loved and soothed him even as his meltdown shamed him. And finally, these last three years, the growing anger and dissatisfaction. His growing fears consuming him until that's all that existed for him.

He wanted her. He needed her. "I love you, baby."

She continued to stare in stony silence, her knuckles clenched white.

She could be his if he said yes. They could stop fighting. She'd be happy, but they could never return to what they once had. A man's fear did terrible things. It ate him up inside. It twisted his feelings. One day he might end up resenting her for forcing his hand. Eventually, he might even hate her.

It was easier to have *her* hate him.

So he said it, uttered the only thing he could. "I don't want another child."

The words rang in his head like a death knell, sealing the fate on their marriage and their love.

SEVEN

SHE WANTED TO cry, scream, rant, rave, demand. She wanted to hit him, kick him, bite him. Anything to get rid of this hot knot of anger and pain strangling her. How could he do this to her? Why? The line between love and hate was indeed thin, and right now, she'd fallen off the line right into the hate side.

But Connie didn't do any of the things she thought about. Instead, she let her gaze ride his naked body with as much disdain as she could muster.

"Tonight I'm sleeping in Peter's bed. Tomorrow I'll clean up the sewing room and you can start sleeping on the day bed."

"Connie, please, let's—"

She held up a hand. "You've made your bed, now lie in it."

She'd made her own bed, too. "We'll talk about divorce after Taylor and Jace's wedding. There's too much to do right now for me to even think about it."

Then she turned and left him standing naked in the bathroom. In Peter's room, she fell asleep without a single tear. She was too angry for tears. She'd do all her crying after the wedding. After she decided whether she'd divorce him or stay with him for the kids' sake.

Whatever she ended up doing, the love, happiness, and passion of the last two days was gone forever.

THAT WAS THE problem with ultimatums. You made them thinking you were going to get the answer you wanted.

In those few moments Mitch stared silently, Connie had vindicating visions of him on his knees, begging her forgiveness, then throwing her birth control pills down the toilet.

A week later, she still couldn't quite believe he hadn't done just that. She wouldn't think about that now. She'd concentrate on her anger. All the bad things started with Lou's death. But Mitch had had three years to work it out. She'd offered solace, he hadn't accepted it. Instead, he lied, he broke his promises, and he didn't trust her. Even just one of those transgressions would kill any marriage.

A vice tightened around her heart.

"Connie, you're messing up the roses."

Evelyn's voice brought her back to the moment. Connie stared down at the red splatter on the white icing.

"Sorry." She was a good cake decorator, and she wanted to make the cake perfect for Taylor's wedding. But it looked more like a Rorschach paint splatter than a rose. She scooped off the splotch, smoothed the layer of frosting, then started again.

Evelyn was putting the finishing touches on the last batch of appetizers. They'd been cooking for a week now. But today, the day before the wedding, Taylor was absent. She couldn't see the cake. That would be bad luck. She was at home finishing the lasagnas. The food wasn't gourmet, but it was inexpensive and good. Taylor made the absolute best lasagna. Even the newcomer, Randi, had her assignment. She said she couldn't cook, so they had her cut up the cheese for crackers and the vegetables for dipping. There was something comforting about the camaraderie of the Jackson womenfolk getting everything ready. At least it would have been serene if Mitch hadn't torn her heart out.

"I've never known anyone that can make a wedding cake look so pretty." Randi sucked at her finger where she'd accidentally nicked herself with the knife.

"It's easy," Connie said. "A steady hand and a careful eye." Which is why she'd muffed the rose. She wasn't steady, and she wasn't being careful. A broken heart wreaked havoc on cake decoration.

With the last of the sausage rolls in the oven—they'd reheat them at the hall—Evelyn stood by the freezer door.

"Heavens above, I forgot to get the spinach for the dip."

"I'll go get it," Randi offered.

Evelyn flapped a hand. "No, no, you finish chopping the veggies, then start on cubing the French bread. It won't take me more than a few minutes."

The kitchen was silent once more as Evelyn's car roared away.

"Connie, can I ask you a question?"

"Sure."

Randi was almost family, or she soon would be if the way David looked at her meant anything. Connie figured the girl had the right to ask whatever she wanted. As long as it wasn't about Mitch and the awkward state of their marriage.

Could she really leave him? Or was it a threat to get him to toe the line? Connie wasn't sure. The only thing she did know with any amount of certainty was that life without Mitch would lose its joy, except for the kids.

"David told me about Lou. And I don't want to say the wrong thing. He said I couldn't possibly say the wrong thing, that after three years all of you had worked out your issues over Lou's passing." Randi dipped her blond head, concentrating on bite-sizing the cauliflower. "I really don't want to upset Evelyn or Taylor by making some stupid remark tomorrow."

Connie smiled, trying her best to bury her own inner turmoil. Yep, this girl was meant for David, sweet and caring and worried about other people's feelings.

"I have to admit that things were a bit dicey for a while." She started another rose. "Gosh, even as recently as a couple of months ago when Taylor and Jace first started . . ." She hesitated. How did one describe what Taylor and Jace had started doing? "When they started dating." Which wasn't really correct because they'd never dated. They'd started sleeping together. Well, not sleeping. She sighed. "David was a little upset about the whole thing."

Randi laughed. "The way David tells it, he went ballistic and said a lot of really hurtful things."

Connie raised a brow. David had come a long way if he was admitting that aloud. But then, he'd been a different man since meeting Randi. He'd lost that somber, angry facade he'd worn since Lou died.

"You *could* say he was upset." Freaked and ballistic described it, though Connie hadn't actually witnessed the event, only heard about it from Evelyn. "But you know, that seemed to fix everything for everyone." She shrugged. "Well, not fix exactly. But it was like the turning point where everyone could finally put him to rest and move on, if you know what I mean." Except for Mitch.

"Oh. That's good to hear. David seemed to think Mitch was still having problems, what with popping all those antacids and downing heavy-duty aspirin like it was candy."

Connie just stared at her, the icing tube still in her hand. "He's a worrywart. He's always been like that."

"Oh." Randi sliced another carrot. "David seemed to think it had gotten a lot worse lately."

David. He'd been telling everyone how they'd screwed up since Lou died. Where did he get off talking about them to Randi? Connie sucked in a breath, willing herself to calm down.

"I'm sorry, Connie. This isn't any of my business. I really just wanted to ask your advice to make sure I didn't say the wrong thing. And now I've said the wrong thing."

"It's all right." But nothing was right. Mitch had always managed their money closely, but after Lou died, he'd gotten downright maniacal about her spending. A few times, she'd risen in the night to find him sitting at the kitchen table pouring over bills and statements. Antacids and extra-strength aspirin had become a regular on the grocery list. That's when he'd started squawking about not being ready for another baby, too.

And she'd answered his fears with anger.

"I'm glad everything's better. It was a terrible tragedy. I don't have any brothers or sisters, but I can imagine how that would devastate a family, especially the way it happened. But *your* family," Randi spread her hands, "well, I'm totally amazed at how you've all helped each other through the grief. Most families would have fallen apart. But you guys"—she shrugged helplessly, as if she couldn't find the right words—"wow."

Randi's little speech said a lot about her own family, but it said a lot more about what Connie had done. Or *hadn't* done. Something cringed inside her. She and Mitch had never talked through his feelings about Lou's death. She'd told him he needed a psychiatrist, and when he denied it, she'd told herself it was out of her hands. All she'd ever *done* for him was get angry at his penny-pinching ways and his refusal to have another child.

Randi was looking at her, the vegetable knife still in her hand as if she expected some sort of comment.

"Yeah, this is a great family." She felt sick. All the praise Randi had heaped on the family didn't cover Connie's own actions. But Randi needed reassurance right now.

"And you don't have to worry about saying anything that will upset Evelyn or Taylor. Evelyn's ecstatic that Jace and Taylor are together."

She barely heard Randi's answer.

She'd been so stuck in her own needs and wants that she'd let Mitch stew in his grief for three years without even trying to help. Even though she'd *known* he needed help.

Her heart contracted. She'd been so selfish. But realizing that now didn't fix her marriage. She still wanted a baby. And Mitch didn't. She didn't see a compromise anywhere in that.

*   *   *

MITCH ACHED. HIS head, his eyes, his heart.

Connie was so beautiful in her bridesmaid dress, pale pink satin that made her skin glow and left her legs bare. Taylor had chosen a style that Connie could use again, for a cocktail party or an evening out at a fancy restaurant.

Connie wouldn't be wearing it with him. She hadn't talked to him, other than what was necessary, about the kids, the wedding, or a chore that needed doing. Even as he'd walked her back down the aisle after the vows, she hadn't said a word and she left him the moment they reached the church steps. He knew Connie inside and out, knew her moods, when she was PMSing, when she was happy, and when she was angry. The anger had lasted a week. Then suddenly, last night, before the wedding, it changed. His wife showed a side he wasn't sure he'd ever seen before. She'd seemed lost in her thoughts, moving in a daze.

And that's why he ached. Her mind was going round and round about how she would leave him, who would get the kids, whether they'd have joint custody, how they'd split the possessions accumulated over the years.

She could have everything. All he wanted was the right to see Rina and Peter as often as he could.

Yet a tiny voice in his head kept whispering: *Tell her you didn't mean it, tell her you want a baby.*

It wouldn't work. She wouldn't believe him. And God, he wouldn't really mean it. Fear would eat at his gut and his soul and in a short time they'd be right back where they'd started.

But she was so beautiful. On the dance floor, Connie held Rina in one arm, chubby legs wrapped around her mother's waist, and with the other hand, she gripped Peter's fingers.

It was the mother-and-child dance. Mom was out there with David doing . . . what was that dance? The Funky Chicken? Even Dad had been persuaded to take to the floor with Randi. That girl was a little weird, sweet but weird. Her skirt was skintight and her blouse was made of spandex. But at least it was white.

The DJ played oldies and elevator music because it was

easiest for everyone to listen and dance to, young and old. Taylor was on the dance floor, too, with Brian and Jamey, each one holding a hand as they danced. She hadn't chosen a traditional white wedding gown, but a cream-colored dress that also could be used for other occasions.

"She's gorgeous, isn't she?" Jace set his champagne back down on the table.

"Yeah. Freaking gorgeous." The dull ache became a jackhammer in his chest. He knew Jace was talking about Taylor, eyes only for his new wife.

Mitch had eyes only for his own wife and children.

"She doesn't look pregnant, does she?"

Mitch whipped his head around, almost giving himself a crick in the neck. "What? Connie's not pregnant."

Jace sighed and gave Mitch a long, slow shake of the head. "Taylor. She's six weeks."

Jesus H. Christ. "Are you an idiot or something? You only just got married."

Jace eyed him.

"Sorry, I didn't mean that the way it sounded. I was just shocked." He spread his hands, begging forgiveness for the idiocy that had fallen from his mouth. "Really. I'm sorry."

Jace suddenly smiled. Man, he was happy, manic even. Maybe he needed drugs. "Aren't you going to congratulate me?"

Mitch had no business criticizing his brother's choice even if it wasn't one he'd make for himself. "Congratulations. But isn't she going to murder you for spilling the beans?"

Jace smiled, watching her float across the dance floor with her sons bound tightly to her. "Yeah. She's going to freaking skin me alive. But I couldn't keep the secret anymore."

Jace had been the party guy, sowing his wild oats from one end of Willoughby to the other. Until Lou died. The perpetual shit-eating grin had died that day, too. So many parts of the family had been put in the ground right along with Lou. The expression on Jace's face was neither the shit-eating grin nor the somber smile that never reached his eyes. This was different.

It was the smile Mitch knew had been on his face when Connie told him about Peter. Then Rina. How he'd felt when he first saw his babies in Connie's arms, nursing at her breast.

It was something he would never have again.

"Do you know what you're getting into?"

"Yeah, Mitch, I know. Diapers and sleepless nights. And holding my newborn in the palm of my hand."

"Start saving now. It's a lot of money."

"Lou did it. You did it. I will, too."

"Yeah." He stared at Connie. He wasn't sure how he was going to hang around watching Taylor grow with Jace's kid. How he was going to bear witness to their happiness while his own crumbled to dust. For a moment, he almost hated his brother for having the thing he couldn't have, for being able to watch the woman he loved grow beautiful with his child inside her. To bring that baby into the world and lavish it with love.

"Taylor thinks Connie should have a baby at the same time."

"What the hell?" He wanted to puke.

Jace shook his head. "Some weird female thing. Like how they always have to go to the restroom together."

"We're not having any more kids." His voice was flat, without emotion.

So flat, Jace stared at him a moment. "But you always said you were going to have a big family."

"That was Connie's idea. Not mine."

"No, that was you, Mitch. I remember at your wedding. I thought you were crazy." He paused. "But now I see it from a whole different angle."

"Right. In a few months, you'll see it from the financial angle, and you'll realize how crazy it is."

"I'm not worried about the money. We'll get by."

"Get by, Jace? Are you freaking nuts? You gotta provide. You can't just hope you're going to 'get by.'"

"Mitch, what's wrong with you?"

He realized his hands were bunched into fists, and his cheeks ached with muscle tension. He did his best to relax.

"Life just made me change my plans, that's all."

"Are you happy about the change?"

"What's happiness got to do with it? A man does what he's got to do. He outgrows those youthful fantasies."

He'd outgrown his youthful fantasies, all right, and lost his wife and kids in the process.

"It's not a youthful fantasy, Mitch. It's a helluva big responsibility, but I'm willing to do it with Taylor, for us."

"Yeah, well, it's different for you. You and she don't have kids together, so I can understand you wanting a baby. But Connie and I have Rina and Peter." But God, he'd dreamed of watching Connie grow full with his child once more, dreamed of seeing her nestle the baby to her breasts. Dreamed of watching that baby grow, teaching him or her, reading stories, and throwing baseballs. Swimming lessons and love and laughter.

His dreams died the day Lou did.

"I'm really happy for you, man, but I'm not doing it again."

Connie twirled on the dance floor, laughing down into Rina's smiling face and whirling Peter across the parquet.

He'd lost everything the day Lou died. Because this day, the day his marriage ended had its roots in Lou's death.

It was almost as if he'd laid himself in the ground right alongside his brother. Given up his hopes, his dreams, his ambitions. Everything became about money, about the future.

He was so damn worried about the future that he'd destroyed his present.

"Mitch, you look a little green around the gills. Had too much champagne?"

No. He'd had too much worrying. Too many hours lying awake at night imagining everything that could go wrong.

"I'm fine."

Jace nudged him. "Dance is almost over. Don't tell Taylor I told you."

"And you told me because?" He spread his hands.

Jace looked at him as if his anxieties were tattooed on his forehead. "Why do you think I told you, Mitch?"

Hell, it didn't take a genius to read a guy's mind. It took a baby brother who'd suddenly taken the plunge himself. Jace was trying to tell him things could work out if he had faith.

Mitch didn't answer.

Finally, Jace shook his head and turned back to watch David and their mom herding the kids back to the table while Taylor and Connie headed for the restroom.

A tender smile creased his brother's mouth. He looked like a guy impossibly, magnificently in love.

"What'd I tell you? Women always have to do things together. You gotta love 'em."

Mitch did. He loved Connie with all his heart. And he'd given her up because he was afraid. What kind of coward did that make him?

EIGHT

TAYLOR TACKLED HER the minute they were alone in the ladies' room. "All right, spill. What's wrong."

"Nothing's wrong." Connie wouldn't spoil Taylor's day, not for anything.

"You are such a fibber. You've been dragging the whole week. And you haven't danced with Mitch once today."

"Let's talk about it later." She barely managed to keep the darn quiver out of her lip.

"Let's talk about it now. I can't run around all happy-happy when I know something's wrong." Taylor squeezed her hand.

And the awful reality just burst out despite her best intentions. "I think Mitch and I might be getting a divorce."

"Oh, Connie." Taylor flopped down in front of the vanity like a hot air balloon without any hot air. "I was afraid you were going to say that."

Divorce didn't feel right. Life without Mitch didn't feel right. Even life with him coming to take the kids on weekends. No, no, no. That's not how she'd envisioned them all.

"Is this because of the baby?" Taylor wasn't stupid.

"He says he doesn't want any more kids. I don't think I can

live with that." She sank down on the stool next to her sister-in-law twice over.

"So, it's a deal-breaker, huh?"

Connie pulled her bottom lip between her teeth and stared at herself in the mirror. "He doesn't trust me. He was checking up on me to make sure I took my birth control pills."

Taylor freshened her lipstick, then made sure no excess color made it to her teeth. "You can't forgive him for that?"

"I don't know," she murmured. "He broke his promise to me about having a big family, and then he didn't trust me. How can we have a good marriage if he doesn't trust me?" How could they have a good marriage if she couldn't even help him through the grief of his brother's death? "Do you miss Lou?" she whispered. It was a terrible question to ask, a terrible thing to say on Taylor's wedding day, but she couldn't help herself.

Taylor put her hand over Connie's trembling fingers. "After he died, I thought life was over. Everything changed. I didn't know exactly where to turn. I'd never imagined myself alone. But I've moved on. And I love Jace with all my heart." She pressed Connie's hand harder. "I have to tell you. We're going to have a baby. I'm six weeks along."

Her body flushed, her skin heated, and her head swam. Spots danced before her eyes, and she thought she might faint.

"I know that must hurt you, Connie, especially now."

It didn't hurt. It devastated. She was going to drown, her soul washing away with the pain.

She and Mitch would never have another child.

Tears suddenly gushed. Taylor put her arms around her shoulders and tugged her head down.

"I'm going to get makeup all over your dress."

"Don't worry about it, sweetie, just let it all out."

Rina was starting first grade in the fall. The house would be empty. All day. Every day, except weekends. How would she survive those long empty days with no one to take care of?

"Can I babysit, Taylor?"

"Of course. I'm going to need you."

"Thanks."

"Will you remarry so you can have more children?"

Connie pulled away, swiped at her eyes, and simply stared at Taylor. It was the most ridiculous question she'd ever heard. She'd never marry again. Never. She couldn't bear another man in her bed. There was only Mitch. There would only ever be Mitch.

"Of course not. Mitch was it for me."

"But if you're leaving him because he doesn't want to have any more kids, but then you're not planning to get remarried so there won't ever be any more kids . . ." Taylor trailed off. "Oh yeah, it's because he broke his promise and didn't trust you."

Connie looked at her toes, her shaking hands, then finally brought her gaze level with Taylor's. It was time to admit the truth. She'd ruined her own marriage.

"I've been very selfish."

"How?"

"I wanted what I wanted, and I expected Mitch to fall in line. It's like we were both going off and doing our own thing, and not paying attention to what was going on between us." She hiccuped. "I don't think I ever *really* talked to him about how Lou's death affected him. When he said he was worried about where the money for another baby would come from, I pooh-poohed him. I didn't take into account how Lou's death made him terrified he couldn't take care of us." She dropped her head in her hands. "I mean, I *heard* what he was saying, but I never really gave his fears any credence. I just got angrier and angrier every time he put off the question of another baby. I got angry with him for not trusting me, but *I* never listened to *him*. I never gave his fears any importance."

Taylor put an arm around her shoulder. "We all get caught up in our own stuff. It's okay. But maybe you guys need to talk before you rush into this divorce thing."

She blotted beneath her eyes. "Ya think?" Their problems might not be fixable, but they *had* to talk. Of that much, Connie was sure.

"Yeah, I think." Taylor put her lipstick back in the little beaded bag that matched her dress. "Now that that's all settled, I have a big favor to ask."

"Anything." Something to take her mind off her troubles.

"Jace took care of the champagne, but I forgot to get the strawberries. Can you just nip out for a bit, get some, then drop them off at the hotel? I want everything laid out when we get there."

Strawberries and champagne. She and Mitch had strawberries and champagne on their wedding night. She almost started bawling all over again.

But she didn't. This was Taylor's day, and she'd already taken more of it than she should have.

"Sure. Don't leave until I get back, okay?"

JACE SENT HIM over to the hotel with a bottle of champagne to ice. His little brother wanted everything to be ready when the reception ended. Of course, he could have had the hotel guest services do it, but Jace said he didn't trust them.

All right, he was entitled to be a freak on his wedding day. After all, he was married and an expectant father all in a very short period of time.

Taylor and Lou had sent a bottle of champagne to the room for his and Connie's wedding night. Strawberries, too. Connie had loved that.

The now familiar ache closed around his chest.

She'd disappeared after going to the restroom for-freaking-ever with Taylor. He'd wanted to talk to her, tell her . . . what? That he'd changed his mind? That he'd rather cut off his right nut than live without her? That he'd give her a baby and live with his fears because living without her was impossible?

He didn't know. But he hoped to God he found her once he got back to the reception.

The card key beeped him in. Man. Jace had spared no expense. A breakfast nook complete with table and chairs sat on a raised platform next to the window, in just the right spot to receive the morning sun. A leather couch and chair faced the fireplace, although at this time of year, who would want a fire? The bed was draped in a thick blue comforter with a mountain of pillows at the head.

He remembered his honeymoon suite. A dinky room with a dinky bed that was hard as a rock. They hadn't even been able to fit in the shower together. He'd bet the bathroom in this joint had a Jacuzzi tub and a two-headed shower. All right, he and Connie had been young and without a lot of money, but he knew he'd been overly cheap. Connie had deserved better. She deserved a wedding night in a room like this, but she hadn't complained about what she got.

The complaining started later. After he'd broken his promise about the baby.

Hell, he needed to ice the champagne and get back to the reception to find Connie. He'd asked his mom to take the kids so that he and Connie could hash this whole thing out.

Shit. Mom was taking Brian and Jamey. He'd be sticking her with all four kids. But hell, he and Connie needed to talk.

Stepping down into what constituted the living room, he reached for the ice bucket.

It sat next to the leather sofa, the ice already in it. Unmelted. A basket of strawberries lay on the coffee table next to two crystal flutes.

"What the hell?" Mitch plopped the champagne into the ice. Someone had already set the hotel staff to work.

He heard water running in the bathroom.

Holy shit. Taylor was already here, and she'd brought her own strawberries.

She probably thought he was Jace.

He hoped to hell she was dressed when she came out of that bathroom, or they'd both get the shock of their lives.

A vision in pale pink satin stepped into the hallway and his heart started racing.

"Mitch, what are you doing here?"

He held up the champagne. "And what are you doing here?"

Connie pointed to the coffee table. "Strawberries."

The phone rang. Mitch snapped it up.

"Here's the gig, buddy, you've got the champagne and the strawberries. Now start patching things up. Or I'll send Mom over there to straighten you two out."

"Jace. What the hell's going on?"

He heard a little scuffle, then Taylor came on the line. "We decided that we want to start out our married life in our own bed in our home, not some silly old hotel room. So we figured you and Connie could put the room to use. No sense wasting it."

"You can't give us your honeymoon suite."

"We can and we did. And Evelyn's taking all four kids so you don't have to worry about anything."

"Taylor."

"We've got eyes, and we know something's not right. So you and Connie sit down and fix it, you hear?"

Then she hung up. He stared at the receiver, the dial tone loud in the room.

"They gave us their room."

"Mitch, I didn't get them to do this."

"I know."

"But I did tell Taylor we were having some . . . issues."

Jesus. At least she didn't tell Taylor we're divorcing.

"I've been doing a lot of thinking."

He stepped closer and put a finger over her lips. "You don't have to explain. You were right. I broke the promise."

"That wasn't what I was going to say, Mitch."

He stared at her, his heart thumping so hard it hurt.

"I was going to say that I let you down."

"You let me down?" The idea was so preposterous, all he could do was repeat it. She'd been right in everything she'd said. He'd destroyed the plan they'd made when they first got married; he hadn't trusted her not to trick him; he'd even gone so far as to stop making love to her to ease the hole growing in his gut.

"None of this was your fault, Connie."

She shook her head. "I never listened to how hard Lou's death hit you. It's still eating at you."

He thought about the hours he lay awake, all the nights in the last three years where he'd floundered, trying to think of a way to protect her and the kids. He'd had sudden, inexplicable death rammed down his throat, and he wanted to make sure Connie didn't have to worry about a thing if something happened to him.

But something had happened to him anyway. He'd lost himself. Lost his dreams. He'd lost Connie.

"We can't go on the way we were, Mitch."

A fierce ache ripped through his abdomen and his head at the same time. He prayed for antacids and extra-strength aspirin. "Please don't leave me."

She put her hand to his cheek. "I'm not going to leave you, Mitch. I love you."

He was dreaming. Floating in some fairy-tale land. Any minute he'd wake up and find himself asleep on the daybed in the sewing room.

"I've been a terrible wife."

He opened his mouth to interrupt.

She covered his lips with her hand. "Will you please shut up long enough for me to say this or I might just forget all about it because I'm very self-oriented, you know."

He kissed her palm. If this was a dream, he never wanted to wake up. His soul would be ripped from him if he lost her.

Connie straightened her shoulders, her breasts straining the bodice of her dress. "Here goes. I didn't pay attention to how badly you felt." She shrugged, drawing his eye to her bare shoulder above the dress. "Oh sure, there were the couple of times where you cried, right after he died, and I held you, and that was so wonderful because I felt like I was doing something for you. Then we had that fight about whether or not you should go talk with someone, and I guess I just didn't know how to deal with it all. So I gave up. And you just tucked it away inside."

His grief had unmanned him. He'd actually been ashamed of letting her see those tears. He'd never let it happen again. Instead, he'd lain awake at night, plotting how he'd make everything safe for her future. But he'd started fighting with her more and more. *The* fight had only been the worst one.

"I didn't pay attention. I was so caught up in what I wanted. Another baby. Like we planned. It got worse when Rina started kindergarten and the house was so empty half the day."

"Connie."

She stamped her foot. He almost smiled. This was his Connie, feisty as hell even when she was apologizing. Every organ in his body threatened to burst with fear and joy.

"I haven't paid attention to you for three years, and I'm sorry. Will you forgive me?"

He gathered her close, buried his face in her hair, breathing her sweet woman scent. "I forgive you," he whispered.

"But I still want another baby, Mitch."

His heart stuttered, then stopped completely. And he knew this was the moment. He either reclaimed the dream, went on with his life, or lost everything. She'd said she wouldn't leave him, but whether she stayed or she went, he was the one killing himself slowly with worry and anxiety.

He was speechless with hope, overcome by fear.

Connie pulled back, framed his face in her hands, and ___ his gaze. "I don't want to give up our dream."

___ ___ ___ ___ble of saying anything.

___ Poor, poor Mitch. "You don't

___ I want. Marriage

___ A big

He seemed incapa___
She shook her head sadly. ___
I'm not leaving. I'm fighting for what I ___
to you. Beautiful, wonderful sex like we had last week. A ___
family which is what we always wanted. I want our house and
___ filled with our children. I want us to come to some
___ us both.
___

They either had another child or they didn't. It *was* black or white. Hadn't she said that to Taylor only a few short months ago? But black and white didn't mean a marriage had to end. "I'll help you understand my point of view if you help me understand yours. Somehow, we'll work it out. I know we can together." She touched her lips lightly to his. "Please don't leave me, either, Mitch. Please help me."

He closed his eyes, leaning his forehead to hers. His breath bathed her cheek. She would die without him. For years she'd taken what they shared for granted, never realizing how fragile love really was. She'd never forget that again.

"I've forgotten how to live, Connie." He held her tight, and his body shook. "I've been so damn scared of dying and leaving you destitute, of leaving the kids, that I destroyed all the good things we had."

She pushed back, cupping his face once more in her hands. "I pray to God you will be here for us, but I'm not a child, Mitch. I can take care of myself and the kids with or without you. I can do whatever's necessary."

"I know. It's just another disservice I did you. Forgive me?" He whispered the final question.

"Of course I do."

He held her, squeezed her until her ribs felt as if they'd crack, but it was so unbelievably good. She clung to him, wrapping her arms as far as they would go.

Mitch reveled in her for a full minute, a moment in time in which he realized what he had to do, what he *wanted* to do.

"I want a baby, Connie. I want our dream." Jace was ng. They would make it through. Their d_____ so worth the sacrifice. God, he'd almost_____ Connie had pla_____ _____ dreams were worth the _____ _____ thrown away everything he and lost *her* to his fears. Life wouldn't be worth living without her. She leaned back, staring at him, shifting her gaze from eye "You're not just saying that to make me feel better?" ____ng I won't let my fears crush our dreams _____ He cupped ____ *_o, not just yours.*" _____ choices.

his palm. "But I'm not sure I'll ever stop worrying completely. Can you live with that?"

"Do you mean it in your heart, Mitch? No regrets later?"

"No regrets. I want another baby with you, Connie. More than anything else. I want to let go of my fears and watch you grow with our child."

"Oh, Mitchie, I love you."

"I love you, too, baby."

She pulled back and cocked her head. "Do I still have to shop at three grocery stores so I get all the best specials?"

"Yes."

"What about the washing machine?"

"I'll fix it. After all, I fixed the toilet."

She bit her lip. "That's okay. Can I have a new car?"

He almost smiled. "Something used. You don't need new with all the bells and whistles."

"Speaking of bells and whistles, what about sex toys? I saw this really cool—"

He slapped his hand over her mouth. "Don't tell me. Make it a surprise."

"So I can spend the money?"

"Better yet, you can use the handcuffs on me."

"Oh, Mitchie."

"Let's make a baby," he whispered.

"Now?"

"Yeah. Remember that scene in *The Godfather* where Sonny did the bridesmaid up against the door?" Connie had rewound to that spot several times.

"I remember. It made me hot."

"Well, let's pretend." Then he hauled her up his body, pulled her legs around his waist, tore her panties, and carried her to the door.

"Do you think someone will hear us out in the hall?"

"Only if you scream like when I put the cuffs on you."

He fumbled with the zipper on his tux slacks, hoisted her higher against the door, then thrust hard and deep inside her.

"Oh, Mitchie."

"Oh, baby."

Life would never be perfect. There would always be bills and new cars and washing machines that needed replacing. But as long as he had Connie, he'd weather it all just fine.

EPILOGUE

EVELYN SAT ON a deck chair in her backyard and watched her boys and their wives, her grandchildren and her husband. And Randi. Evelyn had a good feeling that soon she'd get to plan another wedding. That boy of hers couldn't keep his hands off Randi. Touchy-feely was a good thing. Kept a marriage healthy. Heavens, it had kept Evelyn's marriage healthy.

Jace and Taylor had one night on their own, then rushed to the family barbecue, their first as a married couple. She'd made a lovely bride, both times, but she simply glowed with Jace by her side, the two boys running around, playing Cowboys and Indians. Yes, despite the advent of aliens, Space Invaders, the Internet, and video games, Cowboys and Indians had never truly lost its universal appeal.

Taylor suddenly clapped her hands. "Everyone, we'd like your attention."

It took a moment for the boys and Rina to settle down.

Taylor turned to Brian and Jamey. "I really want to thank you guys for keeping our secret." The boys beamed. Taylor and Jace had arrived before anyone else and closeted themselves in the back bedroom with the two boys.

Evelyn's heart beat a little faster, her palms got sweaty, and her tummy fluttered with all the wonderful possibilities. She clutched Arthur's hand. He squeezed back.

Taylor kissed her husband on the cheek. "You tell them."

Jace's face split with a grin wider than heaven. "We're going to have a baby."

Evelyn burst into tears, great sobs that filled her soul.

"Mom." Jace went down in front of her chair. "You're not supposed to cry."

"I'll cry if I want to. My baby having a baby," she sniffled. He gathered her into his arms. "Tears of joy, Mom?"

"Heavens, yes." She cupped her son's cheeks. "I've never been happier."

He kissed her sweetly, rose, then gathered his new wife and sons to him. This was a new Jace: a man; a hero; a proud and happy father-to-be. A family.

Evelyn exchanged a look with her daughter-in-law. "I'm so happy for you, Taylor."

"Thank you, Evelyn." Taylor was a special woman. She'd survived a terrible tragedy, and somehow, some way, she'd come through it still with more love to give.

David pulled Randi in front of him, resting his chin on the top of her head. "Since we're making announcements, I might as well join in. Randi says she wouldn't mind being my wife."

Randi, the prettiest blonde Evelyn had ever seen, elbowed David in the ribs. "That is not what I said."

David laughed. He laughed a lot these days. "I forgot. You said yes, but only if the dog could still sleep on the bed."

"She's part of my family, too." Randi huffed.

The girl was as cute as a bug. She'd make a wonderful mother. But she did need to learn how to cook. Evelyn piped up in the middle of their teasing.

"If the dog is family, then next time you need to bring her to the barbecue."

Randi beamed, and Evelyn knew she'd said exactly the right thing. "Congratulations, dear, and welcome to the family."

"All right, you guys are outdoing me." Mitch swung Rina up in the air. "How do feel about having a new baby brother or sister, munchkin?"

"Ewww," she squealed. "No boys."

"Ewww," Peter added. "No girls. Dad, we're gonna be out-numbered if it's a girl."

Mitch smiled. Then he tipped his head and shot Connie what was clearly a lascivious grin. "If it's the wrong sex, Pe-ter, your mom and I will just have to make another one."

Evelyn popped to her feet. Gravity just couldn't keep her down. "You're pregnant, too, Connie?"

Connie blushed. "Not yet. But we're trying."

"Oh my. Heavens." Evelyn put her hands to her cheeks and sniffled.

Arthur put his arm across her shoulder, hugged her close, and saved her from making a fool of herself by bursting into sobs of joy for a second time in five minutes.

"I'm hungry," he declared. "Can we start the hamburgers?"

The kids chimed in, chanting their desires. Evelyn's boys tossed for who got to do the cooking. Randi, Taylor, and Con-nie trooped into the kitchen for the condiments, side dishes, plates, and utensils.

Evelyn just stood for a moment in the shelter of her hus-band's arms.

"Lou would be happy that everything's worked out," she whispered against his chest.

"Yeah, Lou's looking down, and he's happy," Arthur agreed.

She'd miss her eldest like the dickens until she got to see him again up in heaven. But until that day, life was as perfect as could be down here on earth.

ABOUT THE AUTHOR

For **Jasmine Haynes**, storytelling has always been a passion. With a bachelor's degree in accounting, she has worked in the high-tech Silicon Valley for the last twenty years. She and her husband live with their cat, Eddie Munster, and Star, the mighty moose-hunting dog. Jasmine's pastimes, when not writing her heart out, are hiking in the redwoods and taking long walks on the beach. Jasmine also writes as Jennifer Skully and JB Skully.

She loves to hear from her readers. Visit her website at www.skullybuzz.com; e-mail her at skully@skullybuzz.com; or write to her at P.O. Box 66738, Scotts Valley, CA 95067.